Whispers of the Heart

A Story of Love, Betrayal and Deception

By
Julie Deborah

Grosvenor House
Publishing Limited

The right of Julie Deborah to be identified as the author of this
work has been asserted in accordance with Section 78
of the Copyright, Designs and Patents Act 1988

The book cover is copyright to Julie Deborah
Cover design by Geoffrey Sleiman

This book is published by
Grosvenor House Publishing Ltd
Link House
140 The Broadway, Tolworth, Surrey, KT6 7HT.
www.grosvenorhousepublishing.co.uk

This book is a work of fiction. Any resemblance to
people or events, past or present, is purely coincidental.

A CIP record for this book
is available from the British Library

ISBN 978-1-83615-202-6
eBook ISBN 978-1-83615-203-3

Connect with Julie Deborah
Instagram - @yourjourney_yourtestimony
Email - juliedeborahauthor@gmail.com

Dedication

"And we know that all things work together
for good to those who love God,
to those who are called according to His purpose."

– Romans 8:28

To our Lord God Almighty,
who assigns, equips and prepares us for every good work,
to Him be all the Glory,
Honour and Praise Forever and Ever.
Amen.

Acknowledgements

To God Almighty, for making this book possible.
It is by your Grace and Mercy, Lord. Father, I Thank You!

To my sister, Vivian, thank you for being a caring sister and
for always praying for me.

To Janice Donowa, thank you so much for your incredible support
(reading pages upon pages of this book and providing feedback),
encouragement, input, and prayer. God bless you!

To my Prayer Partners and Everyone who continuously prayed for
me and encouraged me during this journey, I thank you all!

Reviews for Whispers of the Heart

"Whispers of the Heart is a beautifully written novel that balances cultural authenticity with universal emotions. You crafted a heartfelt story that invites readers to empathize with your characters' struggles and triumphs. This book will resonate with those who appreciate evocative storytelling and an intimate look at family and societal dynamics in Nigeria."

—Annie T

"Whispers of the Heart is such an apt title for this debut novel. It invites the reader to look beyond mere words, to discover the hidden motive of each character, as they endeavour to experience the longing of their hearts. Filled with enlightening insights into culture, friendship and the sacrifices made to uphold family traditions, this beautifully written novel reminds us that in everything there is purpose."

—Janice Donowa

Chapter 1

"Jesus, you too good, you too good, you too good,
I no go lie. You take my life, make am sweet,
you change am sotey, people dey see.
Na wetin I go give you but all my life,
I go live my life to give you praise"

('You Too Good,' Written by Julie Deborah)

Onome lifted her head slightly as she listened to the lyrics of the song drifting from their neighbour's compound. Beads of sweat trickled down her forehead, landing on the sandy ground. The music grew louder than before—they must have brought the speaker outside, she thought. It was a usual Sunday routine for the Odafe family to blast music as soon as they returned from church.

"You take my life, make am sweet, you change am sotey people dey see. Na wetin I go give you but all my life, I go live my life to give you praise," she heard herself sing along. She sighed suddenly and stood upright, placing her right hand on her waist. It was a hot day—too hot, in fact. She was tired. Stretching a little, she noticed a female voice singing the same lyrics, over and over again. She wondered if it was one of the children. She quickly went up on her toes to gaze across the medium-high fence, trying to see who was singing, but couldn't spot anyone. She huffed as she came down on her feet, wiping some more sweat off her forehead.

She placed her hand on her waist again and took a deep breath. The music had once helped her work—it had even made her dance

1

a few times—but now it felt as unbearable as the scorching heat of the sun. As she stared at the fence separating her from the Odafe's compound, she heard a chicken crow. Her face twisted into a frown.

She heard the chicken crow for the second time. This time, she turned to look at it, she could not understand why the chicken was crowing at this time of the day. She sucked her teeth in frustration and raised her right thumb to her forehead, wiping away the sweat before brushing it off on the top of her dress, which was now soaked and clinging to her skin. She tugged at the top of her dress, pulling it slightly away from her body. A wrapper *(a piece of cloth, worn around the waist)* was tied over the dress, and she wasn't ready to take it off just yet. She huffed again. Of all the days to wear the thickest, long-sleeved dress in her wardrobe, she thought. Taking a deep breath, she paused and looked around. She had been cutting firewood sticks for some time, and now she was tired.

Contemplating whether to rest in the shade of a nearby tree for some time, the chicken crowed for the third time, this time she could not help but frown at it annoyingly. She could not understand why the chicken was crowing so much, after all, it was resting under the shade of a tree, while she was the one standing in the heat. Sucking her teeth, she glared at the chicken. "Abeg, just keep quiet there," she said angrily.

She sighed, why is she speaking to a chicken that cannot answer back? She shook her head. It was an extremely hot day, and there was no breeze to help make it bearable. She stared at the pile of firewood; this is unnecessary work sef, she thought. Why her mother insists on cooking with firewood for parties and special occasions, she will never understand. She almost hissed as she looked down again at the firewood she had cut.

"This should be enough for one week," she muttered to herself.

She bent down and began gathering the pieces of firewood sticks she had been cutting into a bundle. She took a piece of rope she had brought with her and proceeded to tie the bundle together. Once done, she slowly untied the cloth wrapped around her waist, folded it into a bun, and placed it on top of her head. Bending down again, she placed both hands beneath the firewood and lifted it, balancing it on the bun atop her head. She checked to ensure it was securely positioned, then slowly bent down to pick up the cutlass.

Fortunately, she didn't have to go far to gather firewood; she only needed to go to the back of the compound, where trees had been cut down. Turning gently, she walked slowly—it wasn't a long distance to the area where the firewood was stored. Once there, she carefully dropped the cutlass on the ground, then slowly lowered the firewood from her head, placing it on the floor. She sighed as she removed the bun-shaped wrapper from her head and tossed it to the ground.

She quickly untied the bundle of firewood and gently stacked it one piece at a time in the storage area. When she finished, she picked up the cutlass and placed it on top of the stacked wood. She looked around to make sure everything was in order and nodded to herself. Noticing that she was still dripping with sweat, she picked up the wrapper from the ground and wiped her face. At this point, she didn't mind that it had a bit of sand on it, which was now stuck to her sweaty face. She sighed once more; she quickly tied the wrapper back around her waist and began walking toward the house.

Upon entering the kitchen, she looked around to see what was left to do. The kitchen had been swept, and there were no dishes left in the sink or anywhere else. Earlier, she had quickly fried some bean buns for breakfast with pap, pre-prepared some chicken to be cooked later in the afternoon, filled the drums with water, and had now gathered some firewood. She sighed as she slumped into the only chair by the backdoor entrance of the kitchen and closed her eyes.

It is finished!" she exclaimed. Suddenly, a nice, cool breeze blew in.

"Ohhh yes!" she exclaimed again, shutting her eyes and holding the dress away from her body as the breeze swept through the door of the side entrance. The wind rustled the leaves on the trees, bringing a cool breeze into the kitchen.

"At last," she thought, stretching her legs out and rolling up the sleeves of her dress. She relaxed in the chair, a little smile slowly forming on her lips.

She hadn't sat for more than a few minutes when she heard her name.

"Onome..."

Her eyes shot open. She frowned and grumbled quietly, "Ohhh... ehn, what is it now?" She heard her name again, quite loudly this time, accompanied by the sound of feet stamping on the floor. Of course, it was her mother calling, but she chose not to answer immediately.

"Onome," she called again, the third time. "Are you not in the kitchen?" she said in an angry tone.

"Ma! Yes, I am here," Onome answered. *How did she know I was in the kitchen?* She kissed her teeth quietly as she slowly stood up from the chair, dragging her feet out of the kitchen as she knew her mother would not come to the kitchen to meet her. The kitchen was only a few steps from the living room where her mother's voice was coming from.

She slowed her pace as she entered the living room and stood facing her mother, who was standing there with her hands on her waist and a tight frown on her face. Her mother looked her up and down.

"Where have you been?"

"I have been here."

"Where?" she asked.

Pointing to the direction of the kitchen, "I was at the back, cutting firewood."

"But I came to the kitchen and called your name, I did not hear you."

"I was at the back," Onome said again.

"Ehnn," her mother said, looking her up and down again. Her eyes lingered on Onome's forearm. Onome could see the look of disgust on her face. Onome slowly pulled down her dress sleeves.

"Have you gone to the market?" her mother asked as she turned her gaze back to her face.

"Market? No, I haven't...I thought you went to the market yesterday?" Onome said, frowning slightly.

Her mother stared at her for a second. Onome could immediately tell when her mother gave one of those looks that meant, *'You are asking for trouble.'*

"Go to the market now. I left a list and some money on that table since this morning," she said, pointing at the small table in the living room. Onome glanced over at the table. The list must have magically appeared, because she did not see a list or money there earlier, she thought to herself.

"Where is Rukevwe?" She went on to ask.

"She is in the room," Onome replied, her eyes still locked on the list and money on the table. *Where could her younger sister be if not in the room sleeping?* she thought to herself.

"She is not there, I have checked. Where has she gone? Her mother asked again.

Glancing at the door to the room she shared with her sister, Onome said, "I don't know," shrugging her shoulders with a frown.

"Ehnn, you don't know?" her mother asked. Onome shook her head in response and quickly looked away.

"You don't know where your sister is?" It was a statement, and she didn't wait for a response. She kissed her teeth, turned away, and started to walk to her room but then stopped suddenly, turning back to her.

"Ehnn, for the Bushmeat *(Grasscutter)*, make sure you go to Oga Amadi's store to buy them ooh. I already told him to keep two fresh bushmeat for me."

Onome was frowning as she nodded her head in response. *Oh no, Grasscutter,* she thought angrily. *That horrible meat. She finds them scary; they have hair on their back that are like spikes and have very tough skin. They taste nice when cooked, but they're ugly and hard to clean.* She hated cleaning them.

"Madam," her mother's voice interrupted her thoughts. "Make sure the bushmeat is fresh ooh," her mother said, pulling one of her ears as she continued. Her mother did that when she was emphasising something that she did not want her to miss. "I want two big ones and very fresh. Do you hear me?"

"Yes, ma," Onome replied, almost grumbling as she picked the list from the table. Her mother looked around the living room as if looking for something to complain about as she always does. She took a deep breath and then walked into her room and shut the door.

Onome sighed and threw the list back on the table. She sat angrily on a nearby chair, putting her hand under her chin. Tears formed in her eyes; she was tired. She thought she had finished all the chores for the day. It was Sunday and she was hoping she would be able to meet with Prisca and her other friends at the town square. She had been up since 6 o'clock this morning. She had been working all day, and now she was so tired. Her gaze moved to the clock on the wall opposite her, it was now exactly 1 o'clock. She took a deep breath, fighting back the tears that threatened to roll down her cheeks.

"Do this, do that. I don't know what she wants from me," she muttered, wiping off the tears that flowed down her cheeks. She kissed her teeth and angrily reached to grab the list and money from the table.

She looked at the list again. As usual, it was a long list of things she was sure her mother did not need right now. She noticed her mother hadn't written whether she wanted the bushmeat cleaned. As she stared at this one item, she started to think. *This is good,* she thought. *I can buy two cleaned bushmeat, and I won't have to clean them.* Every other item on the list was going to be quick and easy to buy. She smiled to herself and nodded.

She quickly looked down at her dress. It had a few stains and was a little dusty from picking the firewood. It was also a bit wet from sweat. Pulling up her sleeves, she stared at the reason for her long-sleeved dress—the rash all over her forearms. There were some new ones, and they were not pleasant to look at. They were creeping up to her shoulders now.

She sighed. It seemed the sweat from the heat was making it worse. *Her mother must have seen it too,* she thought. Her mother never liked to see it. It was always agreed that it wasn't good for her to expose her arms since it could be infectious and might spread to someone else. They had discussed what she was allowed to do— keep her arms covered both inside and outside the house.

The rash had first appeared on her arm when she was in the first year of secondary school. At first, she thought it was caused by the bath soap she was using at the time. She had switched to another brand, but it only got worse. In the following months and years, the rash continued to spread, creeping up her forearms and across her back. The doctors had been unable to treat it or explain what it was and why it kept spreading.

She had even tried to treat it herself using tree herbs recommended by some of her aunties, but those only made it worse. Fortunately, no one in the house had been affected by it, and the rules that had been placed on her had relaxed over the years. Yet, she had grown ashamed of her arms and kept them covered with long-sleeved clothing. Apart from her family and her best friend, no one knew about the rash on her skin.

She sighed as she pulled her sleeves back down. Taking her mind off it, she stood up and untied the wrapper from her waist. She couldn't be bothered to change; the dress would dry quickly in the heat anyway, and the market was only twenty minutes away by local Motorbus. The earlier she went to the market, the earlier she could return and join Prisca at the town square, she thought.

Quickly counting the money her mother had provided, she realised she wasn't sure her mother had factored in transportation costs. She would have to haggle with the Motorbus conductor to make sure she had enough for the ride there and back.

Standing up immediately, she shoved the list and the money into her dress pocket. She rushed back to the kitchen and picked up one of her mother's market baskets. Deciding to leave through the kitchen's back door, it was quicker to reach the compound gate that way, she walked out of the house, almost forgetting to shut the door behind her.

She walked briskly toward the compound gate, her steps quick and purposeful. Near the gate, the security man, Musa, was sitting on the floor, his ear bent toward a small, crackling radio. A sudden burst of laughter escaped him, likely in response to something amusing the presenter had said.

Onome hoped she could slip past him unnoticed, but just as she neared the gate, Musa looked up and spotted her.

"Good afternoon, Onome!" he called out cheerfully.

She responded with a quick nod and a wave of her hand, signalling she was in a hurry. Without breaking her stride, she pushed through the gate and stepped out onto the road.

"Ah, Onome, wetin happen nah? You dey vex? You no go greet me today?"

She stopped not wanting to be disrespectful as he was quite an elderly man. "Sorry, Oga Musa. I no dey vex ooh. Good afternoon."

Musa was their security man or gateman, as they were titled in Nigeria. Musa has been with them for many years. He started working for them when Onome was 8 years old. He was very tall, skinny, and much older, which was similar to most men his age in the town. Musa was uneducated and thus spoke in broken English. She has known him to be a good and kind man, who has become so close to the family. He never married but had three grown children whom he would sometimes take time to go and visit.

"Ehn, good afternoon, my dear," Musa said, fanning his body with the little cloth that was on his shoulder. "Your face just dey strong like say you dey vex. Nah make I ask ooh."

"I dey fine," Onome replied, forcing a small smile. "Na just the sun. E hot well well today ooh," she responded this time in broken English.

"Na true, the sun just hot well well today," Musa replied, looking at the basket she was holding. "You carry basket? You dey comot?"

"Uhm… yes, I am going to the market."

"Okay, take am easy ooh, the sun dey very hot today."

She smiled. "Okay," she said turning away almost quickly to continue out through the gate, when she literally bumped into someone walking towards her.

"Oh!" she exclaimed. She looked up and quickly realised who it was.

"Sorry, ma."

Aunty Omerie had her head down, gently rubbing her toes.

"Sorry, ma. I did not see you."

She was well-dressed; she must have been coming from church, maybe. Aunty Omerie was her father's first wife—yes, his first wife. Her father had three wives, and her mother was the third.

She raised her head, her face looking slightly pained. She reached down again to rub her right foot.

"Sorry, ma," Onome said. She had stepped on Aunty Omerie's toe. She was wearing her slippers, so she was hoping she did not injure her toe.

"It's okay," Omerie raised her hand to signify it was fine

"But where are you rushing to this afternoon?" Omerie asked, raising her head to look at her now.

"Ma, I... I'm going to the market."

"Ehn... Okay." She paused for a second, her eyes had gone to Onome's dress. "Have you been cooking?"

"Ehh... No, ma. I was cleaning the house and picking firewood from the backyard. I just want to rush to the market to buy some things and come back early."

"Okay, but don't you want to change your dress?"

Onome looked down at her dress again, raising up her head to her aunty. She did not know what to say.

"Anyway, it is okay, my dear," Omerie said, placing one of her hands on Onome's shoulder. "Which market are you going to?"

"Uju market, it is not far."

"Okay, no problem. Go well, my dear," she said, bidding her goodbye.

"Okay, Aunty. Thank you." She turned to leave but was a little concerned. "Ermm, Aunty, is your toe hurting you?"

"Ermm..." Aunty Omerie hesitated as she looked at her toe. "Don't worry, it will be okay. I will see you later."

Onome watched as Omerie tightened her face as she tried to walk a little.

"Sorry, ma." She reached over to hold her. "Let me go and get some Vaseline to rub on your toe." Onome was about to go back into her mother's quarters to get the Vaseline.

"No, no, no, it is fine," she said, starting to walk a bit. "See, it's already getting better. Don't worry, eh, just be on your way," she added, patting her on the back.

"Okay, ma," Onome said, a little unsure whether to leave. She started to walk away but then turned back. "Okay, bye-bye, ma."

"Okay, bye-bye," Aunty Omerie replied.

Onome walked slowly through the gate of the compound and turned back to look at her Aunty again. She could tell her thoughts were elsewhere as she started having a conversation with Musa now. This made Onome sigh in relief. As soon as she was through the gate and outside the compound, she started walking quickly again.

In no time, she could see the town square. As she approached, she noticed it was quite busy, as usual—it was a Sunday after all. She saw a group of young boys playing football and recognised them as boys from her school. She was tempted to join. On another part of the square, she saw a group of girls sitting and giggling as they watched the boys. A separate group, about her age, was sitting under a tree listening to a tall man. She didn't need to be told who it was—it was Pastor Maxwell, one of the junior pastors at their family church. She noticed her sister was there too. She should have known her sister would be out playing as usual. Rukevwe was only three years younger than her, although she always liked to act as though she were older. She was very stubborn.

Onome's eyes glanced around the group, and she also noticed her best friend, Prisca. It was as if Prisca could sense her staring at her; upon noticing Onome, she became excited and beckoned for her to join them quickly. Onome shook her head and lifted the shopping basket to show she was going to the market. She saw Prisca say something to Pastor Maxwell, who nodded, and then she left the group and ran over to her.

Prisca came near and stopped. "I have been waiting for you, where are you going?" she asked, looking down at the basket.

"I am going to the market," Onome said, kissing her teeth loudly, with a little disappointment in her voice.

Prisca looked at her, confused. "I thought we said we would meet here?" she said, a little out of breath.

"I know, but I have to go to the market. My mother asked me to buy somethings."

"Ehnn..." Prisca said, looking at her basket. "Which market are you going to?"

"Uju market. You know it's not too far. I think I will take the Motorbus or maybe a Motorbike so that I can get there quickly and come back quickly," she said, a bit unsure.

"If I may suggest, I think a Motorbike will be quicker sha. Just make sure when you come back, you join us."

"Ehnn... what is happening now?" Onome asked, turning to look at the group under the tree.

"Well, we are listening to Pastor Maxwell teaching us an interesting topic. You know how much I like the things he teaches," Prisca said, winking at Onome with a smile.

"Of course, I know," Onome said, shaking her head. "You and this Pastor shaa…" They both laughed playfully. Prisca has liked Pastor Maxwell since he came into the town eight months ago. She was always gushing about his sermons, how inspirational he was, and how kind he seemed to everyone. Every time he spoke, she would praise his words, often mimicking his gestures when she spoke about him. Onome couldn't help but tease her about it, but deep down, she knew Prisca had developed a real admiration for him.

"But why are you people outside today with the children?" Onome asked, looking again at the large group gathering.

"There is no electricity at the moment, so Pastor Maxwell said we should take the children's meeting to the square. At least we can sit under the tree, get some breeze, and more children can join us."

"Oh, okay." Onome looked at the children. "It looks like you have many children today."

Prisca turned to look. "Yes ooh, we have some children who joined newly today."

"That is good."

"Yes ooh, we thank God. It was Pastor Maxwell's good idea," Prisca said, smiling deeply.

"See you, see how you are smiling," Onome said while pushing her on the shoulder playfully. Prisca was giggling now. "Okay ooh, please let me rush so I can come back quickly. I will come and join you people later."

"Okay, then. Please try and come back quick ooh, I have gist for you," Prisca whispered.

"What gist again, madam? And why are you whispering?"

"Not now, just go and come back first, I will tell you. I don't want anyone else to hear," Prisca said, looking around.

"Ah ah, I don't understand, but there is nobody near us."

"It is about Erioma. She is back from holiday and has now joined the choir, imagine." Prisca kissed her teeth and shook her head.

Erioma was Prisca's nemesis. She was a Senior to them, attending University in the city and comes home from time to time. Prisca had always had the impression that Erioma had eyes for Pastor Maxwell.

"Is this the gist?" Onome asked, disappointed.

"No naah. Anyway, just go and come back, I will tell you later."

Onome looked at her strangely and sighed. "Okay, you and your gist shaa…"

"Anyway, I have to go back now. I will see you when you come back" Prisca smiled as she proceeded to turn around and walk away but turned back again "Ehn, wait ooh, this your dress is stained ooh, maybe you should go and change it."

"I know, I just need to go to the market. I will change it before I come, don't worry."

Okay, we'll see later then," Prisca said, waving goodbye as she ran back to join the group. Onome watched as Pastor Maxwell glanced at her when she joined them again, then suddenly raised his gaze, his eyes locking with hers. Onome immediately looked away and started walking. The last thing she wanted was for Pastor Maxwell to call her over. She quickened her pace; she hadn't been to church services in a long time, and she wasn't ready to explain it to him. She had always found it strange speaking with him, he was seven years older than they were and a very serious man (a Pastor). Too serious, in fact, she thought. He was well respected by most people in the town and very friendly with many of the families.

Onome paused to look at her dress, maybe she should have changed it. She sighed. Well, it's too late now; she had to rush to the market. She really wanted to join them at the square later. As she continued walking quickly, she wondered what gist Prisca had for her. This was not the first time Erioma had come to town; she always came and went. Although, if she wasn't mistaken, this was the first time she had shown interest and joined the choir. She wondered what else had happened.

She took a deep breath. Prisca always had some gist. If it wasn't about her darling Pastor, it would be about what was going on in the town. She shook her head. Her friend always had stories to tell, mostly the town gossip, which tended to be true. Well, whatever gist it was, it could wait until later. She swung the basket as she carried on walking. The sooner she got to the bus stop, the sooner she would be out of the sun for a short while.

Upon reaching the bus stop, she saw a Motorbus parked by the side. She ran quickly and was able to board the Motorbus immediately. It was going to Uju market, which made her happy. As she got on, she noticed an empty seat by the window, sat down, and immediately felt the breeze. She closed her eyes, what a relief. Hopefully, the market will go well, she still has to do a lot of haggling, to get the Motorbus back, she thought to herself. Hmm, she took a deep breath. God help her.

Chapter 2

Omerie turned to see if Onome was out of sight. once she was sure Onome was gone, she bent down again to rub her big toe.

Madam, sorry ooh. The leg dey pain you? Make I go bring Rub *(Rub was a brand of ointment used to relieve muscle pain, joint aches, sprains, and minor injuries.)*

"No, no, it is okay. I just need to massage it small, but it is okay."

"Okay, ma."

Omerie carried on walking into the compound. She noticed it had been swept clean, and the grass had been cut.

"Ah, Musa, nah you cut the grass? You try ooh. You cut the grass well today."

"Yes, ma. Thank you, ma." Omerie watched as he looked away smiling.

"But I think we still need to cut the grass a little lower," she said, pointing to some grass growing around one of the trees in the compound. She walked over to it. "Cut am like this," she said, bending down and placing her hand to show the height the grass should be.

"Okay, ma. No wahala, I go cut am."

"Just trim around it small and it will be fine."

"Yes, madam, I go cut am very low," he said, getting up and wiping his hands on his trousers. "I go do am now."

"No, no, finish wetin you dey do." Omerie stopped him as he put the radio away. "You can do it later, just listen to the football match."

"No, madam, I go do am now."

"Musa, don't worry. Listen to the football match, okay? I know how much you like football. You can cut it later," she insisted.

"Okay, ma" he laughed. "Nah Nigeria dey play ooh."

"Is that so? Are they winning?" she asked.

"Dem dey try, ma, but dem never score shaa…"

"Ehn, well, I hope they win because I know that will make people happy in this town," she said as she started walking slowly.

"Ah, yes ooh. Thank you, ma, I go cut the grass well well."

"Okay ooh, Musa, enjoy the football match," Omerie said, waving at him as she started to make her way to her quarters, which was at the back.

"Omerie!" Omerie jolted as she heard a voice call her name. Of course, she recognised the voice of her husband. She turned to look; he was standing just outside his quarters. She had been only a few steps from the gate, deep in thought, and hadn't even noticed him standing there. His quarters was the first building people would see upon entering the compound. It was a medium-sized house, built specifically for him and to his liking. It was well-furnished, with two bedrooms, a living room, and a kitchen. It was where he hosted his guests, laid his head to rest, and entertained each of his wives. It was a place she rarely visited these days.

"Chief…?" She hurried toward him. "Chief" is what everyone calls him—an honourable title given to a few men in the town to honour them. As she drew closer, she noticed there were two chairs and a table with a bottle of brandy on it.

"Chief, good afternoon. I hope all is well," she said, lowering her eyes to avoid his gaze.

"Good afternoon," he replied, glancing around the compound. "Why is the compound quiet? Where is everybody?"

"Ah, it's Sunday. I am sure the children are out playing. There is an event in the square today."

"I see. Okay. Ermm, come and sit down. I need to speak to you," he said, pointing to one of the chairs. He slowly walked to sit in one of the chairs. She took the chair next to him as she watched him open the bottle of brandy and pour himself a large amount into the glass. He quickly took a sip, making a sound with his lips. She had known him long enough to recognise that he did that when he tasted something he enjoyed. She sat still, waiting for him to tell her the reason he had asked her to sit with him. She wondered why her husband had invited her to join him this Sunday. She watched as he took another sip of the brandy.

Now she was worried. Why did Chief need alcohol to discuss whatever was on his mind? *This is highly unusual,* she thought to herself. Now she was curious; she moved slightly on the chair, and she was closely facing him now. She could literally feel her heart starting to beat faster through her blouse.

He leaned back in the chair. "It is very hot today," he said, trying to make small talk. He never makes small talk. She nodded her head in response.

"When was your last wives' meeting?" he asked, not looking at her."

"Yesterday evening, Chief."

"I see. Well, you will have a meeting again, immediately."

"Ah, okay. Is anything the matter?"

"Everything is fine," Chief replied.

"Okay, Chief." Omerie bent her head slightly to the left, avoiding his gaze. He looked around quickly, as if to check that no one was nearby. He cleared his throat, hesitated, and pretended to be slightly distracted by a leaf that had dropped from the tree near his quarters.

"Listen," he finally said, leaning forward a little. "I'm soon to take another wife."

Another wife?" Her eyes widened; her tone filled with shock.

"Yes, of course..." Chief said firmly as he glanced at her. "I still don't have a son. Or are you blind?" His voice sounded a little irritated.

Omerie lowered her head in silence. He continued, taking no notice of it.

"I married Rume so many years ago. All I have are two girls. Two girls! No more children for how many years now. She has become boring, all she does is demand money. I want money for this, I want money for that." He kissed his teeth. "She cannot cook sef. Her food has never tasted nice."

Omerie raised her eyebrows in surprise. She took a deep breath but remained silent.

"Anyway," Chief continued "I just wanted to let you know that I have decided to take a new wife. I'll marry her in two weeks' time; she is from the Eseri village." Chief's gaze now was fixed on Omerie as he told her his plans to marry a new wife. The surprise was written all over her face, but she remained silent. Thankfully, he did not care for a response, his mind was already made up. He carried on, "I have already gone to see her family, they will be coming here for the introduction. You must prepare for her arrival and inform the other wives, they must be on their best behaviour, or I will return them to their father's house." His tone was serious now. He wanted his wives to know that this new bride was important to him. Omerie said nothing still.

"Are you listening to me?" he asked

"Yes, of course, Chief." Omerie raised her gaze to look at him now.

"Okay, then what do you have to say?"

"Well, Chief, I have heard you. We will prepare for her arrival, and I will inform the other wives and their children," she said, "Is there anything specific you want us to do or prepare for that day?" she asked placing her hands together on her thigh.

He relaxed back on the chair. She could see he was thinking.

"Ermm... No," he said, shaking his head.

There was silence between them now. It felt like a long silence, and he looked like he was deep in thought.

"Is that all Chief?"

"Yes, that is all for now. You can go and start preparing now," he said, almost dismissively.

"Okay, Chief." Omerie stood up and turned to leave.

"Ome," Chief called to her. She was surprised; he called her by his favourite name for her; he had not called her that in a long time. His tone was unbelievably soft too.

She turned around to face him. "Yes, Chief," was all she could say as she stood looking at him.

Chief just sat there, staring at her. She thought she saw gentleness in his eyes, and his hand moved slowly but then stopped.

There was silence between them for what felt like eternity. His gaze later shifted to the glass of brandy on the table. He immediately waved his hands to dismiss her. "Nothing, you can go."

"Okay, Chief, rest well." He did not respond as he poured more brandy into his half-filled glass. She turned and hurried away, tears beginning to form in her eyes. She rushed off, not wanting Chief to see the tears that were just about to fall down her cheeks. She walked quickly; her quarters were at the back of the compound. Her hands were over her lips now as the tears streamed down her face. When she reached her front door, she heard voices. She paused a few steps away and quickly wiped away the tears with her wrapper. Thankfully, the curtain was drawn, so no one saw or heard her. When she was sure her face was dry, she walked toward the front door, pulled aside the curtain, and entered the house. She saw Eno, her niece, who was living with her, standing beside a woman talking. Omerie soon realised it was her close friend, Ufuoma.

"Ah, Ufuoma, you are here. I did not know you were coming." She bent to give Ufuoma a hug. "When did you come?" she asked as she took a seat next to her friend.

"Not long at all. I said let me come and see you today as my husband is away."

"Welcome ooh," Omerie said, smiling a little. She and Ufuoma have been friends since childhood. They had known each other since secondary school.

"Thank you," Ufuoma replied.

"Eno, please help me get your aunty something to drink." Turning to Ufuoma. "What would you like to drink?"

"If you have a bottle of chilled coke, that will be good, please. The weather is just too hot today," Ufuoma said and started to fan herself with her blouse.

"Okay. Eno, get her a cold bottle of coke from the fridge," Omerie instructed her niece.

"Ufuoma, Ufuoma," Omerie called to her friend playfully. "How are you?"

"I am fine ooh, my sister."

"You are looking fresh. These two weeks you spent with your mother in the village must have been good for you ooh," Omerie said, looking Ufuoma up and down.

Ufuoma laughed. "You know my mother, nah... Always complaining that I don't eat well. This time, she was complaining that I've lost weight, so she decided to feed me. What can I do but eat? Is it not my mother?" They both laughed then.

"How is everything shaa?"

"Well, we are okay, we are okay" she replied finding it difficult to contain her emotions.

"Are you sure you are okay? You are not your usual self." Ufuoma was looking at her closely now.

Omerie sighed. "I am fine, my sister."

"Look, I know you and I saw your face when you came in just now. I know you are not fine." Ufuoma leaned forward. "Your eyes are red. You have been crying, haven't you?" She shook her head, relaxing back on the chair. Omerie said nothing.

"Ome, what is the matter?" Ufuoma asked with a concerned tone now.

"My sister," Omerie said, sighing and shaking her head. She took a breath before telling Ufuoma was had just happened.

Chapter 3

Chief was deep in thought as he sat outside his quarters, sipping his brandy. He could hear the voices coming from Musa's radio, the football commentator sounding disappointed, as it seemed Nigeria had missed another opportunity to score. Hmm, disappointed. That was how he had been feeling for some time. His third wife, Rume, was becoming a nightmare, always talking about things he had no interest in. Just last night, he had kicked her out of his room and told her never to set foot in there again. Women! He turned to look at Omerie, who seemed to almost be running to her quarters. "Hmmm..." He sighed. Of all his wives, she was his first and his favourite. He loved her, but after seven years of marriage with no children, his parents forced him to take another wife. Omerie, as always, had been understanding that night when he finally plucked up the courage to mention it to her.

They had returned from her favourite eatery, and he told her that she deserved a treat for being such a supportive wife. He wasn't well off when they got married. He knew his father was waiting for him to finish university before introducing him fully to the family business. His father was a trader—he sold beer and other soft drinks. At the time, he wasn't well known, but the business was thriving, and they were comfortable. He had liked Omerie from the moment they met. She had come to his father's store to buy drinks for her father. He had heard her voice while inside, arranging the crates of drinks at the back of the store. There was something soft and warm about her voice that made him want to see what the girl with the lovely voice looked like.

He left the crates he was arranging and came to the front to see her face. As he approached, he noticed how beautiful she was—fair in complexion, slightly tall, with lovely eyes. She was wearing a flowery dress, and her hair was neatly plaited to the back. She was talking to one of the sales assistants, and he noticed her lovely smile as she spoke. He listened to their conversation; she had come to buy three crates of soft drinks and mentioned that she would need help carrying them to her house. The sales assistant said it would be difficult since he had to stay back at the store. At that point, he came back to reality and stepped in, supporting the assistant. He explained that the assistant needed to stay in the store but that he could help her with the crates. She smiled at him in gratitude, and he smiled back.

She assured him that her father's house was not too far, just 20 minutes away. He didn't care; he would carry the crates as far as she wanted. He loaded the crates onto a wheelbarrow and gestured for her to lead the way. The wheelbarrow was heavy, and he was thankful for that, it would make the journey longer. He soon found himself sweating heavily as he pushed the barrow. Making conversation was a challenge, but he tried. She was shy, which made her even more beautiful to him. He must have asked a hundred questions that day. He knew right then that he would marry her.

As they talked, he made sure she knew that he would be the owner of the shop one day. Three years later, they were married. He had just finished university and was still doing his National Youth Service Corps (NYSC), and he was afraid he had waited too long, other men were interested in her. So, he married her quickly.

That night when they had arrived from her favourite eatery, he said they should sit outside as there was a sweet cool breeze, and they could watch the night stars together. She loved it when he was sweet like that. She joined him as he invited her to sit and rest her head on his shoulder. They had sat there quietly for a while. He had been telling himself that tonight, he had to tell her—and he had to do it quickly. Slightly worried that she might have fallen asleep, he gently lifted her head and kissed her cheek.

"Ome, are you sleeping?" he asked softly, gazing at her face.

"No, I'm just enjoying the cool breeze," she replied, sitting up straight, stretching a little, and then resting her head back on his shoulder. He cleared his throat. "Ome, there's something I need to tell you."

She sat up immediately, hearing the seriousness in his voice. "What is it?"

He cleared his throat again and took her hand, trying to speak. "Emm......" but he stopped.

"Ah, this one that you are struggling to tell me, what is the matter, Emmanuel?" she asked, sensing his hesitation. She could tell he was worried now as he struggled to speak. He looked down as she waited patiently. He took a deep breath.

"Ome, you know my father has been insisting that I take a new wife, and he won't let me have any peace." He waited for a response but realising that none was coming, he continued, "Emm...Well, I have agreed to take a second wife." He was still looking down but trying to see her reaction by the side of his eye.

She had removed her hands from his and leaned back on the tiny chair they were both sharing, turning her face away. Both hands were folded over her chest, and she seemed deep in thought. He remembered wondering what she was thinking. His taking a second wife was something his family often mentioned, even in her presence. He stared at her—was she thinking about leaving? He could not bear to lose her. He needed her to stand by him through this. He knew it was selfish, but he could not do this without her.

He took her face, gently trying to turn it toward him.

"Ome, please look at me," he pleaded.

Brushing his hand away, she turned her face again, refusing to look at him. He reached out once more, this time holding her chin as he gently turned her face toward him.

"Ome, please don't be annoyed with me, please." He pressed his face towards hers. "I need to do this. I can't fight with my family anymore. Ome, I promise you, once I have some children, they will leave us alone and we can have a quiet and peaceful life."

She laughed softly. "A peaceful life? You must be joking."

"Yes, my family will leave us alone," he said, wanting to assure her.

She shook her head slightly and was silent for a bit. "Emmanuel, I thought you were a Christian?" He did not reply. She leaned over to him, "We said we would continue to pray about this, God is the one that gives children, don't you believe this anymore?"

"Ehh, yes, of course, I believe, but what can I do ehn? My father is threatening to disown me if I do not do as he says. Ome, what can I do?" he said pleading.

Omerie took a deep breath. "Well, anyway, Emmanuel, you know I am a Christian. I cannot stay with you in marriage if you are going to marry another wife. I can't." She turned away again, this time facing the wall with a frown on her face.

"Ah, Ome, but you know I cannot live without you, you have to stay with me. I cannot do this without you. You know this is not my desire. My parents are insisting that I take another wife so that I can have an heir, a son to carry my name. I must do this for my family; otherwise, my father will disinherit me."

She was quiet for a while. She folded her hands on her chest and took a deep breath.

"Emmanuel, if you feel you must do this, then I will support you. No matter what happens, I will still love you. You are my husband and if you wish for me to stay with you, I will." She couldn't look at him.

"Ome, thank you. I love you." He pulled her towards him and kissed her cheeks over and over again.

He smiled softly, remembering how the night had ended. That was many years ago. A second wife had become a third, and now he was marrying Amaka, an Igbo girl. If his parents were alive, they would have been against him marrying outside their tribe. He almost laughed at the thought of his father having a heart attack and his mother pretending to faint just to draw the attention of the neighbours.

Chief smiled, pausing from his thought. "Parents and their trouble," he muttered, shrugging off the thought.

Amaka was a nice young girl, beautiful. She was 22 years old, and he was 59. At first, he felt uncomfortable taking her as his wife, but he was desperate. He needs a son. A young girl like Amaka was more likely to bear him an heir, or two. Yes, he needs a male child. None of his three wives had been able to give him a son all these years.

He was beginning to think it might be a curse. But no, why should he be cursed? They simply could not bear him a son, and that was that.

Chief sighed. If only Omerie had not been barren—32 years, no children, not even one. He had to take action. He could not stop now; he could not turn back. It was much too late.

Amaka will be his wife in a few weeks. She would produce a male child and make him feel like a man.

"Yes, Chief Emmanuel Akpofure will be a man again," Chief said out loud.

He looked around, worried that someone might have heard him. Shaking his head, he picked up his glass of brandy and took a sip. Setting it down, he leaned back in his chair, his mind drifting to the tasks that still needed to be done for the traditional marriage.

Just as he reached for his glass of brandy for another sip.

Oh no, not her, he thought as he saw Rume approaching.

Chapter 4

Rume angrily slammed the front door to her quarters and sank heavily into a chair in the living room. She rested her chin on her hand, rocking back and forth.

"Imagine," she hissed to herself, frowning.

"Me, Rume." She pointed a finger at her chest as she continued to speak. "Chief is just treating me anyhow." She paused and then laughed sarcastically, clapping her hands together and leaning back in the chair with her arms folded across her chest.

She replayed the event in her mind. She had seen Chief outside, enjoying his usual Sunday relaxation with his brandy. Last night had ended badly—Chief had complained again that there was too much salt in the Egusi soup she had prepared. She had noticed that he was always complaining about her cooking. Today it was too much pepper, tomorrow it would be too little salt, or not enough vegetable.

Last night, she was just tired of his complaints. She shouted and told him to go cook the Egusi himself; after all, some of his friends were doing that at their own home. He didn't take it well. He had risen from the dining table, clearly annoyed that she had spoken to him that way. He'd told her to leave his quarters immediately and to take her plate of Egusi and Pounded Yam with her. She hissed and, picking up everything she had prepared, she stormed off.

But this morning, she woke up thinking it was not a good thing to have done. Things had not been going well between them, and she was getting frustrated. She had tried, but it seemed like nothing she did, pleased him anymore.

Nevertheless, she knew that no matter how she felt, she still needed to apologise, it was the custom. Her mother would always say to her, "Dis nah our custom ooh. Wife no suppose rude to e husband. She must treat am well ... like say e be King, no matter wetin e do."

She could hear her mother's words ringing in her mind. By the afternoon, she couldn't take it anymore. She decided to go and apologise to him. She had her bath, put on a nice wrapper and blouse—she chose a figure-hugging blouse and tied the wrapper tightly around her waist. He could never resist her. No matter how angry he was with her, she always seemed to win him back. She already knew what to do.

As she approached him while he was sipping his brandy, she smiled from ear to ear. He looked away, a serious frown on his face, but she wasn't deterred by it. Men! She thought, always wanting their women to beg them.

"Ah, Chief, Chief!" she remembered saying as she walked over to bend down and give him a hug. He raised his hand to stop her.

"What is this nonsense, ehn?" he had said, looking at her angrily.

Ah, Chief, are you still vexed with me, ehn?" she had asked, looking at him. He said nothing.

"Chief, Chief," she had said playfully, bending down to stroke his chin. He had knocked her hand away.

"Look here my friend, you better leave here, you hear me?" He hissed. He stood up, took his bottle of brandy and glass, and walked into the quarters.

"Ah, Chief, which kind of vexation be this one, ehn?" she said, following him inside. He did not answer. He walked into his room, shut the door, and locked it. She knocked a few times, apologising again and again but did not get an answer. She turned around and saw the maid pretending she was cleaning.

"You! What kind of cleaning are you doing there!?" she raised her voice in anger. "Will you get out of there!"

She watched as the maid quickly hurried away. Hissing in frustration, she kissed her teeth, glared at the door to Chief's room once more, and stormed off.

She was on her feet now, having finished recollecting what had happened. She began pacing the living room when a knock sounded at the front door.

"Yes, who is there?" she almost yelled.

There was no response. She marched to the door, yanked the curtain aside, and flung it open angrily. Standing outside was Eno, the first wife's *(Omerie's)* niece.

Rume looked her up and down.

"Yes?"

"Good afternoon, ma," Eno greeted, kneeling slightly—a gesture of respect for elders. Rume did not respond. She just stared at Eno, waiting to hear why she was at her front door.

"Ma, Aunty Omerie said I should tell you that there is an urgent meeting... ermm... she said you should come and join them at her place."

Rume just continued to stare at her. The girl took a step back unsure what to do now.

"Is that all?" Rume eventually said.

"Yes, ma."

Rume hissed, turned, and shut the door. She dropped onto the chair again.

"What nonsense meeting?" she muttered, leaning back. "Madam meeting, she won't go and give birth to children like her mates." She kissed her teeth.

She had just started to relax when she suddenly leaned forward in the chair. Wait. If she didn't go for this so-called meeting, that woman wouldn't hesitate to tell Chief. And given the current situation, it would be twice as hard to win him back.

She sighed. The last thing she wanted was to sit with the other wives to discuss anything. She knew they didn't like her. They had only pretended when she was first brought into the house. It hadn't taken long for them to show their true colours.

Always scheming, always looking for ways to spoil Chief's mind about her. But they haven't succeeded. She is still Chief's favourite.

Rume stood up. Well, her and Chief might be having this small problem, but it was nothing she couldn't handle.

Her wrapper had come loose. She tied it again, this time tightly. "Let them see and be jealous," she said to herself.

She glanced around the living room as if looking for something to take with her. Then she shook her head.

In no time, she was out the door, making her way to Omerie's quarters.

Chapter 5

The market was bustling with activity. Onome had just finished buying the last item on her mother's list. She now had everything her mother had requested, although she wasn't entirely sure she had picked the right peppers.

On the list, her mother had written red peppers, but Onome had added some yellow and green peppers, thinking their colours might add more flavour—or at least make the dish look prettier.

With the ingredients carefully placed in the basket, she turned and began to make her way home.

The narrow passage between the market stalls was crowded, forcing her to walk carefully to avoid bumping into people or knocking over items. Shops and stalls lined both sides, and the sharp smell of raw meat hit her nose as she passed by the butchers' section.

Suddenly, her eyes landed on a stall displaying beautiful dresses. One, in particular, caught her attention. It hung just outside the shop, its soft fabric swaying gently in the breeze.

Onome moved closer, running her fingers over the material. It felt smooth, almost silky. A smile spread across her face as she admired it. Her birthday was coming up, and oh, how lovely it would be to own this dress.

Just as she was imagining herself wearing it, a cheerful voice interrupted her thoughts.

"Customer! Welcome ooh! You wan buy? We get your size, fine, fine colours!"

Startled, Onome quickly withdrew her hand from the dress and took a small step back.

"No, ma," she said politely. "I was just looking at it."

"Looking at it? Which kain English be that?" the woman snapped, narrowing her eyes. "You no wan buy am, but you dey touch am? Abeg, if you no wan buy, make you no touch am, you hear? Abi you wan spoil am?"

Onome flinched at the sharpness in the woman's voice. She quickly stepped back, clutching her basket tightly.

"No, ma, I no wan spoil am. Abeg, no vex," Onome said, her voice barely above a whisper.

The woman hissed and adjusted the dress on its hanger. "Abeg, shift make better customer see road."

Onome turned away from the shop and continued to make her way through the narrow passage. She admired the shops as she passed, but then she glanced at her watch and realised the time—it was already 4 o'clock!

How did time fly so fast?

Quickly, she picked up her pace. If she hurried, she could be home in thirty minutes. That would give her plenty of time to drop the basket and meet Prisca at the square—hopefully, Prisca was still there.

Emerging from the market, Onome spotted a motorbus. She hopped in, relieved to find it wasn't crowded. Thankfully, the roads were clear of traffic, and she reached her stop in no time.

As soon as she got off, she started walking briskly, almost running. She was halfway down the street when, snap! Her slippers broke.

"Oh no!" she groaned, bending to pick them up. Why now?

This was one of her favourite slippers. She hissed in frustration, inspecting the damage. She'd have to get the shoe repairer to fix it, but that wasn't happening today. For now, she'd have to walk barefoot.

She winced as the hot ground scorched her feet. The sun was still high, and the road felt like fire. Her only option was to run.

"Onome!"

The voice interrupted her thoughts, sharp and impatient. She froze at the junction leading to the narrow road that cut straight to her father's house.

"Onome!"

This time it was louder. She turned reluctantly and groaned. Beatrice.

Oh no, not now.

Beatrice, her cousin, stood at the corner, one hand planted firmly on her waist, the other waving in the air.

"Onome! So. you didn't hear me calling you? Ehn? Are you deaf?" Beatrice demanded, her frown deepening.

Onome huffed under her breath. "Sister, I am not deaf ooh," she muttered.

"Come on, keep quiet!" Beatrice snapped, eyeing her from head to toe. "Rubbish."

She hissed loudly, rolling her eyes before folding her arms across her chest.

Onome looked away, her face tightening with anger. She was not in the mood for an argument.

"Abeg, take."

Beatrice shoved a bag into Onome's hands.

"What is this?" Onome asked, gripping the bag tightly.

"Ask me," Beatrice snapped, hissing as she turned and walked away without another word.

Onome shook her head, watching her cousin's retreating figure. Beatrice was so rude.

Yet, Onome couldn't deny it, Beatrice was beautiful. Her skin glowed, smooth and fair. Her hair, long and perfectly kept, always looked like it had just been styled. And those clothes—always expensive, always stylish.

Onome sighed. She often wondered where Beatrice got the money for such things. Clothes like that weren't cheap.

Unlike Beatrice, Onome never wore fancy outfits. Her mother never bought her anything nice; no clothes, no accessories, nothing.

She clicked her tongue in frustration, her thoughts interrupted by the sound of Beatrice's voice. She was already up the road, greeting a family that passed by.

Onome's stomach tightened. She quickly lowered her head. If Beatrice knew them, then they probably knew their family too.

She wasn't in the mood to see or greet anyone right now.

Pretending to search for something inside the bag, she focused her eyes downward and fiddled with its contents.

The family walked by without saying a word.

Onome exhaled, relieved.

Onome raised her head, careful not to turn and look at the family as they passed. She could still see Beatrice a short distance away, strutting confidently as always.

Onome clicked her tongue in irritation.

"One day," she thought. "One day, she won't be able to push me around."

The thought lingered, growing stronger. "One day, very soon."

She kept walking, her bare feet pressing into the hot sand. Each step burned, but she refused to quicken her pace. She couldn't bear the thought of Beatrice turning around and laughing at her.

Onome straightened her shoulders and continued, forcing herself to keep going despite the heat searing her soles.

***

Two weeks later, it was Onome's birthday. For the first time in years, her mother had decided that, this year, she and her sister should have a small get-together. Their birthdays were just days apart, and Rukevwe had also finished her exams. Excitement filled the air as they had been up early to start preparing.

"Onome!"

She knew that voice. Rising quickly from where she was blowing air into the firewood, Onome looked up and saw Aunty Omerie standing a short distance away, her kind face framed by a warm smile.

"Yes, Ma!" Onome answered, wiping her hands as she walked toward her. There was always something about Aunty Omerie's voice that made her heart skip with excitement.

"Yes, Ma?"

"Onome, it's your birthday today."

"Ah... yes, Ma! You remembered?" Onome's face lit up. "Mama is going to cook my favourite food today—some delicious jollof rice with fried plantain and chicken! They're even preparing the fattest chicken in the compound for me today!"

Omerie chuckled softly. "Excellent... that is good. I've also asked Eric to get some cow meat from the market. I already told Oga Monday to cut it nicely and fry it to make suya for your guests this evening."

"Ah! Thank you, Ma!" Onome dropped to her knees, grabbing Omerie's leg in excitement.

"Ah, stand up, stand up!" Omerie said, quickly lifting her to her feet. "Come, come, I have something for you."

"Something for me, Ma?" Onome's eyes widened, her excitement bubbling over.

Omerie took her hand and began to lead her away from the cooking area.

They walked toward Omerie's quarters at the back of the house. As soon as they entered, Onome's senses were flooded with the soft, fragrant scent of fresh flowers. She immediately noticed a small bouquet of colourful blooms resting by the side of a wooden chair.

The room smelled lovely. The windows were open, and a cool morning breeze danced through the curtains.

"Onome, sit down. I'll be right back."

Onome obeyed, still overwhelmed by the sweet smell of the flowers and how homely Aunty Omerie's quarters felt. Not that this was her first time there, but it always seemed different somehow. The house was immaculately clean, and Onome couldn't resist running her fingers across the stool beside her chair to check for dust. Of course, it was spotless.

She leaned back into the chair, letting out a soft sigh. It was so comfortable—nothing like the stiff, imported chair at their house that always made her bottom hurt. Her mother claimed it had come all the way from China, though Onome often wondered who her mother could possibly know in China. As far as she knew, the farthest her mother had ever travelled was to Drury Village to visit her sister.

Omerie reappeared, holding a bag.

"Here, this is for you."

Onome's eyes widened. "For me? All this?"

She hadn't even opened the bag, but her excitement bubbled over.

"Open it," Omerie urged, smiling.

Onome rushed to untie the bag, her hands trembling slightly. When she saw what was inside, her mouth dropped open.

"This is for me?" She clutched the bag tightly to her chest, eyes wide with disbelief.

"Ma, this is very expensive. Are you sure you want me to have them?"

"Of course! They're yours now," Omerie said, patting her shoulder. "This is my gift to you today. Maybe you can wear one of the dresses this evening, and you can take the materials to the girls in my shop. Let them sew some nice styles for you."

Onome's face lit up. "Ah, thank you, Ma! Thank you, thank you!" She knelt quickly to show her gratitude.

"It's okay, Onome. Get up, get up!" Omerie pulled her to her feet. "You don't know you're becoming a woman now? Very soon, you'll be the apple of one man's eye. Or don't you know?"

Onome blushed deeply, looking down at her feet.

"Ah... no, Ma... no."

"What do you mean 'no'?" Omerie teased, laughing. "Are you not a fine girl?"

Onome shifted nervously, still looking down. Omerie must have noticed her discomfort because she quickly changed the subject.

"Okay, so with the materials, what will you make? Maybe a skirt and blouse or a dress?"

"Ermm... I'm not sure yet," Onome replied, smiling now. "But I know it'll be the latest style in town!"

She grinned, already envisioning herself in something beautiful.

"Latest style, ehn?" Omerie laughed softly. "So which one is that now? You young girls these days." She waved her hand dismissively. "Anyway, do whatever you like with them, but let me see them when they're ready, ehn?"

Omerie smiled as she watched Onome run her hands through the materials, already lost in thought.

"Thank you, Ma!" Onome knelt before her again.

"Ah, I said it's enough now. Get up—it's nothing. If I don't give these things to you, who will I give them to?" Omerie shrugged her shoulders, her words trailing off.

Onome knew what that shrug meant—something unspoken, a deeper thought Omerie didn't care to share. But Onome also knew this wasn't the time to ask questions.

"Okay, Ma. Let me go; Mama must be looking for me now."

"Alright. I'll come and celebrate with you later. Just make sure you leave the breast of the chicken for me, o!"

"Bye, Ma! Thank you!" Onome knelt slightly again and slowly walked out of the quarters. But the moment she stepped outside, her lips spread into a big smile. She hurried toward the back of her mother's quarters, eager to show Rukevwe.

In her haste, she nearly bumped into her mother, who was coming around the back of the house.

Her mother pushed her back sharply. "What is it? Where are you rushing to, ehn?" Without waiting for a reply, she continued, "How many times have I told you to watch where you're going?"

"Sorry..." Onome mumbled, her hand instinctively covering her lips as she raised her head slightly to meet her mother's gaze.

Her mother's eyes swept over her, irritation already clear on her face. Then her gaze fell to the bag in Onome's hands.

"Where are you coming from? And what is this?" She snatched the bag from Onome and began rifling through it.

"Ermm... these are some things that Aunty Omerie gave me just now." Onome shifted nervously. "She said it's my birthday gift."

Her mother's hands kept moving, pulling the contents out one by one.

"Gave you what as a birthday gift? These things?"

The disbelief in her voice stung. Onome's excitement began to waver as she watched her mother's reaction.

She watched as her mother's gaze was first on her and then flicked back to the materials. Her mother's fingers clenched tightly around the fabric as she exhaled sharply, before shoving the materials back into the bag.

"What is it? Do you not like them?" Onome asked, sensing her mother was lost in her thoughts again.

Her mother kissed her teeth, her irritation palpable. "Just go inside, start cooking the rice, and prepare the chicken."

"But Mary *(their maid)* is going to make the rice and chicken. You said you'd cook the rice because it's my birthday."

"Cook what? Which rice? So now I'm your cook?" Rume's voice was sharp, her frustration spilling over.

"Noooo," Onome replied, her tone tinged with disappointment. "I'll cook it," she said, turning to leave, but then she remembered something. "I'll call Ese and Omoefe to come and help *(Ese and Omoefe; her half-sisters from her father's second marriage. Who were slightly older than her.)*

"Help with what, eh? Why do you want to bring those children here? Dis pikin *(child)*… Why do you just like trouble?"

Onome folded her arms across her chest, grumbling slightly. "I can't cook all the food and do everything before the guests start arriving ooh."

Her mother stared at her, clearly unimpressed.

"Ehn, you know this town ooh. They'll laugh at us if they come and we're still cooking the food." Onome leaned against the front door, her arms still crossed, eyes flicking toward her mother. "Chief Olorma's family is coming ooh. They said you invited them. You know them and their bad mouth…" She pretended to turn away, as though she were about to walk to the kitchen.

She knew exactly what to say to make her mother cave. Her mother was a proud woman—everything had to be the best and perfect. The best food, the best clothes, and the finest things. She couldn't stand being late, and she hated the thought of keeping guests waiting.

"My friend, will you come back here? Are you talking with your back to me?" Rume pulled Onome by her dress. Onome nearly lost her balance as she felt herself being dragged to face her mother. Once she was steady, she looked up at her mother, who gave her a sharp, disapproving glare.

With a deep sigh, Rume hissed. "Go and call them. Just make sure they don't enter my kitchen. I am warning you oh!" She raised a finger and pointed at Onome, her voice firm. "If I see them in the kitchen…" she trailed off, her words hanging in the air.

"Yes, ma," Onome replied, her head bent as she smiled, grateful for her mother's concession. She quickly turned to leave, but then she remembered the gift from Aunty Omerie. Scratching her hair nervously, she hesitated.

"Mama..." she began, then paused, unsure. "Emmm... the bag. Let me take it inside."

"My friend, leave here and go and do what you need to do!" Rume hissed again, dismissing her with a wave of her hand.

Onome slowly walked away, reluctantly leaving. Her heart sank as she realised that her mother still had the beautiful dresses and materials Aunty Omerie had given her. *God, please don't let her take them away*, Onome prayed silently. She kicked the sand beneath her feet in frustration. No one in this town has dresses like those. When she wore them, she'd be the envy of the town.

A small skip escaped her as she smiled, comforted by the thought of her party and the beautiful gift she had received. She hoped, more than anything, that her mother would leave her with this one joy.

Chapter 6

The celebration was in full swing. The band played lively tunes while the children danced with joy. Everyone was dressed in their finest clothes, and Onome couldn't help but notice how rare such celebrations were in this small town. Not many could afford to throw birthday parties every year, and she was grateful to her mother for that. It was one of the few things she had always insisted on—hosting a big party each year. But Onome knew it wasn't entirely for her benefit. It was her mother's way of celebrating herself and showing off. But even so, Onome couldn't deny the feeling of excitement.

At 18, she was on the verge of adulthood. She daydreamed about the day she would be old enough to marry... marry Michael.

Yes, Michael! The man of her dreams. He was older, 24 years old, and though he had never noticed her, Onome's heart couldn't let go of the idea that one day, he would. He liked Beatrice, her cousin who lived in her father's quarters. Beatrice was of course beautiful; fair-skinned, glowing, and effortlessly charming. She could turn any man's head, and Michael was no exception. But Onome knew deep down that Beatrice and Michael were not meant to be. *They didn't look good together,* Onome told herself. Michael would be better off with her, that's what she believed. One day, when the scales fell from Michael's eyes, he would finally notice her.

Michael will surely notice me one day. Maybe today, she thought, glancing down at her dress; it was one of the dresses that Aunty Omerie had given her. She had worn it with care, feeling elegant. Ese had helped her plait her hair, and Onome couldn't help but admire herself.

Hopefully, tonight will be the night.

She had prepared the best Jollof rice Michael had ever tasted, and she would serve him his meal in one of her mother's designer dishes. *Hmm...* She smiled at the thought. *Michael will notice me tonight.*

Though she hadn't seen him yet, she knew he might be coming. Ese had overheard Beatrice saying earlier that Michael was coming to visit her today. Apparently, he had bought Beatrice a gold bracelet she had been asking for and would give it to her tonight. The thought of Beatrice with a gold bracelet made Onome's stomach churn. *A gold bracelet? Why her?* She clenched her fists tightly.

Please, God, let Michael notice me today. She whispered silently to herself, her hopes rising despite the gnawing jealousy she felt.

"Happy birthday!" Ese and Omoefe seemed to appear out of nowhere, tickling Onome all over.

"Haha...please stop...stop...if I laugh too much, I'll wee on myself and ruin my dress!" Onome gasped between bursts of laughter.

"You had better not," Ese teased, her voice dropping to a whisper. "You know your darling Michael is here."

"Michael is here?" Onome straightened up immediately, brushing invisible dust off her dress. "Where is he? Omoefe, is he coming this way?"

"Calm down, Sisiyoko," Ese said, using the nickname they'd given Onome. "I saw him with Beatrice earlier. Sorry o, but they were holding hands sha....and standing close to each other." She leaned a bit closer to Onome.

Onome frowned, trying to mask her jealousy. "What do you mean 'close'? Like how?"

"Well, you know, the kind of thing actors do in the movies." Ese pressed her lips to her hand, imitating a kiss.

"Oh no, Ese, abeg, stop," Onome hissed, feeling a knot of frustration tighten in her chest.

"Ah, see ooh, they're coming!" Omoefe suddenly spoke, hitting them both to be quiet. "Be quiet now."

The three of them quickly composed themselves, eyes fixed on Beatrice and Michael as they walked toward them. Beatrice's face was a picture of irritation, a silent acknowledgment that she knew they had been gossiping about her. Michael, on the other hand, was smiling. At first, Onome thought it was directed at her, but soon she realised he was just amused by the look on Beatrice's face.

"Welcome!" Ese greeted, curtsying slightly.

Onome turned to look at her, raising an eyebrow. 'Welcome'? Who says 'welcome'? she thought. She shook her head, knowing full well it sounded silly, but they were all nervous.

"Ese, how are you? You're looking nice this evening with your lovely dress," Michael said, smiling warmly as he playfully touched her cheek.

Ese blushed deeply, clearly flustered.

"Good evening, you're welcome," Onome quickly added, her voice high-pitched as she swayed nervously from side to side, hands pressed together like a nervous puppy. She wondered what his reply would be. Would he touch her cheek like he did with Ese? Would he run his fingers through her hair and tell her she looked beautiful today? Would he hug her since it was her birthday? Or would he...?

"Onome, happy birthday!" Michael interrupted her thoughts. "This place is packed! You're a very popular girl."

No touch. No compliment. No hug. That was disappointing. Onome's smile faltered, her eyes dropping to the floor in silent disappointment.

Beatrice slid her hand into his, flashing a smug smile. "Popular girl...haha...these are some of the ruffians from the other town. There's no important person here," she said, laughing loudly.

Ese, Omoefe, and Onome exchanged glances, their faces darkening with a shared frustration. It was clear from their glares that they didn't find Beatrice's comment funny. Yet, Beatrice laughed on, completely oblivious to the fact that no one was joining her in the joke.

"Actually, I think you're mistaken ooh," Michael interjected, pointing with a casual air. "Chief Omega's children are here, all eight of them. He's the chairman of Shell Petroleum in Warri, Delta State. In fact, there are two of his sons over there." He gestured toward two young boys who looked slightly out of place, scanning the crowd.

"I don't know them," Beatrice responded immediately, rolling her eyes in exasperation. "Anyway, let's go. I made your favourite meal, Ogbono soup and pounded yam. Let's go quickly before it gets cold." She began tugging at him as she turned to leave.

"Okay, Beatrice, we must go then." Michael smiled back at Onome. "Onome, I'll save some space for your Jollof rice. I've heard you're the queen of Jollof rice around here." He laughed, but his words were rushed as Beatrice continued pulling him away. He waved over his shoulder, still holding her hand, and with a final smile, he added, "I'll see you all later."

Beatrice was giggling now, her hand firmly clasped in Michael's as they walked off.

Ese and Omoefe giggled in imitation, but Onome's face hardened. So, he won't be eating her Jollof rice after all, she thought bitterly.

"This Sister Beatrice sef," Omoefe finally spoke, her voice dripping with sarcasm. "Chief Omega's children are not the only popular ones in this town, you know. Elohor Duro's father is the chairman of the Council of Education, and his four children are here too." She pointed toward a group sitting together, their nervous expressions betraying their unease.

Omoefe's gaze flicked over to the children, her face contorting with laughter. "Although, with their outfits, it looks like the tailor must not have been paid on time," she added, her voice rich with amusement. "Look at the yellow dresses they're wearing, the material is not fine at all. The shoulder pad sef, is terrible! And the boys, ha! The tailor must have given up halfway through styling their sleeves." She burst out laughing, but then realised she was the only one enjoying the joke.

"That was quite draining shaa," Ese said, still catching her breath from the excitement of the previous encounter. She turned toward Onome, who had found a log of wood to sit on beneath a tree. "Come on, Onome. He said he'll save space for your Jollof rice. Isn't that great?"

Onome gave a small, nonchalant shrug, her eyes trained on the ground. "Hmm... I don't think so," she muttered. "You know Sister Beatrice. After hearing that, she'll probably feed him so much pounded yam that he won't even remember the word 'Jollof rice'." She looked over at Omoefe, rolling her eyes.

Omoefe walked over to join them, shaking her head in disbelief. "Honestly, Onome, you're so dramatic," she teased. "It's just food nah. Forget about Beatrice."

Ese, standing next to her, attempted to kick Omoefe but missed by a wide margin. "Shut up," she grumbled, crossing her arms.

Onome remained silent, her thoughts lingering on Michael, but she couldn't shake the feeling that it was all slipping out of her reach.

"Listen, Onome!" Omoefe suddenly brightened. "They're playing your favourite song! 'Shake your body,' 'shake your body now!'" She began singing and shimmying her shoulders, laughing. "Come on, let's go dance. Forget about Beatrice and her wahala. 'Shake your body ooh!'"

Ese grinned and grabbed Onome's hand. "Let's go. You know, you're the queen of Jollof rice. Don't let anyone take that crown from you."

Onome couldn't help but smile at her sisters' antics. For a moment, the weight on her shoulders lightened. Maybe dancing would make her forget all about Michael and Beatrice, at least for a little while.

There was something in the way Omoefe moved; awkward and graceless for a girl her age, that made Onome burst into laughter, jumping to her feet.

"Omoefe, seriously, you are the worst dancer in this town!" Onome exclaimed, laughing hard as she shoved Omoefe out of the way. "You should be ashamed. What kind of nonsense is this?"

Omoefe stumbled, pretending to be offended, but Onome wasn't finished. "Listen, Aunty Omerie said that the way young women should dance is soft and gentle, like this." She raised her arms gracefully, waving them in the air, before placing both hands on her hips. Then, with a slow, measured step, she moved one foot back, then brought it forward again, then swayed to the side with a fluid motion.

Ese and Omoefe roared with laughter, doubling over in fits of giggles. "Sisiyoko!" they teased, unable to control themselves.

Onome couldn't help but laugh too, her hips swaying as she continued to lead the impromptu dance. She felt a sense of ease and freedom that only dancing could bring, and before long, all three of them were dancing together, heading toward the open space in the compound where the party was happening. The music, the laughter, the movement, it was all so lively, so full of life.

But even amidst the joyful chaos, Onome's mind kept wandering back to Michael. *Michael will come back,* she reassured herself, smiling as she made her way through the crowd. Tonight was her night, after all. It was her birthday, and nothing, not even the distractions or her doubts, was going to take that away from her.

***

It was 9 o'clock, and the moon was out now. Onome was getting tired; she had been dancing with Prisca and some of the other girls for a while. Michael had not returned since he was dragged away by Beatrice hours ago. Onome sighed and turned to the other end of the compound, where she saw Ese doing her famous waist twisting with Oke, a boy from the town. Ese had a huge crush on him, and Onome was convinced he liked her too. She smiled, at least that was going well. However, Omoefe was nowhere to be found. Onome also hadn't seen Aunty Omerie this evening. Maybe the wives were having their weekly meeting. Perhaps she should go to the house to check on the food she had set aside for Michael. It would be embarrassing if he came back and there was nothing left. She was still hopeful.

She reached the front door and noticed it was shut for some strange reason. She hoped they hadn't locked her out. Suddenly, she heard voices and wondered if the wives were having a meeting. But no, she thought the meetings always took place at Aunty Omerie's house. She decided to press her ear against the door and listen for any sounds. At first, she didn't hear anything, but then she pressed her ear harder and heard a man's voice.

"Rume, this is small naah. Let me tell you, see what I will give you if you agree to this ehnn....it will be big."

"Chief, this is too much to ask of me. People will wonder why I agreed to this. You don't have a good reputation in this town, and you know it. People will talk." Onome could hear her mother's voice now. She sounded annoyed.

"Chief, see, you are 65, older than my husband. Ah, no naah, Chief, this is too much."

What are they talking about? Who is this man calling her mother by her first name and sitting in their living room?

"Rume, listen to me." This man was sounding desperate. "Listen, you know me and you know I have the resources to settle you, and I'll settle you. You will not lack anything for the rest of your life, I promise you."

"Chief, I know...I know... but how do I convince my husband that this is the right decision? He will not believe my intentions are pure... the..." Rume hesitated. "Chief the settlement will have to be big ooh, it has to be big for this sort of arrangement."

"Now you are talking. Yes. Listen, no problem, name your price... Chief Oge is able to meet your demands, whatever they are."

"Chief, this is not a small thing you are asking. It will cost you ooh."

What are they talking about? She wished they could get straight to the point already. She looked around her; she thought she heard someone coming. When she saw no one, she pressed her ear to the door again. This was interesting; scary, yet exciting. She had never been one to listen to any of her mother's discussions before but right now, she could not help herself, something was going on and she wanted to know why her mother was having a discussion with this stranger and a man at this time of the night.

"Okay, name your price. How much?"

"Well, for now, 500,000 naira and then the list which I'll provide later.

"Hahaha...." The stranger laughed. "Only 500,000? Okay, I will give you the money tomorrow first thing, as long as you agree for me to marry Onome."

***

Onome didn't know how long she had been running. She came to a complete stop, dropping to her knees. She put her hands on her cheeks, they were wet. She had been crying and hadn't even realised it. She let the tears stream down her face now; she couldn't control it. What had she just heard? No... no, it couldn't be. It must be a mistake. It was probably just her imagination again. Her mother didn't just agree to hand her over to that stranger she called "Chief"... or did she? No. She stood up. "It cannot be... of course not." She turned to look behind her. How far had she gotten away from the compound? She wasn't too far, she realised. She could almost see the gate to the compound, and it was still open. She took a deep breath. She didn't want to stop running, but eventually, she had to. And she did.

It must be one of those funny jokes, she thought. Surely, her mother wouldn't do this. *She loves me*, she said aloud, trying to reassure herself. "I have to go back. I'm sure I didn't hear correctly. I've never known Mama to do something like this. It will be interesting to find out who came up with this one." She wiped the tears off her face and started walking back home.

She was walking away from the square when she saw Michael approaching. Her heart started to beat fast. *Has he seen me?* She saw Michael smiling, but then the look on his face shifted into concern as he came closer.

"Onome, is everything alright?" He came close and touched her arm.

She quickly pulled away from him. "I'm fine, brother."

"Wait, let me see your face." He reached out to touch her face. "Have you been crying?"

"No, brother. I just had sand in my eye and used some water to wash it out."

He didn't believe her. "What's wrong? Did somebody do something or say something to make you cry?" His tone was full of care and concern as he moved closer.

"No, brother... nobody did anything to me."

"Onome, stop calling me 'brother.' You can call me Michael." He was holding her hand now. His hand felt so soft. "Come, tell me what's wrong. I was looking for you earlier. Ese said you were dancing, and I didn't want to spoil your fun..." He paused, waiting for a response. When none came, he asked, "Is everything okay?"

He was much too close now. She could smell his fresh breath. He had been chewing gum.

"Brother... erm... Michael." Calling him by his name felt unusual, yet intimate and sweet. "I am fine. Did you want your Jollof rice?" She tried to pull away again, feeling shy. Her heart was beating uncontrollably, and her legs were threatening to give way.

He smiled, sensing she was uncomfortable, so he pulled away from her slightly. "Onome, always thinking of others." He smiled. "Hmm... well, I want some rice to take home with me." His hands moved to remove something from her hair, and then they dropped to her cheeks. He murmured something under his breath.

"What?" she asked.

He didn't reply. There was an awkward silence between them, and she wasn't sure whether to start walking to the house to get his food or ask him to explain what he meant. She wanted to speak but couldn't find the words. She crossed her arms over her chest and looked away from him.

"Okay, since you say you're fine, I'll leave you for now," he finally broke the silence.

"But brother... don't... don't you want the rice anymore?" She stuttered, confused by his sudden decision to leave.

"Erm, don't worry about it. I'll come tomorrow. I'm sure it will taste just as good as it does today. So, I'll see you tomorrow." He started to step away from her.

"Bro... Michael..." she called desperately.

This made him stop. She hesitated slightly, struggling to speak. What did she want to say to him? To tell him that her mother was in discussions with a 65-year-old man for her hand in marriage? To tell him she was in love with him and had been since Beatrice introduced him to the family three years ago? She tried to speak again but couldn't get the words out. *Oh God, please help me*, her heart cried.

He walked back to her now.

"You want to ask me something?" It was as if he knew, because it felt more like a statement than a question.

"Are you going to marry Sister Beatrice?" Her hand instinctively went over her mouth. Of all the things she could have said, she couldn't believe she had asked him that.

He chuckled, and she wasn't sure why he thought it was funny. "Aha," he said, smiling. "Why are you asking?"

She shrugged, unable to come up with a response. She hadn't expected him to ask her that. He took both of her hands in his.

"Why do you want to know… eh?"

He moved closer now, still holding her hands. She silently prayed that he couldn't feel her hands shaking, and her legs were threatening to give way again. She took a small step back, and he let go of her hands. She felt a wave of relief. She let out a sigh and hadn't realised she had stopped breathing.

"I don't know yet," he replied, still looking at her. "I like Beatrice, and my father thinks she'll make a great wife for me." He paused before asking, "What do you think?"

"Me?" She hadn't expected him to ask her this. She shrugged. "Brother, I don't know about these things ooh." She was gazing at the sandy road.

"Onome, you do. I'm sure you do." He bent his head slightly to look into her eyes. "I want to know what you think, eh? Please, tell me." His tone was soft now, and there was something in his voice that made her believe he was serious.

She decided to be brave, raising her head to meet his gaze.

"Well, I only know what I've heard people say..." She turned away slightly. "...they say there are wise men, and there are men who are foolish. They say wise men make wise decisions. I think you, brother, are not a foolish man..." She shook her head reassuringly. "I think you're very smart and intelligent." She wasn't sure why she said this, but she continued. "Erm... and I think you know things, and you'll make the right decision when the time comes."

She looked up slightly, hoping to gauge his reaction. It seemed her response pleased him, because he pulled her towards him and hugged her. He planted a kiss on her forehead, and then another. She was surprised and froze, unsure how to react. This wasn't the response she had expected. She had watched a few movies, and from what she had seen, actors sometimes kissed their girlfriends like this. Surely, this must be a good thing, she told herself.

"Are you okay?" he asked.

"Yes, brother."

He looked at her with a playful, yet warning expression in his eyes, reminding her of what he had said before.

"...Michael," she said, smiling.

He smiled also, pinching her cheeks softly.

"What are you doing tomorrow," he asked, almost immediately.

"Me?" it was a silly question, and she knew it.

He looked around them. "I don't see anyone around us or is there a ghost here?" he laughed.

She laughed too, relaxing now.

"Tomorrow is Sunday..." she said. He gave her a puzzled look.

"But that's not a problem," he replied. "Okay, see ehn... what if you meet me tomorrow? You can wait for me in the afternoon by the guava tree outside that big field, opposite the palm wine shop."

She wasn't sure what to say. He wanted them to meet tomorrow? By the guava tree? Why? What about Sister Beatrice?

He didn't wait for her to respond.

"Let's meet at 2 o'clock, ehn? I have to go now so my mother doesn't get worried." He kissed her forehead again. "Make sure you bring me the food ooh. I'll be waiting for you."

He playfully touched her cheek, then hugged her. With a smile, he quickly turned away to walk home.

She stood there for a moment, watching him. His figure slowly faded into the dark part of the road. Suddenly, she heard a voice say, "Go home, Onome."

She smiled, turning around and beginning to make her way back to the compound. She touched her forehead, remembering his lips had just been there. She still couldn't believe it; Michael kissed her.

She knew she would not be able to sleep tonight. Michael kissed her! She couldn't wait to tell Prisca. Prisca would be so envious. Pastor Maxwell hadn't even held Prisca's hand, let alone kissed her forehead.

***

The party was over, and the remaining guests had left; actually, they rushed out after her father shouted at Musa to make sure the gate was locked. Onome stepped into the living room, where her mother, Rume, was pacing back and forth.

"Madam, well done ooh," Rume said sarcastically, clapping her hands. Onome stood still.

"Where have you been?" her tone was sharp and filled with anger.

"Nowhere ooh," Onome mumbled.

"Nowhere? My friend, I said where have you been? Do you know what time it is? You think you can just leave my door unlocked while you wander around the town? So, you've grown wings, ehn?" her tone was still filled with anger. "Madam birthday party; so, you can leave the compound with your friends at this time abi?"

"No ooh, I was at... at..." Onome struggled to come up with an excuse.

Rume stared at her for a long time, and the silence made Onome uneasy. Normally, her mother would have already raised her hand to slap her.

"You know what? No problem..." Rume paused for a second. "First thing tomorrow morning, I want you to run an errand for me. Make sure you're up at 6 o'clock, because we have work to do. Do you hear me?" She pulled at Onome's ear to emphasise the seriousness of the message.

"Yes, ma."

"Where's Rukevwe? Is she still outside?"

"Emm... I didn't see her outside."

Rume said nothing, just eyed her up and down. She hissed, turned her back, and started walking to her room. Onome let out a quiet sigh. Why did her mother always give her trouble? It seemed like nothing she did could please her. She took a deep breath and turned toward the kitchen.

"Come... come... so I'm supposed to lock the door for you now, eh?" Rume's voice stopped her in her tracks, and Onome quickly turned to see her mother had spun around again. From her tone, it was clear it wasn't really a question.

She quickly walked to lock the front door, praying that Rukevwe was inside for her sake. With the door securely locked, she turned around again, but her mother had already retreated to her room. Onome closed her eyes for a brief moment, taking a deep breath.

Why was she angry, though? She thought. Wasn't she the one who had been discussing giving her to an old man in marriage for a huge sum of money? She glared at the door to her mother's room, kissed her teeth, and turned away to head to the her bedroom.

Chapter 7

Rume couldn't sleep. She kept tossing and turning, thoughts swirling in her mind. She hadn't exactly been waiting for this day—the day when a man would come to ask for her daughter's hand in marriage. Yet, it had arrived unexpectedly, with only one choice: Chief Oge.

"Chief Oge... my daughter's husband?" she murmured to herself, throwing back the covers and getting out of bed. She walked to the window and looked out. The full moon hung in the sky, but it didn't mean anything to her right now. She sighed.

Chief Oge was rich, very popular, with friends in high places. If he married Onome, doors would open for her, she thought. Everyone in the town would know her name. Even her husband would appreciate her, her daughter marrying a man who was more than her husband's caliber. The other wives would respect her. But wait a minute, what about this new girl her husband was supposed to marry—this young girl from the next town? Hmm... this could be a challenge. Well, she would cross that bridge when she got there. She assured herself. This can only work to my benefit. Everyone will know me in this town.

She walked back to sit at the edge of the bed. Onome would marry Chief Oge; this was her one chance to become the most popular woman in the town. She smiled, thinking about how much money he had promised her and the list of things she planned to buy. She smiled again, her finger resting between her teeth.

She wasn't exactly the same age as Onome when she first met Chief, but she was still young—only 19 at the time and fresh out of secondary school. Most of her friends had gone or were preparing to go to university in the city, making plans for their future. But she had no choice. She wanted to continue her education, but her parents were very poor. It had been a great challenge for them to send her to secondary school. She couldn't even count how many times she'd been sent home for unpaid fees. It was no use asking her parents for help; they had already said they couldn't send her to university. She had two younger siblings in school as well. It was no surprise—her father was a farmer, and her mother sold whatever crops her father could harvest at the market.

The only option left was marriage, and that wasn't a problem. She thought it was better than selling vegetables at the market or working on the farm with her father.

There were a few suitors at the time, and Chief Emmanuel was one of them. She couldn't help but notice how handsome and tall he was. He never came alone when visiting her family; he always brought an elder with him and gifts of food, which were a blessing to her family. At the time, she had a boyfriend named Richard. He was kind and gentle, with big plans for the future ahead. He often spoke of all his dreams, how he hoped to one day have a business and employ men to work for him. Richard had a profession as an "Okada" driver *(An "Okada" driver is someone who uses a motorcycle to transport passengers for a fare)*; and although she loved him, she knew that great ideas wouldn't put food on the table for her family. Her parents didn't take him seriously either.

She remembered how Richard cried when she told him she had decided to marry the Chief. He begged her to change her mind, but she had told him her mind was made up. She couldn't watch her family suffer any longer, and there was nothing Richard could do to help.

She remembered how Richard tried to stop her from leaving. He begged her to give him more time, to not end what they had. "True love," he said.

She had laughed, shouting, "Richard, is love going to feed my family?"

She struggled to pull away from his embrace. As she walked away, she heard him calling her name. He ran after her, continuing to beg, but she pushed him away, refusing to look back. Even though tears were rolling down her cheeks, she didn't look back. She loved him.

After that day, Richard tried to reach out to her many times. He wrote several letters, but she never opened them.

"Richard..." she whispered his name now, wondering what had become of him. Did he ever fulfill his plans? Did he ever find success?

She sighed, bringing herself back to the present and laying back on the bed as she pulled the covers over herself. Taking a deep breath, she tried desperately to sleep, but her mind refused to quiet down. *I can't think about this tonight,* she told herself. *This is something Mama Omote can help me with.* Yes, Mama Omote would know what to do. Nodding to herself, she resolved to visit her as soon as possible. It had been a while since she'd last seen her. As she stared at the ceiling, her eyes wide open, memories of how she had first met Mama Omote came rushing back.

She was visiting her mother a few years after her marriage to Chief, having just suffered a second miscarriage. She decided to visit her mother and confide in her about what was going on. She had only been there a couple of days when her aunty *(her mother's sister)* came to visit. That day, her mother was expecting her aunty and had prepared something for all of them to have lunch together. They finished eating, and she decided to help clear the dishes when her aunty started asking questions. Her aunt was being inquisitive, asking about her marriage and what was going on.

"Rume, you're looking lean. Are you not eating in your husband's house?"

She pretended she didn't hear as she took the dishes to the kitchen. She decided not to go back into the living room but instead opened the kitchen door and sat outside on a chair under a mango tree. It was a warm, breezy afternoon. She decided to sit outside for a while and drown her sorrows. She could feel the tears starting to well up again, face down; she began to sob gently.

Suddenly, she felt a hand on her shoulder; she didn't look up—she couldn't.

"Ah ah, Rume, what is the matter?" It was her aunty.

Rume shook her head, still bent, unable to speak.

"What's wrong, eh? Come on, talk to me, Rume. I'm your aunty; you can trust me," she said, sitting on a stool next to her. She pulled Rume up slightly and wiped the tear from her face. "Come on, tell me."

"Aunty, I'm tired," she said, still sobbing.

"Tired? What's happening? Are the wives giving you problems?"

"No, I don't have any problems with the wives—just the usual disagreements," she said, taking a deep breath and shaking her head. "Aunty, I've had two miscarriages now." She started crying, this time lowering her head onto her aunt's lap.

"Shh... don't cry. It's okay, it's okay."

"It's not okay. I know Chief married me because none of his wives have been able to bear him a son. He wants a son. Right now, I only have one child, a girl. I need to be able to bear him a son. I don't know what to do, I don't know what to do, aunty."

She was sobbing now. Her aunt tried to console her, rocking her back and forth as she rested her head on her lap. There was a pause.

"Don't worry, my dear, I can help you."

Rume raised her head, wiping the tears off her face.

"How, aunty?"

"Do you want to have a son for Chief?"

"Yes, of course, I am desperate."

"Desperate?"

"I cannot bear the thought of being laughed at. Besides, Chief is getting impatient with all the miscarriages."

"Okay, relax, this is not a problem at all."

"Really, aunty?" Rume's eyes widened as she heard this.

"Look, just be ready now. I will need to stay here tonight so we can do this successfully. You must promise me not to tell anyone about this, sha. Not even my sister. Do you hear?"

Rume looked at her aunty, confused. "But why shouldn't I tell my mother?"

"I will tell you on our way." Her aunty was now on her feet. "Oya, get up, wash your face, then come and join us in the living room."

Her aunt gently pulled her to her feet. "We have to think of a way to tell my sister that I have to spend the night because... hmmm..." She paused. "Okay, what you will do is... say you want us to go and buy something in the market tomorrow."

"Like what?"

"You will have to make something up. Anyway, let's go back inside before your mother comes."

They both slowly walked back inside. Her aunty went to join her mother in the living room while Rume quickly went to the bathroom to wash her face and freshen up. When she joined them in the living room, they were watching a Nigerian movie. Her mother looked up at her suspiciously but said nothing. Rume decided to sit next to her aunty. She had been thinking about what lie to tell her mother to convince her that her aunty should stay. Then it came to her—her mother always wanted her to buy an expensive wrapper. Well, it wasn't that expensive; she just hated the fact that since she married Chief, her mother saw her as a money tree, where she could stand in front and ask for anything, and she would get it.

"Mama, I think we should go to Main Market tomorrow to buy that wrapper you were telling me about."

"Ehn, you mean it?" Her mother's eyes were full of excitement.

"Yes, Mama, I will buy it for you."

"You'll buy that wrapper for me!" Her mother jumped from her chair and started to dance. "Ayea..."

Rume turned to her aunty, shrugging her shoulders, unsure how to bring her in.

"Aunty, you should come with us tomorrow naah."

Her mother stopped dancing, a little frown on her face.

"Ehmm...but your aunty suppose go back today o. Na only the children dey house sef, so she no go fit stay this night."

"That one na true Rume, I no go fit go with una tomorrow."

"Ah ah, Aunty, you have a housemaid; your housemaid can look after the children naah. It's just one night ooh."

Her aunt laughed. Rume thought her aunt wasn't making the lie easy.

"Rume, you have to ask your mother if I can stay."

Her mother paused for a few seconds. "Ehn, well, you no bi my sister?" her mother raised up her hands in resignation. "You fit stay shaa... but nah only me Rume go buy wrapper for ooh."

They laughed.

"Okay, good. I need to buy somethings sef and main market would be good for me."

"So, we are all going tomorrow," Rume said, relieved as she was not sure if she had any more lies up her sleeves.

"Me, I go get my wrapper tomorrow." Her mother started dancing with a huge smile on her face

Rume looked at her aunty, her aunt looked at her and nodded, a sign to say well done. Her aunty got up soon after.

"I need to go to the phone center to call my husband and tell him that I will not be home until tomorrow."

"Okay. Aunty, I think I will come with you, I have to go and visit a friend of mine. I promised I would visit her before I go back," Rume said.

"Haba, everybody dey comot? Nobody won watch this interesting movie?"

"Mama, maybe later, let me get going now so I can come back early."

"Okay ooh, me I go watch am by myself." Her mother sat back down.

"Aunty, please let me quickly change, I will be back soon."

"Okay, I will wait but hurry up ooh."

Rume went to her room to change into something simple. As she changed, she began to think; she had no idea where her aunt was taking her. Should she be concerned? Her aunt had always been a close family member, supportive and helpful whenever the family was in need. But why didn't she want Rume to tell her mother? Was there something suspicious about this? No, Rume shook her head, dismissing the thought.

All she knew was that she was desperate. She wanted more children, sons specifically. She had been married to Chief for three years, and they had just one daughter. Chief was growing impatient. She would do anything to hold a son in her arms. It had to happen, and it had to happen soon. After giving up her university education to marry Chief, with all the promises he made to her if she gave him a son, she deserved every bit of it. She had not sacrificed everything to end up with nothing. She would not let that happen because she could not bear a son. Never!

She would go with her aunt. If this would solve the problem, she had to try. She had nothing to lose. She hurried to get dressed and took a small handbag with some money, remembering the advice to never go anywhere empty-handed. Once she was sure she had everything she needed, she looked at herself in the mirror one last time.

But why? Why is she going through this? She brushed the thought aside. It was time to go.

***

"Should we hire a car?" They had been standing in the sun for some time now, waiting for a Motorbus.

"My dear, the fewer people that know about this, the better."

"Aunty, please, where exactly are we going?"

"You don't need to worry. I'm not taking you to any strange place... we just need to keep this between us. It will take us just two hours to get there."

"Two hours!" she exclaimed. "Ah, aunty, that is far!" She folded her arms across her chest like a little girl.

"Since when did two hours become too far, ehn? Now that you've married Chief and have a driver to take you around, you're complaining, abi? Madam, sorry ooh," her aunty said, clicking her tongue and looking away.

Just then, the Motorbus arrived. Fortunately, it wasn't too busy, and they quickly got on and took their seats. Rume was frowning. The journey hadn't even started, and she was already tired. It was 3 o'clock in the afternoon, it was hot, and she was sweating. Her handkerchief was already soaked. She might as well ask her aunt to tell her where they were going; they had to talk about something.

"Aunty, please tell me where we are going, abeg."

"Ahh, Rume! So, you don't trust me? Nawa ooh."

"I do, aunty. But I need to know where I'm going. If you were in my position, wouldn't you want to know where you're going?"

Her aunty took a deep breath.

"Okay, okay, I'll tell you." She looked around to make sure they didn't know anyone on the Motorbus. "Move closer." Rume shifted closer to her aunt.

Her aunty glanced around again. "I'm taking you to see a prophetess," she whispered.

"A Prophetess!" Rume exclaimed.

"Shh!" Her aunty placed her hand over her lips, signalling for her to keep her voice down.

"Sorry, aunty," Rume said, covering her mouth. There was a short silence. "So, we're going to a church?"

Her aunty chuckled. "Ah, no, we're not going to a church. We're going to her house."

"Okay." Rume sighed with relief. "Aunty, you're funny. Why were you keeping it a secret? I thought you were taking me somewhere in the bush." Rume chuckled.

"Keep your voice down now, Rume," her aunt said as she looked around again.

Rume turned to look around the Motorbus too. She wasn't sure why her aunt kept looking; she was sure no one knew them on the Motorbus.

"But we're not discussing anything bad. People go to see prophets these days," Rume said, her voice lowered.

"Rume, like I said, there are things you don't want people to know."

Rume looked at her aunt strangely. "I still don't understand."

"You're married to Chief, a well-known and respected man in your town and even in places you may not know. Do you want people to know that his wife went to see a prophetess?"

"Ermm... well, I don't think so."

"Ehn... this is what I'm saying."

There was silence. Rume was still thinking. Surely, if it would resolve the issue, then what would it matter?

"Anyway, let's talk about something else. How's your store? Your mother said you had a storekeeper who stole from you. Is that true?"

Rume went on to discuss it. Two hours passed quickly. The journey wasn't too bad, and they arrived at the town. It looked like an up-and-coming area; the roads were made of concrete and were smooth, unlike her parents' town, which was just filled with sand. Her aunt led the way as they walked, coming to a narrow street with houses on both sides. The houses were a good size and decent. They walked for a short while until they almost reached the end of the street.

They came to a house; a medium-sized bungalow painted cream, with a small verandah that had two chairs and a medium-sized stool between them.

If this was the house, it looked much better than Rume had imagined a prophetess would live in. Her aunt knocked softly, but there was no response. She knocked again, then for the third time, much harder than the second.

"Who be that?" they heard a woman's voice. "I say, who be that?" she repeated, slightly impatient.

The door swung open, revealing a woman; skinny, tall, with braided hair, wearing a long white dress. Rume wasn't sure why she was wearing a white dress that almost reached the floor. The woman was staring at her now, looking from her body and slowly down to her feet. Rume followed her gaze, unsure of what was going through her mind. It seemed like she hadn't even noticed her aunt. Rume took a step back from the door.

Then she heard her aunt's voice.

"Mama Omote, it's me. Ah, you don't remember me again?"

"Rosemary! Sorry, my dear, I didn't even see you," the woman laughed softly. "Please come in, come in."

Rume waited for her aunt to go in first. To her surprise, the house was nicely decorated and smelled very pleasant.

She waited for them to sit, then the prophetess called for her maid, who came running out.

"What can I offer you? I have soft drinks, anything you want, I have in my fridge," she said, laughing softly.

They both looked at each other.

"What would you like to drink?" the Prophetess asked.

"I'm okay," Rume said, shaking her head.

"My dear, not even a cup of cold water? After travelling in the hot sun, you must have some water to quench your thirst!"

Rume stayed quiet.

"Don't mind her, she's shy. She will have water, and I will have some Fanta."

The maid rushed back inside, having made a note.

"You are welcome," the Prophetess said to them as she sat down.

"Thank you, ma," Rume's auntie said.

"I wasn't expecting anyone today at all. I was even going to leave to visit one of my clients, but God knew you were coming to see me," she laughed softly.

"Ah, thank God, we met you, ma. Sorry, I didn't inform you; it wasn't planned, it's an emergency."

"An emergency! I hope everything is alright with the family?"

"Everything is fine, ma."

The maid walked in with their drinks, placed them on the stool next to them, and stepped away to go back inside.

"Actually, Ma, I am here because of my sister's daughter," her aunt turned to look at Rume.

"Okay. So, this is your relative?"

"Yes, ma," her aunt beckoned for Rume to speak.

"Good afternoon, ma," was all Rume could say. She was a little nervous.

The prophetess was staring at her with a smile on her face.

"You are welcome, my dear."

"Thank you, ma."

There was a brief silence. Her aunt turned to her and continued.

"Emm... ma, as I said before, it is something that needs an immediate solution. I will let her speak so she can say what she wants."

Oh no, she couldn't believe her aunt wanted her to tell the prophetess the situation. Where was she going to start? How much should she share?

Her thoughts were soon interrupted by the prophetess.

"My dear, don't be afraid. Tell me, what is the problem?"

Rume first cleared her throat.

"Emm... I want children."

"You want children?"

Rume just nodded.

"Are you married?"

"Yes, ma."

"For how long?"

"For 3 years, ma."

"You see, ma..." Her aunt interrupted, seeking to help elaborate on the matter. "She has been married for three years and has one child. She has been trying to have more children, but she has had some miscarriages, which is causing great strain on the marriage."

"Oh, my dear, I am so sorry."

There was silence.

"Come, my dear, come closer. Let me look at you."

Rume became nervous again. She was feeling uncomfortable. She looked at her aunt, who nodded to her and whispered, "Go, don't worry."

"Come, my dear, don't be afraid. I don't know why you are afraid. I want to help you."

She sat down next to her.

"Give me your hand."

Rume stretched out her left arm.

"No, give me your right hand."

The prophetess took her hand. For a minute, she just stared at her palm, then proceeded to stroke each line on her palm. It made Rume extremely nervous and uncomfortable. Fortunately, it didn't last for long.

"My daughter, you should never have married him."

"What?" Rume gasped.

The prophetess looked at her and said again, "This Chief Akpofure, you should never have married him."

"How do you know his name?" Rume turned to look at her aunt again.

"My dear, never mind about that. What you want now is more children."

Rume was quiet.

"Yes. I want male children."

"Good. Okay, we have to go somewhere. We can't do it all here. I will go and get my bag. Finish your drink; I will soon be back." She didn't wait for a response as she hurried out of the room.

Rume watched her leave, then immediately rushed back to sit beside her aunt.

"Aunty, what is going on? To tell you the truth, I am confused. I..."

"Rume, you are worrying too much. I've told you to relax. This lady is a well-known prophetess. She has helped so many people, including myself."

"Who are these people, Aunty?"

"Would you be happy if I told other people your secret?"

"No, of course not."

"So why are you asking me to tell you about others?"

Rume sat back on the chair and sighed.

"It's going to be alright, Rume. Just do as she tells you, and it will be fine. You'll see."

Rume said nothing. She reached for her glass of water.

The prophetess came back into the room.

"Oya, let's get going. I want to take you somewhere..."

Rume was tired of asking questions now. She proceeded to get her bag as she and her aunt got ready to go with the prophetess. She would have to trust her aunt, and if this prophetess said it could be done, then she would go along with it.

And so began her relationship with the prophetess, whom she has come to know as Mama Omote.

Chapter 8

Onome shut the door quietly, her mother was having her siesta. She was thankful for the moment of peace, as it gave her the perfect opportunity to sneak out of the house. She hurried towards the gate, finally slipping out of the compound. Her mind was focused on Michael. She couldn't wait to see him; she had spent the entire night wondering what he wanted to say to her. She must hurry, she thought. It wasn't good to keep a man waiting. She'd learned that from a romantic movie she watched at Prisca's house.

Onome didn't have time to tell Prisca all that had happened, but she knew she'd have plenty of juicy details to share with her next time they met. Her pace quickened as she made her way to the main road. Fortunately, it wasn't far, though it was in a semi-popular area. The area with the guava tree was hidden behind all the shops, a place not many people knew about. Onome was familiar with it because she and Prisca often went there to hide away and gossip. She wondered how Michael had learned about the spot. Perhaps he went there with Beatrice, she thought.

She hadn't seen Beatrice around the compound today. Most of the children went to the local church on Sundays and later gathered in the town square to play. Not Onome, though. She always had to stay behind to do all the house chores and cook. She sighed. She hoped her mother would take a long time with her siesta. She would have to come up with a believable excuse for where she had gone, but she'd cross that bridge when the time came.

As she continued walking, she could hear the swish of her dress. She had worn another beautiful long-sleeved dress, a gift from Auntie Omerie. Thankfully, the sun wasn't out today, and it was much cooler than usual. She wondered what time it was as she neared the area with the guava tree. Hopefully, she wasn't late.

And then she saw him. Michael was already there, sitting back against the tree, eyes closed, relaxed. Her footsteps must have startled him because he jerked, his eyes snapping open as he saw her approaching. A smile spread across his face as he lifted himself off the tree and stood.

"Ah, Onome, you're here! I was beginning to think you weren't coming anymore." Michael said, dusting the sand and grass off his trousers. He walked toward her, taking both her hands. "I'm happy you came."

She felt shy again, lowering her gaze to the grass and saying nothing.

"Oya, come, come. Let's sit down," he beckoned, leading her by the hand towards the tree.

"Brother, I can't stay too long. My mother is just resting. I have to get back before she wakes up."

"Ah, won't you relax first? You just got here. Let's sit down for a while, okay?" His voice held a touch of disappointment.

"Sorry," Onome apologised, sensing the sadness in his tone.

She sat next to him under the tree. Silence settled between them, but it felt like an eternity to Onome.

"So, how are you?" he asked, smiling.

"I'm fine."

"How's school?"

"School is fine."

"You must be in your final year of secondary school, right?"

"We just finished our SSCE exams *(The SSCE (Senior School Certificate Examination).*"

"So, I have finished now," she replied, looking down and nervously fiddling with her fingers.

"Ah, yes... yes, you've finished secondary school now."

"Yes."

"That's good. Now it's time for you to write JAMB *(Joint Admissions and Matriculation Board).*"

"I hope you're preparing well?"

"Yes, I was even revising with some past exam papers last night."

"That's good. Have you decided which university you want to go to?"

She raised her head now with a huge smile on her face.

"Yes, I want to go to Unilag *(University of Lagos, Nigeria)*."

"I can see you are excited about this."

She nodded, still smiling.

"What do you know about Unilag?"

"Ermm…our neighbour, Mr. Odafe's daughter, goes there, and she has told us about Unilag. It is a very big university."

"Ah, okay, so you know her?" there was something in his voice as he said that.

"Whenever she is in town, she comes to the church Sunday school to help teach."

"I see," he said looking away now, he seemed to be lost in his own thoughts.

There was silence again for a few more seconds

"Ermm… Onome," he eventually ended the silence.

"Yes, brother"

"I have told you not to call me brother."

"Sorry."

"Why were you crying yesterday?"

There was a pause. Should she tell him? What would he say? What would he do? Besides, she wasn't sure if she had heard correctly. She would have to wait and see if her mother decides to speak to her about it.

"It was nothing."

"I know that's not true. Something happened last night, something that made you cry. Come on, tell me," he pleaded softly.

"Brother…"

"Michael," he said, correcting her.

"Brother… Michael, I…"

"No, just call me Michael."

She hesitated for a moment. "Michael," she said, looking away, now shy.

"Good. You see, that wasn't hard, was it?"

Onome smiled as she lowered her gaze playfully.

"You know you have a beautiful smile, eh?" His tone was soft now.

Her smile widened even more. His hand lowered to her chin as he slowly lifted her face.

"You are beautiful. Do you know that?" His voice was almost a whisper now, his tone even softer.

She shrugged her shoulders and tried to move her face away, but his hand was firm.

"You are so shy. I like your shyness. It's what I like about you the most."

"You like me?" she asked, surprised.

Michael smiled.

"What's not to like?"

She looked at him now, and he was moving closer.

"I like you," he said, stroking her cheek.

She felt a tightening in her stomach. He had just said he liked her. She smiled again, this time looking down as she managed to pull her face away. He continued to gently caress her cheek. He seemed to have moved even closer; she could feel his breath on her cheek. She was nervous now but managed to speak.

"What about Sister Beatrice? Don't you like her too?"

Michael stopped brushing her cheek. There was silence. She raised her head, which seemed to catch him off guard. He frowned, but his expression suddenly turned to a smile when he saw she was staring at him.

"Beatrice? You want to know if I like Beatrice?"

"I hear she's your girlfriend and that you're planning on marrying her."

He started laughing, so hard that his head went back. She frowned, annoyed. Why was he laughing? She tried to stand up, but he placed both hands on her sides to stop her.

"Wait, wait now."

She turned away from him.

"Don't be like this. Come, look at me."

She refused. To tell the truth, she was now regretting coming to see him this afternoon. She was confused. What was going on here?

He just said he likes her, but how could that be possible when he also just said he likes Beatrice? How?

"Come, look at me, please," he whispered now. His voice was so soft. She turned to look at him. His face was much closer now, his gaze slowly moving from her lips to her eyes.

"You are very beautiful."

She couldn't move. She had never been told this by any boy before. She could see his face slowly coming closer. Her heart was beating fast.

"Close your eyes," he said.

Why? she wondered. What does he want to do? Deep down, she knew. She was scared. She could feel her stomach tighten as she began to slowly shut her eyes. She could feel his breath on her face now, just then, she held her breath...

"Onome," she suddenly heard someone call her name. It was a male voice.

She opened her eyes quickly and turned to see who it was. It was Pastor Maxwell. She quickly jumped to her feet, dusting the sand off her dress.

Oh God! she thought. How did he discover this place? What had he seen? Oh God! she kept shouting in her head. He was walking toward them now, a stern look, on his face. How did he see them? She thought they were clearly hidden. Michael was up too, dusting the grass off his trousers. Pastor Maxwell had walked up to them now, and he seemed to be staring inquisitively.

"Onome," he called again, but quietly this time.

"Good afternoon, sir," she said, lowering her knees slightly.

"Good afternoon," he replied, turning his gaze to Michael, who then greeted him.

"What are you people doing here?" he asked, his tone inquisitive as he gazed firmly at Michael.

There was silence for a bit.

"Em... Pastor, we were just discussing her studies. She's going to be taking her JAMB exams soon, and I was just helping her," Michael quickly responded, frowning.

"Ehen... okay, I see. Where are your study materials?" he asked, looking at Onome as he spoke.

"We were discussing an English subject, so we don't really need the study materials for that," Michael quickly answered again, his tone defensive.

"Is that so?" Pastor Maxwell responded sarcastically, his gaze moving from Michael to Onome.

Onome had her eyes to the floor. She could not believe the lies coming out of Michael's mouth, and to a Pastor, no less. Pastor Maxwell kept staring at them.

"Onome, I am on my way to your house to see your father. In fact, I'm glad I saw you. I was going to ask to see you, as there's something I want to discuss with you."

"Oh, okay, sir," was all she could respond.

"We can walk together to your house, so I can discuss it with you.

"Yes, sir"

She slowly turned to look at Michael, who seemed to be at a loss for words now. Pastor Maxwell beckoned for her to lead the way. She raised her hand to bid Michael goodbye. He had his hands in his trouser pockets, his gaze fixed on Pastor Maxwell, frowning. Pastor Maxwell, on the other hand, was looking at her, waiting for her to begin walking.

There was something in Michael's look that caused her to pause for a moment, but she quickly turned away and made a move.

"Yes, sir," she said for no reason as she hurried away from Michael.

They started to walk slowly, side by side, toward the main road leading to her house. She turned back slightly to see if Michael was still there, but he was not. She felt a pang of disappointment. She had hoped he would still be standing there, waiting to wave her goodbye. She turned back, a little frown forming on her face.

They walked silently for a while. Pastor Maxwell must have looked at her a few times, as though wanting to start a conversation, but he didn't. She was confused. He said there was something he wanted to discuss with her, but what could it be?

In the eight months, Pastor Maxwell had been in town, she had probably only spoken to him a few times, just the usual greetings. While she was contemplating whether to ask him something, they came across two families who knew him well. As the Youth Pastor in the popular church in town, he was well-known. He stopped to greet them.

She stood a small distance away and watched. He was generally greeted with a hug or a handshake. He was much loved in the town. She greeted them too, as that was a way of showing respect. When he was done, he beckoned for her to continue walking.

They walked in silence again. After a few minutes, he broke it.

"Ermm... Onome, I've been meaning to ask you, why do you no longer come to the Sunday classes?"

"Oh, why don't I come to the Sunday classes?" She repeated the question, unsure why he was asking.

"Yes."

"Emm... my mother wants me to do some housework most Sundays, so I cannot come anymore."

"So, you can't do that another day?"

"Ermm... that's the day she wants me to do it."

"I see." He paused for a few seconds. "Well, that's a shame, because I could see that you were starting to enjoy being at church each Sunday."

There was an awkward silence again.

"Okay," he said, as if something came to mind. "What about Wednesday evenings? Do you do anything on Wednesday evenings?"

"Wednesday? No, sir," she said, shaking her head.

"Okay, very good. We have our evening teaching and prayer service with young people, like yourself, on Wednesdays at 6 o'clock in the evening. Maybe you can join us? I'm sure you'd like it."

"Ermm... okay."

"I know you'll need to check with your father and mother first, but I can speak to them to get their permission for you."

"Oh no, sir," she said almost immediately, with a shaky tone. He almost stopped to stare at her. She paused just to get herself together.

"I'll ask my mother if I can come."

"Okay. Anyway, just let me know if you need me to speak to her."

"Okay, sir," she replied.

She couldn't see herself going to him for help. She was afraid of him, and she didn't know why. Prisca spoke so highly of him, but all Onome could see was a tall man who hardly smiled. He was always so serious.

He looked at her like there was something else he wanted to say, but they were approaching the compound now. It was late afternoon, and the gate was still open.

As they walked into the compound, they could hear her father's voice. She noticed her father sitting outside the verandah of his quarters. His driver was with him. A small table sat before them with some bottles of alcohol and glasses.

As they approached the verandah, her father quickly looked up and noticed them.

"Ah ah, Pastor, Pastor, you are here!" her father said.

"Good afternoon, Chief," Pastor Maxwell greeted from afar, bending his knee slightly in a gesture of respect.

Normally, she would have walked straight to her mother's quarters, but since she was with the Pastor and had not seen her father today, she continued to walk with him as he climbed the stairs to the verandah.

"Good afternoon, how are you?" her father asked, stretching out his hand for a handshake.

"I'm well, sir. I'm well," Pastor Maxwell replied as they shook hands. He then turned to shake the driver's hand, who had stood up by now.

"Eric, my brother, how are you?"

"Fine, my brother."

"I hope you and your family are well, sir?" Pastor Maxwell asked her father.

"We are living ooh, we are living," her father said, looking around. "Onome, go and bring a chair from inside for the Pastor to sit."

"I can go and bring it, Chief," Pastor Maxwell offered.

"Ah, no ooh, for what naah? Wait here—today you will drink brandy with me. Onome, go inside and bring one chair," he said again.

"Yes, Papa. Good afternoon, Papa," she greeted.

"Ehhen, good afternoon, my dear," he responded as she rushed inside his quarters to get a chair.

She returned soon after, placing the chair beside Pastor Maxwell.

"Thank you," he said, looking at her with a smile.

She stepped back as he sat down.

"So, Pastor, what do you want to drink? I have in front of me a special brandy," her father said.

"Ah no, sir. I am fine, sir. I am okay," Pastor Maxwell chuckled.

"You don't want anything to drink? Why?" He didn't wait for a response. "I know you don't drink alcohol, but there are soft drinks. You have to drink something."

"Okay, sir, if you insist."

"I insist ooh, you must drink something. What will you drink?"

"I will have a bottle of Coke, sir."

"Coke? Ehn, no problem. We get that one. Oya, Onome..."

"Sir," she responded almost immediately.

"Go and bring one bottle of chilled..." he tried to use his hand to explain what he meant. "...Coke for Pastor."

"Okay, sir."

"Make sure it's chilled ooh," he emphasised.

As Onome walked inside the quarters to the kitchen, she heard Pastor Maxwell laugh. He must have said something funny because they both laughed.

Her father had taken a liking to Pastor Maxwell. This was not the first time he had come to see her father. They seemed to have developed a good relationship since he came to the town a few months ago.

She walked straight into the kitchen, where the maid was sitting. They exchanged pleasantries as Onome opened the tall fridge.

There were only a few soft drinks at the bottom of the fridge. Fortunately, there was a bottle of Coke; but it was not as 'chilled' as her father had requested. She took it anyway and quickly grabbed a bottle opener.

Back outside, she set the bottle of Coke carefully on the table in front of Pastor Maxwell. Fortunately, they were deep in conversation, so her father didn't ask how chilled it was.

She opened the bottle of Coke. From what her father was saying, it was clear their conversation was about marriage.

"...just make sure I am the first person you tell ooh. Ehn?"

Pastor Maxwell chuckled. "Of course, sir."

"We have so many beautiful girls in this town, even in my house sef, so I don't know why you are wasting time," her father laughed and immediately turned to look at Onome.

"Onome!"

"Yes, Papa."

"You and the Pastor see each other for road?"

"Emm..." She froze, unsure what to say. She turned to look at Pastor Maxwell. Would he tell her father that he saw her under a tree with a boy?

"Yes sir, yes sir," he quickly responded, sipping his drink, not looking at her.

"You have bought your JAMB form?" her father asked.

"Yes, Sir, I bought it last week."

"Ehn...okay," he turned to the Pastor. "You see this JAMB sef ehn, it's just a useless exam. They just want to use this exam to chop our money and keep our children at home. Very useless," he said, reaching for his glass of brandy. "They fail you and then say come back in six months. Rubbish." He took a gulp.

There was silence now.

"Papa, is there anything else you want me to do?"

"Emm...no, you fit go," he waved her off.

She didn't look at Pastor Maxwell as she left them, walking away quickly. She could hear Pastor Maxwell breaking the silence, and then her father chuckled. A conversation began again. As soon as she knew she was out of their sight, she sighed, slowing down and relaxing a bit. That was awkward. She was glad to be out of there. Unfortunately, the day had not turned out as she had imagined or hoped.

Seeing Michael ended up being a surprise; his actions were a bit strange. The way he kept looking at her, stroking her cheeks and her face; she could still feel his hand on her cheek. She smiled. Her face had never been touched before by any boy in the town. She remembered him saying she was beautiful.

72

"I'm beautiful," she said out loud, smiling. "He likes me. He really likes me," she thought to herself. She wanted to skip. She almost did. She couldn't wait to tell Prisca all about it.

As she approached her mother's quarters, she saw her sitting outside with a known family friend, Mrs. Ufuoma, her mother's best friend. They were sitting very close and whispering. They noticed her and adjusted themselves. They quietly stared as she walked closer and closer. She felt nervous; the way they both were looking at her made her think they must have been talking about her.

"Good afternoon, ma." Onome greeted Mrs. Ufuoma

"Onome, good afternoon. How are you, my dear?"

"Fine, ma."

"Onome, you are getting big ooh and looking fine."

Onome smiled, looking downwards.

"One nice man, a township man, will soon come and marry you and take you away from us ooh."

"Abeg, which township man! In other words, a village man will marry my daughter, ehn? Abeg, leave that one. Let us discuss something else." Rume said, hissing.

Mrs. Ufuoma was laughing.

"Onome, go to the kitchen. There's a bag there. I want you to take it to Mama Emeka's house. She is waiting for it."

"You want me to go now?"

"Yes, go now. She has been waiting since morning. In fact, I wanted to send you to her place earlier, but I could not find you. Where did you go?"

"I didn't go anywhere."

Rume looked at her suspiciously. "You didn't go anywhere? Were you inside the house?" she asked curiously.

Onome looked at her. *Why is this woman stressing me for goodness' sake?* she thought but said nothing. Rume kissed her teeth.

"Anyway, continue to lie. You will not bring me shame here, you hear me?"

There was silence now.

"I will go and carry the bag to Mama Emeka's house."

Onome could feel her mother's piercing eyes as she walked away. She could sense her mother's stare digging into her back.

She decided to pause as she entered the living room. The living room window was open, and she could hear their voices as they continued their chat, whispering again. Surely, they must be talking about her. Desperately wanting to know, she walked gently and softly to stand close to the open window. She could hear them now.

"In fact, you have been relegated. What are you going to do now?" Mrs. Ufuoma whispered.

"My dear, don't worry. I know what to do. Just relax. Do you see me panicking?"

"Ah, no! In fact, I have never seen you so calm."

"Exactly. Like I told you, I know what to do."

"I trust you naah, Rume. Is it not you?"

"Just relax."

There was silence now. Onome could not make out what was happening. *Well, they are not talking about me,* she thought. She tiptoed away from the window and walked to the kitchen to get the bag her mother mentioned.

On opening the kitchen door, she saw Rukevwe, who was just about to put a big swallow in her mouth *(swallow is a starchy dough-like dish that is eaten with soups or stews)*.

"Ah, Rukevwe, you are here?"

"Yes! What is it?" Rukevwe asked.

"So, you're in the house? Why didn't Mama ask you to take this bag to Mama Emeka's house?"

"Which bag?" Rukevwe looked at her, confused.

Onome walked over to see the so-called bag. "This bag," she said, pointing at a large sack her mother had called a bag. It was a huge sack. She tried to lift it but dropped it immediately—it was too heavy.

"Me, I don't know about any bag, abeg," her sister said, turning back to her food.

"Well, we have to deliver this together because it's too heavy for one person to carry."

"Ah, me I cannot follow you ooh. I have to read for my exams. Plus, Mama didn't send me," Rukevwe said, taking another handful of swallow.

"Mama didn't send me," Onome mocked her sister's tone angrily. "So, thirty minutes of not reading will make you fail your exam, abi?"

Rukevwe didn't respond. Instead, she licked her fingers and grabbed another cut of the swallow. Onome kissed her teeth loudly this time. She needed to figure out how to carry the bag to Mama Emeka's house by herself.

She went to the back of the kitchen to see if anything could help. After looking around, she spotted a wheelbarrow filled with firewood. She unloaded the firewood onto the ground and pushed the wheelbarrow to the kitchen door. She went inside, dragged the sack outside, and with all the strength she could muster, hoisted it onto the wheelbarrow.

She noticed Rukevwe watching her out of the corner of her eye, but she wasn't expecting any help—not that her sister would offer, anyway. Once the sack was safely balanced, Onome began pushing the wheelbarrow slowly and carefully. If she moved too fast, it would topple over.

As she pushed from the back of the house, the wheelbarrow made a loud squeaky sound. She came up behind her mother and Mrs. Ufuoma, who both turned to see what was causing the noise.

"What is this? Where are you going with that wheelbarrow?" her mother asked.

"I can't carry the sack. It's too heavy. See, it's heavy!" Onome said, trying to lift it to show her.

"So, you cannot carry it? Oya, push it from here to the house then."

"Ah, don't break your back ooh, Onome. Can you not carry it?" Mrs. Ufuoma asked. "It's too heavy naah."

"Abeg, leave it," her mother waved dismissively. "Was I not carrying heavier loads than this at her age? Let her learn before she goes to her husband's house."

Her mother turned away.

Onome sighed and lifted the wheelbarrow by its handles, rolling it past them.

"Take it easy ooh, my dear. Don't fall ooh," Mrs. Ufuoma called out with concern in her voice.

Onome was too annoyed to respond. She noticed her mother's eyes following her as she slowly rolled it past them. Approaching the gate, she thought about her father and Pastor Maxwell sitting outside. She wondered what her father would say.

As she neared the gate, it was quiet. She peeped quickly. The verandah was empty, except for the table and an empty Coke bottle. *Pastor Maxwell must have finished his drink quickly,* she thought.

She could hear her father's voice inside, though she couldn't make out what he was saying.

Finally, at the gate, she put down the wheelbarrow to rest. She was already feeling tired, and there was still a long way to go before reaching Mama Emeka's house.

Musa is not at the gate this evening. Where could he be? she wondered. She had hoped to ask him for help.

The compound was unusually quiet. There was no one around to assist her. She took a deep breath, lifted the wheelbarrow again, and pushed it out through the gate. Just as she turned it toward the street, she noticed Pastor Maxwell not far off. He was talking to some children.

She hesitated, debating whether to keep pushing or wait until he was gone. Deciding to move slowly, she hoped he would finish greeting the children before noticing her.

Unfortunately, the squeaky wheelbarrow caught his attention. He looked up, saw her, and quickly walked toward her with a questioning look on his face.

Onome stopped pushing as he came closer.

"Onome, what is this? Why are you pushing this wheelbarrow?"

Onome brushed her hand across her forehead. She was already tired from pushing the wheelbarrow this far. She tried to respond but could only look at Pastor Maxwell and then back at the sack inside the wheelbarrow. He reached to lift the sack and put it back down.

"This sack is heavy. Where are you carrying this to?"

"My mother told me to take it to Mama Emeka's house." Mama Emeka was well-known in the town for her generosity.

"Ah, Mama Emeka. Where is her house again?"

76

"It's just after *the main market,* near the *old church building with the green gate.*"

"Ah, yes, I know that place." He quickly picked up the sack and placed it over his shoulder. "Okay, let's go. I will help you carry it, and you can lead the way."

She stood there staring at him and the sack resting on his shoulder.

"Come on, go and leave the wheelbarrow by the gate," he said in a commanding tone.

She snapped out of her thoughts and rushed off to do as he said. He watched her as she hurried back to meet him, then beckoned for her to lead the way.

"Thank you, sir," was all she could say.

"No problem. Let's go," he said, adjusting the sack as they walked. "I think you packed this sack too heavy. You should have asked the male maid to help you carry and deliver it."

She kept quiet. She did not tell him it was her mother who packed the sack. She was just happy for the help.

"You are lucky I was still here and saw you. I don't know how you would have rolled that wheelbarrow all the way past the main market."

She kept quiet again. Pastor Maxwell looked over at her as they walked.

"Well, we are not going to go on this journey in silence; otherwise, it will be a really boring journey." He adjusted the sack again. She paused, thinking of something to say, but thankfully, he began to speak again.

"Did you manage to ask your mother about coming to join us on Wednesday?"

"Not yet."

"Try to speak to her soon. You don't want to miss any Wednesday."

"What are you going to be teaching?"

"We will be teaching many things; we will study the Bible; teach about Jesus Christ; how to follow him, how to pray, and how to live a holy life. You must come; you will learn many things."

"Okay," was all she could say.

"Do you know Jesus?" he asked.

"Yes," she said, lowering her gaze, unsure. But yes, she knew Jesus. They talked about him every Sunday.

"Anyway, don't worry; you will learn more about him," he said.

She nodded without saying anything. They continued to walk in silence.

"I see your aunty most Sundays. Why do you not come with her?" he asked, breaking the silence. She had so many aunties that she was not sure who he was talking about. He did not wait for her to respond as he continued, "I remember you used to come before with Prisca. What happened?"

"I help my mother on Sundays now, sir. So, I can't come."

"Ah, I remember you said that. Okay, I see. But did you enjoy it when you came?"

"Yes, sir, I did."

"What did you enjoy about it?"

"Hmm, I enjoyed the music."

"The music!" he laughed. "Is that all?"

"Emm...." She started to scratch her hair nervously.

"You like the choir?"

"Yes, they are very good," she said, smiling.

"Okay, then why don't you join the choir?"

"Me?" she exclaimed.

"Yes, of course, you. Why not?"

"Ah, no sir, I cannot sing ooh."

"Ehnn, really? Have you tried?"

"Ermm.... no sir."

"So, you don't know if you can sing?" he asked.

She was silent, her hand went to scratch her head, unsure how to respond.

"Anyway, you can learn, you know. We have somebody that teaches people to sing," he said, now breathing heavily. It seemed the sack was getting too heavy for him.

Just then, they came to a part where there was a field, and they could see some young boys playing football. He dropped the sack immediately.

"Stay here and watch it, I'm coming."

He began to run into the field, and as soon as the boys saw him, they stopped, shouted his name, and ran to greet him. He stood talking to them, then took the ball from one of them and started kicking. He played with them for a few minutes until he was able to score a goal. He ran around them with his hands up and began to run back to her with a huge smile on his face as he shouted, "Until next time!"

He stopped as he came close. He was looking at her, but she looked away.

"I enjoyed that," he said as he picked up the sack again.

"Oya, let's go."

They continued to make their way. She noticed from the corner of her eye that Pastor Maxwell was now sweating, but he kept the sack on his shoulder. He had been carrying the sack on the same shoulder. She wondered why he was so excited about playing football with the boys.

"Look at me, I'm sweating!" he stopped, still carrying the sack on his shoulder. He raised his left hand to wipe his face. "This is my exercise today," he laughed.

Onome smiled.

"By the way, we haven't finished our conversation. Where did we stop?"

"I don't remember," she lied.

"I remember. You liked the music and the choir, right?"

"Yes."

"What else?"

Onome proceeded to tell him what she remembered when she used to attend the Sunday services. The more he asked her questions, the more she spoke. As they walked and talked, he laughed out loud at some of her responses. He seemed to laugh quite easily, she noticed. Onome began to relax with him. This was the first time she had ever spoken with Pastor Maxwell at length, and she was beginning to think that maybe Prisca was right, he was a kind man.

He stopped a few times to greet people and place the sack down. She didn't mind; she was happy to have help. What would she have done if he wasn't right outside her compound at that very time?

Chapter 9

It was the morning of Chief's traditional marriage. Omerie had been up since 5 o'clock, pacing up and down her room before stepping outside to help begin the preparations. There was a lot to be done. Omerie had delegated some of the day's activities to the wives. It was her responsibility to ensure everything went as planned. The compound was busy: some of the canopies were up and ready, the women were already cooking, she knew they would need some extra hands to help and had hired some additional women to help with several other tasks. All the children were up; some were playing around the compound with some of the other women's children, while the others hung around the cooking corner, hoping for a full plate of food before the afternoon's event.

Omerie sighed. Chief was getting a fourth wife. She had been involved in so many of these ceremonies that she could plan them with her eyes closed. She closed her eyes and took a deep breath. It was a lovely sunny morning, with a cool breeze, but it was still very hot.

"Good morning ooh."

Omerie opened her eyes sharply; it was Ugo, a woman from the next compound. Ugo walked past Omerie, heading toward the cooking corner to join the other women. They were soon laughing out loud, and Omerie could only wonder what the joke was. She was briefly tempted to stroll across the compound and join in the usual morning gossip, but there was no time for that. She was due to see Chief to go through the day's arrangements as soon as possible. As much as Omerie wasn't looking forward to it, she desperately wanted to get it out of the way. Something inside her knew that he needed her. She knew he would be nervous, although he would never admit he needed her.

Lost in her thoughts, Omerie almost bumped into Ngozi, one of the neighbours.

"Oh, Ngozi, sorry, I did not see you."

Ngozi looked her up and down. "I was wondering when we were going to see you."

"You're here early."

"I came to see if you need any help with anything."

"Ah, thank you, Ngozi. Chief hired so many people for today, so I doubt there will be anything for you to do."

"Hmmm, okay, no problem. This one you have that look on your face, I take it you're not happy about the day?" Ngozi had a strange smile on her face. Without waiting for Omerie to reply, she added, "Anyway, I'll just join the women who are cooking. You never know if they'll need help with anything."

Omerie wanted to tell her to go home, but she knew it would lead to an extended discussion, and she did not have the time.

"Okay, no problem. I'll come there later."

"Okay, well, I've also just been to Chief's house, and some of the elders are there," Ngozi said, looking Omerie up and down again. "Are you going there?"

"Yes, I am going there now."

"Okay, well, we'll see each other later then," she bid her goodbye as she hurried off to the cooking corner.

Omerie sighed. *Ngozi! Madam wahala*, she thought. She laughed softly to herself before starting to walk toward Chief's house. As she approached, she noticed a few of the elders, sitting outside, already drinking. It was 11 o'clock. Typical. As usual, it was what they knew best.

"My elders, you are here. Good morning, and welcome," she greeted them as she approached.

"Ah, good morning, our wife!" They all responded simultaneously.

"See how beautiful you are, our wife," one of them said, his gaze lowering as he looked her over. Omerie could tell he was slightly drunk and was disgusted by his perverted look.

"You are welcome," she replied.

"This is a good bottle of palm wine. Your husband is a good man," he said, laughing as he managed to tear his eyes away from her. "Come and join us, our wife," he beckoned, tapping the only available chair next to him.

"Thank you, sir, but Chief has sent for me, and I cannot keep him waiting," she politely declined. "Please, enjoy yourselves, and there is more palm wine inside if this one is not enough," she added sarcastically, bending her knee slightly to signify her exit.

"You are welcome, my elders," she said once more. She hurried inside the house. As she approached the living room, she noticed the maids were still cleaning. Chief must have told them to do it again. They all knelt slightly to greet her, but she waved at them and continued to walk toward Chief's room.

Upon reaching the door, she hesitated and pressed her ear gently to the door to listen in. She didn't want to interrupt in case he had a guest inside. There was silence. She knocked softly, but there was no answer. She knocked again but didn't wait for a response before opening the door. Her first thought upon entering the room was that it was empty, but then she noticed Chief standing by the window, looking outside. She approached him. He seemed to be deep in thought.

"Chief," she called to him. This startled him, making him jump slightly with a frown on his face.

"Sorry, Chief. I knocked twice, and there was no answer, so I opened the door to see if you were in here," she paused. He nodded his head but didn't say anything, instead he returned to looking out the window.

"Chief, is everything alright?" she asked, walking slowly toward him.

He turned away from the window and walked slowly to the bed. He sat down and motioned for her to do the same. "Omerie, shut the door and sit down," he said.

Omerie didn't realise she had left the door open. She obeyed without hesitation. This would be a quick discussion, she thought; he was not in a good mood, and she wanted to get out of there as fast as she could. She decided it was best to inform him about the progress of getting things ready.

"Chief, everything is almost set up and ready..." He held up his hand to signal silence. She stopped. The silence seemed to stretch on for ages before Chief spoke.

"How long?" he asked. Omerie was confused by the question.

"Chief, how long?" was all she could mutter.

"Yes, how long have I waited? How long have I waited for a son, ehnn? I'm almost 60 years old; I have no male child. I have three wives, and none of them can bear me a son, just girls—girls, girls, girls. Are they going to carry my name? Tell me, who will carry my name?"

Omerie remained silent. Chief kissed his teeth.

"Now I'm marrying Amaka. What guarantees do I have that she will give me a son, ehnn?" He shook his head.

"Emmanuel..." Omerie hadn't called him by his name in years. He looked up at her, surprised.

"Why are you worried? Amaka is a young girl; she comes from a family of men. Her only sister is married and has four healthy boys. So don't worry, she will surely bear you a male child."

Chief huffed, stood up, and walked to the window. "It's the same thing I thought when I married Mabel; it was taking too long for her to conceive, so I had to marry Rume. Eventually, she became pregnant, but she was only able to bear me two girls and no more children since then," he hissed. "What is going on? My enemies are just laughing at me," he said, throwing his hands in the air.

She walked over and placed her hand on his shoulder. "God forbid, your enemies will not laugh at you. Please, try not to worry, Chief. It will be okay."

Chief huffed again as he stared out the window. There was a long moment of silence.

"You know, you say this to me all the time," he shook his head.

He turned away from the window and grabbed both her hands. "Why have you put up with this, Ome?"

Omerie tried to pull her hands away, but he held them tight. "Tell me, why do you put up with this?" His tone was hard and firm.

"Chief, you are my husband. When I married you, it was for better or for worse," she sighed, then continued. "I promised you that I wouldn't leave you, that's why I am still here." Her face was turned away from him. He gently let go of her hands and turned from her. She also moved away, not wanting him to see the tears that had rolled down her face.

"I have no choice, you know that."

She eyed him, slightly annoyed, but stayed quiet for a while. "I understand," was all she could say.

He stood away from her, and his silence made her uncomfortable.

"Chief, you've come a long way, and even though Rume and Mabel did not bear you a son, trust your current choice, ehnn?"

He turned to look at her now. Omerie continued. "This time it is different; she is from another tribe and a young girl. I'm sure she will bear you a male child," her hand was on his shoulder now.

He smiled. "Ome, you always know what to say to me."

He turned fully to face her. She quickly lowered her eyes, unable to look at him. He put his hand under her chin, lifting her face. She looked up at him. His expression was soft, softer than she had seen in a long time. He was different today; warmer, softer. The look in his eyes reminded her of when he first asked her to marry him. She tried to pull away; this felt strange, and it troubled her. He refused to let her go, pulling her closer. He reached up to run his hands through her plaited hair, cupping one of her cheeks. He bent down, and she started to speak.

"Emmanuel..."

"Shh..."

"Emma..." she tried to speak again

"Shh...it's okay"

Her heart began to beat quite fast. He was going to kiss her. She was unsure of what to do; just then, she closed her eyes and waited.

***

"This is not what we agreed upon at our last wives' meeting! You must be joking if you think I will just sit down and allow you to change things now!"

"Rume, why are you trying to cause trouble? This is what Chief wants," Mabel replied.

"Liar ooh! I say liar!" Rume snapped.

Omerie had just stepped out of Chief's bedroom and was heading toward the living room when she heard the commotion.

"Who is lying?" Mabel asked.

"Listen to me, there's no way I'll allow this to happen. Do you hear me?" Rume's voice was rising now.

"What's going on? Please, keep your voice down. Do you want Chief to come out?" Omerie hurried toward them.

Rume glanced at Omerie, then turned away. "I don't care if Chief comes out. You people are trying me," she said, raising her voice again.

Some of the housemaids stopped what they were doing and stood still, listening in.

"I just told you; Chief is the one who asked for this. Omerie knows this," Mabel tried to calm the situation.

"Mabel, what is going on here?" Omerie asked.

"Rume is..." Mabel started to explain, but Rume interrupted, kissing her teeth. Mabel turned to look at Omerie. "She is not happy with the new wife arrangement."

"Rume, please, I know you're not happy, but it affects all of us. Mabel and I aren't happy either, but this is what Chief wants," Omerie tried to reason with her.

"No, no, I don't agree. How can I not see my husband for two months? And why is it starting when it's my turn to cook his meals and spend time with him?" Rume hissed. "Two of you have had your turn, how convenient. Look, let me tell you, Omerie, you can say what you want, but I will speak to Chief myself."

"Speak to me about what?" Chief's firm voice suddenly cut through the room.

All the wives fell silent. Chief walked towards them and stood next to Omerie.

"Speak to me about what, Rume?" His voice was rough as he locked eyes with her.

Rume slowly walked toward him, smiling as she lifted her hand to place it on his shoulder.

"My honourable husband, I'm sorry our discussion brought you out of your room. Ermm... can we talk privately?" she asked, her voice soft.

"Say what you need to say now, I don't have time for this. It's my marriage ceremony today," Chief replied, his tone growing firmer.

"Mabel and Omerie, will you excuse us?" Rume said, eyeing the other wives.

"No, you will stay here and listen," Chief snapped, turning to look at them.

Omerie and Mabel quickly fell silent.

Chief turned back to Rume, removing her hand from his shoulder. "Speak now, Rume. I don't have time."

"Chief, what you are doing is not right. How can you say that because of your new wife, you don't want to see us for two months? It's not fair! What about our needs? What about our..." Rume folded her arms over her chest.

"Rume..." Chief interrupted, his tone sharp. "Is this why you were raising your voice and disturbing everyone in this compound?"

"Ah ah, Chief, did I shout? How can you say I am disturbing everybody?" Rume pointed to herself, her voice filled with disbelief. "I was just..."

"Now listen here... Ome," Chief turned abruptly to Omerie. "I have told you what I want with my new wife. Make sure no one disturbs me." He faced the others. "Now, I'll say this once: Leave this place now and make sure everything is ready for today. I don't want anyone disturbing me. If I see you here trying to cause trouble Rume..." He said pointing at her, then he turned and walked away, slamming the door to his room behind him.

Tears welled up in Rume's eyes as she stared at the shut door. Just then, Omerie reached out to her, placing a hand on her shoulder.

"Rume, it's okay…"

Rume quickly brushed her hand off her shoulder. "Don't touch me!" She glared at Omerie with fury. "Nonsense." She hissed and stomped off.

Omerie lowered her gaze, sighed, and shook her head.

"Please don't mind her, ehnn. Let's go, we have work to do," Mabel said, urging Omerie to follow.

Omerie hesitated, but Mabel tugged at her arm. "Chief will be angry if he sees us here. Also, we still have a lot to do. Come, let's go."

Omerie smiled at Mabel and motioned for her to go ahead. As Mabel left, Omerie turned back toward the door to Chief's room. Tears slowly began to roll down her cheeks, but she quickly wiped them away. Just then, Chief's driver walked in from the kitchen and saw her. He paused, staring for a moment. She quickly looked away, hurrying to leave.

"Good afternoon, ma," Eric, the driver, greeted.

"Good afternoon, Eric," Omerie said quickly, walking out.

Outside, Mabel was already waiting for her. The compound was now bustling with activity; with cooks and workers preparing for the event. As Omerie took it all in, she heard Eric's voice from behind.

"Madam, sorry to disturb you, but I need to ask where you want me to put the chairs that were brought in."

Omerie paused for a second before responding. "Sorry, what did you say?"

"Emm, sorry, madam, Chief ordered some chairs, and I'm not sure where to put them."

"Oh, okay. Leave them where they are for now. I'll let you know where to put them later, ehn?"

"Okay, ma." He still stood as though he had something more to say.

"Anything else?"

"Emm… no, nothing, ma."

"Okay. I'll be with the cooks if anyone is looking for me." She turned to Mabel. "Please go check on the canopies. They should all be up by now."

"Okay." Mabel hurried off.

Omerie turned around again to see Eric still standing there, staring at her with a concerned look.

"Madam, is everything alright?"

"I'm fine Eric, thank you. Please go and continue with your work, today is a busy day."

Eric nodded. "Yes, ma."

She watched as he slowly walked back into the house, his figure disappearing inside. Turning away, she surveyed the packed compound again, but the noise and bustle felt overwhelming. She didn't want to be part of it right now; she needed some time to herself. Her quarters didn't feel like a safe place either; somebody might come looking for her there.

Slowly, she made her way to a quiet spot between two plants, hidden from view. She sat on the pavement, her body curling inward as she placed her face between her thighs. At that moment, she wanted to scream, but all that escaped her was a small, strangled sound before the tears began to flow.

Chapter 10

Rume paced back and forth in her living room, her eyes flicking to the clock on the wall. It was 3 o'clock. Mama Omote was supposed to be here by now. She had made sure the children were out until 6, not wanting them to overhear the conversation she was about to have. It had been almost two months since Chief's marriage, and since then, he had become a ghost in their lives. He hadn't seen any of his other wives or eaten their food. Two weeks after the marriage, he called a meeting to announce that his new young wife would be cooking and staying in his quarters indefinitely. Rume tried to protest, but Chief cut her off, as he always did, and dismissed them, forbidding them from coming near his quarters unless absolutely urgent. He even provided a list of what he deemed urgent.

Rume was done. She couldn't take it anymore. She needed help, and she needed it fast. Just then, a knock on the door broke her thoughts.

"Is anybody home?"

Rume instantly recognised Mama Omote's voice, clear and familiar. "I'm here o," she called out, rushing to the door. It was already open, but the curtain was drawn. Pushing it aside, Rume smiled as she saw Mama Omote standing there.

"Come in, come in, ma."

Mama Omote was holding a small basket as she entered the house slowly.

"Let me carry that, ma," Rume offered, reaching for the basket.

"I was beginning to think I wouldn't see you today," Rume added, her voice laced with relief.

"Sorry, I had to see someone at the next town, and it took some time to find a motorbus," Mama Omote explained, her voice warm but tired.

"Well, thank you for coming ooh, ma. Please sit down. Let me get you some cold water. I know you must be thirsty; the sun is hot today"

"Oh yes, please." Mama Omote pointed to the basket still in Rume's hand. "There are some garden eggs in there. I bought them for you. Maybe you can put them in the fridge."

Rume peeked into the basket, her eyes widening at the sight of the fresh produce. "Ah, this is a lot ooh," she said, pulling out a few to examine them. "They're big ones. Thank you, ma." She paused, her expression softening. "Let me get you some water." Then, as an afterthought, she added, "Do you want a cold drink?"

"No, my dear, water is just fine."

"Okay, I'm coming. Please, just relax."

Rume hurried into the kitchen and returned shortly with a large glass of cold water, placing it carefully on a stool near Mama Omote.

"Thank you, my dear."

Rume sat down on a nearby chair, watching as Mama Omote drank deeply. She was clearly parched. Mama Omote sighed with relief after taking a long gulp.

"Yes, I feel better now."

Rume smiled as she took the empty glass from her. "The house is quiet today. Where are the children?"

"I sent them out," Rume replied.

"I see. I haven't seen them in a while. How are they?"

"They're fine, ma," Rume said, a slight smile playing at her lips, though her heart felt heavy.

"Onome must be big now," Mama Omote said, her voice warm.

"Ah, she's very big, like her mouth," Rume replied with a tired smile.

Mama Omote laughed, the sound lightening the tension in the room.

"Rume, I'm sorry, but I can't stay long. I still need to go to the next town to see someone."

"Ehnn, I see," Rume said, her tone shifting. "In that case, we need to start talking now."

She stood and moved quickly to shut the front door.

"I just want to make sure nobody hears us," she added, her voice low. "You know the other wives and their children, they like to sneak around, listening to other people's discussions."

Mama Omote nodded knowingly as Rume checked the windows, shuttering them slightly.

"Won't it be too hot?" Mama Omote asked.

"I will turn on the fan," Rume replied, hurrying to switch it on before sitting down again. She cleared her throat, her hands fidgeting nervously.

"Mama Omote, I need your help, please."

"Ehnn... okay. What's going on?"

"Things are not going well for me at all."

"Is that so? Okay, tell me what has happened."

Rume hesitated, her eyes darting to the floor before meeting Mama Omote's gaze. "Chief has totally lost interest in me."

"Are you serious?"

"He has married another wife. It's not just that he married someone else—that surprised me, but I could have lived with it. What troubles me is... I thought the love he had for me was too strong for this." Her voice broke slightly. "Now, he doesn't want to see me, hear from me, or even eat my food anymore."

"Ah, ah! Just you?"

"Well, it's all of us," Rume admitted, waving her hand dismissively. "But I'm not concerned about the other wives." She leaned forward, desperation in her eyes. "Ma, I thought you said he'd love me forever! That he'd always listen to my voice. I don't understand."

Mama Omote studied her for a moment.

"When did you find out he was getting married?"

"Well... he was very quiet about it. He only told us two weeks before the marriage."

"Two weeks?" Mama Omote's voice rose slightly. "And you didn't come to me immediately?"

"I... I... well, I was just confused. I wasn't sure what was going on."

"You should have come to me immediately!" Mama Omote snapped. "You should have informed me so we could investigate."

Rume fell silent, standing abruptly and walking toward the dining table. She paused, then turned back slowly.

"Ma, but you said I shouldn't worry, that I had him under my thumb forever. What happened?" Her voice trembled, and her eyes searched Mama Omote's face for answers.

Mama Omote exhaled, shaking her head.

"My dear, I told you that if everything went well, he would love you forever. Something must have gone wrong somewhere."

"But what could have gone wrong?" Rume's voice cracked. "I did everything you asked me to do, every month."

"Are you sure?" Mama Omote asked, with a doubtful tone. Rume knew what she was thinking. Many years ago, Mama Omote had given her instructions to follow, in order to bear a male child, but she had failed to follow them correctly... but no, not this time. She was careful and hadn't made any mistakes.

"Yes! I did exactly what you told me."

Silence fell between them, heavy and uncomfortable.

"What about him?" Mama Omote finally asked, her brow furrowed. "Has he done something different?"

"Nothing," Rume said. "His routine didn't change; well, not until his marriage."

"Something has changed," Mama Omote murmured, leaning forward, hand on her chin.

Rume turned back and sank into her chair, her shoulders sagging.

"Ma, you have to help me," she pleaded. "I can't afford for things to fall apart like this now. I've come too far to just be relegated like this, just cast aside."

"Rume, relax."

"How can I relax? He has a new wife now. I thought I would be his last and that he would give me all his attention. I still have not given him a son. I'm too old now anyway."

"Are you going to listen to me?"

"Sorry, Ma." She took a deep breath, putting her hands over her face. "I just don't know what to do now."

Mama Omote leaned forward in her chair. "It is going to be okay, my dear. Don't worry. Listen to me. It's not too late. We can still do something about it. I cannot do anything here now, but I will go home. Come to me in two days, and I will tell you what to do."

"Two days?"

"Yes, just make sure you come to me in two days. I need some time to prepare what you need."

"Okay, no problem."

"For now, don't fight with him. Don't cause any trouble. Don't let anything or anyone provoke you to anger, and make sure he doesn't find out about this. Do you hear?"

"No problem, Ma."

There was silence.

"You still look worried. What is it?"

"He has been with her for two months now. We hardly see her, so she must be pregnant by now. What if she bears him a son?"

"Well, if that's the case, it cannot be avoided."

Rume stared at Mama Omote with wide eyes. She knew Mama Omote could see the look of fear and worry on her face.

"Can you stop her from getting pregnant?" Rume asked.

"No, that is not possible."

Rume frowned. "So, it cannot be avoided?" Mama Omote shook her head.

Rume still had a frown on her face.

"What is important now is that you are the one he prefers out of all his wives. Is that not so?"

Rume nodded.

"Okay, then let us forget about her being pregnant and concentrate on the next plan of action."

Rume sighed and leaned back in her seat.

"There is something else."

"Really? What is it?"

"Hmmm... it's about Onome. A Chief came some time ago to ask for her hand in marriage. Now he is saying he wants to marry her for his nephew that lives in Germany."

"Germany? That is great. Abroad!"

"Yes, he lives abroad."

"Ehnnn, that is interesting. How old is he?"

"Twenty-eight years."

"A twenty-eight-year-old man! No wife, living abroad? What has he been doing in Germany all this time?"

"Well, he said he went there to further his education and then started working. Now he has made some money and wants to marry a good girl."

"Ah, that's wonderful. Onome is a good girl, and I know how much you like a rich man." Mama Omote laughed softly. "But come ooh, where did the Chief see Onome or find out about her?"

"He said he has seen her a few times at her friend Prisca's place. Apparently, he knows their family. He said he always sees Onome helping Prisca and her mother, and that she would make a good wife for his nephew."

"What did you say?"

"Well, first of all, I silently thanked God that the Chief decided to marry her for his nephew, because I don't know how I would have explained it to my husband," she said, a playful grin spreading across her face. They both chuckled. "Anyway, umm... there's one thing I need to talk to you about."

"Okay."

"Onome has just finished secondary school. Even if my husband decides to send her to university, I want her to marry first, and then when she is in her husband's house, she can go to university there."

Rume knew Mama Omote was watching her closely. She had better come out with the rest of it.

"I want her to marry and leave this house. She just reminds me of the mistake I made. I think the earlier I can get her out of this house, the better for me." Rume was frowning again.

Mama Omote sighed thoughtfully. She leaned back in her chair with her hand on her chin. Rume was staring at her intently, waiting for a response. Mama Omote was in deep thought for a while.

"Well, if she marries this man, it means she will have to relocate far away to Germany, which is not a bad idea."

"Exactly. That is what I was thinking."

"Have you told Chief yet?"

"No, not at all. I wanted to speak to you first. Besides, with the recent development with Chief, this has to wait until we put a plan into action."

"Ah, that's true. Well, if you want to know my thoughts, I think you should go ahead and agree to the marriage. Chief will agree too. That is not a problem. Just make sure you come to me as I have said."

"No problem. I will be there."

"Good," Mama Omote replied. "Is there anything else you want to discuss with me? Because I still have to go to the next town to see someone before I make my way home."

"No, nothing, Ma. If I remember anything else, I will mention it when I come and see you in two days."

"Okay, then." Mama Omote slowly stood up.

"Ma, please wait! I'm coming," Rume said as she rushed away to her room." She came back, holding a brown envelope. She raised Mama Omote's right hand and pressed the envelope into it. "Ma, please manage this. You know I haven't seen you in a few months."

Mama Omote held the envelope with both hands, feeling its weight. "Ah! This envelope is thick and heavy," she said with excitement.

"Ma, it's just something small from me."

"Ah! Thank you very much, my daughter. Thank you."

"No problem, ma. You know you're my second mother nah."

"Thank God I took a big bag today. I better keep it at the bottom of my bag. I don't want these area boys to steal it." She smiled as she placed it deep into her bag. "I'm grateful," she said, walking towards the door.

Rume!"

"Yes, ma."

"Stay well."

"Yes, ma."

"Don't let anything worry you at all."

"Okay, ma. I'll walk you to the gate, ma."

"Okay."

They both stepped out, and Rume shut the door behind her.

"I noticed that your side of the house has been painted again," Mama Omote said.

"Ah, yes. I told Chief that the paint was wearing off and that I wanted it painted again. He just called the painter, and they did it very well."

"It looks nice and new."

"I'm thinking of asking Chief to change the furniture in the living room sef." She lowered her voice to a whisper. "Especially with Onome's marriage ceremony coming up. I don't want my in-laws to come and meet that old furniture."

"That furniture is not old."

"Ah, ma, it is ooh."

"Rume, don't make me laugh."

"Well, Chief will change it."

"Of course, you are his favourite."

"I am his favourite," she replied softly, though with a slight bit of uncertainty.

They both grew quiet as they turned towards Mabel's quarters. It was the only other quarter close to Chief's. Rume noticed the children outside. Some of their daughters were getting their hair plaited. Omerie and Mabel were sitting, watching them as they talked.

They had to walk past them to get to the compound gate. The women noticed them.

"Good afternoon," the wives said at once.

Rume whispered to Mama Omote, "Don't say anything to them."

"Why? This isn't the first time I'm seeing them."

"Good afternoon, ma. How are you, ma?"

The greeting came again. Rume turned to see who was speaking. It was one of the women plaiting the children's hair. She seemed to be addressing Mama Omote. Mama Omote turned and looked up as well.

"Ah! Good afternoon, my dear. How are you?"

Rume had to stop and listen as they exchanged pleasantries. She avoided looking at the other wives, fully conscious that they were watching her. It suddenly grew quiet. The children seemed to have stopped talking. Those who weren't sneaking glances at her from the corners of their eyes had their heads bent, focused on getting their hair plaited with extensions.

The children had never really warmed up to her, she had never given them a chance to. When she married Chief, the wives had welcomed her warmly. They were friendly, bringing gifts to her quarters and promising to work together to have a happy family because that was what Chief wanted.

They would stay together until late in the evening, on days when Chief was out of town. They would eat together, laugh together, and would each share their personal stories. Things were good for a few months until she became pregnant. That's when everything changed.

With the pleasantries over, Mama Omote turned and signalled for them to continue walking. They headed toward the compound gate, neither noticing how fast their steps had become.

"That woman who greeted you, how do you know her, ma?" Rume asked curiously.

"I know her mother well. She lives near me."

"I see." Rume's expression shifted. She was concerned by this information. If the woman's mother knew Mama Omote, then she likely knew what Mama Omote did, and that meant she could share that information with the wives.

Rume didn't realise she had stopped walking as they were both standing at the gate.

"Okay, let me hurry. I'm already late."

"Okay, ma. Let me walk you to the motor park."

"No, don't worry. I'll manage. I'll see you the day after tomorrow, ehnn. Bye-bye ooh!" She hurried off.

"Bye-bye, ma," Rume called after her.

Rume stood watching as Mama Omote hurried off. She turned away and began walking back to her quarters. A roar of laughter erupted from the wives. She turned to look at them, but no one was facing her. Still, she couldn't help but feel that they were talking about her.

She sucked her teeth in annoyance. *As usual, they just can't help gossiping about me,* she thought. *They're jealous—always have been. Always wanting to know my business.*

Hmm…the woman that greeted Mama Omote, I wonder how much she knows about her, she thought.

Rume had always been careful about her meetings with Mama Omote, always introducing her as a distant aunty. It had been easy to maintain the lie since her family lived in a faraway town and Mama Omote wasn't known in this town. But now there was someone who knew Mama Omote well and also knew this family.

Rume was certain the wives had already asked questions. And what if they have put two and two together? What if they now know that Mama Omote is not her aunty?

Back inside, Rume sat down, resting her chin on her hand as her mind raced.

What if they now know that Mama Omote, is a Prophetess?

She shot to her feet, pacing the room. Mama Omote had been coming here for years. What if that woman has told them everything? Rume's hand flew to cover her mouth.

This is really concerning, she thought as she walked slowly back to the chair and sat down.

"It's not possible," she whispered to herself. "As if I don't already have enough problems."

Just then, she heard footsteps approaching the front door. She quickly stood up.

"Who is there?"

"Mama, it's me."

Rume glanced around the living room, making sure nothing was out of place. Onome stepped in slowly, carrying a small paper bag.

"Mama, it's me ooh," she repeated, smiling. "Look, Prisca's mother gave us some plantain."

Rume stared at the bag and the bunch of plantains inside. She let out a sigh of irritation.

"Abeg, just take it to the kitchen and leave it there."

"Yes, ma."

"Drop it and come back."

"Okay."

She watched as Onome bowed her head as she slowly carried the bunch of plantain to the kitchen. She returned quickly, standing with her hands behind her.

"Sit down," she said, pointing at the chair opposite her. She watched as Onome slowly sat down.

"There is something I need us to discuss."

"Okay."

"You have finished secondary school now," Rume began, pausing briefly. "I know you've already told your father that you want to further your education."

"Yes," Onome replied.

"Good. Me too, I've been thinking about that." She paused again, giving Onome a chance to respond.

"You know it's not easy to pass JAMB these days. Some people have been buying JAMB application forms for years now, and they still haven't been able to pass it," she said, shaking her head. "Imagine, years! Is it not true?"

Onome nodded silently.

"Ehnn. Okay, now listen. I think we can avoid all that stress. There's a way around it, a much better way. A way for you to get the best education, one that nobody in this town can even dream of having. Would you not like that?"

"Yes. But how... I don't understand..."

"Good! Now you're talking." Rume leaned in slightly, her voice lowering. "Like I said, I've been thinking about this, and we've found the perfect solution."

She paused again, letting her words sink in before continuing.

"You will go to university abroad."

"Abroad?" Onome's eyes widened as she gasped, covering her mouth with both hands.

Rume smiled, satisfied with the reaction.

"Yes, abroad—Germany."

"Germany?!" Onome's voice rose in disbelief. "How is that possible?"

"It's possible. Don't worry about that."

"Ah, but Mama, they don't even speak English there ooh!"

"You'll learn. Don't you want to go abroad?"

"Yes ooh, yes."

Rume tilted her head slightly, noting the hesitation in Onome's voice. Her last "yes" had sounded a bit shaky.

"Good," Rume said firmly. "Okay, now listen to me very carefully."

She leaned forward, beckoning Onome to come closer.

"There's this Chief Oge—do you know him?"

Onome shook her head.

"Well, he knows you. Anyway, it does not matter. He has a nephew in Germany; he wants to marry you and take you to Germany."

"Marry me!?"

"Yes ooh, marry you and take you to Germany. Abroad, overseas, can you imagine? On top of that, he'll pay for you to further your education there." Rume smiled. "You see how God has blessed us, ehnn?" She laughed softly.

She watched as Onome stood up quickly, her face twisting into a huge frown.

"Mama, no, no, no! I don't want to marry anybody," Onome said, folding her arms across her chest and looking away.

"What do you mean by that?" Rume asked, her voice calm but firm.

"Mama, I don't want to marry anybody. I just want to finish my education first," Onome responded, still refusing to meet her mother's gaze.

Rume was silent for a moment, her eyes scanning Onome's face. She always knew this daughter would be a challenge, but if she was to succeed, she needed to tread carefully. "Onome, sit down," she said softly.

Onome shook her head, "I don't want to sit down."

Rume stood up, walking gently to Onome's side, and placed both hands on her shoulders. "Sit down, sit down now. Are we fighting?" she asked, her tone persuasive but calm. Finally, Onome sat down. Once she was seated, Rume sat beside her.

"Don't be in a rush to throw this opportunity away, my daughter. I've brought something to you today, and you're saying no without even thinking about it or asking me questions."

Onome took a deep breath. "Calm down. Let's talk this through now. Look, Chief is a good man, and his nephew is also a good man. They have money; you'll be taken care of and the whole family too. Don't you want that for us?"

"Yes, Mama," Onome said quietly, "but I don't want to marry now. I want to go to university, like my mates are doing. I don't mind if it's in the city."

"We're talking about abroad here, and you're talking about the city. Do you think your mates wouldn't want to go abroad instead of studying in the city? Do you know how many people would kill for this kind of opportunity? You're talking about the city, but what is the city compared to Germany, ehnn? You'll marry a man from abroad and go there; you'll become an overseas girl. Think about it."

Onome didn't respond, still frowning, her face turned away.

"Onome, this will be good for you and for this family. Think about your sister. Your sister could have the same life as you. You'll open the way for her to go abroad and study, and she could marry another overseas man."

Rume paused, a realisation dawning on her. "Think of your sister. Don't you want the best for her too?"

"Of course, I want the best for my sister."

"Good." Rume smiled. "Listen to me, Onome, this is a great opportunity. Trust me."

She noticed Onome's breathing slow down a bit, a sign that her words were beginning to reach her daughter.

"Does Papa know?"

"I think it's better if we tell him together."

Onome paused for a while, then suddenly got up.

"Mama, I don't want to marry now. I don't care about going to university abroad. This is my hometown, I will stay here and go to university here."

"Shut up! What do you know? I'm telling you something important, and you're talking nonsense! 'Ermm, I don't want to marry, I don't want to go abroad.' Nonsense!" Rume shouted at Onome. "Listen to me! You will marry! You will marry, or this house won't contain the two of us! Do you hear me?"

"I've said my mind ooh. Me, I don't want to marry," Onome replied firmly.

"Get out of here before I deal with you!" Rume barked.

Onome grumbled as she walked away, still muttering, "I don't want to marry ooh. I want to go to university ooh."

"Come back here!" Rume called after her.

Onome stopped in her tracks.

"I said, come here!" Rume's voice was sharp. Onome slowly walked back toward her mother. Rume reached into her bag and pulled out a small brown bottle.

"Take this," she said, pressing the bottle into Onome's hand.

Onome stared at the bottle; confusion written all over her face. "What is this?"

"This is for the rash on your body. It will clear it up completely. You need to bathe with it twice a day, or it won't work," Rume instructed, her tone firm.

Onome continued to eye the bottle suspiciously. "Mama, is this from the chemist? There's no name on the bottle."

"Madam investigator!" Rume snapped. "Yes, it's from the chemist. The man said it's his own product, and that's why it doesn't have a name. Other people have used it, and it worked for them."

Onome looked at the bottle, still unsure.

"If you like, continue to look at the bottle and wonder why it doesn't have a name. You won't go now and bathe with it." Rume hissed, walking away. "You like to see your body like that, abi? You won't clear your skin before you get married?"

Onome shook her head and huffed. "Mama, I don't want to get married ooh. I want to go to university." She tugged at her ear, trying to make her point clear.

"Get out of here before I slap you!" Rume snapped. She watched as Onome stomped away, but Rume's anger wasn't finished. "Okay, wait for me. I will deal with you. You'll see!" She hissed again. "Nonsense."

She slumped into a chair, fuming with frustration. As she sat there, she glanced at the clock on the wall, it was 6 o'clock. "Everybody is just frustrating me in this house," she muttered. "I need to go somewhere to clear my mind."

She paused for a moment, considering. "I need to speak to someone," she thought aloud. "But where? Who can I go to?"

Suddenly, a thought struck her. She stood up quickly, snatched her handbag off the dining table, and called out to Onome.

"Onome!"

"Ma!" Onome responded from the other room.

"I'm going out. If anyone asks for me, tell them I'm sleeping," Rume said quickly, hurrying out of the house.

As she made her way toward Mrs. Ufuoma's house, she took a deep breath, hoping the conversation she was about to have would help her make sense of everything.

Chapter 11

W hat's in all these bags again?" Omerie sounded tired, her voice tinged with frustration as she picked up another heavy paper bag from the floor. Just when she thought she'd finished sorting everything, another bag would appear. It felt like they'd been at this for hours. She'd been on her feet all this time. Meat-sharing day was always hectic. Chief had made it a tradition to order different types of meat once a month; chicken, beef *(cow)*, goat, bushmeat *(Grasscutter)*, you name it. These would then be divided among the wives according to the size of their households. The day was always busy, with the wives, children, and housemaids all gathering as the meat was shared.

However, today was different. The other wives were absent. Chief was with his new wife, resting. Mabel had taken her daughters to visit her parents in the village. Rume, as usual, was nowhere to be found, leaving Onome with the task of ensuring she received her share. As the first wife and the oldest, Omerie was responsible for dividing the meat and giving each wife their portion. She was sure these were the last bags to sort.

"These are the bags with the goat meat, ma," said Eric, Chief's driver, as he started to open each bag.

"So, there are four bags?" Omerie asked, her hands on her hips.

"Five bags, ma," Eric corrected, counting them for her.

"Okay, don't open them," she said, stopping him. "I'll tell you which one to place with each wife's share and for their quarters." Omerie stepped back, eyeing each bag as she tried to gauge their weight. She then began carrying the bags, placing them by the stack of food items that had already been divided.

"Let me help you, ma." Eric quickly moved to take one of the bags from her hands.

She proceeded to tell him where to place each one. Finally, it was done.

"Okay, now you can start taking them to each house," Omerie said to one of the maids, nodding at Onome to take theirs. She watched as Onome knelt slightly, thanking her before picking up one of the bags, with Eric helping her.

"Okay, help clear away all the rubbish. Bring me the broom," she added. She began sweeping the area with the other maid, and it took a bit of time before everything was finished. She told the maids they could retire for the evening. They thanked her, and Omerie heard a sigh of relief as they turned to leave.

She was very tired now, walking to her quarters. As she approached the house, she saw Eric standing at her front door, her portion of the food items on the floor beside him.

"Eric, you're still here?" she asked, looking at the bags in front of him. "But I told the maid to take the things and put them inside."

"The door is locked, ma. I told them I'd take it inside for you," Eric replied.

Omerie stood there, looking at him as he stared directly at her. She touched the side of her wrapper, realising the keys were still there.

"Ah, I didn't even know I locked the door," she said, shaking her head. "Let me open it." She inserted the key into the lock, and as soon as the door opened, she pushed it and stepped inside the living room. Eric helped hold the door open as she walked in to switch on the light.

"Where do you want them, ma?"

"Erm... just leave them here on the floor for now. I'll take them into the kitchen and arrange them later." Eric nodded but then went ahead and carried everything into the kitchen. She was about to stop him but then decided not to. She watched as he took the first set of bags and then came back for the rest.

"This is the last one, ma," he said, picking up the final bag.

"Thank you very much. Well done, ehn," she said, watching him nod in response as he took the bags and disappeared into the kitchen.

"No problem, ma," he replied, returning to the living room. Omerie noticed he wiped the sweat from his forehead. She could see the tiredness in his eyes as his gaze dropped, his hands dirty from all the work. She saw him hesitate, unsure whether to ask for something to wipe his hands with.

"You can wash your hands in the kitchen sink," she said quickly.

"Thank you, ma." Eric walked back into the kitchen.

"The soap is there," she called out, raising her voice slightly.

"Okay, ma."

As she arranged things in the living room, he returned, standing for a moment before she noticed him staring at her. She tried to move a chair back, but he quickly stepped forward to help.

"Let me carry it, ma. It's heavy." He lifted the chair and placed it where she wanted it.

"Eric, thank you, but you know..." she hesitated, picking up a piece of dirty paper from the floor, "I can do things myself around my own house."

"I'm sorry, ma, I don't mean to interfere. I grew up with three sisters, ma. I did the heavy lifting in the house." His tone was apologetic, a slight nervousness in his voice.

"Ah, are you the only man?"

"Yes, ma."

"You received a lot of petting then," she joked, looking around the living room again to check if everything was in order.

"Ah, no ooh," he chuckled. "No petting for me at all, ma, there was no time for that."

She looked up at him, seeing him standing still, his hands stretched behind him, looking a bit nervous.

"How are your father and mother?"

"My father and mother are late."

"Oh, I'm so sorry. I didn't know. Sorry, ehn."

"No problem, ma. They passed away a few years ago."

"So, you've been taking care of your sisters." It was a statement, not a question, as it made sense to her now.

"Yes, ma. Two of them have finished university now. There's just one left to go."

"Thank God ooh! Well done, ehn. It's not easy."

"Yes, ma, it's not." He let out a slow laugh.

Omerie smiled, but then turned away, her eyes scanning the living room once more. For some reason, she felt like something was out of place, but she couldn't figure out what.

"Is there anything else I can help with, ma?"

"Erm... no, you should go home and rest. You've been here since 8 this morning."

"No problem at all, ma. I can still help if you need anything."

"No. It's okay. You should go home and rest. Besides, you look tired. I'm sure Chief will need you to run some errands for him tomorrow."

"Yes, ma. Goodnight, ma." He made his way to the door, walking slowly, his shoulders slumped. Omerie thought he must be exhausted. She glanced at the time, it was almost 8 o'clock.

She looked back at him again as he stepped outside, turning around to shut the door in front of him.

"Eric," she called to him.

"Yes, ma?" He stopped and looked up at her.

"Have you eaten?"

"No, ma, but I will go to the local canteen, ma."

"Local canteen?! Come, come, let me give you something."

"Ah, no, ma. I will go to the canteen, ma."

"No, no, you will not go to the local canteen. I have plenty of food in the house, no one will eat them. Come in and sit down."

She watched him hesitate a little, but then he nodded. "Okay, ma."

She guessed he was very hungry and desperately needed something to eat. He took off his shoes again, leaving them outside, and walked back inside. As he turned to shut the door, she spoke again.

"You can leave the front door open," she told him as she walked away to the kitchen.

"Yes, ma." He pushed open the door, leaving it ajar, and walked slowly toward the kitchen.

"Go and sit down at the dining. I will prepare the food," she said as she saw him looking in.

"Please let me help, ma," he walked in.

"Help? How? Do you want to prepare the pounded yam?" she asked, laughing softly.

"Ah, ma, I can do it. I cook at home."

"Is that so?" she said, moving around to get what she needed. He moved slowly into the kitchen.

"So, your sisters don't know how to cook?" she asked as she bent down to pick up some yam from the side of the cooker.

"They can cook, ma, but because they were in school, I wanted them to concentrate on their education. So, I started to learn how to cook for myself." He had a little proud smile on his face as he stepped fully into the kitchen and stood a few steps away from her.

"So, you can cook soup and make pounded yam?" she said, starting to peel the yam skin.

"Ah, yes, ma." He smiled again.

She dropped the knife and turned to look at him. He was still smiling.

"Let me help, ma," he said, almost pleading.

She sighed. She knew he wouldn't let it be.

"Don't worry. Rest today from cooking. But if you're looking for something to do, then help me take the pot of soup from the fridge and put it on the stove." She turned back to continue peeling the yam skin.

"Okay, ma." He rushed over to the fridge, and she could tell he was happy to be doing something.

"After that, you can set the table with water and plates."

"Yes, ma." He walked over and placed the pot on one of the burners, quickly making his way out of the kitchen.

She went on to cut the yam into small pieces, washed them, placed them in the pot, and set the pot on the stove. She lit the burner for the soup. Eric was preparing the table, coming in from time to time to pick up something or ask a question. Once everything was done, she asked him to sit down while she got on with preparing the food. After some time, the food was ready. She called for him and asked him to help take it to the dining room. He looked more tired now, and she could tell he was very hungry. Maybe she should have allowed him to go to the canteen after all. What was she thinking, asking him to wait until she prepared something?

He was standing by the table now as she brought in a bowl of water for washing hands. She had already brought in his share of the food and placed it on the table.

"You can sit down and eat ooh," she pointed at the plates in front of him.

"Thank you, ma." He quickly sat down, washed his hands in the bowl of water beside him, and began to eat. She came back with her share and sat opposite him. As she watched him do a quick swallow, she almost felt sorry for him.

"Eric," she called.

"Yes, ma?" He paused, with a formed pounded yam prepared for swallowing.

"Wait a minute, let us quickly pray before you continue eating, ehn?"

"Yes, ma. Sorry, ma," he said apologetically.

Omerie said a quick blessing over the food and signalled to him to continue eating. He resumed, but this time slowly, molding and swallowing at a much slower pace than earlier. She noticed that he was watching her as he ate, swallowing at the same time as her. They continued to eat in silence. She didn't say anything because she knew how hungry he was.

At some point, he forgot himself and began to lick the soup off his fingers. He stopped suddenly when he became aware of what he was doing. She watched as he adjusted himself and cleared his throat.

"Sorry, ma."

"Why are you sorry? Please eat, don't worry."

He smiled a little, reached for the glass of water beside him, and took a drink.

"This food is very sweet, ma," he said with a smile as he placed the glass down.

"Thank you."

He took a few swallows and reached out for a drink again. Placing the glass down, he said, "Ma, is Eno not around? Because I have not seen her since."

"Oh, Eno, she went to stay with my sister. She is coming back next week."

"Ah, okay."

There was silence now as they continued eating.

"Hmm, this one you are asking about Eno, so I hope all is well," she said with a small smile.

"Ah, ma, everything is fine. I was just asking because we have not seen her recently," he smiled.

"Ah, who is the 'we'?"

"Ma, you mean the 'we'?"

"Yes, you said we have not seen her recently, so I am wondering who is the 'we.'"

"Ma, the 'we' is just all of us in this place... this compound," he stuttered, his head half down as he spoke. She could tell he was nervous now, as he had stopped eating his food.

"Abeg, eat your food. I was just joking," she chuckled. He smiled softly; his head still bent down as he continued to eat.

"You have never been married?" she asked, noticing that he did not have a wedding ring.

"Ermm... ma, I was married before ooh, some years ago, but... ermm..." he hesitated. "My wife left me."

"Oh no, sorry to hear that," she said, pausing from her food to look at him.

"No problem, ma." He stared at the food, not eating. "Ermm, things were too tough for her."

They were both silent for some time.

"Do you have any children?" she asked now, with some curiosity.

"No, ma, no children," he said, his voice heavy with pain.

She was tempted to press further but thought otherwise.

There was silence now, each not even eating their food. Omerie looked at him and saw that he was just staring at his plate of food. He looked somewhat sad, and there was something in his tone that made her want to probe some more. But, because she was his madam, he would answer her even if he didn't want to. Deep down inside, she felt it wasn't the right thing to do.

"Well, don't worry," she said, taking a deep breath. "You are still a young man. You will find another good woman to marry and have children one day," she said reassuringly.

He smiled. "Ma, to be honest, I have tried to find a good woman, but since my parents died and I had to take care of my sisters, nobody wants to settle with a man with such responsibilities."

"Ah, don't think like that. Did you not go to school?"

"I did, ma, but not up to university, so I could not find better work," he said, his voice tinged with slight frustration.

"Ah ah but are you not working now?" she asked him, unsure of what he was saying.

"Well... erm... yes, ma," he said hesitantly.

She took a deep breath. Even though he didn't say it outright, she knew what he meant. The work of a driver was not considered "proper" work in society. But he was lucky to have something at all in this small town, and if anyone could find work that enabled them to support three sisters through school, then he should be proud. Not many people could boast of this.

"Well, there is still plenty of time, and there are still good women out there. You are young, so don't give up."

He laughed, shaking his head slightly. "Ma, I am 45 years old."

"So! Ah ah, at 45, you are still a young man. Abeg, don't worry, you will find a good wife. You still have time."

"Yes, ma," he nodded, smiling now.

"Are you a Christian?"

"Yes, I am a Christian, ma."

"Ehnn, okay. Do you pray?"

"Yes ma, I pray," he hesitated, "ermm... sometimes."

She looked at him, and they both laughed.

"I try, ma," he said, smiling softly.

"Okay, well, you have to pray more and ask God for a good wife."

"Yes, ma."

"Which church do you go to?"

"Ah, well, the only one we have in my area, ma."

"You mean Christ Our Redeemer? Ah, I have been there at least twice. How come I have not seen you there?"

"I go when I can, ma."

She shook her head as she smiled at him. "Are you sure?"

"I try, ma." He said these words again, this time with a smile even bigger than the last. She was looking at him now, he had a beautiful smile. Eric had been with them for three years now. He was a good driver, and Omerie had always considered him to be a good man with good manners and character. She could not understand why any woman would want to leave such a man. Yes, he was a driver, but he had a job and could bring money to the home and take care of the family.

She had noticed that he had been very helpful to her lately, and she had her suspicions. He was looking for a wife, and maybe he had found one in her niece, Eno. Maybe this was why he kept being so helpful to her, she thought. She had been observing him for a while. He would make a good husband, and Eno would make a good wife. But would her sister agree? A driver? This would not sit well with her sister at all.

She pondered these thoughts, not realising how long they had been quiet or how long she had been staring at him. When she suddenly came to this realisation, she noticed he was staring back at her. She adjusted herself in her seat quickly.

"Please finish your food, I have been asking you many questions, and it is getting late." Just then, she looked at the time; it was now approaching 10 o'clock.

"Erm... ma, is it okay if I take the rest home?"

"Don't worry about the time. Finish your food, please."

"Actually, ma, I want to go and quickly catch the bus home, as my place is far."

"Ah, okay. Let me pack the remaining food for you." She was up on her feet now.

"Thank you, ma."

She took the plates and walked to the kitchen. She paused as she placed the plates on the counter. She knew it was getting late, but she had asked him to stay and continue eating. She didn't have to ask herself why. It was nice to have company. Eno had been gone for a week and a half now, and it was getting a bit lonely. Even worse was that she hadn't had any private time with Chief for over two months.

She sighed. Eric was right—he needed to go and catch the bus home. She brought out some food containers and proceeded to serve the soup and pounded yam into them. Just then, he came in with the rest of the plates from the table.

"Ah, don't worry about that, I'll pack them later."

"Please, ma, let me help you clear the table and wash the plates. You cooked the food, please let me help. It's the only thing I can do." He didn't wait for her to respond. He went back to clear the dining table, then came back to the kitchen to start washing the dishes. By that time, she had finished putting the food into the containers; she had added some more meat, soup, and pounded yam, just so that he had more to eat later.

He finished washing the dishes, and she waited until he had dried his hands before handing him a bag with the containers of food.

"Ah, thank you, ma," he smiled as he took the bag. He proceeded to the living room, and she followed. He walked quickly to the door. She watched as he slowly put on his shoes. Once done, he looked at her.

"Goodnight, ma. Thank you for the food, ma."

"Good night, safe journey o." She watched as he turned his back, stepped through the door, and left. She walked to the door and looked out, watching as he hurried away. He was walking like someone who was being chased. She almost chuckled.

She smiled to herself as she turned to go back inside, but then she thought she heard footsteps at the back of the house. She turned to look around, but there was no one there. It was dark at the back, with only a little light showing the shadow of the large tree behind the house. She stared hard again, thinking she saw a shadow or figure behind the tree, but once again, there was nothing there.

She quickly turned around, shut the door, and locked it. For some reason, she felt afraid, but why? This wasn't the first time she had stayed alone in her quarters. Besides, the compound had

113

always been safe. She shrugged her shoulders as she walked back to the kitchen. She glanced at the dining table and noticed how neat it was. He had cleared and cleaned it. She smiled. Yes, indeed, he would make a good husband for Eno.

She walked into the kitchen and saw the foodstuffs Eric had helped her bring in were on the floor. She sighed, not wanting to leave this undone. She began opening each bag, arranging the food items in the kitchen cupboard, and placing the meat in the freezer. Once done, she turned off the lights in the kitchen, walked into the living room, glanced around, and saw everything was in order. She switched off the living room lights and walked to her bedroom to prepare for her bath and get ready for bed.

Chapter 12

C hief was pacing up and down the corridor of the hospital. His new wife, Amaka, had been with the doctor for over 45 minutes now, and he was becoming anxious. Why was it taking so long? He went back to sit down, placing his hands between his knees. His fingers trembled, and he couldn't stop them from shaking.

It had been several months since his marriage to Amaka. He had kept her to himself these past few months, partly because she was young, and he didn't want her mingling with the other wives. He was concerned they might have a negative influence on her. But the main reason he had kept her so secluded was that he wanted her pregnant quickly. He had made up his mind; everything had to happen fast. He wasn't getting any younger at 59 years old.

He had planned everything carefully, assigning a maid to take care of her needs and keep her company, ensuring she ate properly and did no work. So far, everything has been going smoothly. Amaka had been feeling unwell for some time now, and Chief had decided to take her out of town to see the best doctors, to make sure everything was alright. After years with his other wives, he was convinced Amaka was pregnant, but he needed the doctor's confirmation.

Chief stood up again, preparing to pace once more. At that moment, the door to the room finally opened, and the doctor stepped out. Chief almost ran to him.

"Doctor, what is happening? Is everything fine?"

"Chief, relax. Everything is fine," the doctor said, trying to calm him down. "Please, let's go into my office."

The doctor led the way to his office, which was just a few steps away. Once inside, the doctor gestured for Chief to sit. Chief sat down quickly, still feeling anxious.

"Doctor, talk to me," he said, not waiting for the doctor to sit.

"Chief, your wife is fine. I told the nurses to give her some fruit and for her to rest for now."

"Okay..." he said, glancing at the doctor, his face reflecting a desire for more information.

"Chief, we've done some tests, and everything is fine. In fact, we have good news for you, sir. Your wife is two months pregnant. Congratulations!" The doctor smiled and extended his hand for a handshake.

"Thank you, doctor," Chief replied, shaking his hand. "That's good, very good," he added, still holding onto the doctor's hand. "Erm, doctor, please... is it a boy or a girl?"

"Ah, Chief, we don't have that information yet."

"Ah? What do you mean?" Chief asked, finally releasing the doctor's hand.

"Sir, we can't know that yet, but we'll be able to tell you once the baby is born. That's not a problem." The doctor spoke reassuringly.

"When the baby is born? No, no, no, I can't wait that long!" Chief shook his head. "Look, doctor..." he leaned forward, resting his hand on the desk and looking straight at the doctor. "You can tell me. You have that... erm... what do you call it? That system... yes, that thing you can use to check, abi?"

"Ah, no Chief, I'm sorry. We don't have that kind of technology here."

"What? You don't have that kind of technology here? What kind of hospital is this?" The doctor remained silent. "But my friend, who directed me here, told me you were one of the best hospitals around! Or is that not true?"

"Yes, sir, we are one of the top hospitals in this city."

"Okay, I see. So how come you don't have the equipment, or as you call it, the technology, to find out?" Chief asked, impatience creeping into his voice.

"Chief, we don't have it yet."

"You don't have it yet?" Chief clicked his tongue. "Why?" He didn't wait for a response. "Okay, so which hospital has that kind of technology?"

"Sir, to be honest, that kind of technology is expensive. It costs millions of naira, and we're still a growing hospital. We hope to acquire it soon."

"I see." Chief paused, his impatience rising again. "So, which hospital has it?"

"Ah, Chief, I really don't know. There are some other hospitals that are bigger than ours that might have it, but I'm not sure which ones, sir."

Chief looked at the doctor suspiciously. He leaned back in the chair, crossing his arms over his chest and shaking his head with visible disappointment. His friend had recommended this hospital, and he had travelled over three hours to get here, only to be told this. This was the most important thing right now. He needed to know. There would be no surprises this time. Is it a boy or not? Simple question, right?

"Chief, I hope everything is alright?" the doctor asked, noticing Chief's agitation.

Chief looked at him, trying to calm his frustration. As much as he was disappointed, he needed the doctor's help to find out which hospital had the technology he needed. He leaned forward, resting his hands on the desk.

"Erm... doctor, please, I need your help. I need to know which hospital has this information. Please, help me."

"Chief, I really don't know."

"Doctor, I know you know. You just don't want to tell me."

"Sir..." The doctor seemed hesitant, but Chief's tone was firm.

"Relax, doctor. Listen..." Chief moved even closer to the desk, his voice lowering. "If it's money you want, I have money. Let's talk."

The doctor shook his head, dismissing the offer.

"Doctor, doctor, I said relax. Is it not just the two of us here? What are you afraid of? I'm offering you money. Come on, talk to me."

The doctor fell silent, clearly thinking it over. Chief could see the doctor was wrestling with the decision.

"Okay, Chief, it's no problem. What are you offering?"

"Ah, now you're talking, doctor. Okay, for the information you'll give me, I'll offer you 10,000 naira."

"Ah, no Chief, that's too small. Please, add more."

"Relax, doctor. Is it not for the small information you want to give me?"

"Yes, Chief, I know, but if anyone finds out, I could lose my job. Please understand," the doctor said, his frown deepening.

"Isn't it just the two of us here? Will I go and report you?"

"Chief, this is dangerous for me. Please, consider it and add more. Let's make it 30,000 naira, sir."

"30,000 naira?" Chief exclaimed. "For just information?" He watched the doctor shrug, resigned to the situation.

"But, sir, it's a risky affair."

"Okay, let's make it 15,000 naira. I'll give you the money here and now."

The doctor hesitated, still unsure.

"Also, I'll make sure my wife gives birth here. This will be our hospital from now on, and I'll tell all my friends about this place."

The doctor thought it over for a moment, his expression softening. He took a deep breath and nodded.

"Okay, sir. Give me some time to make some enquiries. Please, wait here." The doctor stood up. "Do you want anything? Tea? Water?"

"Tea? You serve that here?" Chief was surprised.

"Of course, sir. We offer a lot of things." The doctor smiled, waiting for an answer.

"Okay, then let me have tea."

"Alright, I'll tell the nurse to bring it. Meanwhile, please relax here. I'll be back soon."

"No problem, doctor."

Chief watched him hurry off, then leaned back in the chair, letting out a deep breath. A smile slowly spread across his face. Good, no time to waste. He was going to get the information he needed. He definitely wasn't going to wait until the baby was born to find out. The sooner he knew, the better.

A few moments later, the nurse entered, holding a cup of tea.

"Your tea, sir," she gently placed it on the table. "Should I add sugar and milk, sir?" she asked, standing near the door, ready to leave.

"No, don't worry," Chief said dismissively as the nurse left the room.

Chief took another sip of his tea, enjoying the warmth, when the doctor walked in. He was holding a folded piece of paper in his hand.

"You have something for me, doctor?"

The doctor sat down, still clutching the paper.

"Yes, sir, but you need to give me what you promised first."

Chief took a deep breath, a little frustrated with how things were going. He reached for his small bag, quickly counting out 15,000 naira. He handed it over to the doctor, watching closely as the doctor counted the money again. When he was satisfied, the doctor handed over the folded paper.

Chief quickly opened it. On it was the address of a hospital and the name of a doctor.

"So, this is the doctor I need to speak to?" Chief asked.

"Yes, he's my friend. He will take care of you, don't worry."

"Okay," Chief said, standing up.

"Ah, Chief, you're leaving already? You didn't finish your tea."

"No time to waste, doctor. I have to go. Thank you." He shook the doctor's hand.

"But your wife needs to rest, sir."

"Doctor, she can rest at home," Chief replied, the sense of urgency in his tone clear. With the information in hand, he walked out of the office.

As he headed toward his wife's room, he glanced at the address on the piece of paper. It was going to be another five-hour drive to the hospital. But it had to be done, and it had to be done quickly.

He opened the door to her room and saw Amaka sitting up on the bed, eating some fruit. Her face immediately stiffened when she saw him, and she avoided his gaze. He walked toward her and sat down on the side of the bed.

"My dear, how are you feeling?" His voice was soft, laced with concern.

"Fine," she responded coldly.

Chief paused, sensing the tension between them. She'd been in a bad mood all morning.

"Did the doctor tell you?" he asked gently.

"Yes," she replied, her tone colder than before.

He lifted his hand to touch her face, but she flinched slightly, moving away from his touch. Just then, a noise broke the silence. He turned around and saw their maid standing at the door, holding a bottle of water.

"Is that for your madam?" he asked as he stood up.

"Yes, sir," the maid answered, stepping into the room.

"Okay, give it to her, and help her dress. We're leaving the hospital now."

He walked out of the room, and not long after, they were standing by the front doors of the hospital. Chief saw Eric sitting on a bench outside, waiting. He called out to him, asking him to bring the car around.

As they waited, Chief glanced at Amaka. She was staring into space, her face set in a deep frown, arms folded tightly over her chest. She hadn't said much lately. In the few months they'd been married, she had grown quieter and quieter. Chief didn't mind too much, as long as she stuck to the arrangement. She would give him male children, and he would support her family; an arrangement that worked fine in his mind.

The car pulled up, and the maid helped Amaka into the back seat. The maid took a seat in the front.

Chief called out to Eric.

"Yes, sir?"

"Do you know the way to Lagos?"

"Lagos, sir?" Eric's brow furrowed slightly.

"Yes, Lagos. Do you know the way from here?"

"Yes, sir. I haven't been there in a while, but I remember the way."

"Good. We're going to Lagos. I'll tell you the area when we get closer." Chief opened the car door.

"Emm... sir," Eric said hesitantly.

"Lagos is five hours away, sir. We won't get there until very late at night or even early morning, sir. It's risky to travel there at night, sir."

Chief pondered what he had said. Indeed, it was a long drive, and they would have to eat and use the toilet, which meant they would get there very late at night. He put his hand on his chin, deep in thought. How was he going to do this? He wanted all of this to be done in secret. He sighed.

"Okay, you are right. Take us back to the house. But here is what we will do—you will get ready for Lagos tomorrow. Come early so we can leave early and get there early."

"Okay, sir."

"Make sure you don't tell anyone about this trip or even mention this journey. Do you hear me?"

"Yes, sir."

He got in the car, once again disappointed. It seemed the plan would not be possible today. As much as he desperately wanted to get to Lagos as soon as possible, he had to make sure it was safe. He sighed as they drove off on their journey back to the house. He could hear his fingers tapping the handle of the door by his side. He was deep in thought.

"Chief."

He turned to look at his wife, who had not said much during the journey.

"Please, I would like to go and see my mother."

"No problem. You will go. Eric will take you when you want to go."

"I would like to go tomorrow."

"Tomorrow!?" he exclaimed with a frown.

"Yes, Chief."

Chief was shaking his head now as he turned away, briefly looking out the window.

"Ermm, my dear, you will have to go another day."

"Chief, please. I have not seen my family for months now. At least let me go see my mother, especially now that I am pregnant."

"Listen, my dear," he said, turning to face her now. "We have to keep this a secret for now. You cannot tell anyone you are pregnant."

"But why, Chief?"

"It is too early to tell anyone."

"But I am going to be showing very soon. People will be able to tell."

"Well, I will think of something we can do."

Amaka sighed. "Please let me go and see my mother. Please," her voice almost tearful.

Chief shook his head. "My dear, tomorrow is not good."

"Please, Chief, please..." she begged, now starting to tear up.

"No, my dear. I said tomorrow is not good. You will go another time."

She started to sob gently. She turned her face away as she sobbed, head down. Chief looked out the window, trying not to notice her. The sobs became louder and louder, and it was starting to become too much for him to bear. He looked over at her, took a deep breath, and reached over to gently move her toward him, placing her head on his chest.

"Don't cry, okay? Don't cry. You see, the reason I said not tomorrow is because I want us to go to Lagos tomorrow."

"Lagos? What are we going to do in Lagos?"

"We are going to a special hospital to do a proper check-up to make sure you and the.... our baby are fine, okay? Immediately we come back from Lagos, I will tell Eric to take you to spend a few days with them okay."

She nodded and started to smile now. "Now dry your eyes, okay? You know crying is not good for the baby."

She wiped the tears from her face.

"Eric, we'll stop to get something to eat—the usual place."

"Okay, sir."

Chief figured they might as well eat something. After stopping to eat, they continued the journey. Amaka's mood had softened, and she was beginning to talk to him again. He wondered if not seeing her parents was the reason for her coldness toward him. Anyway, he had assured her that she would visit them after their trip to Lagos.

They eventually arrived at the compound early in the evening. The gate was wide open, but Musa was nowhere in sight. They drove straight in. As the car stopped, Chief noticed a man sitting outside his quarters. Omerie was with him. When Chief looked closely, he recognised his good friend, Alfred.

As Chief stepped out of the car, his friend stood.

"Alfred, you're here?"

"Yes ooh! I came to see you."

"Welcome."

Chief turned to the maid who had travelled with them. "Take madam to the room now."

He saw Omerie approaching but stopped suddenly. He turned to watch the maid lead Amaka inside. Then he turned to Eric.

"Eric."

"Yes, sir."

"Park the car and go home. Remember what I said about tomorrow."

"Yes, sir."

Chief called to his friend, "Alfred! Long time no see." They shook hands. "Welcome. How's the family?" he asked, gesturing for him to sit.

"The family is well. We thank God."

He waved Omerie away, as she was standing nearby.

"Welcome, Chief."

"Thank you." He looked at her again, his eyes questioning why she was still there.

"I was keeping Alfred company before you arrived," she said quickly.

"Yes ooh! Your wife has been taking good care of me. I've been here for over an hour," Alfred added.

"I see. Okay, Alfred, let's go inside."

"There's no electricity, Chief," Omerie interrupted.

"Ah ah, this NEPA! They're just punishing us in this town. There's never any light," Alfred said, echoing Chief's thoughts.

Chief sighed. "My brother, what can we do? Well, let's stay outside then. Please, let's prepare something for you to eat."

"I've already eaten. I told you—your wife has been taking care of me," Alfred laughed.

"Ah, you've been well taken care of!" Chief said, now sitting down.

"Chief, should I ask them to prepare something for you to eat?" Omerie asked.

"No, no. I've already eaten," he replied. "Alfred, we must get you a proper drink."

"Ah, isn't this proper enough?" Alfred asked, pointing to his half-finished bottle of Star beer.

"That's not proper for you. I know you like brandy," Chief teased playfully. "Akpevwe!" Chief called out to the maid.

"Chief, don't worry. Let me go and get it."

"No, no, don't worry. You go and rest now. I'll talk with Alfred." He waved her away.

"O... okay," she replied hesitantly. Chief turned to look at her.

"Ehen... our wife, thank you ooh!" Alfred said.

Chief watched as Omerie walked back toward her quarters.

"Chief, Chief!"

"Alfred, stop calling me 'Chief.' You're like my brother."

Alfred laughed. "We must give respect to whom respect is due. It's your title."

"You're my brother. Stop calling me Chief!" he insisted. "Anyway, my brother, it's been a long-time ooh!"

"It's you! When was the last time you came to my house?"

"My dear brother, I'm sorry. I've just been busy."

"Of course! Busy enjoying your new young wife," Alfred teased, laughing and winking.

"Ah ah! Am I not supposed to enjoy my new wife? Am I supposed to suffer?"

"No, of course not. God forbid!"

"Exactly."

The maid returned, placing the brandy and two glasses on the table.

"This is what you like," Chief said, referring to the brandy as he poured a glass and handed it to Alfred. "Taste this."

Alfred tasted it and smacked his lips, nodding in approval.

"Chief, this is good brandy." They both laughed.

"I know your type of drink, Alfred. What is Star beer?" Chief laughed again, pouring more brandy for both of them.

They sat back, sipping the brandy, each acknowledging its great taste with satisfied sounds.

"Speaking of your new wife… how is she? Is everything okay with the other wives?"

"Well, she's okay. Everything is okay."

"That's good. There is peace. Ah, you know I was worried your last wife would make trouble. I'm surprised she hasn't."

"Who? You mean Rume?"

"Yes, of course."

"I have barred her from my quarters."

"You mean it?"

"Yes." He took a sip of brandy and leaned forward, lowering his voice. "In fact, I told them all that I will not be eating any food or seeing any of them for two months. It's now three months."

"So, you took my advice?"

"Yes naah."

"Good!"

Chief leaned even closer, whispering. "And it worked."

"You mean…?"

"Yes."

"You have confirmed it?"

"Yes, of course. Where do you think I'm coming from?" It was a rhetorical question.

"That is good news. Congratulations!"

"Shh…." Chief said, placing two fingers on his lips as he looked around to make sure no one was nearby. "Lower your voice. No one knows."

"Sorry," Alfred said, also looking around. He shook Chief's hand and whispered congratulations again. They both raised their glasses of brandy, smiling widely as they sipped.

"This is good news. Did you go to that hospital I told you about?"

"Ermm… yes, I was actually going to come and see you, so thank God you are here."

"Okay."

"I went to the hospital you mentioned, but they couldn't give me the information."

"Ah, but why?"

"Well, the doctor I spoke to said they don't have the equipment or something."

"They don't have the equipment. What equipment is that? In that big hospital?"

"Well, that's what he said."

"But I thought they would have it."

"You thought? But you told me they have it, like you knew they had it."

"Well, it's a big hospital, and when I went there, they had some big, big equipment."

"Big equipment?" Chief chuckled.

"Yes, things I have not seen before," Alfred said, laughing.

"So, because of that, you just thought they have 'the equipment' to do the..."

"Yes naah!"

Chief paused, looking at him strangely.

"Would you not have thought the same thing?"

Chief shook his head. "It is a very expensive hospital, very expensive."

"It's all those big equipment plus the power they need to operate them. That's why it is expensive."

Chief looked at his friend again, wondering if he was 'alright.' He sat back, enjoying his drink. He shook his head again. There was silence for some time.

"I know some people in that town who can get us the correct information."

"No, don't worry. Leave it."

"Leave it? But why?"

Chief kept shaking his head from side to side as he relaxed back in his chair. "I got some information from the doctor about a hospital that can provide the information I need."

"Ehn, that's good, very good," he said in a lowered tone, taking a quick sip of his drink. "Emmanuel, you must go there quickly. Don't waste time."

Chief nodded in agreement, but he thought to himself that he had to keep the next part of his plan a secret. Alfred had been a loyal friend, and in fact, he was following Alfred's own advice—'tell no one about your plans.'

"Emmanuel," Alfred leaned forward now, "what if... what if..."

"Do not say it," Chief warned, looking firmly at him.

"Sorry, you are right. Let us be positive," Alfred said as he relaxed back into the chair. It seemed like a very long silence before they started to talk about other things. They sat outside even after the power came back on. They drank brandy, shared stories, and laughed until almost late at night.

Alfred bid Chief goodbye, staggering as he walked to the gate. He was drunk. Chief stood and watched as he spoke briefly to Musa before going through the open gate. Chief smiled to himself now. Alfred was a good friend. He sighed, now feeling a bit dizzy. He called the maid to clear the table outside and take the chairs inside the house. As he proceeded indoors, he decided he was going to sit for a while and have some more brandy.

He told the maid to bring back the brandy and a glass. Suffice it to say, he was exhausted. It had been a long day, and tomorrow was going to be even more tiring. He sat down as the maid brought back the drink.

He poured just a little brandy into the glass. *Lagos!* he thought, sighing, already dreading how busy tomorrow was going to be. He took a tiny sip, leaned back in the chair, and rested his head against its side. Covering his eyes with one hand, he let out another sigh.

It felt like only five minutes later when he heard a knock on the door and someone calling his name. He lifted his hand from his eyes and looked toward the door. It was Omerie, standing there and looking at him. Her hand was lightly holding the door.

"Chief, I hope I am not disturbing you?"

"Omerie? I thought you were at your place," he asked, frowning.

"Yes, I was at my place, but I heard Alfred leaving, so I rushed here quickly."

He was confused. *Why was she here? What did she want?*

"Chief, I need to talk to you," she said immediately.

He huffed and leaned back in the chair again. "Please, it has to wait," he said, without even waiting for her response. "I am tired. I want to rest. We can talk tomorrow."

"Emmanuel, please, this cannot wait. I have to talk to you now."

He turned to look at her. She had called him by his first name. She only did that when it was very serious. But he was tired.

"Omerie, it has to wait until tomorrow." He got up now, turning away from her and walking toward his room.

"No, Emmanuel, no... it cannot wait!"

He stopped and turned around quickly to look at her. He hadn't heard her use that tone of voice in years, angry and firm. He stared at her for a bit. Her face was slightly turned away, but he could see the tears rolling down her cheeks. He took a deep breath and walked back to the chair, sitting down again. Refusing to look directly at her, he watched her every move from the corner of his eye.

"Okay, what is it?" he asked, a bit irritated.

He watched as she wiped her tears, took a deep breath, closed the front door, and then sat down in the chair opposite him. She looked around briefly, as if making sure no one else was in the room.

"Emmanuel... I... I... I am pregnant," she blurted out.

"What?" he exclaimed loudly.

"I said... I am pregnant."

He looked at her and then shook his head. He must be drunk. He thought he had heard her say she was pregnant. He paused for a second and then started to laugh. His laughter grew louder and louder.

"I must be drunk," he said, turning to look at her now. "I think I am hearing things."

But she wasn't laughing. Her face showed surprise at his behaviour, which made him stop laughing. Now, he was confused. He watched as she shrugged her shoulders, folded her arms, and looked down at the floor.

"Well, Emmanuel, I'm glad you're happy. I am still in shock. First, I was shocked, then confused, but the doctor confirmed it."

She reached into the side of her wrapper and brought out something. "Here is the result, Emmanuel."

He saw the envelope in her hand. She stepped closer, grabbed his right hand, placed the envelope in it, and then walked back to sit down. He stared at it for a few seconds before slowly opening it. He pulled out a piece of paper and saw that it was from a hospital, a doctor's report. As he read, his eyes widened. The results stated that she was pregnant; three months, in fact.

He looked back at her, his mouth slightly open.

No way, he thought.

He tried to speak but no words came out. He stood up and started pacing slowly. "It cannot be," he thought to himself. "How can it be?"

He read the report again and must have paced in one spot before hearing her call his name.

"Chief... Chief."

She was on her feet too, stepping closer. He looked up at her, his mouth still slightly open. The words were still not coming. His mind was racing.

No, it can't be possible. She is 55 years old. Surely, 55-year-old women do not... cannot get pregnant, he thought.

"Chief, what is it? Why are you looking at me like that?"

He turned away and quickly walked back to sit down. Grabbing his glass, he took a gulp. She had walked back to sit opposite him again.

"Chief, say something."

He could hear the desperation in her voice. He took a deep breath.

"Omerie, are you sure? How can this be? How is this possible?" he managed to say.

"Chief, the truth is, I do not know," she paused briefly. "I have been feeling very sick these last few weeks, but I thought it was malaria. I bought malaria tablets from the chemist and was taking them, but I was still feeling sick. So, I went to the doctor to check what was wrong and to ask him to give me proper malaria tablets. The doctor asked me to explain how I was feeling and for how long. Then he said he needed to carry out some tests.

"They did all the tests and asked me to come back in three days for the results. The doctor gave me something to stop the vomiting, and I left. When I went back, he told me it wasn't malaria, that I was pregnant."

She paused to catch her breath. She had been talking nonstop.

"Calm down, Omerie, calm down."

He watched her take a deep breath and try to settle down.

"The document said you are three months pregnant?!" He was asking a question rather than stating it, and it seemed she knew what he meant.

"Chief, have you forgotten the day of your traditional marriage to...?"

"Oh, of course," was all he could say. "Is the doctor sure?"

"Yes Chief, you know we have known him for years. He would not lie to me. I asked the same questions you have, and he answered and confirmed that I am pregnant. Emmanuel, don't you believe me?"

"I believe you, Omerie, but you have to understand this is something that does not happen. So, I am really shocked and confused."

She nodded her head in agreement. "But have you forgotten that God can do anything?" He did not respond. "Emmanuel, God has done it. I am going to have a child. We are going to have a child, after all these years." This time she had a huge smile on her face, her arms wrapped over her belly.

He looked at her now. He could see the tears, but they were happy tears. He was still in shock. He looked down at her stomach. *She is pregnant? Omerie is pregnant?*

Chapter 13

Onome could hear the choir singing as she approached the church. She was slightly late. The service had started at 6 o'clock, and it was now 6:15. She had hoped to arrive earlier, but she had taken the longest route to get to the church this evening. She was hoping, even praying, that she would see Michael. It had been a few months since she last saw him, which was quite unusual. He hadn't even been to the house to see Beatrice in the compound.

She knew he sometimes stayed in the city, where his father had some businesses, but he had never been away for this long before. Ever since their last meeting, she had been thinking about him every single day. She was slightly worried and hoped everything was fine.

Maybe they've broken up, she thought. That would surely explain why he hadn't been to the compound. *Could he have broken up with her because he now realises he doesn't love her? What if that's the reason?—What if he now knows that he loves me?*

She smiled at the thought but quickly frowned. *Then why hasn't he asked to see me again?* Her mind went back to their last meeting at the guava tree. Oh, if only Pastor Maxwell hadn't seen them that day. She sighed deeply.

The singing grew louder as she neared the side entrance of the church. She had been told this was where the group would be meeting. It was a smaller building, but the room was large enough to seat hundreds of people.

Fortunately, the door was slightly open. She slowly pushed it wider and stepped inside. It was loud, filled with music and the voices of the choir. She entered quietly, though no one could hear or see her come in. It was a full house. She could see most of her agemates and some familiar faces from town, all singing and dancing joyfully.

She slid onto one of the benches at the back and joined the singing right away. Her eyes wandered toward the choir. She spotted Prisca, beaming with a big smile as she belted out each line of the song. Prisca clearly loved this. She talked about singing all the time.

Even though Onome liked singing too, she was too shy. She felt she lacked the confidence to stand in front of people and sing. But she loved the choir, their uniform especially. She often wondered how she would look in the white blouse and blue skirt the girls wore. Still, she didn't see it happening.

A sudden clearing of the throat into the microphone interrupted her thoughts. From the very back, she couldn't see everything happening at the front. But she recognised the voice on the mic, it was Pastor Maxwell.

The choir brought the song to an end as Pastor Maxwell cleared his throat again, testing the mic. Onome moved a few seats forward. She didn't know why, but she wanted to see clearly.

He stood at the front, dressed in formal clothes, as he always did on Sundays. He looked serious as he slowly paced back and forth. The instruments were still playing softly as he began to repeat the lyrics of the song.

"Do you believe it?" he asked the congregation. "Do you believe that Jesus is King of Kings and Lord of Lords?"

A few people shouted, "Yes, amen!" followed by clapping and cheers.

He instructed everyone to close their eyes, to block out distractions, forget the challenges of the day, and remember why they had come this evening.

Onome closed her eyes but immediately found herself asking why she was there. Her thoughts drifted back to Michael. Deep down, she had hoped he would be here. Prisca had mentioned seeing him at a few evening prayer meetings, but Onome had looked around. There was no sign of him.

She sighed and tried to focus. Pastor Maxwell's voice rang out again, loud and clear through the microphone.

"Do not get distracted. You are here now. Focus on the words of this song and open your mouth, talk to God..."

She decided to do as they had been told. She listened carefully as Pastor Maxwell recited the words of the song. Closing her eyes, she let the lyrics wash over her as he repeated them over and over:

"Your Name is greater than the mountain that I see,
Your Name is stronger and can still the stormy sea,
Your Name is powerful, all the earth bow down before You,
Your Name is Jesus, Your Name is Jesus."

('Your Name Is Jesus', Written by Julie Deborah)

After singing the song a few more times, Pastor Maxwell beckoned the choir to stop and asked everyone to take their seats. The instruments went silent, and the choir slowly walked back to their seats.

Onome decided to look around the church again. Now that everyone was seated, it was much easier to see people. As her eyes scanned the room, they landed on the far side to her left, and there they were.

Sister Beatrice. Sitting with Michael.

Her heart jumped. At first, she felt relief. He was alive. Nothing bad had happened to him as she had feared. But the relief quickly faded, replaced by a deep, sharp pain. He was sitting with Beatrice.

She was a few seats behind them, on another row, so they hadn't noticed her. She could see them clearly, and that was all she did throughout the service, watch them.

She watched how they laughed when Pastor Maxwell made some jokes, how Michael smiled at her now and then, and how Beatrice placed her hand over his, smiling as they listened to the sermon.

The pain she felt pierced through her heart like a knife. All these months, she had been worried, missing him, thinking about their last meeting; the way he had looked at her, smiled at her and played with her cheeks.

Now, seeing him happy, sitting with Beatrice, looking into her eyes, and sharing laughs, made Onome question everything. *Was it all a lie?* she wondered. *Surely, he cannot like her too?*

She couldn't stop staring at him. Then, as if he could feel her gaze, he suddenly turned to look around. Onome quickly looked away, pretending to focus on her unopened Bible.

When she raised her head again, he was looking back at Pastor Maxwell. She let out a deep breath, wondering if he had seen her.

She tried to concentrate on the sermon, but her mind kept drifting. Pastor Maxwell spoke for what felt like an hour and a half before wrapping up the service.

The choir sang one more song, and when they finished, he encouraged everyone to stay back for a little while to greet each other.

Onome turned to glance at Michael and Beatrice again. They were still talking to the people around them.

Suddenly, she felt a tap on her shoulder. Turning around, she saw a tall boy, no, a man standing just behind her.

"Hello," he said with a smile.

"Hello," she greeted back.

"I am Boniface, what is your name?"

"My name is Onome."

"Ono...me," he tried to pronounce her name, smiling. "Did I get it right?" he asked, his smile widening as he spoke.

She nodded slightly, offering a small smile in return. She didn't know what else to say. Talking to men had never been her strong suit.

Nervously, she glanced toward the choir, hoping to spot Prisca and beckon her over to rescue her from this awkward exchange, but Prisca was nowhere to be found.

"Is this your first time here?" he asked, seemingly unaware of her discomfort.

"Yes, it is," she replied quickly.

"Ah, okay. Me too."

An uncomfortable silence followed. He kept looking at her, still smiling. She rubbed her palms together, then blurted out, "Ermm... I have to go find my friend now."

"Ah, okay."

"Bye," she said quickly and turned to leave.

"Excuse me, Ono...me."

She stopped and turned back, trying to hide her frustration.

"Will you be here next week?"

"Ermm... I'm not sure."

"Okay, well... maybe I'll see you."

"Okay, see you." She turned away again, this time walking off as quickly as she could without looking back.

Weaving through the crowd, she scanned the room for Prisca. Spotting a group of choir members, she approached them and asked about her friend's whereabouts. They pointed toward the side of the platform.

Following their directions, she saw Prisca chatting with some other girls and Pastor Maxwell. She hesitated. She wasn't sure if she wanted to see Pastor Maxwell, at least not yet.

As she stood there debating, she heard a laugh she would recognise anywhere, Michael's.

Her heart skipped. She didn't need to turn to confirm it was him, but she did anyway.

When she looked, he was staring right at her.

He was standing with a small group, but Beatrice wasn't there. He smiled and waved.

She smiled faintly but didn't wave back. Turning away, she hurried toward Prisca, tapping her on the shoulder. Prisca turned, eyes lighting up with excitement.

"You're here!" Prisca squealed, pulling her into a hug.

Her loud excitement drew the attention of the group, and suddenly, all eyes were on Onome.

"I waited for you outside. I didn't think you were coming anymore," Prisca said.

"I was late," Onome replied quietly, now feeling self-conscious under the group's stares.

The others turned back to their conversation, but Pastor Maxwell had already noticed her.

"It's good you could make it, Onome," Pastor Maxwell said, smiling warmly. "How did you find the service?"

"Erm... good, sir," she mumbled, feeling guilty since she hadn't paid attention to any of it.

"Good? Okay." He nodded, still smiling.

"I think it was very powerful, sir," one of the girls chimed in loudly.

Pastor Maxwell turned his attention to her, and the conversation resumed with the group.

Seizing the moment, Onome pulled Prisca aside, eager to talk to her alone.

"Where are we going?" Prisca asked as Onome led her away.

"We can talk here," Onome said, stopping when she felt they were far enough from the group.

Prisca frowned. "Why are you acting like this?"

"I don't want anyone to hear what we're discussing, please," Onome whispered, her voice urgent.

"Okay, let's talk quickly and then go back to join the group," Prisca said, turning quickly to glance at the group.

"Has he said anything?" Onome asked, lifting her chin to show she was referring to Pastor Maxwell.

"Ermm... no, not yet. But..." her voice filled with excitement again. "He came to see my parents two days ago."

"Really?"

"Yes!" she said, a huge smile spreading across her face. "He came to ask them if they would allow me to take on more responsibility in the church, to help with the children's play this Christmas." She reached out to hold Onome's hand in excitement.

"Ah, that's an improvement ooh!"

"You're telling me! I'm so happy. He is also leading, so he'll always be there with me." She raised her hand for a high-five, and they both laughed as they slapped palms.

"It's just all these other girls, they won't leave him alone," Prisca hissed, turning to look at the group again. Onome also turned to look. There was now a long queue that hadn't been there before, with everyone seemingly wanting 'prayer.' Some were holding paper bags, and she guessed they were filled with cooked food for the Pastor. She looked at Pastor Maxwell, his eyes were closed as he prayed for the person in front of him. What could Prisca and these other girls see that she couldn't? Prisca had been interested in Pastor Maxwell since he joined the church and came to town. She joined the Youth choir and the Children's Ministry department just to be close to him, hoping one day he'd notice her. From this conversation, it seemed she might just be getting what she wanted.

She turned back to her friend. "Don't worry, Prisca, you're a beautiful girl, I'm sure you've stolen his heart," she smiled and winked. They both laughed.

"I hope so ooh," Prisca said, turning away again.

"Well, yours is good, but for me, it's really not happening."

"What do you mean?" Prisca asked, shifting her attention back to Onome.

"See..." she turned to glance toward one side of the room. "Brother Michael is here."

"Ah, but I told you he comes here naah."

"But I haven't seen him for almost two months now. I thought he was out of town."

"Out of town? Nooo... he's been coming here."

"Are you serious?" Onome exclaimed.

"Yes naah."

Onome hesitated for a moment, then decided to ask anyway.

"Does he always come with... emm... you know?" she hesitated, looking toward them. "You know naah... Beatrice," she whispered her name.

"Emm... well, I don't know. To be honest, I'm not sure, plus I don't check."

"Thank you!" Onome said, rolling her eyes.

"Why are you thanking me?" Prisca chuckled.

"I'm just thanking you... you're my friend... thank you for making sure you informed me."

Prisca laughed out loud. "Onome, you're not serious. I'm in the choir; I can't be checking on people here. I have to concentrate on my ministry abeg ooh."

"Oh, yes, ministry. I can see you concentrating on your ministry," Onome teased, and they both started laughing, knowing exactly what she meant.

"What's so funny?" a voice asked.

Onome turned around to see Michael standing just two feet away, a small smile on his face. The laughter stopped immediately, and Onome suddenly felt shy. She turned to Prisca, silently asking for help. Prisca got the message.

"We were just laughing about something that happened yesterday," Prisca said with a grin.

"Really? What happened?" he asked, clearly intrigued.

Onome's eyes widened as she stared at Prisca. What was she going to say now?

"Ah, you won't find it funny. It is actually quite embarrassing," Prisca said, shaking her head.

Ah, very good, Onome thought, smiling at Prisca. Michael just nodded, then turned his attention to Onome.

"Onome, long time, no see. How are you?" His voice was soft and caring.

"I'm fine," she said, refusing to look at him. Just then, Prisca's name was called, and she excused herself, leaving Onome alone with Michael. He moved closer now.

"Onome, you look well. How are you?" he asked again.

"I'm fine," she replied, her mind set. *I'm not going to talk much. I just want him to know I'm annoyed*, she thought.

"I've really missed you," he said, smiling. She didn't respond, but she could tell from the corner of her eye that he was staring at her intensely.

"Haven't you missed me?" he asked.

She didn't answer, keeping her head down, eyes on the floor.

"So; you haven't missed me?" he asked again, his voice carrying a slight note of disappointment. She raised her head to look at him. He was smiling, his expression soft. Surely, he must love her, she thought.

"I have missed you too. I thought something had happened to you," she couldn't believe she said those words.

"Aww... you were worried about me?" he smiled. She lowered her face again, blushing.

"Sorry, I made you worry. You see, I've been so busy I didn't even have time to come and see Bea... you," he said, catching himself.

She knew exactly what he meant—Beatrice. Suddenly, her shyness faded as she spoke up.

"No need to apologise. You were busy. Well, at least you're okay now, and that's what matters. Now you and Sister Beatrice can see each other," she managed a tight smile.

"And I can see you too, Onome. Truly, I know you don't believe me," his voice softened again, low and sincere. "I really missed you ooh. I've been hoping to see you after that day we met, but things just got so busy for me. Even look at me..." he said, pointing to his body. "I've lost weight."

She glanced at him as he pointed to himself, feeling shy again.

"See!" he smiled, still pointing at his body. She smiled but quickly looked away.

"Michael," came a firm tone. They both knew who it was. Beatrice was walking toward them, a frown on her face. She came to an abrupt stop just by his side.

"Please, let's go. I have something to do early tomorrow morning," she said, not acknowledging Onome.

"Okay, I saw that you're still talking to your friends, so I came over to talk to Onome," he said, pointing to her. Beatrice quickly glanced at Onome.

"Good evening, sister," Onome greeted.

Beatrice just nodded at her, then pulled Michael's arm, her expression softening as she leaned towards him, batting her eyes. "Baby, please let's go now."

Onome turned away, looking toward Prisca, who was standing not too far from them. She heard Michael say, "Okay." As he turned away from her, he said, "Onome, take care of yourself, okay? I'll see you soon."

She didn't respond. He waved at her as he took Beatrice's hand. Onome watched them walk away, holding hands, with Beatrice laughing at something Michael had said. She continued to watch as they exited the room together.

She turned her gaze back to Prisca, who was now helping with cleaning and clearing. The room was starting to empty, with most of the youths leaving for home. Onome walked over to Prisca and some of the other choir members.

"Can I help? Is there anything I can do?" she asked wanting to get her mind off what just happened.

"Ermm....well you could check the sitting area to see if people left anything behind and also pick up every paper and clean any dirt there."

"Okay," she went through the sitting area, doing just that. It was actually an easy task, as there wasn't much dirt. As she moved through the seats and got to the front of the room, she could hear Pastor Maxwell's voice. He was now at the main entrance, saying farewell to some of the young boys. She was right behind him now, praying and hoping he wouldn't notice her. She bent down, pretending to search for dirt that wasn't there. There was a table filled with books, and she quickly rushed to it, pretending to look at the books. From the corner of her eye, she saw him turn around and spot her. He stopped for a second, looking at her, and she saw his lips curl into a smile. She refused to look up, pretending to stay focused on cleaning one particular spot.

"Onome, you can take one book from the table, it's free," he said. She glanced at him.

"Sir, any book here?"

"Yes, any book, just one. It's free. Make sure you choose wisely," he said, smiling before turning away and walking out of the main room. She guessed he must've gone into his office. She breathed a sigh of relief. For some strange reason, she didn't want to speak to him. Something about him made her heart race uncontrollably. He left her speechless, for reasons she couldn't explain. She was grateful he went to his office; it made sense for her to leave as soon as possible before he came back out.

She turned back to the table of books. There were so many to choose from. She saw the "Take one book for free and be blessed" sign on the table. She took a deep breath. How does one choose? He'd said to choose wisely. The pressure was on. Maybe not today, she thought, and turned away from the table. Just then, she saw Prisca walking toward her. "Oh, good," she thought to herself, "she must be ready to go now."

"Have you finished?" Prisca asked.

"Yes, I've checked all the seats. Are you ready to go now?"

"Ermm... not yet. Have you seen Pastor Maxwell at all? Did he go outside?"

"No, he went through those doors to the back."

"Ah, to his office. Okay, please wait for me here while I go and say goodbye," she said, her voice playful, a smile on her face. Onome shook her head from side to side.

"Imagine," Onome whispered.

"Just wait, I'll be back," Prisca said, walking away quickly. Onome turned around, looking around the room. There were just two girls and a boy from the choir still talking in a corner. She glanced at the clock on the wall, it was almost 8:30 pm. She was sure her mother would still be at the wives' meeting, which was held every Wednesday evening. However, she wanted to be home before it finished. She turned back to the table of books. One book caught her eye this time. She turned it around to read the summary, she read the first line: *"A story of a woman who found Jesus Christ and was miraculously healed from her sickness."* Hmm, this one looks interesting, she thought. *I'll take this one.* She quickly placed it in her bag and then decided to sit and wait for Prisca. She hadn't been sitting long before Prisca came out, shaking her head. Onome stood up quickly, concern on her face.

"What is it?" she asked as Prisca walked toward her.

"Nothing. He was with a boy in the office. It seems they were discussing something private, so I couldn't say goodbye."

"Ah, okay. I was wondering what happened."

Prisca led the way as she walked out of the room. Onome was about to ask where her little bag was but noticed it hanging in front of her. They hadn't stepped out for more than a minute when Prisca started again.

"You see the thing about Pastor Maxwell," she said angrily, swinging her handbag from side to side. "You hardly get him alone. He's always doing one thing after another, either with one person or a group of people," she hissed and continued, "I heard that sometimes he stays in his office till late at night, attending to people. Even these small girls, trying to book appointments to see him," she shook her head. "That's how these girls keep bringing things to him every time."

"Well, I guess that's what pastors are supposed to do," Onome shrugged.

"Well, yes. But I hear he doesn't see them behind closed doors, and a boy always needs to be present outside the room. Well, me, I can't wait to be his wife so he can only eat my food," she smiled. "Can you see how lean he is?"

"I haven't noticed..." Onome tried to reply, but Prisca interrupted.

"You know, they say a good wife takes care of her husband, and the sign of it is how his body looks."

"That is true," she muttered, considering what she had said. "But Prisca, you know pastors fast and pray a lot, so he's probably going to be lean forever shaa."

"Ah, no oh! God forbid, not after I take care of him. My mother told me about this green leaf for cooking Egusi food. If you eat a lot, you'll put on weight fast."

"It looks like you've been doing your homework ooh."

"Of course, naah, I have to prepare. No time to waste!" They both laughed.

"Ehen, Pastor's wife!"

"Ah, of course."

"So, you'll be ready for fasting and praying all the time?"

"Am I not doing it now? It's not a problem at all. I fast every week and go to all the prayer meetings."

"Are you serious?"

"Be there and watch. I've been adopting the 5 P rule."

"Which one is the 5 P rule again?"

"That's what Pastor Maxwell was teaching last week. I have the notes, but I can tell you briefly. You see, Pastor Maxwell explained it like this..."

It was obvious they were only going to talk about Pastor Maxwell until they both said goodbye and headed off to their individual homes. Prisca was still going on, but Onome was far from listening. Today had been a disappointment, to say the least. She wanted to see Michael, and she did, but unfortunately, not in the way she had hoped. Still, she had to admit, she was happy to see him again. She remembered her heart skipping a beat when she saw him staring at her. She remembered his smile, the light on his face. Those were the things that made her love him. Love... wow, she thought, love. Does she love him? Surely, yes. She loved him the very first day she saw him. It was love at first sight. He's all she thinks about, even now more than ever. But she paused in her thoughts. What about Beatrice? Surely Beatrice is his girlfriend. Everyone knows this. Then again, she always talks about him and how he promised to marry her soon. But is there any truth to that? Will Michael marry Sister Beatrice? The thought of it made her face drop slightly. It would break her heart.

"Are you listening to me?" Prisca's voice interrupted her thoughts.

"Sorry, I'm listening."

"Are you sure? This one your face looks sad," pushing her away slightly. "Okay, what did I just say?"

"Erm... you said..." she struggled as Prisca stared at her intently.

"Erm... yes, that's what I said," she chuckled.

"Sorry, Prisca."

"Uh-huh... I hear you, Mrs. Michael," she replied, pushing her slightly with a soft laugh. "We are both in love," she laughed again, this time loudly. Onome managed to laugh slightly. They were quiet now as they continued to walk. They were reaching the side of the road where they both had to say goodnight to each other. Onome was deep in thought again. Marriage... is she ready for it right now, though? She didn't realise she had said it aloud.

"Of course. Well, if you're not, I am ready. If Pastor Maxwell comes right now, I'm ready."

"Ah, Prisca, I thought we were discussing a few weeks ago about going to university to further our education. Have you changed your mind now?"

"Who said you can't marry before going to university? I don't see a problem with that."

"Me, I'm not sure I want to marry before going to university because anything can happen."

"Please, nothing will happen. You worry too much," Prisca said dismissively.

"Well, as for me, I must go to university and graduate before I marry."

"Me, I'm okay with it. I don't want to miss my opportunity to marry the man of my dreams."

"But what if he is okay with it?"

"Me, I'm not okay with it. With all these other girls around him... Ah, no oh!"

Onome shook her head. She should have known she was thinking about Pastor Maxwell. Just then, she wondered what Pastor Maxwell would want. She found it difficult to think of what he would say. He had only been in town for a few months. He was a university graduate, who she heard decided to be a pastor a few years after finishing university. She had always wondered why he chose to train to become a pastor. She heard he had studied engineering at a big city university but decided to go into pastoral ministry. She found it very strange. Why would his parents pay so much money for him to study for a degree, but then allow him to do something totally different? She could not imagine it being acceptable to her father.

"No, no, I will not waste time at all," Prisca was still rambling on. Onome took a deep, tired breath.

"Well, I still think it's something to seriously think about."

"You're obviously not hearing me. Anyway, we are by my street, so I'll see you later. Oh it's Dumebi's birthday this Friday. Are you going?"

"Erm... I don't know yet. You know my mother, she is never tired of giving me housework."

"Ah, sorry ooh. But your mother shaa... does she realise you're older now? You're eighteen."

"That's one of the reasons I want to go to university. Let me just leave the house for her."

"Sorry, dear."

"Please, let's forget about that. Goodnight, I'll see you soon, I hope."

"Well, you can come to my house anytime you're free. You know my mother is always asking after you. She said you've forgotten about her," Prisca was slowly walking away now.

"Ah, please tell her I haven't forgotten about her ooh. I will come and visit."

"No problem. Goodnight." Prisca waved as she quickened her steps down her street.

Onome continued walking for another 15 minutes before reaching home. As she approached the gate, she saw it was shut, but she could hear voices coming from the side of the compound. She knocked a few times until the security man came to open the gate.

"Ah, nah you?" he said as he opened the gate.

"Good evening, Musa," she greeted. She could hear the voices louder now, the noise seeming to come from Aunty Omerie's side. She could also hear her mother's voice, which seemed to be louder than anyone else's.

"Serious trouble dey ooh," she heard Musa say as she quickly hurried there. Not another quarrel, she thought, and decided to pray silently as she approached the back of the house. Some of the children were there; it seemed there had been a fight, as she saw Aunty Mabel and Sister Beatrice standing between her mother and Aunty Omerie. Her sister Rukevwe was by her mother's side, holding tightly to her hand. Her mother was pushing at the women now as she raised her voice.

"Idiot!" her mother shouted. "Useless woman. Go, go and call the father!" Her mother said, clapping her hands towards Aunty Omerie's face. "You think you can deceive us? You cannot deceive me. Fake ooh, fake!"

"Rume, please stop this. Please," she heard Aunty Mabel pleading with her mother from across Aunty Omerie's side.

"No, leave her! Let her talk, let her say whatever she likes," Aunty Omerie said, as Aunty Mabel slowly pulled her back again, pleading with her to please go inside her house. Aunty Omerie seemed to be cooperating.

"I will talk ooh, I will surely talk... Fake pregnancy. Old mama, you think you can deceive me. In short, just wait until I see Chief!" Her mother shouted, raising her hands.

Onome, eventually snapping out of her shock, walked slowly to her mother.

"Mama, please calm down. What has happened?" she asked, slightly scared.

"We shall see," was all her mother said as she walked away, her feet hard on the ground, clearly angry. Rukevwe followed, still holding her hand and murmuring something inaudible. Onome watched as her mother stormed off. She turned to see that Aunty Omerie had now gone inside. She then turned to Beatrice, hoping for someone to tell her what was going on. All she knew was that there was a wives' meeting, but the wives' meeting had never resulted in a fight before. Sure, they'd had a few raised voices, but they had never ended in a fight before.

"Sister Beatrice, please what happened?"

"Do I know for your mother?" she hissed. "Always making trouble." She turned away and walked off. Onome turned to look at Omoefe, who looked puzzled. Koko just shrugged her shoulders and looked away.

Onome glanced towards Aunty Omerie's quarters, wondering if she would step out. She walked slowly to the front door, but it was closed. She could still hear Aunty Mabel's voice, trying to calm her down. Onome decided it wouldn't be right to eavesdrop on their conversation. She turned and started walking back to their house, taking her time. She was worried about how her mother was feeling. Her mother was very angry, and who knows what she might do.

As Onome walked slowly, replaying the argument in her mind, she couldn't stop thinking about the fake pregnancy her mother mentioned. Who was pregnant? Was Aunty Omerie pregnant? Is that why her mother called her an old woman? Too many questions filled her mind. She continued walking and thinking, passing Musa, who was sitting by the gate. As soon as he saw her, he shook his head. Deep down, Onome didn't want to know what he was thinking.

When she reached the front door, she found it closed. She turned the handle slowly, relieved that it wasn't locked, as she had feared. The living room light and ceiling fan were on. She shut the door quietly behind her and locked it. There was no sign of her mother or sister; it was quiet. Onome tiptoed to her mother's room door, where she could hear her mum talking to herself and hissing. She wondered if her sister was inside with her. Onome pressed her ear against the door, but her mother had stopped talking.

146

She paused, unsure whether to knock and ask if everything was okay. She lifted her hand to knock but then changed her mind. If she went into the kitchen and made noise, her mother would surely come out and ask why she was being so loud. That could give Onome a chance to get to the bottom of what had happened at the wives' meeting and why her mother was so angry. And, of course, Onome desperately wanted to know who was pregnant.

She stepped away from the door softly and went into the kitchen. It was as clean as when she left it earlier. She looked around, wondering if there was something she could do. She began opening and shutting the kitchen cabinets noisily. She did this several times, but her mother didn't come out of her room. She then opened and slammed the back door, hoping that might get her attention, but nothing. At that point, Onome gave up. Whatever was going on, her mother was too annoyed to come out tonight.

She opened the back door and stepped outside. It was a cool evening, so she decided to sit for a while. It had been a long, eventful day, and she knew she would be up all night thinking about everything that had happened. Sleep would be hard to come by. She sighed and looked up at the sky. The stars were shining brightly. It was a shame because the evening had turned out to be so unpleasant.

"You missed wahala!" Onome jumped at Rukevwe's voice. Rukevwe was standing at the door, looking down at her.

"What happened?" Onome asked as she stood up.

Her sister grunted, then clicked her tongue before walking outside to join Onome, who waited patiently.

"I was in the room when I heard shouting and quarrelling," Rukevwe said, adding her usual dramatic flair. "Then I heard Mama's voice shouting, 'You are lying!' I ran out quickly to see what was going on. By the time I got there, everyone was already there. Mama had taken off one of her wrappers, and Aunty Mabel was standing between her and Aunty Omerie. Mama was saying all sorts of things about Aunty Omerie."

"What was she saying?" Onome asked, her interest piqued. This was exactly what she needed to hear, she thought.

"Well, she was saying that Aunty was telling lies, that she's lying, that the pregnancy is fake."

147

"Wait, wait, what pregnancy? Who is pregnant?" Onome interrupted.

"Apparently, Aunty Omerie is pregnant," Rukevwe said, folding her arms over her chest.

Onome shook her head, turning it left and right. Did she just hear that right? Aunty Omerie is pregnant?

"I know, me too, I was shocked. I thought I didn't hear Mama right, but then she said it again: 'Fake pregnancy. Who give you belle? Lie, lie.' Me, I was shocked ooh."

Onome shook her head in disbelief. Surely, it was impossible. From what she knew from studying biology in school, Aunty couldn't be pregnant, she was too old. Impossible.

"Did they fight?" Onome asked.

"No ooh, no fighting. We were separating them. But Mama was very angry ooh. I think if not for us, they would have fought."

Onome placed her hand on her chin, thinking. There was silence between them now.

"Where is Papa?" she finally asked.

"They said Papa is out of town with Amaka," Rukevwe answered.

Onome sighed. Out of town? How were they going to resolve this now?

"We don't know when he's coming back," Rukevwe added, as if anticipating her next question.

Onome sighed again. "There's definitely trouble. God help us."

"Did Mama say anything to you when you were walking back?" Rukevwe asked.

"No, she was just talking to herself. I tried to talk to her, but she didn't answer me. She just went to her room and locked the door."

Onome let out a deep breath. "Well, we'll just have to wait and see until tomorrow."

"Well, I have to leave early for school. I'll try Mama in the morning to see if she'll answer. If not, you'll have to tell me what happened."

Onome paused. That was something to look forward to.

"Me, I'm going to sleep," Rukevwe said, turning to walk back into the house. But she stopped. "Wait, do you think it's true?"

"What?"

Rukevwe rolled her eyes. "That Aunty Omerie is pregnant?" she asked.

Blowing her breath out and shrugging her shoulders, Onome replied, "I don't know ooh. Why would Aunty Omerie lie about that?"

"Me, I don't know, but I'm sure we'll find out very soon," Rukevwe said, walking back into the kitchen.

Onome heard the door to their room open and then close. She took a deep breath and sat back down. This is a big one. What is going on? What is going on in this family? It seemed like a lot had been happening, and the children didn't know anything about it. Papa was never around since he married his fourth wife. She hardly saw him. When she would go to his quarters, she was always met by a maid and some sort of security guard appointed by Papa.

She wondered if Papa was aware of the present situation with Aunty Omerie. He must know, she thought. What has he made of it; she wondered. She looked up at the stars again, but they seemed to have disappeared. Scary, she thought. She sighed as her mind went to the evening and Michael. She was glad she saw him, although not in the circumstances she wanted. She liked the fact that he smiled when he saw her. She loved it when he smiled, the thought of it made her smile just then. He said he missed her, so he was thinking about her too.

But Sister Beatrice was there too. Why did he act as if he liked her too? Surely, he couldn't like both her and Sister Beatrice. Sister Beatrice was much more beautiful than her, and she dressed very well. There was no way Onome could compare, but did she even want to, was the question. She could not deny the fact that she was afraid of Beatrice. She was very mean. Onome never knew why Beatrice wasn't like her sisters. There was peace between her and the other sisters, but for some reason, Beatrice didn't like her. She never understood why.

Onome sighed again. Now that Michael was involved, she needed to be careful. But she loved Michael, she thought. What was she going to do? She sighed once again, got up, and walked into the kitchen, shutting the door and locking it. She looked around the kitchen, turned off the lights, and then walked into the room she shared with her sister. Rukevwe was already in bed, fast asleep—or pretending to be. Onome moved around slowly and quietly as she prepared to take her bath.

She quickly had her bath, dressed in her nightgown, and got into bed, raising her head on the pillow. She was not feeling sleepy. She sat up on her bed and opened the drawer by her bedside. She saw the bottle her mother had given her for treating the rashes. She picked up the bottle, opened it, and brought it to her nose. She was expecting it to smell horrible, but it smelled like mint.

She lifted her nightgown and looked at the rashes. She had noticed when taking her bath that they had spread and were still spreading to her chest. Maybe she should try this ointment her mother gave her. This would be the last thing she tried. Who knows, it might cause them to go away. She lifted her nightgown higher. She had already rubbed some body lotion on her skin. She hesitated. Maybe it's not a good idea to mix the two. It's best to rub it on her skin when she has nothing on.

She sighed, placing the bottle back down in the drawer. She had placed the bag she took to the church on top of the drawer. She quickly opened it and saw the book she had taken from the church earlier. She took it out, whispering, "Healing Miracle." She picked up the book, opened it to the introduction, and began to read:

> *"My name is Lillian Cooper, a wife, a mother, and a Minister. You may not know anything about me now, but I promise you, you will know many things by the end of this book. I am about to tell you a story, a story of how I met Jesus Christ and how He healed me."*

Onome raised her pillow and placed it at the top of the bed, resting her back on it as she continued reading.

Chapter 14

What did you say? What nonsense are you telling me?"
Chief sat up straight, his voice now full of anger. It
had been two days since Rume's argument with
Omerie. She had heard that Chief was back, apparently having
taken his new wife to her parents' house for a while. Rume thought
it was the right time to carry out her plan. Chief had been reluctant
to see her, but when she mentioned she had some information that
concerned Omerie's pregnancy, he had invited her into his quarters.

Rume paused for a second as she replayed the story in her head
again. She had been rehearsing it for some time, wanting to get it
just right.

"Chief, I'm not telling you nonsense. What I'm saying is the
truth. Why would I lie to you? What do I have to gain from this? I
said I saw it myself." She watched as Chief looked at her, and she
could tell he didn't believe her.

"Well, Chief, if you don't believe me, then call her and ask her.
Let her deny it in my presence." Rume watched him closely, hoping
this would convince him. He studied her from head to toe, then
stood up, calling out to the maid.

"Go and call Omerie for me. Tell her to come here immediately."
His tone was serious.

"Yes, Sir," the maid responded, rushing out through the front
door. Chief walked over and sat down, visibly angry. He rested his
hand on the armrest, lifted his palm to his chin, and looked away
from Rume. His legs shook slightly. Rume knew him well enough to
know that he was both angry and worried at that moment. She
opened her mouth to speak but changed her mind. Instead, she

relaxed back into the chair. They sat in silence as they waited for Omerie.

It didn't take long for her to arrive. Omerie had a smile on her face at first, but it quickly turned into a frown as she saw Rume. Rume watched as she slowly walked toward Chief and stood beside him.

"Chief, you sent for me? You said to come immediately. Is everything alright?" Omerie asked.

"Sit down," Chief ordered, without looking in her direction. Omerie sat beside him, her voice soft.

"Chief, is anything the matter?"

Rume rolled her eyes, clicking her tongue. *There she goes,* she thought. *Let's see how she tries to get out of this one.*

"Omerie…"

"Yes, Chief?"

"Tell me the truth. Who is responsible for your pregnancy?"

Rume watched as Omerie looked at Chief, confused.

"Chief, what kind of question is this?" she replied, shifting slightly on her seat. "I don't understand."

"Are you deaf? I said, who is responsible for this pregnancy?" Chief's voice rose as he pointed to her stomach.

"Chief, I don't understand what you're asking me."

"What don't you understand? Am I not speaking English?" Chief was yelling now, his tone firm as he pointed to her stomach again. "I said, who is responsible for your…this thing you call pregnancy?"

"Chief, what sort of question is this, ehn?" Omerie stood up now, clearly upset.

Rume, tired of the back-and-forth, finally spoke. "Okay, since you want to pretend you don't understand, let me help you. Who… is…the…owner…of…your…pregnancy?"

She watched as Omerie's eyes widened in shock. Her mouth was slightly open, but no words came out.

"Rume, keep quiet!" Chief shouted at her.

Rume eyed Omerie, who was still in shock from the question.

"I asked you a question," Chief said, his voice firm.

Omerie shook her head, speechless.

"Chief, why are you asking me this question, ehn? You know who is responsible. Who else could be responsible?" Omerie's voice was defensive.

"Is that so?" Chief's tone was cold. "Okay, good. What has my driver been doing at your quarters?" He was on his feet now, his gaze fixed on Omerie. Rume nodded at his question, eager to see how Omerie would respond.

"Your driver?" Omerie looked genuinely surprised. "I don't understand."

"You don't understand?" Chief moved closer to her, pointing a finger at her as he spoke. "Is that the answer you plan to use to explain yourself, ehn?"

"Chief, I really don't understand all these questions. The driver has never come to my quarters unless it's to leave me a message or drop something off. Why would he come to my quarters?" Omerie tried to defend herself.

"Madam liar! Liar!" Rume suddenly stood up, shouting. "What else, ehn? Madam, tell Chief what sort of message he's delivering late at night at your quarters! Tell Chief!" Rume clapped her hands towards Omerie's face as she shouted.

"Oh... so this is your plan, ehn?" Omerie's voice rose, and she faced Rume now, clearly upset. "This is your plan?"

"Which plan? Which plan? I'm saying you should tell Chief the truth. What is his driver always doing at your quarters late at night, ehn?" Rume clapped her hands again, her eyes wide.

"Are you mad, Rume? What kind of nonsense talk is this?" Omerie's voice became sharp, but Rume stood her ground.

"Nonsense talk indeed! I've been seeing you. You think you can hide it from everyone? Nah lie. Oya, Madam Pregnancy, start explaining," Rume shouted, her voice echoing with anger.

"You are stupid, do you hear me?" Omerie yelled. Rume hissed and turned away, her patience wearing thin.

"Chief, are you really listening to this nonsense? Rume just wants to make trouble, but she won't succeed," Omerie said, moving closer to Chief. "She's started again with her madness, and this time I've had enough. Please, tell her to shut up and leave now." Omerie pointed to the door, trying to dismiss Rume.

"Omerie! Shut up!" Chief's voice boomed. "Will you stop avoiding the question, or do you think I'm stupid, ehn?" Without waiting for her response, he continued, "Look here, I'll ask you one last time. Who is responsible for this pregnancy?"

"Chief, it's you! God knows!" Omerie was about to kneel in front of him.

"Ehnn, so, you've been sleeping with my driver, ehn? Is that not so?" Chief's anger flared as he quickly stormed out, calling out for the driver. "Eric! Eric! Where is this useless driver? Eric!" he yelled, his voice getting louder as he rushed outside.

"Chief, please!" Omerie cried out, rushing behind him, trying to stop him. Rume followed behind them, a smile slowly forming on her face. *Yes, o, today we will know the truth,* she thought to herself.

By the time they reached outside, the driver was standing before Chief. Chief immediately pounced on him, slapping him hard across the face.

"You useless man!" Chief shouted, his anger palpable. He grabbed the driver by his shirt. "So, you've been sleeping with my wife?"

Omerie rushed forward, trying to pull Chief's hand off Eric's shirt, but Chief shoved her aside, and she almost fell to the ground. "Tell me now, or I'll deal with you!"

Rume watched, content as the situation unfolded just as she had planned. She smiled slightly, observing Eric, whose hand was still on his face, shocked from the slap.

Chief continued to pull on his shirt. "So, you can't talk, eh? You don't understand?" he barked. Rume watched as the driver's eyes filled with tears and his lips began to quiver.

"Oga, sleep with your wife?" was all the driver managed to say, his voice shaky.

"Ah, so now you can talk, eh? Or maybe you don't understand? I said my wife, yes," Chief retorted angrily.

"Haba, Chief, please! I did not sleep with your wife ooh. How could I do such a thing?" The driver swore before God that it wasn't true.

"Professional liar," Rume sneered, clapping her hands in front of the driver's face. "Tell us what you've been doing at her quarters late at night?"

"Ah, Sir, it's not me ooh," the driver exclaimed, his voice filled with desperation.

"Liar!" Rume shouted. "I've seen you several times coming out of her quarters!"

"Ah, ma!" The driver widened his eyes at Rume, then looked back at Chief. "Please, sir, I have not been sleeping with your wife ooh."

The noise from the commotion had now attracted Musa, who rushed over, and some of the children were starting to gather, curious about what was happening. Chief was still gripping the driver's shirt, his anger barely contained.

"Sir, I go there to help ooh. That's all, sir. I swear, sir," Eric continued to plead, now on his knees.

"Ah, so now you remember that you go there, ehn?" Chief asked sarcastically, his voice laced with mockery.

"Chief, please, please!" Omerie dropped to her knees, pleading. "He's an innocent man! He's innocent of all these lies. He's a good man. The only time he was at my quarters late was when he delivered meat and other food items. I asked him to sit down for food because he was hungry. He had been working all day and hadn't eaten. I gave him food, and it was late. That's the only time he was at my place. Please, Chief, he's innocent." She took a deep breath, her hand on her chest as she spoke quickly.

Chief's breath grew heavy as his gaze flicked from Omerie to the driver, his eyes burning with rage. He turned back to Omerie, who was still kneeling and pleading.

"Emmanuel, please, have I ever lied to you, ehn?" Omerie's voice wavered as she looked up at him. "This is your child I'm carrying. How can you believe this child isn't yours? Please, don't listen to all these lies this wicked woman is telling you." Rume sneered at her, with a nasty look on her face.

Chief's gaze shifted back to Eric, still kneeling and rubbing his hands together, pleading and continuing to insist on his innocence. Rume watched closely, sensing Chief's anger beginning to subside. She drew closer to him, her voice low by his ear.

"Chief, don't listen to them ooh. They're lying to you. Don't believe them. Let me tell you the truth; she's entertained him so many times at the back there. I've seen him coming out of her quarters late at night. They've been doing this for a long time. Don't let them deceive you." She hissed, turning her back to them.

There was a loud gasp from the children who had been quietly listening to the drama unfolding.

"Ah, ma, but you know that's not true na," the driver exclaimed, shaking his head in disbelief.

"Shut up! You liar!" Rume lashed out at him, pushing him by the head with the tip of her finger.

Omerie's eyes filled with tears as she slowly shook her head, her body trembling. She turned to look at Rume, tears now rolling down her cheeks. "Rume, why are you lying? Why? What are you doing this for, ehn?"

"Why am I doing what?" Rume clapped her hands and kissed her teeth, rolling her eyes at Omerie. "So, because I exposed you by telling the truth, ehn?"

"Anyway, you know what? I'm finished with you." Chief said, letting go of Eric's shirt. He pointed towards the gate. "Leave my house immediately. I don't want to see you here again."

Eric, now panicking, prostrated on the ground, begging.

"Musa, get him out of my compound now!" Chief shouted, his voice firm.

"Chief, please, please! I haven't done anything! This is not true!" the driver pleaded, his voice cracking.

"Musa, why are you just standing there? Are you deaf? I said get him out of my compound now!" Chief's voice thundered as his frustration boiled over.

Musa reached down to pull him up. "Sorry, Oga. Oya, my brother, get up, con dey go abeg," Musa said as he began lifting Eric off the floor. The driver continued to beg Chief.

"Get out, my friend! Did you not hear Chief? Come on, get out!" Rume yelled, almost pushing him.

"Madam, abeg, please beg Chief for me, ma. I need this job," he pleaded.

"Musa, if you don't move fast, you will lose your job," Chief said.

"Ah, Oga, no ooh!" Musa began pulling the driver up, urging him to move toward the gate. The driver dusted off his shirt, bent down to show respect to Chief, and raised his gaze to look at Rume, and she noticed that he had tears in his eyes. He turned to look at Omerie.

"I'm sorry, ma," was all he could say as Musa started pushing him toward the gate.

"Get out!" Chief shouted at him as Musa led him slowly to the gate and then out of the compound.

"Ehn! So that is your code language?" Rume said, clapping her hands together and laughing. "Chief, you see them?" she laughed.

Chief quickly turned to look at the children. "What are you people looking at? Will you leave here immediately?" he demanded, watching as they all rushed off, two of them almost running. He hissed, then turned to look at Omerie. She had her head down, tears rushing down her cheeks.

"You..." he paused. "Look at you, you don't have any shame," he paused again for a second. "Since you have refused to tell the truth and confess, I will deal with you in this house." He looked at her, disgusted. "Rubbish," he muttered, walking into his quarters.

Once Chief was out of sight, Rume walked over to Omerie, watching her sob. She laughed; her head leaned back.

"Look at you. I told you, didn't I?" Omerie didn't look up. "I told you that you will see. Now do you see?" Rume asked in a whisper, walking around Omerie before laughing softly. "Pregnant indeed," she huffed, turning around to walk into Chief's quarters.

Chief was back in his chair, this time with a full glass of brandy. The bottle was on the side. He had just taken a gulp when she walked in. She walked slowly toward him.

"Close the door. I don't want to see her face," he said to Rume.

Rume walked to the door, glancing at Omerie, still kneeling and sobbing softly. She eyed her as she shut the door, then turned around to look at Chief. His hand was over his face now. Rume walked over and sat next to him, placing a hand on his shoulder.

"Chief, please don't let her pretense deceive you ooh. She has been doing this for a long time."

Chief moved slightly away from her, causing her hand to drop to her side.

"Rume, leave me alone now. I want to be alone," his tone was cold. She wasn't expecting this. She moved closer to close the space between them.

"Chief, I came to tell you because of my love for you."

"Your love for me? Is that so?" he asked sarcastically.

"Yes naah, Chief, of course, you know I care for you."

He shook his head. "Your love for me?" He turned to look at her now. His eyes were bloodshot, looking like he had been crying too. "You waited all this time to tell me, and you say you love me?"

"Chief, how could I tell you when you ordered us not to come near you for months? How was I supposed to tell you when you didn't even want to see me?"

He looked away, his hand over his face again.

She paused for a few seconds. "What happened, Chief?" she asked softly. "You used to love me. You used to love spending time with me. I would cook your food; we would laugh together and…"

"Please, please, I said I want to be alone. In fact, since you don't want me to rest, I'll go to my room," he stood up with a glass in one hand and the bottle in the other. Rume stood up immediately and rushed to block his way.

"Chief, please don't leave… erm… there's something else I need to talk to you about," she felt she needed to say something to keep him there.

"What is it? Look, let's talk about this later, I'm tired now," he tried to move, but she stood in front of him.

"Please, Chief, this is very important."

"It can wait," he attempted to walk past her, but she didn't move.

"Ah, Chief, it can't ooh, it can't wait," she said, folding her arms across her chest.

"Okay, what is it?"

"Won't you sit down?"

"What is it?" he said harshly.

"Well, it's about Onome. Someone has come for her hand in marriage."

"And?"

Rume gave him a surprised look. "The man wants to take her abroad."

Chief sighed. "And what do you want me to do about it?"

"Well, Chief, they want to come meet you for the introduction and make arrangements."

"Make any arrangement you want. Is she not your daughter?"

"Ah... ah, what is all this? Is she not your daughter too?"

"Rume, I'm tired. I'm going to my room to lie down." He pushed her aside and began walking to his room.

"Chief! Chief!" she called after him.

He continued walking but stopped suddenly. "Don't come and disturb me. I'm warning you, just go to your quarters." He entered his room and slammed the door shut, locking it behind him.

Rume's mouth was wide open. She couldn't believe he had gotten up and walked away, leaving her there. She sighed, clapping her hands together. "Imagine, all this effort for nothing?" she muttered to herself. She shook her head and sat back down, relaxing in the chair. Hand on her chin, she was deep in thought now. She had played everything in her mind before coming to see Chief, but the ending was not what she had envisaged. She had imagined that in the end, she would be resting on Chief's bosom, he would profess his love for her, they would laugh, and he would tell her how much he had missed her. She sighed. Surely, this is not the end? No, this is not the end. She shook her head. She will relax here until he comes back. She is not going anywhere. She did not go through all this effort for nothing.

She called the maid. It was just past midday, and she was hungry. There was no point in going back to her quarters and returning. Chief would probably leave the compound to avoid any conversation.

"Yes, ma," the maid approached.

"Has Chief eaten?"

"No, ma."

"I see. What did you prepare this afternoon?"

"We prepared some swallow, ma, with soup and beef."

"What kind of soup?"

"Egusi soup, ma."

"Okay, no problem. I'll tell you when to bring his food. Just bring me some food to eat now."

"Yes, ma."

She just realised how hungry she was. All the shouting had left her drained. As the maid left, she walked slowly to the room door, pressing her ear to the door. She didn't hear a sound. She sighed and walked to the dining area, sitting down. *Well,* she thought to herself, *he can't stay in there all day. He'll need to come out to eat, and when he does, I'll be here waiting.* Leaning back in the chair, she paused, tapping her lips with her fingers and letting out a soft "Hmm..." This road she'd decided to take, she hoped it wouldn't come back to haunt her. It's too late to turn back now. She hadn't lied; she told herself. Yes, she had seen that useless driver coming out of Omerie's quarters. She had been on her way to the back of Omerie's quarters to do something as instructed by Mama Omote. The door was slightly ajar, and as she moved closer, she could hear them talking and laughing as they ate. She pulled the curtain slightly and peeped in; they were sitting opposite each other. She saw the driver looking at Omerie as she ate. She quietly watched them, continuing to eat and talk. She had then hidden behind a tree when the driver left to go home. She had seen him put on his shoes outside, food in hand, as he left. A leaf had fallen from the tree, just as Omerie was outside, watching the driver leave. Afraid that Omerie might have heard, she quickly moved to hide behind the tree. She prayed that Omerie hadn't noticed her. Thankfully, Omerie went back in and shut the door. Although she hadn't seen anything that night, she was sure something was going on. The driver's eyes told her everything she needed to know.

Her thoughts were interrupted by the maid walking in with a tray of food. The maid placed the tray on the table, but Rume stopped her before she could take the food off the tray.

"Leave it. I'll do it. Go and bring me some water to wash my hands."

As the maid hurried back to the kitchen, Rume placed the food on the table and resumed her thoughts. Omerie was definitely involved with that man, which explained why she never complained about Chief not wanting to see them. Omerie always liked to pretend to be the 'good' wife, but no more. Rume shook her head. She had to expose her for who she truly was. Rume clicked her tongue. She needed to finish this and carry out what she came to do.

Omerie must leave, her time in the compound was over. Chief must throw her out.

The maid returned and placed the rinse bowl of water on the table. Rume washed her hands and handed the bowl back to the maid.

"After you drop this in the kitchen, go and tell Musa that Chief is tired and is now sleeping. No visitors are allowed in the compound, you hear?"

"Yes, ma."

"Hurry up."

"Yes, ma."

She watched as the maid hurried back to the kitchen with the bowl, then quickly came out, and rushed through the front door to deliver the message to Musa. As she watched her disappear through the door, Rume stood up swiftly. If anything was to be done, she knew it had to be done now.

She unfolded the side of her wrapper and brought out a small black bottle she had hidden there. Mama Omote had given her the bottle, which contained a powdery substance, and instructed her to sprinkle some in his food to rekindle his love for her.

"We will see how things change in this compound. Omerie must go," she said with a hiss. She looked at the front door, *"hmm... the maid will soon be back,"* she thought.

"I have to do this quickly", she said, looking at the bottle in her hand once more before rushing to the kitchen.

Chapter 15

"Nawa ooh. This is serious ooh, I feel so sorry for Aunty Omerie," Prisca said.

Onome had just finished sharing the story. They were at Prisca's house; her parents had gone to a party. It had been two weeks since the incident with Papa and Aunty Omerie. The compound had been eerily quiet since then.

"Have you seen her since then?" Prisca asked.

"No, I haven't. I've gone to her quarters to see if she's there, but the door is always closed. I think she has left the compound," Onome replied.

Prisca shook her head. "Poor woman." There was a moment of silence before Prisca spoke again.

"But wait ooh," she said, raising an eyebrow. "Is she really pregnant? Even if it's for the driver?"

"I don't know. But it's not like Aunty Omerie. She's so nice, and I don't think she could do something like that," Onome said dismissively. Aunty Omerie had always been a good aunt, a very caring woman; she was always making sure everything was okay in the compound.

"Hmmm... my sister, you know what they say..." Prisca said, shrugging her shoulders.

"What do they say?" Onome asked.

Prisca shrugged again. "People are not always what they show themselves to be."

"Ah, English. No, I don't believe that. Not Aunty Omerie, she wouldn't do something like that. She goes to church; she's a good person."

"Ah, good keh? Read the Bible, it says no one is good except God."

"No, not Aunty Omerie, not after all these years. She loves my father," Onome said firmly.

"Okay ooh, well..." Prisca shrugged again. "But I'm sorry to say this ooh, but your mother is wicked. It's really not good the way she treated Aunty Omerie," she added, reminding Onome of her mother's actions.

Onome fell silent, feeling ashamed. She knew that Prisca was right, her mother had always treated Aunty Omerie badly. It was clear that her mother hated her, and Onome could never understand why. Aunty Omerie had always been calm, and in fact, that day had been the first time in a long while that she had seen Aunty Omerie upset.

"So, what do you think about the Jollof rice?" Prisca interrupted Onome's thoughts. Onome looked down at the plate of Jollof rice on her lap, realising she had completely forgotten about it. Prisca had just finished cooking it, planning to take some to Pastor Maxwell. She'd also made some chicken and plantain to go with it.

"This one you're quiet, so..." Prisca teased.

Onome took a spoonful of rice. "Prisca, you know your Jollof rice is always sweet. This one is extra sweet, like you put sugar in it."

"Ah, sugar keh?"

They both laughed.

"You put some extra sweetness in this one shaa," Onome laughed again.

"Of course naah!" Prisca winked.

"Pastor Maxwell is really enjoying ooh. All you girls cooking for him."

"Please don't count me with them. I'm just doing this to help feed him. He looks too thin."

"Didn't you say he goes on fasts a lot?"

"Well, that's what he said."

"Okay, so how do you know he's not fasting right now?"

Prisca paused for a moment; Onome was sure she was giving it some thought. She shrugged. "Well, even better. He can break his fast with the Jollof rice," she continued, taking big spoonfuls of the Jollof rice. "It's 4 o'clock now, by the time we get there, it'll be time for him to break his fast," she said, her mouth still full.

Onome laughed. "Ah, madam! You've thought of everything."

"You have to be smart if you're going to marry a Pastor," Prisca smiled as she took another spoonful of rice, then dropped the spoon, picked up a piece of chicken leg and bit into it. She glanced at Onome's plate. "You haven't tasted the chicken yet? Why?"

"I like to eat the chicken at the end."

"At the end? Ah ah, what's that about?" Prisca asked, not waiting for a reply. "Please, forget that. Taste the chicken and let me know if it's nice or too hard," she said as she took another bite of her chicken.

Onome sighed, knowing Prisca wouldn't let her eat in peace. She put down the spoon and took a bite of the large chicken thigh on her plate. It was succulent, soft, even though it was fried. It was delicious, so good that she couldn't help but close her eyes as she chewed.

"I can see you're enjoying it. Look at your face," Prisca chuckled.

"Is it nice?" Prisca asked, smiling.

Onome nodded as her mouth was full, giving a thumbs up.

Prisca laughed. "Look at your mouth!" She pointed at Onome's lips while laughing.

"We need to eat quickly so I can do your hair before I take the food to Pastor Maxwell at the church. I think he's doing counselling today."

"Ah, he does counselling too?" Onome asked, surprised.

"See you, he does almost everything. He's always busy."

"Oh, okay."

"Why? Do you want to go for counselling?" Prisca chuckled as she asked.

"No, I'm just asking," Onome replied.

"Well, maybe you should go for counselling because of your family," Prisca said playfully, chuckling again.

Onome lowered her head, feeling hurt. She knew her family wasn't like most others in the town, very few families had a father with four wives. It didn't help that her mother was known around the town as a wicked and troublesome woman.

"Sorry," Prisca whispered, reaching out to place her hand on Onome's shoulder. "Please don't be angry with me for saying that."

Onome shrugged. "It's okay."

Prisca sighed. "If you ask me, in all seriousness, I think you should go to Pastor Maxwell for advice. He's really good."

Onome didn't respond. She just continued eating the chicken.

"Especially with this new situation with your mother wanting you to get married to that man's nephew in Germany."

"Ah, I can't tell Pastor Maxwell that!"

"Why not?"

Onome shook her head. The thought of speaking to Pastor Maxwell about anything scared her.

"Be shaking your head there. Listen, he gives very good advice, and he keeps everything confidential. Nobody will ever know."

"How do you know?" Onome asked, looking up at Prisca.

"I know," Prisca said, standing up as she finished her food. "I'm so full," she said, slapping her stomach and laughing.

"Me, I'm taking my time, abeg," Onome said, taking another spoonful of Jollof rice and another bite of the chicken. Prisca had gone into the kitchen now. As Onome continued eating, her mind was on what Prisca had said about counselling with Pastor Maxwell. He knew her father—he came to the house quite regularly to see him and Aunty Omerie from time to time. But how much does he really know about the family? Imagine going to him for counselling and telling him her mother wanted her to marry some stranger from abroad. Who's to say that it's truly the man's nephew? It felt too embarrassing; besides, it was too personal. *I don't even know Pastor Maxwell that well*, she thought.

"By the way, are you still thinking it's a bad idea?" Prisca's voice came from the door. She stood there with one hand on her waist, staring down at Onome. "Because this is Germany ooh! My sister, you don't know how many people will kill for an opportunity to go to Germany."

Onome rolled her eyes, slightly annoyed. She just couldn't believe Prisca. "My answer is still no, it hasn't changed."

"Hmm... okay. Well, I really hope you don't regret it ooh," Prisca said, placing her hand on Onome's shoulder. Before Onome could respond, Prisca added, "I think we should go and drop the food off first, then come back and do your hair."

"We? You want me to go there with you?" Onome asked.

Prisca walked into the house without answering. Onome quickly picked up her unfinished plate of rice and followed her. As she entered the kitchen, she saw Prisca dishing some Jollof rice into a hot food container. It was a large container filled with so much rice and chicken already.

"I don't think I can go with you ooh," Onome said, placing her plate in the kitchen sink.

"Why not? It won't take long, naah, please," Prisca pleaded softly.

"Look, I came here so you could do my hair. You know I can't stay out too long today."

"Please, it won't take long. See, I'm almost finished serving it, and besides, it's not far," Prisca said as she arranged some more fried chicken on top of the rice. Onome watched as she rushed to open the fridge and pulled out a large bowl of vegetables.

"Ah, when did you make this, and how come I didn't get any?" Onome asked as she stirred at the bowl, filled with cold but nicely arranged vegetables.

Prisca just chuckled in response. Onome watched as Prisca brought out a plastic food container and quickly transferred some vegetables into it.

"Pastor Maxwell is really enjoying ooh," Onome said, folding her arms across her chest.

It seemed Prisca had stopped listening and was now focusing on placing everything she had prepared in a large carrier bag to make it presentable. Onome sighed as she looked at the plate in the sink, still with some rice and chicken left. She hated wasting food. She looked around the kitchen.

"Do you have any more plastic food containers?" she asked.

"Ermm... check the cupboard on your left," Prisca said as she rushed out of the kitchen. Onome opened the left cupboard, reaching up to grab a plastic food container. She quickly transferred the remaining food into the container. Looking around for a plastic bag, she was still searching when Prisca came back in. Onome noticed that she had changed into a different dress.

"Please, help me zip it up," Prisca said, turning her back to Onome.

"Ah, all this just to drop food?"

"But of course! I had to change; the other dress smelled like food," Prisca replied, pointing to the zipper as if Onome had forgotten where it was. Onome zipped the dress up.

"Should I go there smelling like food?" Prisca added, rushing out of the kitchen again. Onome heard the sound of spraying—no doubt perfume, she guessed. She also heard the sound of shoes hitting the floor.

"This is serious!" Onome chuckled.

Prisca came back and started to arrange some cutlery, a large bottle of cold water, and two bottles of Supermalt in the carrier bag. She picked up the bag, adjusted her dress, and ran her hands through her hair to ensure it was tidy. Onome noticed she was wearing earrings too.

"Oya, are you ready?" Prisca asked Onome.

"But Prisca, this wasn't the plan at all! Look at how you're dressed and then look at me." Onome said, her tone sharp.

"You look..." Prisca hesitated. "...fine."

"I look fine?" Onome asked, raising an eyebrow.

"Yes naah."

"Prisca, you think I don't know when you are lying."

"Ooooh, Onome, you look fine! Let's go! You know I still have to do your hair. Do you want us to come back quickly?" Prisca exclaimed.

Onome sighed. She knew she was not looking her best; her hair wasn't neat because she had come to Prisca specifically for that. She'd thrown on a long-sleeve dress and hadn't even bothered with earrings or perfume. She briefly thought about borrowing some of Prisca's perfume, but then wondered why she would bother. After all, they were going to Pastor Maxwell's. What did she care about how Pastor Maxwell saw her or what he thought? It was obvious that Prisca and Pastor Maxwell made a good power couple, anyway.

"Onome, please naah," Prisca said, her eyes pleading.

Onome sighed again, shrugged her shoulders, and finally said, "Okay, let's go, madam." She pointed to the door, signalling for her to lead the way.

***

They were only a few yards from the church now, having walked briskly the entire way. Onome hadn't had time to think about anything, as Prisca had been talking nonstop. She'd been asking questions over and over again. "Is my dress fine? How's my hair? Please check my breath?" Onome, finally exasperated, replied, "It's enough now, madam, please."

It had been a while since she'd had a conversation with Pastor Maxwell. Even though she'd been attending the Youth Service every Wednesday, she had noticed how busy he always is. There was always a long queue of people waiting to speak with him. Onome remembered running into him when he'd come by to drop off some leaflets with Papa. He'd briefly asked how she was, to which she had responded with a simple "fine." He nodded and smiled before continuing on his way. There was something about Pastor Maxwell that made her nervous every time she saw him, but she couldn't quite figure out why.

As they walked to the back of the church, the sound of children's voices caught their attention. They saw a group of young boys playing football. It took Onome a moment to notice the Senior Pastor sitting outside with two other people. One of them was Pastor Maxwell, and the other was a young man sitting by his side. The Senior Pastor was watching the boys play, while Pastor Maxwell had his head down, reading a book to the other man. As they got closer, the Senior Pastor saw them first, but Pastor Maxwell was still engrossed in his reading.

"Good evening, Sir," they both said simultaneously.

The Senior Pastor studied them for a moment, clearly trying to place their faces. "Ah, good evening, my daughters. How are you?"

"We are fine, Sir," Prisca replied. Onome noticed Prisca's eyes quickly darting to Pastor Maxwell.

"Good afternoon, Pastor Maxwell," Prisca greeted him.

Pastor Maxwell looked up, offering a slight smile. "Ah, Prisca, Onome, welcome," he said, closing the book he was reading and placing it on a stool beside him. He stood up as they stopped just a few steps away, reaching out to give them both a hug. Onome felt it was a bit awkward. The young man that was sitting beside him, smiled as he watched.

Onome glanced at him; his face seemed familiar, and she had the feeling she had seen him before.

"How are you?" Pastor Maxwell asked. Onome wasn't sure if he was addressing her or Prisca, but fortunately, Prisca answered for both of them.

"We are fine, Pastor," Prisca said, swaying slightly.

"Maxwell, please go and bring two chairs from inside," the Senior Pastor instructed.

Pastor Maxwell quickly went inside to fetch the chairs, with the young man following behind to help. Onome watched as both men returned, each carrying a chair. They placed them next to the Senior Pastor's seat, and he motioned for them to sit. Prisca immediately took the seat right next to Pastor Maxwell, a big smile on her face. Onome couldn't help but notice the way Prisca looked at Pastor Maxwell. How Pastor Maxwell didn't already know that Prisca liked him, Onome would never understand.

"Prisca how is your father?" the Senior Pastor asked.

"He is fine, Sir. He said I should greet you whenever I see you," Prisca responded, her eyes bright with enthusiasm.

"Okay, that's good, that's good. Please greet him from me," the Senior Pastor said.

"I will, Sir," Prisca replied, her smile widening.

It was almost Onome's turn now, and she couldn't help but think, well, her family knew the Senior Pastor quite well. He had visited their compound a few times to see her father, though not so much recently. Those duties had been handed over to Pastor Maxwell.

"Onome."

"Yes, Sir. Good evening, Sir." She couldn't help but feel the oddness in her response.

"Good evening, my dear. How is your father?"

"He's fine, Sir." She would be lying if she said her father sent his greetings, or her mother for that matter. There was a pause that seemed to stretch on forever.

"These boys can really play," Prisca remarked, pointing at the young footballers with genuine interest.

Onome was grateful for the break in the awkward silence.

"Ah, these boys, they're our next football champions!" the young man sitting beside Pastor Maxwell said enthusiastically.

"Yes ooh!" The Senior Pastor clapped his hands in excitement.

"Amen," Prisca muttered. Onome was wondering why Prisca had suddenly gone all spiritual.

"Especially that one in front," Prisca continued, "he's really fast."

"Him?" Pastor Maxwell asked, pointing at a young boy in a blue t-shirt. Prisca nodded.

"Ah, he's our next Pele—very fast," Pastor Maxwell said, nodding with approval.

"Abi ooh," the young man added, hoping to get some attention.

Pastor Maxwell caught on. "Ah, sorry, I forgot to introduce you. This is Boniface," he said. "Boniface, you know Prisca, right?"

Boniface nodded, "Yes, of course, she sings in the choir."

"Yes, okay, good," Pastor Maxwell said, before turning to Onome. "And this is Onome, her friend. She just started coming to the Wednesday Youth Fellowship, maybe someday she'll join the choir," he added, his lips curving into a smile as he glanced at her. Onome smiled back, understanding why he mentioned the choir. They had talked about her possibly joining the choir before.

Prisca turned to Onome, her expression slightly confused, and whispered, "You want to join the choir?"

Onome just shrugged, leaving Prisca more confused than before.

"I know her," Boniface suddenly interjected, a smile on his face. He sat forward in his chair, clearly eager to get her attention.

Onome remembered immediately. He was the guy who had tried to speak to her on her first day at the Youth Fellowship. She had run off then, unsure of what to say.

"Oh, okay, so we all know each other now, very good," Pastor Maxwell said, looking around the group.

Boniface was still looking at Onome with a smile. She turned away, not wanting to guess what he was thinking.

"How are you?" he asked her.

"I'm fine, thank you." It seemed like everyone was watching the two of them now, curiosity evident on their faces. Thankfully, the Senior Pastor was engrossed in the football match and exclaimed, "Ah, he almost scored!"

Everyone turned their attention back to the young boys, who were playing with fervor. Onome wasn't really into football, but she never missed an opportunity to watch it during the World Cup or the Olympics. She loved how football had a way of bringing the whole town together, especially during those global events.

As they watched, Onome couldn't help but glance at both Prisca and Pastor Maxwell. This was the first time she had been so close to them, and she couldn't shake the feeling of tension. Onome knew that Prisca had to behave properly with the Senior Pastor there.

Onome was starting to think that Prisca's plans for the food weren't going well. No one had noticed the carrier bag she had brought. It was as if no one even cared. Just as she was about to dwell on it, the Senior Pastor suddenly said, as if reading her mind:

"I see that you brought a bag of food again," he said, pointing at the bag. "Or am I mistaken?"

Again? Onome thought. How many times has Prisca done this? She wondered.

"Yes Sir, we cooked some Jollof rice and chicken today, and Mama said I should bring some to you, Sir, and Pastor Maxwell," she replied. Onome's eyes almost popped out as she listened to Prisca lie.

"Ah, thank your mother for us ooh."

"Yes, Sir," Prisca said, smiling.

"Maxwell, please take the bag inside."

"Yes, Sir." Pastor Maxwell stood up to pick up the bag, but Prisca picked it up slowly and handed it to him.

171

"Erm... let me come and help you. My mother arranged things in different parts for you, and I can explain them," Prisca spoke softly now.

"Okay, no problem," he said, as he carried the bag and led the way in.

They both walked into the house, leaving Onome alone with the Senior Pastor and Boniface, whose gaze had now moved from the children to her. Onome felt her legs shaking; she was very nervous. This was not how she expected this Saturday to be. What was she thinking coming here with Prisca? What does Boniface want sef? He keeps looking at her. What will she even talk about for goodness' sake? Maybe she could talk about the sermon on Wednesday, if only she could remember the sermon topic.

She was still deliberating when the Senior Pastor asked, "My dear, how is your aunty?"

"My aunty?" She was confused. He must have forgotten that her father has many wives, and each was called Aunty.

"Your Aunty Omerie," he clarified, likely noticing the confusion on her face.

"Ermm..." She paused. "She is fine, Sir."

"I have not seen her in the last few weeks."

Onome did not reply. "She must be busy," he said.

"Yes, Sir," was all she could say. Deep down, she hoped he wouldn't ask any more questions about Aunty Omerie or any other member of her family. She wasn't sure how much she could tell him. How could she tell him, in front of everyone, that Aunty Omerie was no longer in the compound? She knew well enough that you do not lie to a pastor, a Senior Pastor for that matter. She always felt that the more senior you are in the church, the closer you are to God. Surely, if she lied to him and he found out, he might report her to God, and that would not be good for her, she thought.

Not that it stopped Prisca. She still couldn't believe the lies Prisca had told. Jollof rice and chicken from her mother. Imagine! Still in her thoughts, still pondering on what she could or couldn't say, she suddenly heard,

"A goal!" The Senior Pastor stood up clapping and cheering.

Boniface stood up also to clap. "Nigerian Pele!" he shouted. Onome had seen from the corner of her eye that he had looked over at her.

Pastor Maxwell rushed out, with Prisca behind him. The group that scored had the goal-scorer, 'Pele' as he was now called—in a huge embrace. Pastor Maxwell was clapping, and Prisca joined in. Onome joined in too, as Pastor Maxwell went over to the children, giving them high fives. He also went over to the losing team to encourage them. Onome couldn't help thinking what a nice person he is.

"These boys are getting better every day," the Senior Pastor said.

"Yes ooh," Pastor Maxwell nodded as he walked back to take his seat.

"You all played so well. Next time, the other team has to score," Pastor Maxwell said, speaking to the losing team.

The Senior Pastor chuckled and then whispered, "They will play seriously now. They will try to score by all means now that they're losing."

Pastor Maxwell and Prisca were sitting down now. Everyone was silent again, watching the young boys play. There was some chatter about how the game was going and who was likely to win. Onome tried to join in even though she knew too little about football. Prisca, on the other hand, was chatting away, impressing the men with her knowledge of football. Apparently, she had three brothers who she played football with from time to time.

Prisca looked over at Onome a couple of times. They both knew she was telling 'little' lies. Onome had never noticed her playing football with her brothers. She knew it was all to impress Pastor Maxwell.

It must have been about 30 minutes later when the Senior Pastor started to yawn. "I am tired," he said.

"You should go and rest, Sir. You have not rested at all since you came back," Pastor Maxwell said.

"It's true," he yawned again and kissed his teeth. "Let me go and sleep," he said, rising slowly. He was an older man. He was her father's age but slimmer and taller.

"Prisca," he called.

"Yes, Sir?"

"This food that you brought will save us today ooh. Maxwell was going to cook something tonight," he laughed, looking at Pastor Maxwell, "but now he can relax and enjoy. No work, abi Maxwell?"

Pastor Maxwell laughed. "Very true, Sir."

"Tell your mother thank you ooh."

"Yes, Sir. I cooked it myself, Sir," Prisca could not help but mention.

"Ah, really?"

"Yes, Sir."

"Ah, so we will enjoy your cooking. Well done, eeh? God will bless you."

"Amen, Sir. Amen," Prisca said with a big smile across her face.

Pastor Maxwell turned to look at Prisca, nodding his head in agreement. Prisca lowered her gaze at that point. Onome could not believe how shy she had become. She could only hope that Pastor Maxwell would make a move very soon and ask Prisca to marry him. That was Prisca's dream, of course. She turned to look at Pastor Maxwell. He was on his feet now.

"Ah, sorry, I forgot. Since you came, I haven't even asked what you'd like to drink," he said, glancing from Prisca to her.

"If you have a bottle of Coke, I don't mind," Prisca quickly replied, a huge smile spreading across her face again.

"Coke, okay. Onome, what will you drink?"

"Erm...I don't really want anything," Onome said hesitantly.

"Ah, why naah?" the Senior Pastor asked, not waiting for her to respond. "You must take something," he insisted. "There is Coke, Fanta, Supermalt, choose anything. I will not be happy if you don't drink something ooh."

She really didn't want anything to drink. What she wanted was to start heading back home. But could she refuse the Senior Pastor? As she battled with her thoughts, Pastor Maxwell suddenly spoke.

"I know she likes Supermalt, so that's what I will bring for her," he said, not waiting for her to respond. He went inside to get the drinks, and Boniface followed closely behind. Onome noticed that

Boniface had been quiet all this time, just listening to the conversation and adding one or two comments here and there.

The Senior Pastor yawned again, this time resting his hand on the door handle to steady himself so he wouldn't fall.

"Well, I'm going to lie down. Maxwell will stay with you all until you go. Please greet your parents for me," he said.

"Yes, Sir. Bye bye, Sir!" Prisca replied.

He waved at them as he walked into the house.

Prisca was smiling as she turned to look at Onome and winked.

"You said we were not going to stay long because you have to do my hair, ehn. What is this naah?" Onome whispered.

"Sorry naah, just relax. Let's finish the drinks, and we'll go," Prisca pleaded, rubbing her palms together as if begging. Onome turned her face away, visibly annoyed, and huffed slightly.

"By the way, this guy Boniface, I think he likes you," Prisca said, smiling and winking at her. "So, you people met each other at fellowship, ehn?"

Onome turned to Prisca. "I don't know why you are winking and getting excited. I don't really know him, and he hasn't told me he likes me or anything."

"Well, me, I'm telling you he likes you. Did you see the way he kept looking at you earlier?"

"Please, keep your voice down," Onome said, glancing towards the door.

She was about to say something else when Pastor Maxwell and Boniface returned with the drinks. Pastor Maxwell held two bottles of soft drinks: a Coke and a Fanta, along with two glasses, while Boniface carried two bottles of Supermalt, a glass, and two straws. They both watched as Pastor Maxwell dragged a stool and placed it in front of them. Prisca quickly stood up to help, taking the glasses from his hand. There was a Bible on the stool, which he removed and placed on the floor beside his chair.

So, this was what he was reading when they arrived, she thought. Each bottle was now carefully set on the stool.

"Thank you," he said to Prisca as he took the glasses from her and gently placed them on the stool. Taking a bottle of Supermalt from Boniface, he set it down in front of Onome.

"Your Supermalt, madam. I didn't ask if you wanted a glass or a straw, so I brought both," he said, smiling at Onome as he placed the glass and straw before her. She managed a tight smile.

"Thank you," she said.

"You are welcome," he replied, reaching into his shirt pocket and bringing out a bottle opener.

"Thank you," she said again.

"You are welcome," he responded.

There was something about his tone this time that made her look up at him again. He had a smile on his face, and there was something in his eyes she couldn't quite figure out. He immediately turned to Prisca.

"Prisca, I know you prefer a glass," he said.

"Ah yes, Pastor, you know me so well," she laughed softly as she took the bottle of Coke from him. "The straw is just too dangerous for my teeth and gums, that's why I don't use straws."

"Are you serious?" Boniface exclaimed as he moved his chair to sit beside Onome. Onome immediately tensed up.

"Why is that?" Pastor Maxwell asked as he proceeded to open the remaining bottles. Then he sat down, now quite close to Prisca, and she loved it.

"It's something that happened to me when I was young," she said and proceeded to tell her childhood story, the story of *"The Girl and the Straw."* Onome thought it was a fitting title, though she braced herself for what she suspected would be a long tale.

And long it was.

They had been there for nearly two hours. Onome had finished drinking her Supermalt so quickly, while Prisca took her time sipping from her glass. She kept telling one story after another. Pastor Maxwell listened patiently. He laughed a few times and tried to get Onome involved in the conversation, but she only said a few words before Prisca was at it again. Onome couldn't help but feel a little bit envious of Prisca. Here she was, having a great time talking to both men. Boniface seemed engrossed in the conversation too.

Onome wished she had this with Michael. She was just too shy, and besides, he was always with Beatrice these days. He would wave to her from afar and smile but wouldn't even wait for her to return the greeting. But she loved him still and wished he loved her. If only Michael was her boyfriend and wanted to marry her instead of a stranger from Germany. She sighed and picked up the bottle of Supermalt, hoping to get the last few drops, but the bottle was empty. She stared at the empty bottle, surprised at how fast she had drunk it.

"You really like Supermalt shaa," it was Boniface. He must have been watching her as she tried to get a few sips from the empty bottle. She looked up at him and smiled.

"Do you want another one?" he asked.

"Oh, no."

"Are you sure? There is more in the fridge ooh."

"No, no. I'm full already," she said, placing her hand over her stomach.

There was silence between them. She sat back in the chair. The children were still playing football. They had been at it for ages.

"Do you like football?" he asked.

Oh no, why was he asking her this, she thought. "Erm...not really" she replied

She wasn't sure how to answer him, so she remained silent. He continued to look at her, waiting for her to speak. She looked up at him again. "I only watch football during the World Cup and the Olympics."

"Ah, like my sisters," he smiled. "They are like professionals when it comes to the World Cup." They both laughed.

"Are you like that too?"

"Who, me? No ooh, I just watch to support Nigeria."

"Okay, me too. So, what sport do you like then?"

He was asking a lot of questions, she thought. She was happy to be having a conversation with someone. She surely would have felt alone since Prisca and Pastor Maxwell were engrossed in their conversation. Boniface continued to ask her questions, and they talked for a while. It took some time before they noticed it had gone quiet at the other end. It was still an hour later before they said goodbye to Pastor Maxwell.

Boniface decided to leave at the same time. Pastor Maxwell hugged them goodbye. Prisca lingered with the hug a little bit longer before letting go. Onome found it awkward again. He always had a smile on his face, but there was something comforting about it.

"We will see you in church on Wednesday, madam," he said as he let her go and turned to give Boniface a handshake. Boniface leaned in to whisper something in his ear.

"We will talk later," Pastor Maxwell said as he patted Boniface on the shoulder. "Come and see me in the office." They both nodded.

"Safe journey home, all of you. Boniface, please make sure they get home safely."

"Yes, of course, Pastor," he said, smiling like he had just won the lottery. He then stretched out his hand to guide them forward. As they began to walk away, Prisca couldn't help saying something to Pastor Maxwell:

"Enjoy the Jollof rice ooh, Pastor."

"Ah, I will ooh. Thank you and say thank you to your mother for us."

"No problem." Prisca was walking slowly. Obviously, she was a bit reluctant to leave. As they turned the corner, Onome looked back at the same time as Prisca. She wanted to wave goodbye. She noticed he was watching them leave, his hands in his pockets and a worried look on his face. They waved at him as they disappeared out into the main street. Onome saw that he didn't wave back but instead stood still, watching them. He must have been deep in thought. Onome wondered what was on his mind.

She turned over to look at Prisca. Her head was down; she didn't look happy. Onome was going to ask why, but she remembered that Boniface was with them.

"So, whose place should we go to first?" he asked, rubbing his hands together with a big smile on his face. Onome turned to look at Prisca, who was miles away and uninterested. Boniface continued to speak as they made their way to Prisca's house.

Once they reached the street leading to Prisca's house, it was as if Prisca had found her voice again.

"Ermm...Onome, please forgive me. I am sorry, but I don't think I can do your hair today anymore. Can you come tomorrow instead?"

"Ah, Prisca, but you said you would do it after we visit Pastor?"

"Yes, I know, but I am sorry. I'm really tired. Please ehn, come tomorrow."

Onome was going to respond angrily but remembered that Boniface was there with them. She was staring at Prisca with so much anger. How could Prisca do this to her? The only reason she went to Prisca's house was to get her hair plaited. She hadn't expected to be dragged to see Pastor Maxwell and spend hours there. After helping her, now Prisca was saying she couldn't do her hair because she was tired. Prisca reached forward, putting her hands around Onome, apologising and promising to make it up to her. Onome noticed that Boniface was watching them, unsure of what to do or say. She sighed and nodded. They both waved goodbye to Prisca and continued walking.

Boniface insisted on walking Onome to her house. She allowed him to walk her to her street and thanked him. She explained that her father wasn't too happy about having men around his compound. That was enough to convince him to say his goodbyes, promising to hopefully see her in church. Onome watched as he walked away, waiting until he was a good distance off before heading to the compound.

Chapter 16

The rocking chair was making a strange noise as it swung back and forth. Omerie had decided to sit outside again this afternoon to spend some time reading the Bible and praying. The chair had begun to make a strange noise as it slowly rocked back and forth. The squeaky sound was starting to trouble her. This had been going on for some time, consistently. Some days it would squeak, and other days, there would be silence. She stopped, and the noise ceased. She stood up and turned to look at the chair.

That's it, she thought. I am going to find out why it is making such a strange noise.

As she tried to lift the chair onto its side and bent down to check, she heard the front gate to the compound open. She raised her head to see who it was. It was her sister, back from the market. She watched as her sister shut the gate behind her and walked toward the house, carrying two heavy nylon bags. Omerie tried to walk over to meet her, wanting to offer some help.

"No, sister, don't worry. Sit down, I can carry them."

"Are you sure?"

"Yes, don't worry. Sit down."

"Okay. Welcome ooh," Omerie said.

"Thank you. Let me go inside, drop these things, and come back."

"Okay."

She watched as her sister disappeared through the front door of the house. Then, she turned back to look at the suspicious chair. She had thought it was suspicious from the day her sister bought it.

But it was comfortable and good for her back. She sighed and sat back down. She decided it was better not to rock it.

There was a cool breeze that afternoon. She closed her eyes. This was one thing she liked about her sister's house: there was always a cool breeze in the afternoon, and there were many plants and trees in the compound. Omerie had been at her sister's house for a few weeks now. Her sister had rushed over a few days after hearing what had happened. She was afraid for her and convinced her that it was best to leave the compound for some time.

Omerie had never been away from the compound for longer than a few days. The only people she would visit were her parents and younger siblings, and Rhoda was one of them. Rhoda was her immediate younger sister who lived only a few hours away in the next town with her husband and children. Fortunately for Rhoda, her husband was married only to her, and she had given him two girls and two boys. Very rarely did Rhoda have marital problems, and even when she did, they were resolved quickly, returning to being the loving husband and wife they had always been.

Sighing, she thought her sister was lucky. *What if she had taken a different path in life?* she wondered. *What if she had not married Chief?*

She heard her sister's footsteps as she walked back to meet her on the verandah and took a seat next to her.

"Eeh!" she exclaimed. "I'm tired."

"You and your buy-buy shaa. I thought you just went to get some fresh fish and goat meat."

"Yes, that is why I went, but then I saw some coconut. I know how much you like Coconut rice," she smiled at Omerie.

"Ah, you too. You and Coconut rice," she said, pointing at her. They both laughed.

"I bought some starch for some Ogwo soup; I want to make it for my husband and some small-small things shaa," she said as she leaned back on the chair, enjoying the afternoon breeze. "Ah, this breeze shaa."

"That's why I am always sitting outside. The breeze is so sweet," Omerie said, closing her eyes as the breeze continued to blow.

There was silence for a while as they sat, enjoying the cool afternoon breeze.

"Sister."

"Hmm…"

"How are you feeling?" Rhoda asked, her voice tinged with concern.

Omerie sighed. "Rhoda, you don't have to keep asking me that question. I've told you, I'm fine."

She turned to look at Rhoda and could tell her sister didn't believe her. "I said I'm fine."

Rhoda shrugged. "Okay, sister."

She paused briefly, then continued, this time with a bit of excitement in her voice. "But sister, you are starting to show small small ooh. Can you see?"

Omerie looked down at her slightly protruding stomach. Slowly, she placed her hand on it and rubbed gently.

"Sister, God is so good," Rhoda said, her smile growing wider. She reached forward and joined Omerie in rubbing her stomach.

Omerie stayed silent, still rubbing her stomach. She was starting to feel emotional. Yes, God had been so good to her. But why did it take so long? Tears began to form in her eyes.

"Sister, please don't cry again."

"Again?"

Rhoda quickly realised what she had said and turned her face away.

"Wait, what do you mean by 'again'?"

"Erm…sister, I heard you when you were crying last night."

Omerie looked at her in surprise. Surely, she hadn't been crying that loud. How did Rhoda hear? She was about to ask when they heard a knock on the compound gate.

"Ah, who is that?"

They both looked at each other, then turned their eyes to the gate. They watched as the security man opened it and spoke to some people. They could hear two male voices.

"Efyon, who is that?" Rhoda shouted.

"Madam, nah one pastor with one man here," Efyon called back. Then he paused to ask the man's name. "E say him name nah Eric, madam. Madam former driver."

"Eric? Who is Eric?" Rhoda asked, turning to Omerie.

"Eric was the name of our former driver."

"Ehen...the one they said you..."

Omerie didn't wait for Rhoda to finish. "Yes, that's the one."

"Ah ah, but what is he doing here?"

Omerie shrugged. "Let him open the gate for them, please."

"Efyon, open the gate!" Rhoda shouted.

The security man opened the gate, and the two men entered the compound. Omerie immediately recognised Eric, but the other man was unfamiliar. As they walked toward the verandah, Omerie noticed Eric had lost weight. He looked very thin, like someone who hadn't eaten well in a while. His face was pale and lean, and his eyes looked sad.

When they were almost at the verandah, the other man greeted them.

"Good afternoon."

Eric quickly followed with his own greeting. "Good afternoon."

"Good afternoon. You are welcome," Rhoda replied before immediately asking, "How can we help you?"

"Ermm...madam, we are sorry for coming without informing you first," the man said hesitantly.

Omerie listened as Rhoda nodded and probed further. "Please, how did you even know this place?"

"Ermm...ma, my brother has brought madam here several times," he said, pointing to Eric.

Omerie looked at them but said nothing. Rhoda continued. "Ehn, I see. But how did you know she was here? We didn't tell anybody that she was coming here."

"Ermm...ma, please don't be angry. We asked one of madam's girls, who works at her sewing machine shop, and she told us."

Rhoda turned to Omerie. "Can you imagine those girls?" she said angrily.

"It's okay, it's okay," Omerie said calmly, touching her sister's arm to pacify her.

"You are welcome...ermm...please, what is your name?" Omerie asked.

"Ma, my name is Pastor Isaac, and of course, you already know my brother Eric. I hope you remember him; he used to drive for you, ma," he said, pointing at Eric again.

"Good afternoon, ma," Eric said again, this time directing his greeting to Omerie.

"Good afternoon, Eric. How are you?" Omerie asked.

"I am fine, ma," he replied softly, immediately looking downwards.

"You see, ma, we just came to see you and hopefully talk to you, ma," the Pastor said, directing his comment to Omerie.

"Is anything the matter?" Rhoda immediately asked. Omerie turned to look at her.

"Rhoda, please let us get them a seat first."

Rhoda looked at them suspiciously before calling to the security man.

"Efyon! Abeg bring two chairs come."

"Yes, ma," the security man said, rising from where he was sitting and rushing to get two chairs. Eric quickly went to help him. Once they brought the chairs and the men were seated, Omerie spoke.

"Please, what may we offer you?" Omerie asked.

"No, nothing, ma. We are okay," the Pastor replied.

"Nothing? Not even water, Pastor?"

"Don't worry, ma. We are fine."

"Okay."

"Ermm... ma, we don't want to waste your time, so we'll just tell you why we are here," the Pastor said, speaking directly to Omerie.

Omerie nodded while Rhoda sat back, just wanting them to get on with it.

"Ermm, you see, ma, I am here to support my brother. We have... I mean, he has come to apologise, ma."

"Apologise?" Omerie asked, looking confused.

"Yes, ma."

"Apologise for what?" She looked from the Pastor to Eric. They glanced at each other before the Pastor continued.

"Madam, if there is anything my brother did to cause any problems between you and Chief, please, ma, forgive him." At that point, Eric went on his knees. She noticed his eyes were teary, and he covered them with his fingers as he whispered, "Please forgive me." It was all he could say.

"Ah, no, no, no. Eric, stand up. Stand up," Omerie said almost commandingly. He remained on his knees. She stood and went over to him.

"Eric, stand up now," she said, trying to lift him up by his hand. Rhoda quickly stepped in.

"Please stand up. You know my sister is pregnant and should not be trying to lift you up."

He quickly stood up and raised his hand to steady her.

"Sorry, ma."

"Sister, sit down," Rhoda commanded.

"Let us all sit down," Omerie said.

"Eh, you first, sister," Rhoda said. They all waited for her to sit before they took their seats.

"I am sorry, ma. I didn't mean to trouble you today, ma," Eric apologised again.

"Eric, you have not troubled me, so don't worry. But I still don't know why you came to apologise. You didn't do anything wrong. So why are you here apologising?"

"Ma..." he hesitated. "You see..." He hesitated again and took a deep breath. The Pastor put a hand on his shoulder to encourage him. He took another deep breath and continued.

"I keep telling myself that if I had respected myself and just taken the food in a plastic container straight away that evening and gone home, then maybe all this would not have happened." He bent his head, tearing up again.

Omerie sighed, shaking her head.

"Well, then I should be saying, if I had respected myself and not offered you food in my house, then this wouldn't have happened."

"No, ma, I don't mean..."

"Eric, I don't know why you are carrying this guilt, ehn. Why are you carrying this guilt? You have not done anything wrong. Please don't worry yourself. There is nothing for me to forgive, so I don't know why you came to apologise."

There was silence for some time before the Pastor spoke.

"Ma, you see, my brother is a person who tries to maintain peace wherever he goes. So, if for any reason he feels he has caused unrest wherever he has been, he will not rest until it is resolved."

"It is not his fault at all. So, there is no need for him to worry, ehn. Eric! Eric!" Omerie called out to him. He raised his head slowly, his eyes now red from the tears.

"Eric, please, it is not your fault, okay? Okay?" She stared into his eyes, wanting him to believe her. He nodded and slowly wiped the tears that had rolled down his cheeks.

The Pastor was tapping him on the shoulder now, whispering words of encouragement. Omerie took that opportunity to look over to her sister. Rhoda was teary now as she looked at Eric. She was not someone who could watch another person shed tears. She was deeply touched by what she was seeing.

Omerie, however, was worried about Eric and how long he had been feeling this way. Is this why he looks so thin and pale, like he has been sick? She wondered how he was faring. Had he found a job yet? She wanted to ask but felt that was not a good time. There was silence now. Hmm…how should she change the topic? Should she ask them if they wanted anything to eat? Well, she could tell they would refuse. As she was still deliberating,

"Well, ma, ermm we must take our leave now," the Pastor said.

"Ah, so soon?" Rhoda spoke quickly.

"I was going to ask my girl to make some food for us. Please stay, let us all eat, ehn. Please."

"Ah," the Pastor laughed nervously. "That is very kind, ma. But we are fasting, ma."

"Fasting?"

"Yes, ma. You see, we have a programme in our church at the moment." The look on both women's faces made him continue.

"Yes, we are on a 21-day fast, ma."

That explains it, thought Omerie. He definitely looks like he hasn't eaten in days.

"Are you serious?" Omerie said.

The Pastor laughed again. "Yes, ma."

"Which church is this?" Omerie asked as she continued to look at Eric.

"It is called Christ Our Redeemer, ma," the Pastor replied. "We are not too far from Ughelli town, near the Military camp."

"Ah, okay. I have seen it," Rhoda said, turning to Omerie. "That is the church that Mama Victoria keeps inviting me to." She turned back to look at them. "My tailor," she clarified to avoid any confusion.

"Ah, we know Mama Victoria well, ma. She has a shop at Benawa Street, abi?"

"Yes, that is her," Rhoda continued her conversation with the Pastor.

Omerie could not help but look over at Eric, surprised he was staring at her, his eyes heavy from crying. He immediately looked away, turning his gaze back to the floor. Omerie could not help but wonder what was on his mind. If only she could ask him.

She heard the Pastor as he stood up, saying, "Okay, ma. Thank you so much, ma."

Eric was up too but now looking at Rhoda. "Thank you, ma, for having us." He lifted his hand, offering a handshake.

"No problem. Please come back anytime," Rhoda said as they shook hands.

Omerie got up too. Eric kept saying repeatedly, "Thank you, ma." Omerie kept nodding each time. They turned to leave, walking to the gate. Omerie watched as the Pastor started to pat Eric on his shoulder again, obviously to encourage him. She watched as they walked out through the gate and out of the compound.

Rhoda sighed as she took her seat. Omerie sat back down also; she could tell her sister was looking at her. She turned to her. "What are you thinking now?"

"It's just the whole thing. I really feel sorry for the driver shaa," her sister said.

"Eric," Omerie said, as if wanting her to know his name.

"Ah, sorry, Eric. Me I don't know him; he is your driver."

Omerie sighed, a bit irritated with her comment.

"At first, I was thinking he was sick. That is why he came here. Did you see the way he looked?" Rhoda continued.

"I don't think he would have come to meet me or try to find me if he was sick. I mean…" she hesitated, "why?" Without waiting for her sister to respond, "Anyway, it's because of the fasting that he looked like that."

"Uhmmm," Rhoda twisted her lips. "Well, his fasting must be different from his Pastor friend because his body didn't look like that shaa."

Omerie huffed at that point. "Abeg, let us forget about it. Let us talk about other things."

"Ah, no need to vex ooh. I was just saying what I observed, that is all," Rhoda said, lifting her hands as if in surrender.

"Well, we know he is going through something, and obviously it is not easy for him."

"Nawa ooh, the way you are talking about the driver, like he's your friend or your son."

"How can he be my son? He is only 10 years younger than me," Omerie said, almost angry.

"Ah, why are you angry all of a sudden?"

Omerie didn't respond but sighed with a hand covering her eyes.

"Sister, is everything alright?" Rhoda asked, now a bit concerned.

"Everything is fine."

"Okay," Rhoda stood up. "I will go and start making the Coconut rice. Do you want it with stew?"

"Ermm…wait…" Omerie paused. "Are you making for yourself too?"

"Ermm…maybe, but I think I want to eat Ogwo and starch with my husband tonight."

"You mean you want to cook Ogwo soup today, too?" Omerie asked, surprised.

"Yes, of course naah. You know how my husband loves Ogwo soup," her sister smiled.

Urhobo men and Ogwo soup, Omerie thought.

"Let me come and help you." Omerie rose slowly from the chair.

"No, no, no. Sit down...I don't need any help. Oke is there and she can help me. You just relax. I will tell you when the food is ready." She said as she immediately walked into the house, not waiting for her to follow.

Omerie sighed and sat back down. Why her sister keeps treating her like an old woman, she will never know. She is only pregnant. Granted, she is 55 and pregnant, but she doesn't even look 55. She relaxed back in the suspicious chair, her mind going back to all that had just happened. She was sad to see Eric so unhappy and in tears. She had never seen a man in so many tears; it took her by surprise. She was always used to him smiling and being of good cheer in Chief's compound. He was always so helpful to her and was always there whenever she needed something done quickly.

She shook her head. She must see him again. Maybe find out about his church and where he lives. She could go and visit him, just to check that he is okay.

But why do you care? A tiny little thought crossed her mind. Good question—why does she care? She shrugged her shoulders. Well, it is her nature to care.

She started to rock the chair back and forth again, and the squeaky sound returned.

Chapter 17

D arling!" Chief jolted from his thoughts when he heard Rume's voice as she entered the room. He was sitting by the window, a glass of brandy in one hand and the bottle in the other. He turned to look at her, watching as she paused, her gaze shifting from one hand to the other.

"Ah ah, Chief! You are drinking again!?" Rume said, concern lacing her voice.

"This?" He raised the glass. "This small thing?" He took a sip, swirled it between his teeth, and swallowed.

"Chief, this is exactly what you said yesterday."

"That was yesterday. This is today." He watched as Rume shook her head; disappointment written all over her face. He took another sip, then glanced at her standing there, one hand on her waist and a frown on her face.

There's something about this woman, he thought to himself. What is it? Her beauty. Yes, it's her beauty. He had married a woman too beautiful to ignore. This woman was just too fine. He thought again, taking another sip of brandy, swallowing loudly.

"Chief, is everything okay?"

He nodded as he put the glass down.

"Anyway, your food is ready. Come, let's go and eat." She turned immediately, waiting for him to rise to his feet.

"My wife," he called to her. She turned to look back at him. "You look so beautiful today. Haba! My Princess. Just look at you." He looked her up and down. She smiled softly, clapping her hands together and placing one hand on her waist again.

"Chief, abeg, you are not serious. Abeg, come let us go and eat. The food is getting cold ooh."

"Leave the food. Oya, come. Come to me. Come and sit down." He tapped his thigh.

"Chief, let us do that later. Let us go and eat."

"I said come naah, come first," he beckoned again, waving her over and tapping his thigh. She paused for a moment, looking at him with uncertainty, then slowly walked toward him. He could see in her eyes that she was of two minds about it. As soon as she was close enough, he pulled her down to sit on his thigh.

"Ehh...yes. Is this not better?" he said, moving forward to kiss her.

"Ah, Chief, your mouth is smelling of brandy!" she exclaimed, rubbing her nose and trying to pull away. But he held her tightly.

"Is brandy not better than mouth odour?" he teased, pulling her close again to kiss her. She kept struggling until she finally loosened herself from his grip. She quickly stood up and walked away.

"Chief, you better behave yourself ooh, or there will be nothing for you tonight, or any night for that matter!" she said, kissing her teeth. He looked at her as she stood there, now frowning with her arms folded across her chest.

"Your food is ready. If you like, come and eat. If you like, continue drinking your brandy. Me, I'm going to the dining table." She stormed off, slamming the door behind her. Chief stared at the door for a while and then burst out laughing.

"Women," he exclaimed, shaking his head. He took the last sip of brandy in the glass. He stood up, then fell back on the chair. He tried again and fell back once more. On the third try, he managed to stand, gripping the handle of the chair for support.

"I am not drunk," he said to himself as he walked slowly to the door. He opened it and proceeded to the dining area. The smell of food hit him immediately. Rume was already seated, dishing some food onto a plate.

"Ah, I was already serving your food. I wasn't sure if you were coming out," she said. He pulled out the chair beside Rume and sat heavily in it. He watched as she finished dishing the soup and placed the plate in front of him.

"It's Egusi soup, your favourite," Rume said, smiling. She proceeded to serve him some pounded yam. He waited for her to pass him the bowl of water to wash his hands. He took a portion of the pounded yam and mixed it with some Egusi soup. He swallowed it and licked his fingers. As he reached for another handful, Rume interrupted.

"Chief, don't rush the food ooh," she said, laughing softly as she dished some food for herself and joined him.

"Ah, my wife, this food is too sweet. I will lick the plate when I finish. Wait and see!" He rushed another handful of pounded yam, mixing it with the soup and swallowing hungrily.

"Chief, please take it easy," she said, taking a portion of swallow herself.

He had never tasted such a delicious meal. Of all the women who had cooked for him, hers was the best. Why had he not known this before? As he rushed through the food, he coughed slightly. He felt Rume place her hand on his back, stroking it gently as she reached for a glass of water to offer him.

"Chief, I said you should slow down. Do you want to choke on pounded yam?"

"Uhmm... let me choke, abeg. Is it not sweet?" he laughed, continuing, but more slowly this time.

As they ate, there was a knock on the door. Chief raised his head and saw Musa peeping through the front door, which had been left slightly ajar for the cool afternoon breeze.

"Musa, what is it?" Chief asked, pausing from his meal.

"Sorry, Oga. Nah Pastor from church dey for gate. E say e wan see you, sir."

"Pastor? Which Pastor? Can't you see Chief is eating? Please tell them to come another time," Rume said, kissing her teeth.

"Ermm... no," Chief said, raising his hand to calm her. "Musa!"

"Yes, Oga."

"Open the gate."

"Yes, sir," Musa said, quickly running off to do as he was told.

"Chief, at least let them wait outside until you finish your food," Rume said, slightly annoyed.

He touched her arm lightly. "Let us eat; they will sit down and wait. Don't worry," he said. "Eat your food."

"Peace be unto this house," a voice called from the front door.

Chief did not recognise the voice. He raised his head to see who it was.

"Good afternoon, Chief. Long time."

It was the Senior Pastor from the local church.

"Ahh... Pastor! Welcome, welcome. Ahh... e don tey ooh," Chief said, quickly dipping his hands in the wash bowl to wash them.

The Senior Pastor stood at the entrance of the living room, waiting to be welcomed in. Chief reached for a napkin to dry his hands, pushed back his chair, and slowly got up to meet him.

"Please come inside, Pastor, come in," he said, watching as the Senior Pastor entered. They shook hands. "Sit down, sit down."

"Thank you, Chief."

The sound of clattering plates drew the Pastor's attention. Chief turned back to see Rume clearing the dishes with a frown on her face.

"You know Rume nah, Pastor," Chief said, pointing to her.

"Ah, yes, of course. Rume, how are you? Good afternoon," he said, smiling and waving at her.

"Good afternoon," she replied coldly before standing up and walking into the kitchen.

Chief, oblivious to her mood, turned back to the Senior Pastor. "Welcome."

"Thank you, Chief."

"This one that you came to see me today," Chief laughed softly, "I hope the church is well."

"Ah," Pastor laughed as well. "We are well ooh, Chief. We are well."

"Eh, okay, good. What should I offer you?"

"Ah, nothing, Chief. I am okay."

"Nothing keh? This one you are visiting me after how many months, you must drink something," Chief insisted. Before the Senior Pastor could protest, he called for the maid. "I know it is only soft drinks you church people drink," Chief chuckled. "What will you drink?"

"Well, Chief, if you insist, I will just have a bottle of Sprite if you have it."

"Yes, we have Sprite," Chief said, turning to the maid, who nodded. "Go and bring one Sprite for Pastor. And go to my room and bring me my bottle of brandy."

The maid hurried off but returned shortly with a Sprite and a bottle of Supermalt.

"Why did you bring Supermalt? I said brandy, not Supermalt. Did you not hear me?" Chief asked, irritated.

"Ermm..." The maid knelt slightly. "Madam said I should not bring the brandy, sir."

"Who?"

"Madam, sir," she said hesitantly.

Rume walked into the room at that moment, standing next to the maid.

"Chief, please drink the Supermalt. It will help digest the food," she said, taking the bottle opener from the maid and dismissing her. She opened the Supermalt first.

"Supermalt is good for your body ooh, Chief. Abi, am I wrong, Pastor?"

The Senior Pastor, looking slightly confused, nodded in agreement.

"Ehnn, let me open your Sprite," Rume continued, leaning forward to open the bottle. "Pastor, should I get you some food? We have Egusi soup and pounded yam," she said, gesturing toward the kitchen.

"Ah, no, no. I am fine, thank you," the Senior Pastor replied, glancing at Chief.

"Okay, no problem. Anyway, let me leave you people to discuss, ehn." Rume began to leave but paused. "Chief, please try not to stay too long ooh. You know the doctor said you need your siesta."

Chief nodded, smiling as he watched her walk away. He turned to the Senior Pastor, still smiling. "This my wife, she can really take care of me," he said, removing the Supermalt bottle cap.

"Pastor, I hope this is okay for you?" Chief said, pointing at the bottle of Sprite.

The Pastor nodded. "Okay, good. Please feel free ooh. Drink your Sprite."

Chief took a sip of the Supermalt, his expression betraying his dislike for the taste. But since Rume said it was good for him; he decided to give it another try. Smiling, he thought about how caring she was.

"Ermm, Chief," the Senior Pastor interrupted his thoughts. "First of all, I want to apologise for not visiting earlier. Things have been very busy. They put me in charge of this town and two others, so I've not had time to come and see you."

"Ah, Pastor, Pastor! You are a big man now. Two other towns?" Chief said, his smile widening. "Congratulations ooh!"

"Ermm... thank you, Chief. It's not easy."

"Well, that's why they promoted you. You can do the job very well."

"Ah, thank you, Chief."

"In fact, congratulations!" Chief raised his bottle of Supermalt in a toast.

"Thank you, Chief," the Pastor said again, raising his Sprite.

They both took a drink. There was silence for a few seconds. The Pastor cleared his throat before speaking.

"Erm, Chief, I came to see you about something," he said, leaning forward in the chair.

"Ehn, okay," Chief responded, setting down the bottle of Supermalt. The Pastor's voice had become serious, and Chief was curious as to why.

"Erm, Chief, please I don't want you to be annoyed with what I want to discuss with you."

"Ah, me? Annoyed? No ooh, Pastor, how can I be angry with you? You are our Pastor naah," Chief laughed softly. "Please, feel free."

The Pastor took a deep breath and continued, "Thank you, Chief. You see, I've known your family for many years."

"Yes, that is true. You're even family to us here in this town," Chief said, laughing softly.

The Pastor smiled a little, "Ah, thank God." He paused briefly. "Chief, as you know, there have been problems over the years, and you and I have always worked together to settle them because that is what we do."

195

Chief was silent now, unsure where the Senior Pastor was going with this conversation. He reached for the Supermalt, deciding to just hold the bottle to keep his hand busy.

"Erm... you see, Chief, your wife came to see me in my office a week ago."

"My wife?" Chief asked, confused.

"Yes, Chief, your wife... Omerie."

Chief nodded his head, "I see," he said, putting down the bottle of Supermalt.

"Chief, she came and narrated to me what happened here some time ago."

"Is that so?"

"Yes, Chief," the Pastor said, shifting further in the chair. "Please, Chief, no matter what has happened, let us try to settle it. There is nothing we cannot settle with God on our side."

Chief remained quiet, slowly placing his hand on his chin.

"You see, Chief, Omerie has been your wife for a long time. You can't believe she will sleep with another man?"

Chief laughed softly, reaching for the Supermalt and taking a gulp. He noticed the Senior Pastor starting to stutter as he continued. Chief raised his eyes to look at him; the Pastor was nervously looking back.

"You see... Chief... Omerie is a good woman and a good wife. You always used to say that God gave you His best in her, so you can't believe she would do what you're thinking or what people are saying she did."

"Is that so?"

"Yes, Chief, or do you not believe so?" Chief didn't respond, his hand firmly under his chin now.

"But Chief, how can Omerie do this thing to you?"

"So, wait..." Chief raised his hand, trying to stop him from speaking further. "You mean you know this because of what she told you, abi?"

"Yes. I mean, no. I know this because I've known this family for years now, and Omerie is a serious church member. There's no way she would do something like that."

"Ah, I see. A serious church member, abi?"

"Yes, Chief. She never misses our church services or prayer meetings."

"Ah, I see, your prayer meetings," Chief said sarcastically.

"Chief, see what God has done as a result; she's now pregnant with your child."

"Whose child?" Chief sat up straight, his tone slightly raised.

"Erm... your child, Chief. Isn't this what you've been praying for?"

"Now, look here, Pastor," Chief raised his voice, leaning forward. "I don't know what Omerie has discussed with you to come and do here today, but you have failed."

"Ah ah, Chief, what do you mean?"

"Did you hear me? You have failed!" Chief shouted.

"Chief, what are you talking about? I don't understand."

"Ehn, you don't understand?" He watched as the Pastor shook his head in confusion. "Listen, if you think you know Omerie very well as a serious church member, ehn, who prays very well in your church, then okay, you can marry her."

"What?"

"What is what? I said you can take her, marry her." Chief was on his feet now.

"Chief, please calm down... calm down."

"I said take her!" he shouted again. "Yes, take her, marry her. Since you know her so well, go and take her and keep her in that your church, you hear me?"

"Chief, what is all this, ehn? Please relax. I didn't mean to make you angry. I just came to see if we can settle this matter. Please sit down, let us talk about this."

"I am not sitting down to talk about anything! In fact, you can leave my house now."

"What! Chief! Leave your house?"

"I said leave my house now, or I will throw you out!" His voice became louder as he pointed to the door. He could hear footsteps, which he knew were Rume's.

"Chief, please, I am sorry. Don't be annoyed with me. Let's settle this matter, please."

"Chief, what is going on? Is everything alright?" Rume was by his side quickly, placing her hands around his shoulders.

"Look, tell this man to leave my house."

"Ah ah, Pastor, what happened? What is this?" she turned to look at the Pastor.

"Madam, I came in peace. Please tell Chief to calm down."

"Which peace? I said, which peace? You came here to make trouble, but like I said to you, you have failed. Now you can leave!"

The Pastor stood up and began to walk towards the front door. As he pulled away the curtains, he turned back. "Please forgive me, Chief. I came in peace. If I offended you, then please forgive me."

"Get out, my friend!" he said, kissing his teeth.

"Please leave, Pastor," Rume added in annoyance too. The Pastor glanced over at her, surprised by her outburst, but said nothing as he left.

"Nonsense Pastor! These people will not mind their business!" Chief sat down furiously, grabbing his Supermalt and drinking it fast like he was thirsty.

"Chief, please calm down," Rume said as she sat next to him. "You know your blood pressure, please calm down, eh?"

"I'm fine. At least he is gone now, stupid Pastor," he hissed again, breathing heavily.

"But what did he say that got you so angry?"

"My dear, please don't worry yourself. It's not important." He watched as Rume paused, glancing over at the front door. He didn't want to get her annoyed by telling her the Pastor came to talk about Omerie.

"Okay, well, Chief, please go and rest now. Let me take you to your room, eh?" she said, pulling him by the arm softly.

"You will come with me?" His anger subsided a little.

"Ooooh, Chief, are you still thinking about that?"

"Why should I not think about that, eh? Are you not my beautiful wife?" He playfully pinched her cheek as he drew her to him. He was now immediately interested in something else.

"Chief, stop now," she tried to pull away.

"Let's go inside," he said, almost pleading.

"Chief, you will not let me rest!" She pushed away from him. He stood up immediately after her. "Look, you know that money I promised you, eh? I will double it."

He watched as Rume paused. "Really! You will double it, Chief?"

"Of course. Let us go to my room," he urged her forward, guiding her towards the room.

"Chief, you must give me double as you said ooh."

"Ah ah, Rume, don't you trust me anymore?" he said as he urged her quickly toward the door. He waited as she opened the door, and he urged her in. He stopped for a moment to call the maid and told her he did not want to be disturbed for the rest of the day. He walked in, closing the door behind him and locking it.

Chapter 18

"**R**ume! Rume!"

Rume jerked as she felt a hand on her shoulder. She opened her eyes, realising she had fallen asleep outside Mama Omote's house, waiting for her to return home.

"Ma, ah," she managed to say, wiping her hand over her face and stretching. The chair she had fallen asleep on was hard. She got up slowly and rubbed her bottom a little.

"Ah, sorry ooh," she saw Mama Omote looking at her strangely. "You are here?"

"Yes, Ma," she yawned and then hissed.

"How long have you been waiting?"

Rume hissed again, tired. "I don't even know."

"Eyaa, sorry. Did you come with public transport?"

"Yes, ma. When I got here, I saw the door was locked."

"Yes, I went to the next town. I didn't know you were coming today, and my girl is not around."

"Sorry, ma."

"Come, let me open the door for us to enter quickly, eh? Sorry," Mama Omote rushed to open the door. "But I didn't know you were coming."

She opened the door to the house, and they both walked in. Rume watched as Mama Omote rushed to clear some clothes off the chairs in the living room and put them on a table next to a sewing machine. Rume, pushing the chair cushion aside, quickly sat down. She watched again as Mama Omote rushed inside to the kitchen. "Let me get you some cold water," she heard her say.

Rume took the opportunity to look around the living room. It was not as tidy as she was used to seeing, but she hadn't been to

Mama Omote's house in a long time. She sat next to the table with the sewing machine. It was quite a large sewing machine, with clothes and some materials on the sides of the table and on top of the machine.

"Ehn... cold water?" Mama Omote came back in with a glass of cold water.

"Yes, thank you, ma". Rume took a sip. "Ah, Ma, are you now a tailor?"

Mama Omote glanced over at the machine. "Oh, the sewing machine?" She walked over to clear the clothes off the machine. "I said let me start doing something ooh."

"You must have a lot of customers with all these materials," she said, pointing at the fabrics.

"Well, we are trying ooh," she brushed her hand through the fabrics and pushed them aside to clear space on the table. She walked and sat down opposite Rume. Rume took another sip of cold water. She could see Mama Omote watching her with a puzzled look on her face, no doubt wondering why she had come without informing her beforehand. She placed the glass down. "Thank you, ma."

Mama Omote nodded. "Ah, no problem, my dear."

"Ma, sorry ooh, I had to come and see you immediately."

"Ehn, I hope everything is alright."

"Ermm..." She took a deep breath. "I don't even know."

"Ah ah, what has happened?"

"Well, I don't know if it's a problem. You see, I did exactly what you told me to do."

"Okay, ehn..." Mama Omote said, waiting for her to continue.

"Ehn... well, his first wife is now out of the house, and I have now moved into Chief's main quarters."

"Good. Very good."

"Yes, Aunty," she nodded in agreement. "I get anything I want now."

Mama Omote laughed. "You mean all the attention and money, abi?"

"Yes ooh," she leaned forward on her chair. "I don't even have to ask for the money, he just looks for any chance to give it to me."

Mama Omote laughed loudly this time.

"Mama, I'm now the madam of the house, just like when I first married him," she smiled with satisfaction. "He does whatever I say."

"Very good, yes! Did I not tell you?" Mama Omote responded again.

Rume nodded in agreement.

"Ehn, so what is the problem?" Mama Omote went on to ask.

"Ermm, Ma, the thing is, my husband has just become a mumu *(an idiot)*. Like, he doesn't have sense at all; he just drinks every day. He doesn't even go to his office anymore," she said, shaking her head. "...and he keeps...he keeps..." she hesitated, ashamed to say it out loud.

"What? What does he keep doing?"

Rume shifted uncomfortably in her chair. "He keeps... wanting to... wanting to sleep with me all the time, ma," she finally said, frowning and putting her head down. Mama Omote burst out laughing. Rume watched, a little bit annoyed. Why is she laughing? Rume thought. It was not funny to her at all.

"Ah, ma, this is serious ooh," she said, turning her face away. Mama Omote stopped laughing, and Rume refused to look at her.

"Rume, wait, I don't understand. Is he not your husband?"

"Ah ah, so? Is that why he won't let me rest?" she said, irritation in her tone. "It's too much, every day, every day, sometimes two or three times a day. What is it!? We are too old for this kind of thing!" She could hear Mama Omote chuckling, and she hissed.

"Ah, ma, this is a serious matter ooh. Please, you must do something." She watched as Mama Omote paused, her expression changing.

"What do you want me to do now, ehn? You said you wanted him to love you, for his attention to be only on you. Did you not get what you wanted?"

"Yes, I said that."

"Okay. So, you were given what you asked for. Is it not so?"

Rume frowned now. "Ma, but he is not supposed to be a mumu now; he drinks all the time. Even the doctor has warned that if he doesn't stop soon, it will damage his liver, and to make matters worse, his business is not going well. He doesn't care; he doesn't even go to the office." She waited for Mama Omote to say something, but she remained quiet. "Ma, please, you have to do something. Please, you have to."

"I don't even understand why you think he's a mumu?"

"Hmmm... he just laughs anyhow; he plays around like a small child. I mean, he's a Chief, and he just behaves and talks like a nobody... like he has no sense."

"Ehhnnn."

"Yes ooh. It's just terrible, ma. Very disgraceful."

Mama Omote shook her head. "Well, Rume, I'm sorry, there's nothing I can do here ooh."

Rume's eyes went wide open.

"I cannot do anything."

"Ah, no, ma, you can do something. You are Mama Omote. I've known you for years; there's nothing you can't find. You can find something, there must be something you can do for me."

"Like what? To do what?"

"Ah, to stop him from drinking and for him to face his work. I can manage the... the other thing," she was still too uncomfortable saying it. She watched as Mama Omote shook her head, putting both hands over her thighs and looking at her intently now. "Rume, you remember when you came to me, I asked you what you wanted to happen, abi?"

"Yes, ma."

"Good. I told you to be sure, that you cannot change your mind once it's done. Is that not so?"

"Ah, ma, I don't remember that ooh," she said, looking away and scratching her head.

"You don't remember? You were sitting on the same chair, and I was looking at you because it was a serious question."

Rume shook her head, signifying she did not remember it happening.

"Well, you can shake your head from now until tomorrow. All I know is that I told you, and I cannot do anything to help you," she said, relaxing back in her chair.

No, no, this is not true, Rume thought to herself. *There must be something Mama Omote can do to change this.* Rume stood up, went over, and kneeled beside Mama Omote. Tears began to form in her eyes now.

"Please, ma, please help me. I know you can help me, please. Please do something. There must be something you can give me. I am begging you."

"You are not hearing me, my daughter. I cannot help you. There is nothing I can give now. I am sorry." Rume kept pleading, her head resting on the arms of the chair beside Mama Omote, crying bitterly now. Mama Omote put her hands over her and stroked her back gently to console her.

"My dear, stop crying. You see, this is not bad at all. You will not lose Chief. Just go home, hide every bottle of alcohol in the house. You can now start going to the office and make sure everything is working fine."

"That is not what I want, ma. You must give me something."

"I don't know why you don't believe me! Have I ever told you this before?"

Rume refused to respond and continued to cry.

"Come sef, are you not a woman? The things I just asked you to do, can't you do them? Ah ah, so many women are doing it in their husbands' houses. Abeg, stop crying, there's nothing I can do now." Mama Omote stood up and walked over to the table with the sewing machine. She began to neatly fold the fabrics and place them on the chair. Just then, there was a knock on the door.

"Ah, who is it now?" The door was open, but there was a curtain between them. Rume immediately stood up and wiped the tears from her face. "Go to the bathroom," Mama Omote said. She quickly rushed away while Mama Omote moved to the door to see who it was.

In the bathroom, there was a mirror above the sink. Rume stood in front of the mirror, staring at herself. Her eyes were swollen and bloodshot now. She quickly splashed cold water over her face a few times, then wiped her face with her wrapper. She raised her face up to the mirror again. Unfortunately, the cold water had done little to help with the redness or the swelling of her eyes.

What was she going to do? She could only hope the knock wasn't for a visitor.

She came out of the bathroom and slowly walked toward the living room, listening for voices. It was certainly a visitor, a woman. She listened carefully to what they were saying, it was a client who had come for her fabric. Rume paused. How was she going to get out of here? This woman couldn't see her like this; she would surely know she had been crying.

As she stood there, a thought came to her, yes, she thought. She lifted her wrapper over her eyes and walked quickly into the living room.

"Ma, the fly has come out, but the eye is really bad ooh. It's now red sef," she interrupted them.

Mama Omote paused for a moment but then understood what she was trying to do. "Ah, sorry my dear. At least it has come out of the eye."

"Yes, ma. I need to go to the chemist quickly so they can give me something to treat the eye, ma," she said, picking up her handbag with one hand while covering her eyes with the other. "Ma, I will come and see you another time," she said, putting on a small fake smile as she rushed out, not even waiting for a response from Mama Omote.

As she walked out of the house and took a few steps away, she carefully tied her wrapper properly around her waist, placing her handbag over her shoulder. She slowed her pace now, her face turning into one of sadness as she processed everything that had happened. Wait, she thought, what just happened at Mama Omote's house? Did she just leave Mama Omote's house with nothing? She had hurried there, thinking Mama Omote was going to give her something. In fact, she was sure Mama Omote would have given her something to take back today to help with the situation. She stopped walking for a second. What would she do now? She shook her head and sighed. There has to be another way, she thought. Well, if Mama Omote won't help, then she'll go to someone else. Mama Omote is not the only Prophetess in the whole state. Yes, she will speak to her friend and find somebody who can help her.

The journey back home didn't feel like two hours, as her mind strategised how she would solve the situation without Mama Omote's help. Upon arriving at the compound, the gate was locked. She knocked on it.

"Musa! Musa!" she called out.

"Yes, Madam," she heard him as he ran toward the gate to open it.

"Why did you lock the gate? It's only 5 o'clock, eh?"

"Madam, thank God say you don come ooh, something dey happen."

"Abeg, open the gate so I can enter!" she shouted, hissing.

"Sorry madam," Musa said as he unlocked the gate, and she walked in. She wasn't interested in what he was saying. She walked quickly, heading towards Chief's quarters. As she approached, she noticed quite a few people gathered outside. There was a man who looked behind when he heard her footsteps. She stared at his face, then stopped and froze. No, it can't be, it cannot be him. His facial features had changed slightly, but she knew—it was him.

"Richard! Richard!" she paused for a second. "What are you doing here?"

He turned his gaze, looking down. She snapped back to reality and then saw it, there were three men kneeling over Chief. His body was on the floor, and the men were trying to lift him up.

"Where is the car? We need to take him to the hospital now!" someone shouted.

Rume dropped her bag and ran over, pushing between the men. "Chief! Chief!" she called out, panic rising in her voice. "No, no!" She reached for his cheeks. "Chief, can you hear me? Chief!" she cried out again. He didn't respond. She dropped to her knees, leaning forward; she pressed her ear to his chest to listen for a heartbeat.

"Madam, please move away, let us take him to the hospital." The men pushed her away as the driver brought the car.

"Chief, please answer me! My husband, please answer me!" Rume cried, tears running down her face. She turned and looked at Richard, rushing to him, grabbing hold of his shirt.

"What have you done to my husband, ehnn?" She shouted at him, her voice shaking with emotion.

Richard tried to pull her hands away from his shirt.

"I said, what did you do, Richard?" she screamed as the tears flowed down her face.

"I didn't do anything, Rume. We saw him like this. Please, leave my shirt," Richard said, still trying to pull her hand away from it.

"You're lying! What did you say to him, ehn?"

"Madam, leave him, he didn't do anything."

She turned to look at the man standing next to them. She recognised him but couldn't remember where. Her eyes followed the men as they tried to get Chief into the car. She quickly released Richard's shirt and rushed over.

"Chief, please answer me!"

"Rume, leave him, let us take him to the hospital," she recognised the voice pleading with her. It was Alfred, Chief's closest friend.

"Alfred, you're here! What happened, eh? What happened to my husband?"

"Let us take him to the hospital first, please." Alfred turned away from her to make sure Chief was now in the car. "Let's go quickly," he said.

She rushed to the front seat. "I'm going with my husband." Alfred got into the back with the other man, whom Rume now remembered as one of the elders in the town. Chief's body was at the back, being held by these two men. Rume reached out to stroke his face. It was still warm, but his breathing was very slow.

"My husband, please don't leave me. I'm sorry." She couldn't hold back the tears; they ran freely down her face.

"He will not die, don't think bad things. Let us get him to the hospital. Oya, driver, fast, fast!" She heard Alfred say.

She hadn't noticed they had already left the compound. As the driver sped as fast as he could, Rume held Chief's hand, her heart filled with dread. She couldn't help but wonder, had Chief had a chance to speak with Richard? But why was Richard at the compound? Why today? Why now?

Chapter 19

Onome watched as the security man opened the gate to her Aunty Rhoda's compound. Pastor Maxwell stepped in first, and she followed behind. It had been a few weeks since the incident with her father, who was still in the hospital. Aunty Omerie wasn't allowed near Chief by her mother's instructions, so Onome was the one who reported back to her, sneaking from the house to the hospital and then to her aunt's house to give a progress report.

Lost in thought, Onome didn't realise how fast Pastor Maxwell was walking, so she quickened her pace to keep up. Over the last few weeks, Pastor Maxwell had become a dear friend to the family. He was very close to Chief and had been deeply disturbed when he learned about his hospitalisation. He visited as often as possible, sometimes even spending the night praying for Chief's recovery. Earlier today, he and the Senior Pastor had gone to visit.

Onome recalled arriving at the hospital and seeing them speaking with the doctor. She assumed they were inquiring about her father's condition. Pastor Maxwell acknowledged her with a nod before continuing to listen to the doctor. Onome had decided not to join them and had walked straight to her father's hospital room. She had brought some food, hoping she could feed him once he woke up.

As she approached the door, a nurse was just coming out. Upon seeing Onome, the nurse quickly shut the door behind her.

"Ah, good afternoon," the nurse greeted.

"Good afternoon," Onome responded.

"You're one of Chief's daughters, right?" The nurse asked, standing by the door with her hand on the handle. Onome nodded.

"I see you brought food for Chief again today," the nurse continued, stretching out her hand to take the bag. Onome instinctively pulled it back.

"No, don't worry. I'll take it inside myself," Onome said, moving away slightly and holding the bag close.

"Erm... sorry, the doctor isn't allowing anyone to see him at the moment."

"But why? Is everything okay?"

"Erm... yes. The doctor just wants Chief to rest. Visitors come every day and make him weak, so the doctor said he needs a few days of rest."

Onome paused for a moment, taking in what the nurse said. "Okay," she finally said, her voice low. The nurse reached for the bag again, and Onome reluctantly handed it over.

"I'll make sure we give it to him right away, as we're serving the afternoon meal now," the nurse said with a reassuring smile.

"Okay," Onome murmured, feeling the disappointment wash over her.

The nurse seemed to notice her mood and gently touched her shoulder. "Don't worry, okay? Chief will be fine. He's doing well."

"Okay," Onome replied, hoping the nurse would leave so she could sneak into the room. She hadn't been able to see her father alone yet; there were always three or four people in the room when she visited, and she was always kept at the back. After observing the visiting hours, she had figured out when the room would be empty, right before lunchtime. She had prepared Egusi soup and pounded yam, just like her father used to enjoy. She remembered how he would praise her cooking, and it made her feel warm inside.

But now, with the door closed to her, she felt defeated.

"He's fine, don't worry. You can try again tomorrow, and I'll ask the doctor for you, okay?" the nurse said, patting her shoulder.

Since she wasn't going to see him now, Onome decided to visit Aunty Omerie to give her an update. As she walked away, she heard her name and knew exactly who it was. She had spoken to him a few times at the hospital and during his visits to the compound. Pastor Maxwell approached her, his face filled with concern. Onome saw his hand rise as if to touch her shoulder, but he seemed to change his mind at the last moment.

"Good afternoon, Pastor Maxwell."

"Good afternoon, Onome. How are you? Were you able to see him?" His voice held a note of genuine concern.

"Erm... no," she said, the disappointment evident in her tone. "They said he needs to rest for a few days."

"Yes, they told us the same thing," Pastor Maxwell replied, his brow furrowing slightly. "But I thought it was just because we're not part of the family."

They stood in silence for a few moments, both feeling the weight of the situation.

"So... how are you feeling? We haven't seen you at church for a while. Are you alright?" Pastor Maxwell asked, his tone shifting to one of deeper concern.

Onome was surprised that Pastor Maxwell had noticed her absence from church. She hadn't had time to attend lately; her mother had been acting strangely over the past few weeks, and they had even called a doctor to check on her. Onome had stayed home to make sure her mother was okay.

"I haven't had any time to come," she said softly.

"I understand," Pastor Maxwell replied. "We've been praying for your family. We're believing that all will be well, okay?"

Onome nodded, but a wave of sadness hit her suddenly, and she could feel tears beginning to well up in her eyes. Just then, the Senior Pastor appeared, joining them in the hallway.

"Ah, Onome, how are you, my dear?" he asked warmly.

"Good afternoon, sir. I'm fine, sir." she replied, though her voice wavered as the tears began to disappear.

"Sorry, eh, it is well. Your father will be alright, you hear?" Senior Pastor said, his tone full of reassurance.

Onome nodded again, not trusting herself to speak, fearing she might burst into uncontrollable tears. She listened to Senior Pastor as he spoke to Pastor Maxwell.

"Maxwell, let me go see one of the members in the other town. I'm already late," Senior Pastor said.

"Ah, okay. Do you want me to drop you, sir?" Pastor Maxwell asked.

"Oh no, it's not far, besides the road is very bad there. I'll see you later this evening, eh?"

"Okay, sir," Maxwell responded.

Senior Pastor placed his hand on Onome's shoulder before turning to leave. "It will be alright, my dear, you hear? Don't worry, eh. I'll come and see your mother in a few days, eh?"

"Yes, sir," Onome said, wiping away the tears that had started to fall.

"Goodbye, eh?" Senior Pastor added as he walked away.

Onome nodded silently, watching him go. But now the tears were no longer just welling up; they were falling, and she couldn't stop them. She quickly pressed her hands over her eyes, hoping to hide the tears.

Pastor Maxwell gently pulled her closer, wrapping his arms around her. He rested her head on his chest, and she began sobbing uncontrollably. "It's okay, don't worry," he whispered softly, shaking her gently as if she were a child. His chin rested on her plaited hair as he continued to whisper, "It is well."

For the first time, Onome didn't find him intimidating or distant. His voice was soothing, his embrace calming, and as the tears flowed, she began to feel a sense of peace. He continued to whisper reassuringly in her ear, "It's well."

She wasn't sure why she had burst into tears. Everyone kept saying her father would be fine, but she wasn't sure. She felt overwhelmed by the situation, especially with how things had been at the compound since her father had been hospitalised.

She had no idea how long they stood there in the hospital hallway. All she knew was that Pastor Maxwell had asked if he could take her home afterward. She told him she needed to see Aunty Omerie to update her on her father's progress, and he had insisted on coming along. Now, here they were, walking into the compound.

***

They were sitting outside Aunty Rhoda's house with Aunty Omerie, enjoying some goat meat pepper soup that she had insisted they have before leaving. Pastor Maxwell had refused at first, but Onome felt he didn't want to offend Aunty Omerie by turning down her food. Onome, on the other hand, was more than happy to enjoy a nice plate of pepper soup. It had been a long time since she'd had hot pepper soup, though she didn't expect it to be so spicy. Aunty Omerie had gone inside to get some bottles of cold water for them and was now walking back slowly.

"Ma, let me help you," Pastor Maxwell quickly dropped his plate and rushed to take the bottles from her. "Ma, please sit down. Don't worry about us; we're fine."

Onome watched as he helped Aunty Omerie to a chair. Once she was seated, he went back to pick up his plate of pepper soup. Onome observed him as he lowered his head and took a spoonful of the soup. He had been quiet since they left the hospital, not saying much during the car ride. All he did was ask for directions. This mood seemed to have carried into the compound. He must have a lot on his mind, she thought. He looked deep in thought still. She turned to look away from him, and just then, she noticed Aunty Omerie looking at her with a smile, rubbing her pregnant belly. Onome quickly lowered her face, staring at her bowl of pepper soup. They continued to eat in silence while Aunty Omerie watched them.

"Hmmm... this one you both aren't talking. It means the pepper soup is very delicious, abi?" Aunty Omerie joked.

"Ah, Ma, I can't complain at all," Pastor Maxwell chuckled, spooning his soup.

"Aunty, it's very nice," was all Onome could say, avoiding her gaze.

"Okay, good. I'm happy because I thought I put too much pepper."

"Ah, no, Ma. It's very nice," Pastor Maxwell said, wiping his nose stylishly. He looked at her and smiled. Onome couldn't help but smile back. They must have stared at each other for a while before he turned to Aunty Omerie.

"Ma, have they told you when you'll give birth?"

"Ah, my dear, very soon ooh."

They continued talking about how she was feeling. Onome used the opportunity to look at Pastor Maxwell. He smiled as he spoke about the baby, and she found herself smiling too. His teeth were white and straight, and when he smiled, his face softened, making him look even more handsome. He spoke with such care and kindness; she had never seen this side of him. Then, she stopped herself. What was she thinking? Why was she thinking about Pastor Maxwell like this? Was she developing feelings for him? Ah, no. Of course not. She adjusted herself in the chair. No, she must not think of him in that way. He was a kind and nice person, that's all. He is Prisca's man, even though he hasn't made his intentions known to her yet. But it's going to happen, she thought. Besides, it's Brother Michael she loved—or Michael, as he told her to call him. Michael hadn't been around at all. Apparently, he had gone back to his father's house in the city and hadn't returned. She heard Beatrice had visited him in the city, but there was still no news about their engagement or marriage. The clicking of plates brought her back to the present. Pastor Maxwell was packing his bowl now.

"I can take yours inside too. Have you finished?"

"Yes, but let me take them in. You're a guest; I'll take them in and wash them." She didn't wait for him to say anything before rushing to take away their plates. She left him to continue talking with Aunty Omerie. When she came back, he was standing, car keys in hand. They both looked up at her as she walked back outside.

"Pastor Maxwell is going ooh. I told him to please help me drop you at home."

"Oh... that's okay, I can go later with a motorbus."

"Motorbus keh? Pastor Maxwell said he can drop you."

"It's okay, I can drop you at home." He was looking at her now, his eyes soft.

"Okay, thank you." They both said their goodbyes to Aunty Omerie and took their leave.

The drive to their house was silent. He mentioned that the pepper soup was delicious, and she smiled as she remembered what he said to her aunt Omerie. Then, silence again. The drive to her house was surprisingly quick. She was thankful, as she wasn't sure what was on his mind. He said his goodbye and waved as he drove off. She watched the car as it slowly drove away, watching it turn onto the next street before she walked into the compound. Musa was sitting by the gate with his arms folded across his chest.

"Good evening, Oga Musa."

"Good evening ooh, welcome," he said, looking straight ahead, not acknowledging her. As she walked in, she noticed the guests sitting outside the verandah of her father's quarters. There were four men and two women, and her mother was with them. They turned to look at her as she was about to walk past, but she quickly turned her face away to focus on heading to her mother's quarters. Then she heard her name.

"Onome, please come."

Oh no, she thought. What is it now? Why is she being called? God only knows what they are discussing in that meeting. She walked toward the verandah. As she approached, she noticed her mother's sister was there, two of the men were village elders, and the other two, she had no idea who they were. She stepped onto the verandah and greeted everyone. Her mother's face was bowed down now, and Onome could see the tears as they dropped, noticing the drops on the floor. Oh God, let nothing bad have happened to her father.

"Onome," a voice interrupted her thoughts. "We have been waiting for you to come. Oya, sit down." Her aunty pointed to a chair beside her.

Onome stared at the chair, shaking her head. "Aunty, I want to stand," she said, too worried to sit.

"No, Onome, we want you to sit down, ehn. Oya, sit down here."

She still did not move. She turned to look at her mother, whose face was still bent low, tears still dropping.

"We want to tell you something important. Just sit down first, my daughter." one of the elders said

"Please, is it Papa? Is it Papa? Is he dead?" she asked, her voice shaking, tears welling up now.

"Oh no, no, my dear. Your father is fine. It's not about your father. Please, come and sit down."

214

Onome breathed a sigh of relief. She walked closer and sat in the chair next to her aunty.

"How are you, Onome?" one of the strangers spoke to her, with an anxious smile on his face. She could not help but look at him strangely.

"I'm fine, sir," she responded, wondering who he was. He was older, as old as her mother, she guessed.

One of the elders cleared his throat, preparing to speak. "Ermm... my daughter, there is a reason why we have called you here."

She nodded, her heart starting to beat again. Oh no, she thought. These men can't be here to talk about marriage, not when her father is in the hospital. How could her mother do this? This cannot be happening. She turned to look at her mother, who had raised her face now, staring straight ahead, looking at an empty space.

"My dear," she heard the elder say, trying to get her attention. "Please, look here."

"My dear, this is not easy for us to tell you," Her aunty reached out and gripped her hands tightly. Onome turned to look at her aunty, wondering what was going on. What ridiculous plans have they hatched now; she wondered.

"Onome, face him naah," her aunty said softly, signalling for her to look at the man speaking.'

She turned to look at the older man.

"My daughter, you see this man here," he pointed to the man who had smiled strangely and asked how she was. "The man is Mr. Richard Okoro from Eseri. He is a businessman from the city. Your mother knows him very well." At that point, her mother started to sob softly.

"Ermm... well... erm... you see this man here," he pointed to the man again. "Ehn... ehn... well, he said he is your father, and your mother has now confirmed it."

Onome looked at him, confused. What was he talking about? He must be confused. She looked at the man he was talking about. She noticed there was a serious look on his face now, and he was nodding at her. It seemed everyone was silent now, waiting for her to respond.

"Please, I don't understand," she managed to say. What is this about? Her mother's sobs were getting louder.

"Mama!" She got up now and walked over to her mother's side, kneeling beside her. "Mama, what is going on? Did you hear what Uncle just said?"

Her aunty started to pull at her hand, trying to get her to sit down.

"I don't want to sit down! What is happening here?" She turned to look at her mother. "Mama, what is going on?" she asked again, louder this time.

Her mother was still staring at the empty space, her eyes bloodshot and filled with tears. Onome reached out and held her arm. "Mama?" Rume turned slowly to look at her.

"Onome," she finally responded, her voice shaky.

"Yes, Mama." Onome watched as tears began to stream down her mother's cheeks.

"It's true. This man is your father."

Onome stared at her mother, her face frozen in shock and confusion.

"No, Mama." She rose from where she had been kneeling. "No! It cannot be. No!"

Those were the last words she heard herself say before everything went blank.

Chapter 20

Chief was lifted slowly from the bed and onto the wheelchair. Once he was carefully seated and the nurses were sure he was comfortable, the female nurse began to push the wheelchair out of the room. Chief took a deep breath as they passed through the hospital front doors. It was a sunny afternoon, and a sweet breeze brushed against his face.

No, he was not going home. This was his daily routine as instructed by the doctor. He was wheeled outside two to three times a week to spend some time outdoors. The doctor believed it would help with his recovery and prepare him to eventually go home.

Home. Chief thought about it with unease. He wasn't sure if he wanted to return to that house. It had been a month since he was admitted to the hospital. At first, he hadn't even known what had happened to him. He only remembered waking up to a crowd of people around his bed, strangers he didn't recognise. He later learned he had been unconscious for two weeks.

"Chief, is this place okay for you, sir?" the nurse asked, snapping him out of his thoughts. Chief looked around and noticed they were now under a tree.

"It is fine, my dear. Thank you."

The nurse smiled. "Sir, I will check on you every 20 minutes, okay?"

Chief nodded. She spread a cloth over his legs to keep him warm and placed a cushion for him to rest his head. She left briefly and returned with a small stool, a bottle of water, and a cup. She poured some water into the cup and set it on the stool.

"I hope this is okay, sir."

"It is fine, my dear. Thank you." As the nurse began to walk away, Chief remembered something.

"Eh, my dear..."

"Yes, sir?"

"What is the time?"

The nurse glanced at her watch. "It is past 2, sir."

He's late, Chief thought. He realised the nurse was still waiting.

"Okay... thank you, ehn."

Although he watched the nurse walk away, his thoughts were elsewhere. *He was late.* Chief's gaze shifted to the hospital gate, where he saw people walking in and out. *He must have been delayed*, he thought. He had sent his new driver on an important errand, and he should have been back by now.

He kept watching until he saw the gate swing open. It was an elderly man with a young girl. A few minutes later, Chief finally saw him.

"Mudiaga!" Chief called out as loudly as he could. When his new driver approached, he was sweating.

"Mudiaga, why are you late?" Chief asked.

"Oga, sorry. Madam send me to drop her mama for motor park."

"Which madam? Which mama?" Chief asked, confused.

"Madam Rume, sir. Her mama come from village, so she talk say make I drop her for motor park to take Motorbus go back village."

"Her mother came into town?"

"Yes, sir. In fact, she don dey there for three days, sir."

Chief paused, pondering what his mother-in-law was doing in the house. She hadn't even come to see him in the hospital. Imagine. A woman he always sent money to, for her upkeep. *In-laws! So selfish and greedy*, he thought.

"Emm...sir, no be small thing dey happen for the house ooh."

"Is that so? What did you hear? What is happening?"

"Oga, the maid tell me say some men come the house, some men from village. Say dem come see madam Rume," he paused.

"Ah, people from my village?"

"I no dey sure, sir. She say old people from village. Dem sit down for your verandah, dey hold meeting."

"Ehhnn. Are you serious?"

"Yes, sir. In fact, dem invite your pikin *(child)* ...emmm...Onome con join the meeting too. But the thing be say she no fit hear wetin dem discuss."

"Nothing at all? They did not hear a single word?"

"No, sir. Dem talk say dem send dem comot for house when di people come."

Chief took a deep breath, wondering what was happening in his house. As he pondered, his driver coughed slightly.

"Okay, you will go and find out more. You hear me?"

"Yes, sir."

"Somebody knows what is happening. Ermm...who do you talk to?" He thought for a moment. "Ah, yes!" he exclaimed. "Musa, the security man." He smiled. "Talk to the security man."

"Okay, sir."

"No. In fact, just bring him to see me, but don't let anybody know ooh."

"Ehenn, tell him I sent you, that he must come with you quick quick. You hear?"

"Yes, sir."

"Good. I must find out what they are hiding from me in that compound," he said. His driver nodded.

"Ehnnn, what about the other thing I asked you to check for me?"

"Hmmm.....oga, me I no know how to tell you this ooh." The driver scratched his head nervously.

"What do you mean?"

"Ah, oga, I dey fear to tell you ooh. You know say your body never strong."

"What sort of nonsense talk is that ehnn? Was it not me who sent you? Did I not give you money to go and find out for me?"

"Yes, sir," he replied nervously again.

"Ehnn, oya talk my friend," Chief said commandingly.

The driver hesitated, took a deep breath, and continued. "Emm, na true dem talk. She dey stay him house and she get belle." He paused, but Chief remained silent, waiting for him to continue.

"I speak to people, wen dey stay near am. Dem say dem don know am even before she marry you. Say na Chief Alfred house she been dey stay before dem con hear say she don marry. Say since she marry, dem don only see am for there two times."

Chief remained quiet.

"Oga?"

"Continue," Chief said.

"Dem say since she come back two months ago, say na Chief Alfred house she don dey stay."

"Did you see him?"

"Ermm...I see am, sir. Dem go dey play love even in front of him wife."

"I see." Chief paused for some time before asking, "Did they say if they knew if the baby is his?"

"Ehn? Sorry, sir. I no understand, sir."

"Is he the father of the baby? Na him get the pikin *(child)*?" Chief repeated in broken English.

"Emm...dat one shaa... dem no fit talk for sure. But dem say e no go surprise dem."

Chief was stroking his lips now; he took a deep breath. This was too hard to believe. So, it is true. Amaka, his wife, was having an affair. But how? When did this happen, and how come he never knew about it? To make matters worse, it was with his dear best friend, Alfred.

This was the nonsense Alfred came to tell him that fateful afternoon. Alfred had come to visit with two elders. Chief had welcomed Alfred cheerfully and even brought out a brand new bottle of brandy. Alfred had refused to drink, but the greedy elders were all too happy to fill their glasses.

Alfred had been quiet for a while. Chief had noticed he wasn't himself, that something was wrong. Chief joked about him having troubles, but Alfred didn't laugh the way he normally would. Instead, he signalled to one of the elders, who then sat up and began to speak.

They had come to discuss an important matter. They wanted things handled amicably and in peace. The elder mentioned Alfred had something to confess, and that was when Alfred spoke. He had been sleeping with Amaka.

At first, Chief thought it was a joke, but Alfred was serious. It had been going on for a while. Amaka had agreed to marry Chief just to spite Alfred for refusing to make her his second wife. But now Amaka was pregnant, and they both knew it. Alfred then claimed the baby was his.

Chief remembered standing up, slapping Alfred hard, and grabbing him by the neck. At that moment, all he could think of was killing him. The elders had stood, trying to stop Chief. Right then, he felt a sharp pain in his chest. He remembered grabbing his chest, struggling to breathe. The pain was sharp; his legs became weak. He dropped to the floor, still struggling to breathe. That was all he could remember. That was when they rushed him to the hospital.

Chief sighed now. Alfred wanted to claim that Amaka's pregnancy was his. They both knew that was a lie. But maybe not, with what Mudiaga had just told him, what if Alfred was telling the truth? He mentioned he was with Amaka before Chief married her. Well, he knew Amaka wasn't a virgin. She had told him the truth, and he hadn't cared about her past. He had focused on making sure she got pregnant quickly, which she did. Unfortunately, he couldn't take her to the hospital in Lagos to find out if the baby was a boy or a girl. That evening, she had cried bitterly, insisting she be allowed to go see her mother and that they could go to Lagos as soon as she returned. He agreed—after all, she was carrying his child.

But now, based on this report from his driver, how could he be sure that the baby she was carrying wasn't for his best friend, Alfred? He took a deep breath. Alfred, someone he had known since their school days. They had grown up together, their family houses close to each other. They had shared everything. How could Alfred do this to him?

He sighed again. No way, he thought. Alfred must answer in a big way. It is not over. "I will deal with him," he murmured.

"Sir, you say wetin?"

"Mudiaga!"

"Yes, sir."

"Did you also go to my wife's sister's place?"

"Yes, sir. Ah, I almost enter trouble there ooh. Ermm... madam sister almost finish me sef, sir."

"Ehnn...what did they say?"

"She say she no go come, sir."

"She said no?" Chief said softly.

"She say no, sir."

"I see." Chief took a deep breath. He had hoped for a different response from Omerie. He thought his being in the hospital would soften her heart.

"Oga, dat her sister shaa. I sure say na she dey prevent am. If not, your wife for come."

Chief nodded. Hmmm...Rhoda. Omerie's difficult and troublesome sister. Rhoda was never a fan of his. Even worse, she had stopped liking him years ago when he decided to marry his second wife. Since then, she had stopped coming to the compound and became one of the people who regularly encouraged Omerie to leave him.

"Mudiaga."

"Yes, sir."

"You will take me there."

"Sir, where you wan go, sir?"

"You will take me to my wife's sister's place."

He saw how the driver stared at him, confused and worried. He then crossed his hands behind him.

"Where is the car?"

"Oga, e dey for house. Make I go bring am?"

Chief paused to think. The doctor would not sign off for him to go out today. At the moment, it was too difficult for him to walk. His legs were still weak; he would need a wheelchair and a nurse. He paused. Well, he could arrange something with the doctor tomorrow. He was sure the doctor would be reluctant at first, but he had known him for a long time. He could talk to him in a way he would understand.

"Mudiaga, you will come with the car tomorrow by 11 o'clock in the morning."

"Yes, Sir. Okay, Sir."

"Make sure you are not late ooh."

"Ah, no Sir," he smiled, scratching his head. "Emm... Sir, wetin I go tell madam? Because she no go gree make I carry the motor ooh."

"Emm... that's true," Chief paused to think. "Okay..." Chief exclaimed, finally having an idea. "You will tell madam that you're taking it for servicing."

"Servicing, Sir?"

"Yes. Tell her that I normally service it every two months, and you need to make sure it's serviced and has petrol in case she needs to use it to pick me from the hospital when I'm discharged."

"Ermm... okay, oga. I go try. You know say madam naah..." he hesitated.

"Madam na wetin?" Chief asked.

"Nothing, Sir," Mudiaga said, looking down.

Chief could have finished the sentence for him, but instead, he took a deep breath. He was deep in thought again. He had to see Omerie. He couldn't believe how badly he had treated her. He couldn't believe he had kicked her out of the compound. For the life of him, he couldn't even remember why he had believed what was said about her.

Omerie had always been a good and faithful wife. She had always stood by his side. God, how would he face her now? Would she forgive him? She must hate him.

It was even worse that she was now living with her sister, Rhoda, who hated him with a passion. Would Rhoda even let him in? He sighed. Well, this was the bridge he had to cross. He must see Omerie; it was now more important than ever that he spoke to her.

Omerie had a soft heart, and if he begged her, she would forgive him. He just needed to figure out how to approach the meeting.

"Mudiaga."

"Yes, Sir."

"You can go now, ehn. I will see you tomorrow."

"Okay, Sir."

"Just make sure you are here by 11 o'clock ooh."

"Yes, Sir. No problem. I go dey here before 11 o'clock sef, dey wait for you."

"Good."

"Ehn... Sir, na which time you want make I bring oga Musa, Sir?"

"Ah, yes, Musa," Chief thought quickly. Today is Thursday. "Bring him on Sunday afternoon, ehn. I will give you some money tomorrow for your transport on Sunday."

"Oga, no wahala, Sir."

"Okay, I will see you tomorrow."

"Okay, Sir. Rest well, Sir."

"Thank you."

Chief watched as the driver walked quickly out of the hospital compound. He began stroking his chin again, thinking hard. He needed a convincing story to tell the doctor so they would let him leave the hospital with a nurse, for a short while.

Hmm... there's nothing money cannot do, he thought. All he had to do was promise the doctor a good amount. Besides, the doctor knew him well; most, if not all, of his children had been born in this very hospital.

He was thirsty now. He turned to look at the cup of water the nurse had left on the stool for him. A leaf had dropped into it, so he threw the water away. Fortunately, the bottle of water beside him was still cold. He poured himself a cupful and relaxed as he took a sip.

His thoughts turned to his dear friend, Alfred. *Hmm... Alfred*, whom he had helped to start a business, whom he had helped train some of his children. *Imagine! He doesn't know who he's dealing with.*

"I will deal with him in this town," Chief muttered to himself.

"Me, Chief Emmanuel Akpofure, in this town! I will show him," he said, taking another sip of water and shaking his head.

He looked at the cup. "So, this is what I have been reduced to, ehn? Just drinking water." He kissed his teeth and set the cup down.

A cool breeze swept through where he was sitting. Chief rested his head on the cushion the nurse had placed there for him; he began thinking and planning how he would deal with Alfred.

Chapter 21

Omerie was startled by the knock on the front door. She hadn't realised she had fallen asleep while watching another Nigerian movie her sister had left playing before leaving to go to her shop. She rubbed her hand over her face to wake herself up. The knock came again, and she called the maid, but Omerie knew she was outside washing some clothes. Slowly, Omerie stood up and made her way to the front door, which was locked. Unlocking and opening it, she was met by the security man, his face covered with sweat.

"Ah, madam, well done ooh. Good afternoon."

"Afternoon, Efyon. Wetin?"

"Madam, abeg no vex ooh. E get one man wey come with big motor for outside. E say e wan see you ma."

"Man with big motor? To see me?" Omerie repeated, puzzled.

"Yes ma. E say e know you well well, ma."

"Are you sure it is not my sister's visitor? Because I don't know anyone with a big car."

"Me, I ask am ma, but e say nah you, nah you e come see."

"What is his name?"

"E say e be Chief."

"Chief who?"

"E no tell me ma, e just say him be Chief. E get woman wey sit down for front seat sef."

"Ah ah," Omerie said, slightly confused. Who could this be? The only Chiefs she knew, *apart from her husband who was in the hospital,* were her husband's friends. None of her husband's friends knew where she was staying. Unless the girls at the shop had opened their big mouths again. She had warned them not to tell anyone where she was staying.

"Madam, make I tell am make e go?"

Omerie looked at the security man, unsure of what to say. They already knew she was here. If she refused to see them, it would be disrespectful, and she would not hear the end of it in this town. She took a deep breath. "Go and open the gate for them."

As he ran off to open it, she slowly walked out and sat on the rocking chair. She watched as the car slowly drove in. First, the front of the car appeared, then the full body. She recognised the white Volvo pulling into the compound. She leaned forward to see who was sitting inside the car. She froze. "No, it cannot be," she spoke out, covering her mouth in shock.

The Volvo parked in front of the house. The woman came out first. Omerie noticed she was wearing a nurse's uniform. The woman quickly walked to the back door. The driver, at the boot of the car, lifted out a wheelchair. He set it down as the nurse opened the back door. They both helped Chief out slowly and sat him in the wheelchair. Omerie leaned forward, her hand over her mouth to hide her gasp, a tiny tear forming in her eye. Chief was being wheeled towards her. She stood up, unsure of what to do. She hadn't seen him in months. He looked so lean and old now. Maybe it was his grey hair; he had gone completely grey, she thought.

She didn't know he had been discharged from the hospital. Onome hadn't mentioned it the last time she was here. Chief was looking at her now, his mouth slightly open. She realised he was looking down at her stomach. She looked down. Her pregnant stomach was much more visible in her Buba attire. She watched as the surprised look on his face turned into a warm smile. Her hand dropped to her stomach. She immediately sat down, turning away.

They wheeled him to the verandah. The greetings of "Good afternoon" rang out like a summer song. Omerie took a deep breath and turned around to answer them.

"Welcome," she said, looking at the driver and then at the nurse. The nurse first checked to ensure both wheels of the chair were steady. Her gaze shifted to Chief, who was now looking at her with something warm in his stare. She recognised this stare. He used to look at her this way when they were happy, in love, and he had eyes only for her.

"Welcome, Chief," she greeted him with a cold tone.

"Thank you." He turned to the driver and nurse. "Go and wait for me in the car."

He hasn't lost his commanding tone, she thought. They both nodded. The nurse first checked that the wheel was steady, and the chair pillow was carefully positioned at his back to give him some comfort.

"Is it okay, sir?" the nurse checked.

"Yes, my dear. Thank you." he smiled as he looked up at her.

Omerie looked away. She wasn't feeling jealous, just irritated. When she turned back again, the nurse had walked away, and Chief was just staring at her. They were silent for a few seconds. Omerie sighed.

"Chief, how are you?" she asked, honestly seeking to know how he was feeling.

He took a deep breath in and out. "I am fine."

She nodded. "When were you discharged from the hospital?"

He hesitated a bit before answering. "I have not been discharged."

"You have not been discharged?" she said, alarmed.

"No," he clasped his palms together.

"Then how were you able to leave the hospital? How..."

"Omerie, so you could not come to visit me in the hospital? Even after I sent my driver to visit you and beg you to come and see me, ehn?"

Omerie looked away, a slight frown coming over her face. How dare he ask such a question? How dare he? After the way he treated her; he practically disowned her as a wife and their unborn child. He never once asked how she was faring with the pregnancy. He never once cared. Now that he almost died, he had the audacity to summon her. How dare he?

Omerie turned to look at him now, the frown much more defined on her face. "Chief, are you really asking me that question?" Her tone was filled with anger. She kissed her teeth as she relaxed back in the chair, arms folded over her stomach. She stared at him angrily. He dropped his gaze now and took a deep breath. *What is he going to say now?* she wondered. He raised his head to look up at her again.

"Omerie, I know that I have done you wrong. I cannot believe that I did what I did. In fact, I do not even remember what happened that day."

"Oh, you cannot remember. So, this is your excuse, ehn?"

"Omerie, it is not an excuse. You see, I just cannot remember anything. I don't remember what I did."

"Hahaha... hmm," she laughed as she clapped her hands together.

"I am telling the truth," he said, almost pleading.

"I hear you," she lifted her hand up to stop him from speaking anymore. "It is okay." She turned her face to the side. Chief placed his hands on the wheels of the chair and rolled it to move closer.

"Chief, abeg," she raised her hand again signalling for him to stop and not come any closer.

He stopped. "Okay. Omerie, please just listen to me," he beckoned to her. She kept quiet, still looking to the side of her. Chief took a deep breath again, clasping his palms together.

"How did this happen to us?" She turned and almost barked at him but stopped. He continued speaking. "All because I wanted to have a son. My father told me that the family lineage would not be complete without a son. At first, I wanted to..." he took a deep breath. "I wanted to please my parents," he paused and shook his head. "But then I started to want it. What is a man without a son?" He put his head down now. "Why did God make you pregnant now? Why not all those years when we spent days and nights at the church begging him to give us a child? All I wanted was just one son. Was that too much for me to ask, ehn?" He raised his head now. She could tell from the corner of her eyes that his gaze was focused on her. She stayed silent still. *Now he wants answers?* She shook her head one more time. One son, now he has four girls. She sighed.

"Omerie," he called her softly. She still refused to look at him. "Omerie," he called again. There was something about his tone of voice that made her look at him. His eyes were filled with tears, and they were flowing down his cheeks. "I am sorry for all the pain I have caused you and our unborn child." He paused, looking down as the tears dropped onto his native attire. I don't know what came over me that day," he continued, his words heavy with remorse. "I don't know why I did what I did or why things have been happening the way they have. Please," his voice broke further, "please forgive me.

She had never seen him like this, not even in the good old days of their marriage. She knew right then that he was not lying; he was truly sorry. But can she forgive him? She had been through all these years, putting up with his crazed desire for a son, wife after wife, each time a female child, which made him even more crazed. His desire made him cold and unbearable. She had watched him as he became proud, making his desire less of a problem, making it a 'right', something he so rightly deserved. After all, she could not bear him a child, let alone a son. He became someone she did not recognise as the man she married, well, not until now. But can she trust him now? *It seems this incident may have weakened him and brought him to his senses. Maybe,* she thought.

"Sister, what is happening?" The sound of her sister's voice brought her back to reality. Rhoda was standing a few steps from them. Omerie had not heard the gate to the compound open or close. Rhoda was standing with her hand on her waist, eyes glaring at Chief. Omerie watched as Chief quickly wiped off the tear drops that lingered on his face before placing his hands on the wheels of the chair, to move away from Omerie.

Slightly turning to look at Rhoda. "Rhoda, good afternoon, how are you?" he said, immediately glancing away, his eyes looking down now. Rhoda's hands dropped from her waist as she recognised Chief. Omerie saw the look on her face: shocked and confused. Rhoda was quiet for a few seconds before she responded.

"Ah, ah, Brother Emmanuel, you have been discharged from hospital?" she said, her tone confused. Rhoda is the only one who has refused to call him Chief. She still referred to him as Brother since she met him years ago when Omerie was still dating him. Chief did not respond.

"Oke!" She called the housemaid. She called so loudly that Omerie felt the baby kick hard. Her voice must have woken the baby. She quickly rested her hand on her pregnant belly, stroking it. She called out to Oke again, much louder now. "Where is this girl?"

"Emm... Rhoda," Omerie said softly. "Please excuse us."

She watched as Rhoda glanced over at Chief and then at her. Just then, the housemaid came out, looking startled to see so many people in the compound.

"Take this inside," Rhoda said, handing the bags she was carrying to the maid. She gave them one more look, saying nothing, before walking behind the maid and disappearing into the house. Omerie kept her eyes on her sister and could tell she wasn't happy. She already knew they would have a lengthy conversation about this later.

Turning to Chief, Omerie noticed his gaze was fixed on her stomach. She was still stroking it absentmindedly but stopped when she caught him staring. That seemed to break his trance. He looked up at her now, his mouth slightly open as if he was about to say something, but then he shut it again.

Taking a deep breath, Omerie adjusted herself slightly in the rocking chair.

"Chief, I've heard what you have to say, but I don't think we can settle this matter today. I..."

"Ome, I know," he interrupted quickly. She noticed he had called her by his favourite short name for her, but she chose to ignore it. She had promised herself she wouldn't fall for his attempts to deceive her into thinking he actually cared.

"Ome, just think about what I said, ehn? Find it in your heart to forgive me, please."

She sighed deeply again.

"Ermm... how are you feeling?" he asked, his eyes drifting back to her stomach.

"I am fine."

"So, you're okay? No problems?" His eyes were on her now.

"No problems at all," she replied, turning away to avoid his gaze.

"That's very good, very good." He smiled. "I'll tell Mudiaga to be on standby in case you need anything."

"Ermm, Chief, that's not necessary. I'm fine."

"I know, Ome, but you never know when you might need something. He can come here, take you to the hospital, or anywhere you need to go."

She sighed again. "Chief, I'm fine. I don't need to go anywhere, and Rhoda is here if I need anything." Her irritation was clear now.

"Okay," he said, raising his hands in surrender. He cleared his throat. Omerie kept her eyes turned away, still avoiding his gaze.

"Ome?" he called softly. She couldn't help but turn to look at him. He was leaning forward in the wheelchair now.

"Emm... please, I want you to come visit me in the hospital... at least sometimes," he said, almost pleading.

She stared at him, and before she knew it, the words slipped from her lips.

"Okay, I will, Chief."

He leaned back, a small smile spreading across his face.

"Thank you," he said, clearly relieved. "Ermm... can I ask one last thing?"

"What is it?"

"Can I... can I touch your stomach?"

She stared at him, then looked down at her protruding stomach. Did he think her pregnancy was fake? Was this his way of confirming it? But could she deny him this? The child was his, after all. Could she really refuse?

She looked back at him, unable to find words, and simply nodded. His face lit up, smiling like an excited child who had just been given his favourite toy. He rolled his wheelchair closer, waiting as she shifted forward in her chair.

She watched as he placed his hand gently on her stomach, his smile widening. She couldn't help but smile too as she observed him. He must be thinking what she often thought that a child they both wanted so badly, one they had prayed for together, was finally coming.

If only he had waited. If only he had believed and continued in hope. But he had wanted a male child. Was he thinking and hoping it was a boy now?

Just then, he whispered softly, "Ogheneruona."

"Ogheneruona?" Omerie repeated. "You're already giving this child a name?"

Chief smiled again and nodded, pressing his hand gently on her stomach.

"God has done this," she said softly, repeating the name in English.

She smiled. She loved the name; it could be for a boy or a girl. Clearly, he didn't care which it was. He really had changed, she thought.

Omerie looked at him, a soft smile lingering on her lips. His eyes, however, were still fixed on her stomach. He was stroking it now, almost mesmerised. She couldn't help but notice the tenderness in his gaze. His eyes were teary.

Something had happened to him, she thought. She couldn't quite put her finger on it, but it felt like a veil had been lifted from his eyes.

She kept watching him as he gently stroked her stomach, quietly repeating the name over and over again.

"Sister!"

Omerie looked up and saw Rhoda standing at the front door, glaring at her. Chief quickly removed his hand, almost as though he'd been caught doing something wrong. Omerie couldn't help but notice how uncomfortable he always seemed whenever Rhoda was around.

"Oke has made some Jollof rice and chicken. There's also Egusi soup and swallow, if Brother wants to eat," Rhoda said. Her tone dropped slightly at the last part, and Omerie didn't miss the way she rolled her eyes.

She turned to look at Chief, but he was already shaking his head.

"No, thank you. I'm fine. In fact..." He adjusted himself on the wheelchair and looked towards the car. "I need to go back to the hospital."

He was already signalling the driver, his voice too low to carry.

"Mudiaga!"

Omerie noticed how weak his voice sounded.

"Where is the driver? Mudiaga!" Rhoda called out in a loud tone.

"Ma!" The driver's voice rang out as he hurried towards them, with the nurse following closely behind.

"Oga." The driver bowed slightly as he reached them.

"I'm ready to go now," Chief said firmly.

"Yes, sir."

Omerie watched as the driver carefully wheeled him off the verandah. The nurse also stepped in to assist.

Everything was moving so fast. Omerie wanted to say something, anything, but the words wouldn't come. She watched as the driver wheeled him toward the car, parked just a short distance away. The driver helped Chief into the car. Omerie stood now, with Rhoda moving to stand beside her.

Chief didn't look back. Omerie suspected it was because Rhoda was there.

Her chest tightened. There was still so much she wanted to ask him, and she hated that Rhoda had interrupted. She watched as the nurse settled into the front seat, and the driver hurried in to start the car. Chief was now seated in the back, but she couldn't see him clearly.

The gate opened. The driver reversed slowly, and just as the car started to roll out, Omerie saw him. He was looking at her.

She raised her hand hesitantly and waved.

He raised his hand too but quickly turned away as the car drove out of the compound.

Tears welled up in Omerie's eyes, though she didn't know why.

Behind her, Rhoda kissed her teeth and walked into the house. Omerie was surprised she didn't say anything. She had expected her sister to bombard her with questions, but for once, she was grateful for the silence.

She was tired.

Her emotions were all over the place, she needed time to make sense of them.

Sinking back into the rocking chair, she let its steady rhythm calm her. As it rocked forward and backward, her mind replayed the meeting with Chief. The surprise of seeing him here. The shock of how frail he looked. She still couldn't believe he had come to visit her when he hadn't even been discharged yet.

He looked so lean, so aged.

And even though she was still angry with him, she had to admit, she was worried.

Despite his attempts to sound strong with his commanding tone, Omerie had seen through it. She knew he was weak. They had told her what the doctor said about his heart, and the truth was, she was deeply thankful that he was still alive.

Just then, Oke appeared on the verandah.

"Ma, madam say make I ask you wetin you wan chop?"

"I will eat Jollof rice."

"Okay, ma. Make I bring am here?"

"Yes, bring it outside."

"Okay, ma."

She watched as Oke disappeared inside. She continued to rock the chair, still pondering some of Chief's words. There were still some things she was unsure of. So, if she decided to forgive him, what would he expect her to do? Come back to the house? That compound? What about Rume? Would she be there? Could she cope with Rume in the compound, with all the lies she had told and the trouble she had caused? It was especially important now that she was carrying their child. Rume was evil, and she could not live under the same roof with that woman. Chief must tell her what decision he intended to make concerning that horrible woman.

She had left the compound that day resolute that she'd had enough. She had tried her best all these years to put up with his selfish desires and unrealistic quest for a son. His plea today seemed to show he had really changed. But had he, really? There were times when he would speak to her privately, telling her he still cared about her. He would shower her with little gifts, but all that would fade away once he entered that phase where he felt overwhelmed by his desires again, making him unbearable.

She took a deep breath. Well, it would not be easy for him this time. They had a lot to discuss if she was going to forgive him. Her forgiveness would have to come with some requirements.

The tables had turned, and she intended to use that to her advantage. She would go and visit him in the hospital soon.

The baby was kicking now. Omerie patted her stomach. "Wait, my dear. Food is coming, ehn." Just then, Oke returned with a tray carrying a plate of Jollof rice and chicken. She noticed there was a separate plate with some plantain. Rhoda knew how much she loved plantain. She could not help but smile. She watched as Oke settled the tray on the wide stool close to her.

Chapter 22

Onome heard the bedroom door open again. From the footsteps, she could tell it was Rukevwe. Onome was lying on the bed, facing the wall. This was the third time Rukevwe had come into the room today to speak to her about something; first it was breakfast, then lunch, and now this. Onome wondered what it was this time.

It had been two weeks since she fainted in front of everyone. She had woken up later, after someone splashed water on her face. She came to in shock, and then the tears followed. Everyone had been worried about her. They decided not to discuss anything further and asked her aunty to take her to their quarters and make sure she was alright.

As they picked her up from the floor, her legs shook and nearly gave way. Her aunty, a strong woman, had supported her as they walked to the house. Once inside, her aunty helped her to the bed and covered her with a wrapper. Onome had burst into tears again, and her aunty spent a long time consoling her, telling her it would be okay. She tried to get her to rest, then went to the kitchen to bring her some cold water. After making her comfortable, her aunty stayed until Onome finally fell asleep.

For the past two weeks, Onome had spent most of her time in bed, barely eating or doing any chores. She stayed in bed whenever she needed to or simply felt like it. She had refused to see her best friend. She'd heard Prisca had come to visit, but she decided not to see her.

Prisca had always been the one she told everything about her family, but this? This was too much. She was too ashamed. Imagine, finding out that her father wasn't really her father. It was too much to bear.

Rukevwe walked over to face her now.

"Onome, aunty is calling you ooh. She said you should come to the living room."

Onome continued to stare at the wall. She didn't blink. She didn't move.

"Onome." Rukevwe sat at the end of the bed now. "Aunty is calling you ooh."

Onome shifted a little and suddenly felt sorry for Rukevwe. How much did she know? Had they told her? Did she understand what was going on? What was she thinking?

Onome took a deep breath. "Abeg, tell aunty I'm sleeping."

"I don't think she will believe me ooh. That's what you said the last time she sent me."

Onome stayed silent again. She didn't care whether her aunty believed her or not. She just didn't want to see anyone. She hadn't seen her mother since that day. Her mother hadn't come to check on her, and Onome hadn't even heard her voice in the house.

She heard Rukevwe hiss as she got up and walked to the door, slamming it shut on her way out. Onome closed her eyes and sighed. This must be hard on Rukevwe too. She was her younger sister. She wasn't good at handling these kinds of things.

Onome sighed again and swung her legs off the bed. She was still wearing her long-sleeved nightgown. She stood up and walked slowly to the door. As she passed the standing mirror, she caught a glimpse of herself and stopped. Her face looked sad. Her eyes were heavy. Her hair was rough and messy. She turned away from the mirror, opened the bedroom door, and stepped out.

The kitchen door was shut. Voices drifted from the living room. She paused, wondering who was in there with her aunty. She hoped it was her mother. Maybe it would be a good thing if she was there, maybe she'd finally get some truth about all of this.

She stepped slowly into the living room. The first person she saw was her aunty, who was turned toward a woman Onome didn't recognise. Why hadn't Rukevwe mentioned that her aunty was with someone?

Then Onome noticed him.

The man.

The one from that day.

The man who had been looking at her strangely.

The man who was supposed to be her father.

She froze. Unable to move.

"Ah, Onome," her aunty stood up and walked over to her. "Rukevwe said you were sleeping. How are you?" She took her hand and slowly led her to a chair. Her aunty made sure she was seated before taking her seat beside the other woman. "How are you?"

"I am fine." The man was looking at her now, having moved to the edge of the chair. Her aunty followed her gaze but said nothing. "Rukevwe said you are not eating, why now, Onome?"

She did not respond but looked down, folding her hands on her thighs, over her lengthy nightgown.

"Onome!"

"Yes, aunty."

"Try to eat something, ehn, so you don't get sick, okay?"

She nodded her head, still looking at her hands. There was a pause for some time. She saw her aunty shift in the chair before speaking. "Ehn, Onome, I... erm... we came today to talk to you." She shifted again. "Your father wanted to come and check on you and talk to you too." Her aunty waited for her to respond, but she said nothing. "Your mother also wanted us to check on you."

She raised her head to look at her aunty. Her mother wanted them to check on her, but why? Where is she? "Where is my mother?" she asked almost immediately.

"She is in the village, with Mama." Onome dropped her gaze again. She watched from the side of her eyes as her aunty turned to the man and beckoned for him to speak.

She saw him rub his palms together, clear his throat, and then he said, "Onome, how are you?"

"I am fine," she said with a frown. *This man is not my father,* she thought to herself. *I already have a father.*

"That is good. We thank God." There was something about his voice, it was gentle and somewhat kind. "Ermm, my name is

Richard Okoro. I knew your mother years ago when we were..." He looked over at her aunty. "Friends," he said, looking back at Onome. "We were boyfriend and girlfriend before she married Chief."

Oh no, Onome thought; her mother was sleeping with him while married to her father? Her father, yes, Chief was her father. But how could he not be her father? He was the one she had known all her life. She frowned; she wasn't sure if she wanted to hear this story. She wasn't ready for it. She didn't realise she was shaking her head from side to side.

"Onome, what is it?" he asked. She raised her gaze to look at him, his face full of questions.

"Nothing, Sir."

He adjusted in his chair, cleared his throat again, and continued. "Well, I didn't see your mother until two months before she married Chief." *So, her mother didn't sleep with him while married*, there was a silent sigh of relief. "She said she was pregnant, and I was the father. I believed her because your mother never lied to me," he paused, turning to her aunty and shaking his head.

"Ermm, look, I think I'll leave it to your mother to tell you the whole story." He rubbed his palm on his trousers. She looked at his hands, which were covered in sweat. But why? she thought.

"I took permission from your mother and the rest of the family to come and talk to you today. I told her I want you to know who I am and that I am your real father." He took a deep breath and continued. "You see, your mother and I agreed I wouldn't tell anyone because of the marriage... erm, I've kept quiet for a long time, but I couldn't lie anymore, so that's why I decided to come and tell everyone." He paused, looking at her, his eyes hoping for a response.

Rubbing her hands together, she asked, "Does my father know?"

He looked over to her aunty and said, "Ermm... Chief does not know. We are trying not to tell him yet because of his condition."

Onome nodded.

"Onome, do you have any questions for your father?" her aunty asked.

She shook her head. She heard him sigh. He leaned forward in his chair again and spoke. "Emm... no problem. Well, what I also

239

came here to do is to tell you that..." He paused and started again. "I've discussed it with your mother, and I want to make sure I take care of you now. So... I will be providing for you and taking care of everything you need—for school, or anything you need." He stopped to see her reaction.

Onome was unsure how to react or what to say. She needed her mother. She needed to see her mother, to hear from her what happened. Why hadn't her mother told her? Was this why her mother had been hostile toward her? Was this why her mother never treated her right, because she reminded her of her relationship with him? So, her mother saw her as a mistake. She had always thought her mother didn't really love her; she loved Rukevwe more. She treated Rukevwe differently—better, in fact. All these years, she had wondered, and now she knew. This was why. Tears began to gather in her eyes.

She saw her aunty quickly stand up and come towards her. "Onome, it's okay, ehn? There's nothing to cry about now, ehn?"

It was easy for her to say. She wasn't the one who had believed a lie all these years.

"Your father is a good man, ehn. He doesn't want any trouble for you. He just wants you to know the truth and provide for you; that's not a bad thing, abi?"

"No, not at all," the other woman eventually spoke. "He just wants you to know. That's all, ehn? Don't cry, my dear." She stood beside her, her hand on her back, patting her. Her aunty was stroking her hand now, moving it back and forth as her long sleeved nightgown slid up and down. Just then she thought about the rash on her skin. Although nothing was revealed, she tugged at the sleeves, drawing them down. They must have noticed she was uncomfortable, as the woman immediately went back to sit, and her aunty sat back down as well.

"Don't cry, ehn?" her aunty said. She nodded, wiping the tears off her face. She was looking down at her hands, clasped tightly between her thighs.

She heard him sigh. "Let us leave her to rest," he said, looking at her aunty.

"Okay, no problem," her aunty replied.

"My dear, let us go," he said to the lady. Onome noticed he had called her "my dear." Is she his wife? she wondered. He stood up at the same time as her. He put his hand in his pocket and brought out a bundle of cash. After counting some of it, he slipped the rest into his back pocket. Then, he walked toward her and extended the money.

"Onome, please take this. It's for your upkeep."

She shook her head, refusing to look up.

"Please take it, it's for your upkeep," he tried again, but she kept shaking her head, this time turning her face away completely.

Her aunty stood up. "Give it to me, I'll make sure she keeps it, ehn." He sighed and handed it over to her aunty.

"We will be going now. I'll come and see you again, ehn," he said to her aunty.

"Onome, I'll come and see you again, by God's grace, ehn? Please take care of yourself, ehn?" She did not respond. He proceeded toward the door, and the other lady placed a hand behind her back.

"Take care, my dear. Eat some food, ehn." She walked to join him at the door as they both left together.

Her aunty sighed as she sat back down again, looking up. She exclaimed, "Ah, na wa ooh," sounding tired. She turned to look at Onome. "Go and bathe. I will make some food for us to eat. I will stay with you people today," she told her, standing up to go to the kitchen. She waited at the door of the kitchen to make sure Onome was leaving to go take her bath. Onome slowly stood up and walked toward the bedroom door. Just as she walked in, her aunty grabbed her hand and pressed the money into it.

"Take it. I don't want to hear you threw it away, do you hear?" She opened the door to the kitchen and shut it.

Onome looked at her hand. It was a bunch of 20 naira notes. It was hard to tell how much it was, but it seemed like a lot of money. Onome walked into the room, placed the money in the side drawer, and shut it. She proceeded to take off her nightgown in preparation for her bath. As she walked to get her towel, she tied it around her chest. As her hands moved across her body, she paused. Her eyes widened as she stretched out her hand, left and then right. She could not see the rash.

She took off the towel to inspect her chest and other parts of her body, no rash. Her eyes widened. "No, it can't be," she whispered. She wiped her eyes and looked again. Still, no rash. She quickly went to the mirror, took off the towel, and inspected her body closely. Everywhere she looked, there were no rash. She turned around a few times. "No rash!" she exclaimed. "No rash!" she said even louder, rubbing her hands all over her arms and untying the towel from her chest. "There is no rash. It has all gone. It has disappeared!" She spoke in disbelief, her voice questioning yet exclaiming at the same time. But how? How? "No, I will not bathe," she said to herself, maybe it will come back, she thought. She looked at her body in the mirror again. There was nothing.

At that moment, she heard Rukevwe outside the door speaking with her aunty. She quickly walked into the bathroom. She looked around; there was no water in the bucket, but there was some in a tiny bowl just by the bucket. She quickly washed her face and threw the rest of the water away. She returned to the room. Rukevwe was still not in; she was still conversing with her aunty by the door. Onome quickly rushed to get a dress from the clothes hanger. It had long sleeves. She dressed in it quickly. She remembered she hadn't put on deodorant. She quickly sprayed some deodorant, and just as she was done, Rukevwe opened the door. Onome didn't say anything. In fact, she avoided looking at Rukevwe, who walked straight to the bathroom. A few minutes later, Rukevwe came out and walked right out of the room.

Onome had been standing facing the rack of clothes, moving her hand through them. She wasn't sure if she could contain her excitement. She wasn't sure how to tell Rukevwe, but what if it's just a temporary thing? What if it comes back? She heard the door close and sighed. She turned away from the clothes and walked back to the full-length mirror. She pulled up the sleeves of the dress, still no sign of the rash. She pulled down the sleeves and sat on the bed, baffled. What happened to the rash? How come they have disappeared?

The door opened again. Rukevwe stood at the door. "Aunty said the food is ready and that you should come and eat." She immediately shut the door. Onome sighed, standing up to look at herself in the mirror once more. She couldn't help but smile. The pain she was feeling about the current situation seemed to have disappeared. She decided to keep it to herself for now, until she was sure she was completely healed.

Her stomach rumbled. She was hungry all of a sudden. She pulled the dress sleeves down further, not realising they had already been pulled to the end. She decided not to tell anyone for now. She smiled again, then opened the door and walked straight to the kitchen to join her aunt and Rukevwe.

Chapter 23

"A re you sure of what you are telling me?"

"Yes, sir. I'm sure, sir."

Chief placed his hand on his lips, pressing them together as he tried to process what Musa was telling him. What was he hearing? Onome, not his daughter? How could this be? He paused... No. He shook his head. Impossible! He was sitting outside the hospital again, at his favourite spot. He took a deep breath as he rested his head on his hand. He could not believe what he had just heard. He raised his head. Musa was watching him intently. He took another deep breath.

"Musa!"

"Yes, sir."

"Where is Madam Rume now?"

"She don carry her bag and don comot since."

"Do you know where she has gone to?"

"No, sir, she no talk where she dey go ooh."

Rubbing his hand over his face, Chief paused for a second, unsure of what to do or say.

"Okay," he managed to mutter. The silence stretched as he fell deep into thought. What is going on? What is happening to his family? Everything seems to be falling apart since he ended up in the hospital. His wife, Amaka, has refused to come back home, and she's now staying with Albert, his best friend. And she's supposed to be pregnant with his child. He had driven his dear wife, Omerie, out of the house for no reason. Now, he's hearing there's a man claiming to be the father of his daughter. How can this be? Who is this man sef?

"Oga, sir," Musa interrupted his thoughts.

He looked up at him.

"E be like say nah Madam be that ooh," Musa said, pointing toward the hospital gate.

A lady was slowly making her way toward them.

Chief saw that Musa's mouth was wide open in surprise. Chief wasn't sure who Musa was referring to, as there was a huge tree in the way. He leaned forward to get a better look. He saw Omerie walking slowly toward them, a young girl by her side.

"Oya, Musa, go and help her quick, quick," he ordered in a commanding tone.

"Yes, sir," Musa quickly rushed over to them and took the bag from the young girl.

"Go and bring a chair from inside, quick," Chief commanded again as they approached him.

"Yes, sir."

He tried to rise from the chair, his legs shaking slightly; he was still weak.

"Chief, please, don't get up, please," Omerie said hurriedly, rushing toward him and placing her hand on his to stop him. He sank back into his seat.

Just then, Musa arrived with a wooden chair.

"Madam, I don bring chair for you," Musa said, setting it down.

"Thank you, Musa."

Chief watched as Omerie lowered herself heavily into the chair.

"Are you okay?" he asked, his voice filled with concern.

"I'm fine," she replied, signalling to the girl beside her to hand her something. The young girl picked up the bag from the floor and passed it to her.

"How did you come?"

"Oh, ermm, we took transport."

"Ah ah, Omerie, but I told you now. I said you could ask the driver to bring you here. He could have brought you, you know, in your condition..."

"Chief, I'm fine, it's not a problem."

"But you're pregnant and..."

"Emmanuel, I'm fine, don't worry," she said, her hand resting on his arm now, a smile on her face.

He went silent, staring at her, taking a deep breath. His dear wife... God, how did he get here? He thought, lowering his head. He listened as Omerie dismissed Musa and the young girl.

"We will call you when we need you, ehn, don't go far ooh."

"Yes, madam," they responded in unison.

"Chief, what is the matter?" she asked. He could hear the concern in her voice. He shook his head; he couldn't bring himself to look at her.

"Emmanuel...?"

"Ome..." He could hear how tearful he sounded. "I feel like I've lost everything." He felt the sob rise, louder and louder. He heard Omerie move the chair closer and place her hands over him as much as she could. He had no idea how long he sobbed, but Omerie just kept her hands on him, stroking him gently. Slowly, he regained his composure. He raised his head and wiped his face with his hospital gown. Omerie still had her hands on him as he leaned back in the chair. Omerie remained quiet. He didn't want to look at her. This was the most she had ever seen him weak and in tears, and he felt so ashamed. He took a deep breath.

"I'm okay," he said, trying to reassure her. "I'm okay," he repeated. She reluctantly withdrew her hands, placing them on her thighs. He watched as she fumbled in her bag, looking for something. She brought out a tissue and handed it to him. He took it, not saying a word, and blew his nose.

It took some time for him to realise that her hand was on his back now, stroking up and down. She passed him some more tissues. He didn't say anything this time, just blew his nose again. She dropped her hand, then reached for the bag they had brought. He looked around for a place to drop the used tissues.

"Bring it, I will put them in the corner here," she pointed to the grass next to her. "We will throw them away when we are leaving." She reached over, took the tissues from him, and placed them on the ground. He became uncomfortable, sensing that she had many questions but wasn't sure when to ask. He had never been like this before; he had never been weak or even in tears. What was happening to him? He took a deep breath and shook his head.

"Ome, I know you're wondering what is going on..."

"Chief, you are right, I want to know what is going on. But for now, let us make sure you are alright, ehn?" she said as she placed her hand on his shoulder. "Have you eaten yet?" she asked as she rested the bag on her lap and started to sift through it.

"No. I told them to bring my food at 1 o'clock," he pulled up the sleeves of his shirt to check the time but he didn't have a watch.

"Okay, well I brought some Egusi soup with pounded yam for you." She brought out a hot food container and the pounded yam wrapped in foil. He watched as she laid them on the small stool in front of him. Everyone knew that Egusi soup was his favourite. He quietly watched as she also took out a bottle of water with a glass and set it by the side of the stool. She was always prepared, he thought. She opened the food container, and he could smell the fresh Egusi, which immediately made him hungry. It was a full bowl of Egusi, and he could already see that it was loaded with assorted meats and filled with green leaves. He continued to watch her as she set everything carefully on the stool before him. He couldn't believe how she was with him today—so loving, so caring. Although Omerie may be angry with him, she never let it stop her from being a loving wife. He had always loved this about her, but for some reason, he couldn't understand how he had lost sight of things, which had brought them to where they were now.

"Oya, wash your hands," she commanded. She had opened the bottle of water and positioned it so he could wash his hands by his side on the grass. Like a little child, he obeyed, raising both his hands, and she gently poured some water over them. After this, he moved the container of Egusi soup and opened the foil wrapped with pounded yam. He liked his swallow on the left and the Egusi soup on the right. He stretched his hand to cut a piece of pounded yam but then stopped. He didn't want to eat it alone; they were both going to eat it together, like old times.

"Ome, wash your hands and join me."

"I have already eaten, Chief. Please eat. It's all for you."

"I want you to join me. Let us eat, just like we used to do," he turned his gaze toward her now. She paused, looking directly into his eyes, then took the bottle of water, and washed her hands.

He adjusted the stool, so it was comfortable for both of them to eat together. As he dipped the swallow into the Egusi, taking a big portion of Egusi and vegetable, he took a swallow. He closed his eyes; it was just as he liked it—hot, full, and sweet.

"You like it?"

He opened his eyes and nodded. "You know me and Egusi soup." He could see her smile from the corner of his eyes. He hadn't seen that soft smile in a long time. He pointed for her to take a piece and some soup. It was strange at first, but after a few bites, they both relaxed and began to talk while they ate together.

Omerie wanted to know when he was going to be discharged. He made up a story about them wanting to keep him for a few more weeks until his legs were strong again. The truth was, he had asked the doctor if he could stay longer. He wasn't ready to go back to his house, not ready to handle everything that was happening now. How could he deal with all of this? Even worse, what he had heard today. Did she know? What would she think? He had forgotten all the troubles as they ate and talked. He tried to concentrate on what Omerie was saying. She was worried they still wanted to keep him, as he had been there too long. She thought it would be better if he went home and was taken care of there.

As they continued to eat and talk, he was feeling a little better. There was something about Omerie that knew what to say or do to just make him feel alright. There was no way he was going back to the house until Omerie moved back.

"Ah, see," she exclaimed, "Egusi everywhere!" They both chuckled as she looked at her hand, now covered with Egusi soup.

"Ah, there is even some bitter leaf on your wrapper!" he said, pointing at a spot on her wrapper. He paused as his gaze was suddenly fixed on her protruding stomach. He could feel it; he could sense it. It was going to be a boy. He noticed she was looking at him. He gave a strange chuckle and turned his gaze back to the food. He noticed her going for the bottled water to wash her hands.

"Ah, wait ooh," he said, his tone playful. "We haven't finished ooh. We have to finish the meat. Oya, let us finish the meat." He put his hand into the bowl and fished out a piece of beef and gave it to her.

"Ah, Chief!" she was shaking her head now. "This one is too big!" she exclaimed but then took it and took a small bite before putting the rest back in the bowl. He smiled, turning back to the bowl of soup, which was almost empty, except for the meat. Yes, he thought to himself, he would not go back to the compound until she returned. Based on how things were going now, he had no doubt she would be moving back soon.

Chapter 24

"R ume, you dey outside there? Rume!" she heard as her mother called out to her from the kitchen. She could hear her footsteps as she made her way toward the kitchen back door. What did her mother want again, for goodness sake? She kissed her teeth as she dipped the dress into the bucket of soapy water and started rubbing her hands on it. She had decided to wash some of her clothes this afternoon. It had been a few weeks now since she came to the village to live with her mother. It was unplanned; after being made to confess to some of the elders from her village and Richard's family the truth about Onome, she just could not remain in the compound. She was sure some of the children and the maids had heard. They had told the maid to leave the compound and told the children to go out or remain inside. But knowing the compound, it was as if the walls had ears, and even worse, the walls talked. No secret was safe in that compound. Of course, they left Musa at the gate. She had cried her eyes out by the end of the discussion. She was tired and ashamed. She could not see herself staying one more day in the compound. She had packed a small bag very late that evening and hurriedly left the compound, not wanting anyone to see her, not even Onome. Onome... her heart sank as she remembered.

"Rume!" Her mother was standing by the door now. She turned her gaze to her mother, her hands still hanging over the dress in the bucket of water. "Ma?"

"Some people from your husband village don come ooh; dem say they get message for you. So, make you come ooh."

"People from Chief's village?" she said, a little confused. But no one from Chief knew she was here. "Mama, who be these people?" she asked her mother.

"I don tell you now, dem say dem be from Chief. Him brother dey with them. Abeg, make you come answer dem. Dem dey for palour dey wait." Her mother turned away, seeming slightly irritated. Rume heard her steps again as she walked slowly out of the kitchen.

Her husband's people? Chief's brother is here? And who are the people he has come with? This cannot be good, she thought to herself. She stood up from the little stool, but wait, how did they know she was here? She shook her head. Well, where else would she be if not at her father's house? She had been here for a few weeks now. Her decision to come and stay in her father's house was because she thought she would have some peace. How wrong was she? She had not had any peace since being here. Her mother constantly sought to understand why she was back home and not in her husband's house. She had begged that they contact the elders to settle any misunderstandings between them. Her mother kept reminding her that she *(her mother)* was in her husband's house and that Rume should go back to her husband's house. Rume took a deep breath. Now, it seemed her husband's house had come to find her. What did they want?

She kissed her teeth as she moved her wet hands to her waist. She didn't want to see anybody. The last she heard from her sister, Chief was still in the hospital. They were obviously here to discuss the matter concerning Richard and Onome. She kissed her teeth again, bending over the bucket. She squeezed the soapy water out of the dress she was washing and placed it in another bucket of clean water. Drying her hands on her wrapper, which was tied around the Buba she wore, she untied it. She adjusted the Buba as she walked into the kitchen.

The living room was only a corridor away from the kitchen. As she walked toward the living room, she could hear some male voices. She stood still for a second, wondering if her mother was with them. She took a deep breath and then slowly walked in. She was met with a cold stare from Chief's brother. Here was a man she barely saw since an outburst they had a few years ago. She never liked him, and he never liked her.

There were two elders sitting by his side. There was silence as everyone just stared at her. Her mother sat in an armchair, looking at her. She stood there for a second, wondering why all of them had come. No one said anything. She quietly walked to a chair and sat down.

"Welcome," she said in Urhobo, not looking at anyone.

"Ehen, my daughter. Thank you." one of the elders said.

***

"We have said all we came to say to you. You must come and tell us why you deceived my brother with a child that is not his own and then tried to kill him."

Rume was up now. "I am not coming, and you cannot force me, you hear?" Her tone was very high. "Was I the one that was forcing him to drink like a fish, ehn? Let me tell you, you people cannot do anything to me, you hear?"

"Okay, we shall see. Let us go," Chief's brother said to the other men. They all stood up, turning toward the door. Her mother had been pleading with them this whole time.

"My in-laws, abeg, make una no go like this aah. Make we settle this matter, abeg."

"Was I the one that made him drink, ehn?" Rume continued to yell at them.

"Is Onome his child?" Chief's brother yelled back at her. "Is she his child?" He turned, yelling back at her. "Prostitute!"

"Who is a prostitute?"

"Ovie, let us go," one of the elders pulled at him, forcing him to turn toward the door.

"You people think you can come here to threaten me? You have failed, you hear, failed!" she yelled, clapping her hands together at them as they stepped out. Her mother pulled at her.

"Rume, wetin dey do you, ehn?" her mother pulled at her. "You no go close this your mouth," her mother whispered.

Rume moved away from her. "No, make dem con force me. I dey here. Rubbish," Rume said as she slammed her bottom hard on the chair and hissed. Her mother had stepped outside now, still pleading with them. A few minutes later, she could hear the engine of a car start, and it drove away. Rume kissed her teeth.

"Nonsense," she said as she placed her hand on the side of the armchair, her palm over her chin, her face with a heavy frown, both legs shaking. Her mother had walked in, and she could see her mother staring at her. She looked away, not caring what could be going through her mind.

"Rume? Na true say Onome no be Chief pikin?" Rume remained silent.

"Rume? No be you I dey talk to?" Rume remained quiet.

"So, you no go answer me?"

"Mama, leave me alone, abeg."

She heard her mother sigh. A few minutes later, she heard her pick up the empty glasses and walked to the kitchen. Soon after, she heard a door close. Rume took a deep breath, leaning back on the chair. These people, she thought, she cannot believe they came to her father's house to insist on her presence at a family meeting to explain Onome's birth and Chief's illness. Imagine! What is their business if she lied to Chief about Onome; it is between her and Chief, a private family matter. But who is she deceiving? "This is a big issue, a big one," she murmured out loud. She held her hand over her face. But why? Why did Richard do this?

Her mind went back to when she found out she was pregnant. It was a few weeks after she had said her goodbye to Richard. The marriage plans were in motion. She had gone with her friend to the tailor to finalise what she wanted. While speaking to the tailor, she became sick. She had been feeling unwell for a few days, but on that day, she was so ill that she had to rush outside to throw up. She had told the tailor that it was malaria symptoms. She had rushed off to her friend Amara's place. She was afraid it was not malaria. Amara had told her to come back in a few days for them to visit a doctor. The doctor later confirmed her fear. She was 6 weeks pregnant.

She had rushed to Richard's place and rained abuses at him, accusing him of intentionally getting her pregnant. He was delighted and talked about them getting married. She had laughed at him. "Never," she had said. She told him she was getting it removed and stormed off. But she knew she would never do it; she was too afraid of things going wrong and losing her life. It was then that Amara helped her work out a plan; she would marry Chief quickly. He was an older man, and he would not suspect anything. She would make him drink a lot the first night, so when he came to consummate the marriage, he would not remember if she was a virgin.

The plan was successful. Chief was so drunk by the time they went to bed. She felt like he was a bit nervous too, hence the heavy drinking. When they woke up the next morning, he was slightly embarrassed. He joked about how the festivities got to him and that he would perform better next time. A few weeks later, she told him she was pregnant. Upon his insistence, they went to clarify in the hospital. She had pleaded with and paid the female doctor some money to lie about the stage of the pregnancy. Everything went well.

Seven months later, she was in the delivery room giving birth to Onome. 'It was 'premature', it was said, but her and the doctor were the only ones that knew the truth. She was, of course, disappointed that it wasn't a male child. She looked like her father, and she hated it—a constant reminder of the man she loved, who was not able to save her from marrying Chief. Richard was too poor to save her. It took her a long time to forget about him. He had threatened to tell everyone, but she had told him the baby was not his and that she had aborted it. She believed he stopped only because he had no money to take care of a child. But he knew the child was his and he didn't want to cause any trouble.

Now, to her surprise, he shows up after 18 years and exposes everything, just as she was planning to get Onome married and move to Germany where no one would have found out. She shook her head and kissed her teeth. Now, Chief's brother and elders are asking her to report to the village to answer questions.

"No, this shame is too much to bear," she stood, pacing the floor. How does she get out of this? Mama Omote, that evil woman, so-called Prophetess, had deceived her after years of spending money on her, love portions, and other concoctions. Oh, thank the Lord she did not kill anybody.

She stopped pacing. A bright idea had come to her. She rushed to sit down again. Yes, she heard her friend Muna *(a friend from secondary school)* now runs a single mother's home in the East somewhere. She can go there, tell her she is looking to start a business, and then after some time explain the situation and start a new life. Muna has always been a good friend to all of them *(a Christian)*. But wait, how can she reach her? She stood up and started pacing up and down again. Mrs. Ufuoma must know. She was the one who told her that Muna now runs a home. If she waits, it will take days. No, she cannot wait to reach her, she thought. These people could come back any day now. She must contact Mrs. Ufuoma immediately. She will know where the home is and give her the address. Yes.

She looked around her suddenly, not sure what she was looking for. She turned around and headed to her room. As she passed her mother's room, she could hear her softly praying. She listened carefully by the door, then stepped back and continued to her room. She swung the door open and rushed quickly to the wardrobe, pulling a bag down. She ruffled through the bag, looking for something. She found it, opened it, and there was cash. She scanned through and nodded her head, then put it back and placed it on the bed.

She quickly reached to the top of the wardrobe for a suitcase, dragged it down, opened it, and started arranging the clothes. There is no time to waste, she thought to herself. The quicker she leaves, the better it will be. Based on Chief's brother's tone, they intend to make trouble for her. Who knows what plans they have in mind? Well, she will not wait to find out. She will make sure she is at the motor park early tomorrow to get a travel vehicle.

She checked the wardrobe to see what was left. She hadn't brought much with her to the village. She doesn't need much, as she plans to start life again. She would get new things. She looked over at the bag of money on her bed. Well, there is enough money to keep her going.

She heard her mother's room door open. She stood still, holding her breath, praying she would not call out to her or come to her room. Thankfully, she did not. She heard her steps walking away. She resumed her packing. She had no intention of telling her mother her plans. She will leave her a letter tonight and pray that she understands. She will also leave her some money, to take care of herself. She paused.

"My children, what about my children?" She stopped packing and sat down on the bed. Rukevwe, her baby girl, is about to finish secondary school. She took a deep breath, and a small tear began to develop. *How did she get here?* She asked herself. So, this is how life has treated her. A tear dropped down her face; all she wanted was to be loved. Is that a bad thing?

Chapter 25

"Ehnn! So, it just disappeared like that?"

"Prisca, I am telling you, it is gone! It has just disappeared.....look...look," she said with a massive smile on her face. "'It has been 2 weeks since I noticed it and it has not come back. See now...see," she pointed to her arms and her hand, raising up her skirt as she laughed. It was the second time she was showing Prisca her arms again. Today, she was wearing a t-shirt and skirt.

"I see, I see," Prisca put on a tight smile, but there was something about her friend's behaviour that seemed odd. She didn't look excited to see her. Onome thought maybe it was because she had just woken up from sleep. She had suggested they sit outside as it was very hot, and there was no electricity that afternoon. Prisca had barely said a word since she arrived. Onome watched as she smiled slowly.

"Well, we thank God. God is good," was all Prisca said. There was an unusual silence after. Prisca had turned away now and was staring as the breeze blew, causing the leaves on the trees to rustle against each other. They had seen each other a few times since her father went into the hospital. Prisca had always been a good support during difficult times for her, cooking and bringing food. But Prisca had not said anything to her about Pastor Maxwell, it was unlike herself. Onome wondered what could be on her mind.

"Prisca, this one you're quiet, is something the matter?"

"Ehn....look Onome, I'm not going to lie to you, we have been friends for a long time," Prisca said, her tone serious. Onome nodded, listening attentively. Prisca's serious tone made Onome feel worried.

"I saw you one Saturday," she paused. "Pastor Maxwell dropped you outside your compound with the church car," she paused again, this time expecting a response.

"Yes, I remember that day." Onome said, waiting for her to continue.

Prisca folded her arms across her chest and shook her head.

"Prisca, what is it? Yes, Pastor Maxwell dropped me off at the compound that day after the hospital. So, what happened?"

"You think I didn't see the way you were smiling and waving him goodbye, ehnn?"

"So, I waved him goodbye, what is wrong with that?"

"Onome, remove your eyes from him, I beg you, ehn?"

"What do you mean, remove your eyes from him? I don't understand at all."

"You are pretending like you don't know what I'm saying." Prisca stood up. "Just because he has been helping your family and has been nice to you, all of a sudden you like him now?"

"See me, see trouble ooh."

"You are the one looking for trouble. Remove your eye, Onome, you hear?" she said, her hands over one ear. "I have told you." With that, she walked into the house, leaving Onome by herself outside. Onome sat for a few minutes, quite surprised. She was not sure what had just happened. Does Prisca think she has a thing for Pastor Maxwell? She paused. She would be lying if she said she didn't think about him, but she knew how Prisca felt about him, and she would never ruin their friendship by doing that. But why would Prisca think she would do that to her? She sighed.

But how had Prisca seen them that day? Was she coming to her house? Because Onome didn't see her on the street. Surely, she didn't notice how she smiled as she waved goodbye to Pastor Maxwell. They had a good time together that day; it was by far the longest they had spent together. That was the day she cried on his shoulder; he was so gentle, holding her and encouraging her. He has been so good to her and her family. Although she had not seen him in a while and wondered where he was. Yes, she had missed him.

Oh no, she thought, her eyes widening. "I think I love him," she whispered, then quickly covered her lips. She quickly stood up, looked inside the house, and saw no sign of Prisca. She called her name, but there was no answer. She sighed and decided maybe she should leave. And she did.

***

As she walked home, Onome decided to take the longer route, which meant passing by the front of the church. It was a Tuesday afternoon, and there was no chance of seeing anyone. She also wanted to stop by the church to say thank you to God and pray. As she approached, she saw two men standing outside. Immediately, she recognised one of them as Pastor Maxwell, and it felt like the ground should open and swallow her. She had really thought no one would be there, especially the pastors. Fortunately, Pastor Maxwell had his back to her, but the other man, who it took her a moment to recognise, was Boniface. She hadn't seen him in a while.

She lowered her head and started walking quickly, hoping they wouldn't recognise her in her shirt and skirt. As she quickly passed by the church, she heard her name being called. At first, she pretended not to hear and kept walking, but then she heard it again, louder this time. It was Boniface. There was no way she could pretend she hadn't heard him now.

She stopped and turned around to look at them. Her gaze immediately landed on Pastor Maxwell, who had a questioning look on his face. Then she turned to Boniface, who had a huge smile on his face. He had turned away from Pastor Maxwell taking a few steps toward her. "I thought it was you! Longest time, Onome. How have you been?"

"I'm fine," she replied, lowering her gaze. Both of them were looking at her, making her feel shy.

"It's good to see you today! I was even at your house some time ago, but your security man wouldn't let me in to see you," Boniface added.

Onome stood frozen for a second. He had come to her house? She was speechless. Fortunately, Pastor Maxwell broke the silence.

"How is everyone?" he asked, his tone soft.

"They're fine," she replied, turning to look at him. There was a softness in his expression, one she was sure she had seen before.

"That's good. They said your father will be discharged very soon," Pastor Maxwell continued.

"Yes, he's getting discharged next week."

"Thank God," Boniface chimed in. "I was coming to check on you, but I couldn't find you." He paused. "That security man of yours shaa."

Pastor Maxwell chuckled. "He does his job well," he joked, and they both laughed. Onome smiled, feeling tense. She wasn't sure how to act around him, especially now that she realised how much she liked him.

"I have to go and attend to someone inside," Pastor Maxwell said. "I'll come and see your family next week, okay?"

"Okay," she managed to respond. He turned to Boniface. "Don't forget about what we discussed."

"I won't forget, Pastor. Thank you," Boniface said as they shook hands. Pastor Maxwell quickly turned and rushed inside.

Onome wasn't sure how long she had been watching him leave until Boniface interrupted. "Our Pastor, he's a very busy man," he said with a smile, gazing at her. She nodded and looked down again.

"Are you going home?" he asked.

"Ehmm..." She hesitated. She wasn't sure now if she should go into the church to pray or head home. She turned to look at the church door, then pointed at it.

"Are you going inside?" Boniface asked, noticing her gesture.

"Ehmm... no, I'm going home," she replied. There was no way she was going into the church now, especially knowing Pastor Maxwell would be inside.

"Okay," Boniface said, hesitating for a moment. "Let me escort you home." He walked down the church steps and stood in front of her. She had forgotten how tall he was. She didn't feel like she could refuse, but she was too confused to say no.

He waited for her to lead the way, and they walked side by side. Just like last time, he started with his questions.

"How have you been coping with your father in the hospital?"

"Well, I've been coping fine. I just keep praying for God to heal him."

"Mm, yes, that's good. We've been praying for your family at church. We thank God he's getting discharged."

"Yes, we thank God."

They walked in silence for a short while.

"I really missed you," he said, his tone serious. Onome almost froze. She wasn't sure how to respond to what he had said. She looked down, slowing her pace.

"Why are you so shy?" he asked.

"I'm not shy," she said, raising her head.

"I know you're shy," he chuckled. She smiled but immediately looked away. Again, there was silence.

"Ehmm... what are you doing at home this afternoon?" he asked, his tone curious.

"I'm going to do some housework and maybe finish reading a book my aunty gave me."

"Ehnn...okay," he said, but she knew there was more coming.

"Will you allow me to buy you a cold drink?"

"Ehmmm..."

"We can go somewhere near your house if you like. We'll have one drink, and you can go home afterward."

"I don't...." she started to say, but he quickly interrupted, "Please, Onome, I have something to tell you. Please, it's very important."

They had both come to a standstill now. Onome was looking away, unsure of what to do with her hands. She folded them against her chest, then put them down by her side, before looking down. "Please naah... I will not take too long."

She took a deep breath. No one had ever asked her or shown any interest in her like this. It seemed like this change in her skin might be having a positive effect. But should she let him buy her a soft drink? He knows Pastor Maxwell. What if he tells him? What will Pastor Maxwell think? She wouldn't want Pastor Maxwell to think she likes Boniface; she wants him to know that she likes him—she loves him, in fact. But what if Boniface has already spoken to Pastor Maxwell about this? He did say to him, *"Don't forget what we discussed."* Maybe it was a code; maybe they were talking about her.

There she was, thinking about Pastor Maxwell. He probably didn't like her, just like Prisca said. He's very nice, and that's why most of the girls like him and want to marry him. For all she knew, he might like Prisca, who was very beautiful and sang in the choir. She was already training to be a Pastor's wife.

Boniface's voice interrupted her thoughts.

"Okay, I don't want to force you. I will walk with you to your compound."

"Ermmm...no, it's okay. I can go with you for a cold drink," she said, and she could see his face light up. A huge smile crossed his face.

"Thank you! Thank you!" he clapped his hands, and they started walking again. "We can go anywhere you like, maybe somewhere near your compound."

Oh no, not near her compound, Onome thought alarmingly. She looked around, then remembered a place just before the square. She mentioned it to him, and thankfully, he was happy with that. He was much happier knowing he could buy her a drink, and they could sit for some time. He would then tell her what he wanted to say.

They walked toward the place, and Boniface continued talking, mainly about the town, transportation, and work. She listened to him, looking at him from time to time. He wasn't a bad-looking man. He was tall, slim, dressed well, and had nice teeth. She didn't know anything else about him, but she thought this talk would give her an opportunity to find out more. She decided to pay attention to what he was saying as they walked.

Upon entering the place, they were offered a table with two chairs. She chose a spot far inside, worried about people she knew seeing them there. They quickly ordered their drinks, which arrived soon after. She had ordered Supermalt, and he had ordered the same. He raised his bottle, and they both cheered. She chuckled at that point.

She took a few sips; it was nice and cold. Resting the bottle on the table, she raised her head to look at him. He was staring at her, smiling. She smiled back and put her head down.

"And you said you're not shy?" he laughed as he took a gulp of his Supermalt. She laughed as well, shaking her head.

"Onome, thank you for coming here with me."

"No problem."

"Ermm...there's something I want to tell you, and I'm hoping you can help me," he said, sounding serious now. She became nervous again. Was she ready for him to tell her how he felt about her? She picked up her Supermalt, placing it on her lips so it would cover her eyes slightly. It felt safer, as it would hide her expression, she hoped.

"You see, I've been trying to talk to you for some time now because I need your help, please."

"My help?"

"Yes, Onome, please. You see, I really like your friend Prisca, and I want to marry her. I really like her ooh, but she will not give me a chance to communicate with her. Every time I see her; she won't allow me to talk to her. I've spoken to Pastor, and he told me to go and pray."

He was still speaking, but her thoughts slowly drowned out his voice. She wasn't sure if he could see the shock on her face. She must have sat in shock for a couple of minutes. The words were pouring out of his mouth, like he couldn't stop himself. She tried to focus, but all she could think was, *Prisca!?* That thought rang loudly in her head. She stared at him, and he was completely unaware of how surprised she was.

You mean I read it wrong? she thought. Why did she think he liked her? Even Prisca thought the same thing.

She could do this, she would just pretend. She had pretended before, so this should be fine. Now, she was listening to him as he continued to talk about how he liked Prisca and how he wanted to marry her.

How could she have missed knowing this!

Well, she should be relieved, she thought. She wasn't sure how she would have responded if he had told her he liked her and wanted a relationship. She was just coming to terms about her feelings for Pastor Maxwell. Although it was a nice feeling, thinking that Boniface admired her; she had never felt that way before. She sometimes wondered if she would ever have an admirer like her friend Prisca.

"Onome," she heard her name, and he was staring at her now with a questioning look on his face. She looked at him, unsure what he was saying.

"Will you help me talk to her?"

Chapter 26

Omerie watched as Chief took a deep breath and stepped out of the car without assistance. They had just arrived at the compound, and it seemed as if the compound was filled with people, but it was just Omerie and all the children who had gathered around to welcome him home. Mabel, his second wife, had been the one to go with the driver to the hospital to pick him up as soon as he was discharged. Omerie had wanted to go, but everyone insisted that she stay home, as she was now too heavy. The children gathered around him to welcome him, each bending their knees slightly as they greeted him. Omerie watched as he spread open his arms to embrace each one, not letting go for a while. He asked each one how they were doing, checking if they had behaved themselves in his absence.

She noticed that Onome had greeted him but had not joined the others in embracing him. She stood a few steps away. Chief hadn't noticed; he was distracted by Ese, Omoefe, Rukevwe, and Beatrice, who hovered around him as he slowly walked to his quarters. Omerie stood eagerly, ready to welcome him home. She had visited him at the hospital a few days before, to hear the doctor explain the results of his tests. The doctor had said his heart was getting stronger and more stable, and his liver was improving since he stopped drinking. Everything was fine.

"Welcome, Chief," she said, smiling as she pointed to the first available chair. They had filled the verandah with plenty of chairs so that everyone in the family could sit with him if they wanted to. She had also made some additional arrangements to the verandah. She had bought a rocking chair similar to the one in her sister's house, making sure to test it so there was no squeaky sound. There was also a nice stool for him to rest his feet on. She wondered if he had noticed. Her thoughts were confirmed soon.

"Ah, you people bought me a new chair?" he asked, staring at the rocking chair for a second.

"Yes, Chief. This one is good for the back, and it also has a stool for you to relax your legs," Omerie said, gently encouraging him to sit.

"Thank you, my dear," he replied as he slowly settled into the chair. It started to rock slowly, and Omerie could see the smile forming on his face. She was glad. The children were taking their seats one by one beside him, eager to ask him questions about what he thought of the chair and the new and improved verandah. As Omerie watched this, she realised how much the family had changed since Chief's incident. Chief had changed significantly; it was as if nearly dying was the eye-opener he needed to recognise his mistakes and want to change everything.

She had decided they would have a family gathering to celebrate his return, with food and drinks for them all. She looked up at Mabel and signalled for her to join her inside. As they walked toward the living room, Omerie stopped by the dining area.

"How did everything go with the doctor?" Omerie asked.

"It went well. The doctor did some checks and said everything is fine."

"Okay, we thank God."

"The doctor also gave me all the tablets," Mabel said, turning to reach for her bag. She unzipped it, brought out a small plastic bag, and handed it to Omerie.

"Ah, it looks like there are plenty ooh," Omerie said as she slowly opened the plastic bag.

"This is also what I thought," Mabel replied. "I asked the doctor, and he said Chief has been taking them in the hospital. He said he just needs to take them only for the next two months."

"Ehnn..." Omerie peeked into the bag. Taking a deep breath, she closed the plastic bag. "Okay, let's keep it in his room. I will ask you how the doctor said we should give them to him later," she said, handing the bag back to Mabel. She watched as Mabel placed it back in her bag.

"Let us go and dish out the food and drinks now, abi?" Omerie asked, beginning to walk slowly toward the kitchen.

"Ehnn, Omerie," Mabel called to her. Omerie stopped and turned to look at Mabel.

"Go and sit down, I beg you. You're heavy now. Please go and rest. I will make sure everything is done," Mabel said, concern in her voice. Omerie sighed. Yes, she needed to sit down. It was getting harder now for her to walk. The doctor had said she should rest now. She looked at Mabel. She had been so helpful to her. They had lived happily since Mabel arrived at the compound. Not that they hadn't had arguments, but her and Mabel had always made amends soon after. She smiled at her.

"Thank you, ehnn... thank you," she said, placing her hand on Mabel's shoulder. Mabel smiled. Omerie walked away from Mabel in the living room and headed to the verandah to join the family. She stood at the door, resting her frame against the doorpost, watching. Beatrice was talking about what had been happening at university. Everyone was listening attentively, smiling. Omerie smiled as she listened, taking in the scene around the verandah. But then she suddenly realised that Onome and Rukevwe were not there. They had been there earlier to welcome their father, but why had they decided to leave? She had noticed that Onome had not gone to hug her father. Omerie shook her head, wondering what could be going on in their minds.

"Omerie, we are coming ooh," she heard Mabel's voice behind her. She immediately walked onto the verandah to give way as Mabel and the maid came with a large hot food container and some plates.

"Ah, Aunty, you did not call me to help you," Beatrice said.

"Don't worry about this. You can go to the kitchen to bring the drinks," Mabel said.

Omerie was watching all this now. She felt a hand on her elbow. She turned and saw that it was Chief.

"Come and sit down," he said softly.

She watched as Omoefe quickly stood up from the chair beside her father. Slowly, she walked to the chair and sat down.

"How are you feeling?" he asked. She could hear a little concern in his voice.

"I am feeling fine," she replied. She noticed his eyes drift down to her stomach.

"Our child is fine," she smiled, placing her hand on her stomach, gently stroking it.

"Chief, it's fried rice today ooh!" Mabel said with excitement

Chief turned his attention to her. Omerie watched as Mabel opened the large food container. It was filled with fried rice—not just any fried rice, but a richly prepared one with vegetables, pieces of goat meat, and more.

"Ah ah!" was all Chief could say.

They laughed. She could see the look of excitement in his eyes. The children stood up to peek into the food container as Mabel dished out some rice for Chief, adding a piece of fried chicken.

Just then, Beatrice came out carrying some drinks from the fridge. Omerie watched as everyone chipped in to make sure Chief was comfortable and had everything he needed.

Omerie smiled. She looked up to the sky and whispered, "God, I thank you."

***

It was late in the evening now. The children had gone to rest for the evening. Omerie watched as Mabel helped Chief take his medicine, handing them to him one by one to ensure none was missed.

Once that was done, Mabel packed the medicine back into the plastic bag. Chief's face showed he had not enjoyed the experience. He drank some more water and shook his head.

"Doh," Omerie said softly.

Chief nodded in response as he placed the glass down. Mabel set the medicine bag next to the glass of water.

"Let me go and put it back in the room," Mabel said, picking up the bag of medicine and walking inside.

Omerie looked at Chief again. "Sorry, ehnn?" she said.

He nodded again, this time with his eyes closed, his head resting back on the chair. They sat quietly.

Mabel came back and stood on the verandah. Omerie saw her look at Chief and then at her. Omerie shook her head, signalling to Mabel not to say anything. Mabel gestured that she was heading to her quarters, and Omerie nodded. She watched as Mabel tiptoed away from the verandah, making her way to her quarters.

Turning back to Chief, Omerie noticed he looked like he was fast asleep. She hesitated, thinking it might not be a good idea for him to sleep there. Maybe she should wake him and ask him to go rest in his room.

"Chief," she said, placing her hand softly on his shoulder.

"Yes, dear," he responded quickly, surprising her.

"Ah, I thought you were sleeping," she said as he opened his eyes.

He took a deep breath and sat up straight. "Ome," he called, his tone suddenly serious.

"Yes, Chief," she replied, slightly worried.

Chief took another deep breath and paused briefly. "I have not seen Onome and Rukevwe today. Are they not in this compound?" he asked, concern lacing his voice.

"Ermm… yes, they are. They came to greet you. Did you not see them?"

"No, I did not," he said, shaking his head.

"They were here," she insisted but noticed the confused look on his face. "Ermm... but they were not here when we were eating," she added quickly, sensing what he was thinking.

He nodded in agreement. "Okay, I did not see them," he responded, sounding curious.

Omerie decided it was best not to have this conversation tonight. Chief had just returned from the hospital and needed time to rest before discussing family matters.

"Ermm Chief, please go inside and rest. You know you were just discharged today, and the doctor said you should try and rest."

He remained silent, a slight frown on his face.

"Chief, is everything okay?" Omerie asked.

"Ome, please tell them to go and call Onome for me," he finally said.

"Okay, I will tell her to come here tomorrow," Omerie replied, relieved that he didn't demand to see her immediately. "Chief, you need to rest," she said, gently patting his hand to encourage him to get up and go inside.

"Ome, do you really think I can sleep in this compound with this weight on me?" he asked, staring at her intently.

"Ah ah, but Emmanuel, this can wait till tomorrow now, ehnn? What is it you want to tell her that cannot wait until morning?" she asked.

Chief shook his head from side to side. "No. No, I will not be able to sleep tonight until I deal with this," he said, leaning back in the rocking chair. "Please tell them to go and call Onome for me now."

She knew there was no point in trying to convince him otherwise, so she called for the maid and asked her to fetch Onome.

As the maid walked away, Omerie looked at Chief, who had rested his head again on the chair. She sighed and leaned back as well.

A few minutes later, the maid returned. "She dey come, ma," she said before disappearing into the house.

They waited a few more minutes. Soon, Omerie saw Onome walking slowly toward them. Beside her, holding tightly to her hand, was Rukevwe.

As they drew closer, Omerie could tell they were crying.

"Onome, Rukevwe, come, come. Don't cry. Come, come," she beckoned to them, but they stood frozen at a distance.

She saw Chief sit up, looking at them. He beckoned to them as well, but they still didn't move closer. Omerie could see the fear in their eyes.

"Onome, you have never disobeyed me," he said. "Come."

This time, he stretched both arms out to her.

Omerie watched as Onome told Rukevwe to wait there. She then walked slowly to her father and quickly knelt before him. Chief immediately enveloped her in his arms, and they began to weep.

"Papa, please..." she sobbed. "Please don't drive me from this compound. You are my father."

Omerie could hear Onome say this over and over again. She hadn't realised she was crying too. She beckoned to Rukevwe, who came closer, and Omerie hugged her tightly.

"Never, my daughter. Never. You hear me? This is your home, you hear me?" Chief said at last, his voice choking with tears.

He looked up and saw Rukevwe. "My pikin," he said, "Come, come."

Rukevwe knelt before him too, and Omerie watched as all three of them sobbed together. She was crying as well—tears of joy.

She hadn't expected things to happen the way they just had, but all she could do was thank God.

Chapter 27

Onome watched as Rukevwe reached down to pick up a broom from the kitchen floor and headed out through the kitchen door. The two of them had been hard at work this afternoon, keeping the house tidy. Onome was making stew for them to have with rice and some plantain. They both loved plantain, and today, they felt like having some. Onome said she would make it while also taking care of some of the house chores.

Rukevwe had been quiet since their meeting with their father a few days ago. It had been a lot for her to handle. She had found out everything on that day. The next day, she had refused to eat, staying in her room after school. She cried so much afterward. Onome knew that the absence of their mother and discovering that her only sister has a different father was just too much for Rukevwe to process.

For Onome, it was all unexpected. Aunty Omerie had informed them that their father was being discharged the day before he arrived, and there was to be a family gathering upon his return. Onome was worried. She knew the day would come, and she had been praying a lot, asking God for help. She had not gone to see her father in the hospital after learning about her biological father. She was afraid to face him, unsure if he would want to see her.

Although Aunty Omerie never said anything, Onome felt that she knew. It was quite evident, one day when Aunty Omerie hugged her for no reason, and Onome cried in her arms as Aunty Omerie assured her that nothing had changed, and she was still a part of the family. Onome felt much better afterward. Aunty Omerie had always been a mother to them, and now that their own mother had left without any news or even to check on them, Aunty Omerie stepped in even more.

Onome could hear Rukevwe sweeping the living room. She could hear her dusting the chairs. They had been getting along well in the last few months, and the challenges they faced had brought them closer together. They had never been this close before, and it felt like their mother's departure had drawn them together.

Onome turned to focus on the pot of stew, which was nearly cooked, and the rice, which was slowly cooking on another stove. She proceeded to chop the plantain. It wouldn't take too long, and she was very hungry, just like Rukevwe. The plantain fried quickly, and the stew and rice were ready. Onome called out for her sister, but she didn't hear back. She called a few more times, then decided to go see where she was.

She wasn't in the living room, so she went outside the house. She saw the broom left by the side of the house and continued walking, but Rukevwe was nowhere to be found. As she walked toward the gate to ask Musa if he had seen her, she heard voices coming from her father's verandah. One voice she immediately recognised. Her heart stopped for a second. No, it couldn't be. She immediately turned to look toward her father's quarters, and there he was—Michael. His back was turned away from her as he sat on a chair facing her father, Aunty Omerie, and Aunty Mabel. She could see Rukevwe standing beside Sister Beatrice.

At that moment, Rukevwe saw her, said something to Sister Beatrice, and immediately left them to walk toward Onome. Onome was still standing there, unsure whether to go over to them or not.

"Are you looking for me?" Rukevwe asked as she drew closer.

"Yes," Onome replied, "I wanted to tell you to come and eat. The food is ready."

"Okay," Rukevwe said, sensing the expression on her sister's face. "It's Brother Michael ooh. You know he wants to marry Sister Beatrice now that she's finished university. He came to tell Papa."

"Ehnn, okay," Onome whispered.

"Anyway, I think Aunty Omerie said they have to wait a few months until Papa is strong enough, but Papa is saying no, that they can marry anytime," Rukevwe added, staring at Onome before turning back to look at the verandah.

"Aren't you going to greet them?" Rukevwe asked.

Onome took a deep breath. Why? she thought. Sister Beatrice still hadn't changed, and Brother Michael—well, she hadn't seen him since that day at the church. She heard he went to the city when Sister Beatrice returned to university. It was clear that he liked her. Onome had missed him at first, but over time, she stopped thinking about him. In fact, she couldn't even remember when her feelings for him faded.

"I'm hungry," Rukevwe interrupted her thoughts. "I can't wait for you," she said as she started to walk away toward their quarters.

Onome was still looking at the verandah. Sister Beatrice had turned to look at her now. She smiled and waved. Onome almost turned to look behind her to see if someone else had stepped into the compound, but since she was close to the gate, she knew Sister Beatrice could only have been waving at her. That seemed to catch everyone's attention. Michael turned around to look. Onome started walking toward the verandah.

Brother Michael had turned back to continue his conversation with Aunty Omerie. As she stepped onto the verandah, Sister Beatrice quickly walked over to her and gave her a big hug.

"Onome, how naah?" she said with a huge smile. Onome was in shock, her hands stuck by her side. Sister Beatrice could see her surprised look.

"Ah, you don't want to hug me? Are we fighting?" Sister Beatrice said playfully.

"Welcome, Sister."

"Thank you," Beatrice said, turning her gaze back to Michael. Michael's eyes were away from Onome. He didn't look up at her.

"Good afternoon, Brother," she greeted him.

"Good afternoon, Onome," he replied with a slight smile. "How are you?" Onome couldn't believe how cold his tone was now. This was the same person who had told her he liked her. He didn't wait for her to respond. His attention turned to Omoefe.

"Omoefe, so when are you going to come to Lagos?" he asked.

"Ah no ooh, my daughter is not going to Lagos yet ooh," Aunty Mabel said, pulling Omoefe toward her bosom.

Everyone burst into laughter, except Onome. She turned to look at Sister Beatrice, who was now looking back at her. She wasn't smiling this time. There was an awkward silence. Onome quickly broke the silence.

"Congratulations, Sister. I heard you're getting married."

"Thank you ooh, he's been disturbing me since," Sister Beatrice laughed, playfully touching Michael's head. Onome noticed that Michael caught her hand as she pulled it back. "Thank God we've finally agreed on a date," Sister Beatrice added, and they both smiled at each other.

"Ehnn... see love wantiti ooh," Omoefe said, laughing softly. Everyone burst into laughter again, and Onome joined in. She thought she would be in tears when this day finally came. The day when she would hear about them getting married. She had always thought she would be in tears, but it wasn't the case. In fact, she was happy for them. The truth was, they were good together. She thought as she looked at them, their hands still locked as they talked about why they had chosen that date.

Onome noticed that Michael hadn't looked at her again. She didn't know why she had thought he was the one. She couldn't deny that he was very handsome, but she had come to realise that he wasn't who she thought he was. Well, she wished them well and would pray for them.

Her thoughts were interrupted by the loud sound of the gate opening. She turned back to see who Musa had opened it for. Her heart skipped a beat. Right then, at the gate, was Pastor Maxwell, smiling as he spoke briefly to Musa and turned away to walk quickly toward them. A broad smile was on his face, and Onome couldn't help but smile as well. She thought he was looking at her. She suddenly looked away.

"Pastor Maxwell, good afternoon," Sister Beatrice walked toward him and gave him a side hug.

"Good afternoon, Beatrice. I was trying not to be late," he said, looking across the verandah. He greeted both aunties. Onome couldn't help but notice how the place lit up with his arrival. Suddenly, he was by her side.

"Onome, how are you?" he said, extending a side hug.

"We've missed you in church ooh. We hope you'll come back soon," he added.

Before she could respond, Sister Beatrice got his attention.

"Uncle, we asked Pastor Maxwell to please come today so that we can all talk and at least make some plans."

"Ehnn?" Chief said. "My Pastor, my Pastor," Chief joked.

Her father had started calling him that now; he had grown even fonder of him. "Oya, let's go inside to the living room,"

Onome watched as Pastor Maxwell and Brother Michael shook hands and walked inside. She had a feeling she wasn't invited, and apparently, so did Omoefe. They both looked at each other, shrugged their shoulders, and chuckled.

"Me, I'm going to eat," Onome said as she made to leave.

"What are you going to eat?"

"Rice and stew with dodo *(plantain)*."

"Ah, dodo! I'm coming ooh. Abeg, you will give me some ooh," Omoefe said, not asking but telling her. They both started walking towards the quarters, with Omoefe asking if it was with chicken or beef. As they conversed, Onome's thoughts drifted back to earlier—*I like him. No, in fact, I love him. I love Pastor Maxwell. I really love him.*

***

A few hours later, they were playing Ludo. Omoefe had already won twice, and Onome had given up. She was watching as Omoefe played with Rukevwe. Then, there was a knock on the door. Onome turned toward it; the door was ajar with the curtain partially blocking the view. She didn't need to guess who it was. She could tell by his tall frame, standing outside. Onome nervously walked towards the door and pulled the curtain away.

He smiled at her. "Onome, sorry ooh, I hope I'm not disturbing you." She shook her head in response, unable to say anything.

"I just wanted to check on you before I leave," he said, pausing slightly. "How are you and Rukevwe keeping?"

At that moment, she wished he would hug her, and that she could burst into tears and tell him everything in her heart. She was lost in her thoughts, but he was waiting for her response.

"We're keeping fine," was all she could manage to say.

"Is everything okay?" he asked, moving a little closer, concern in his voice.

"Yes, everything is fine," she managed a smile.

"Are you sure?"

"Yes, Pastor, everything is okay."

He gave her a suspicious and funny look, making her laugh, which in turn made him smile.

"Good afternoon, Pastor Maxwell!" Rukevwe joined them.

"Rukevwe! I was just asking about you. How are you?"

"I'm fine ooh."

"I hope I didn't disturb you."

"No, not at all. We were just playing Ludo."

"I'm winning!" Omoefe exclaimed from inside.

"I was just feeling sorry for you, Omoefe. Let me tell you ooh," Rukevwe shouted back.

"For where!?" Omoefe had now come to join them by the door. "Pastor Maxwell, come and play naah, let's see if you'll beat me."

Pastor Maxwell laughed. "Madam champion."

"Who wants to try me?" Omoefe swayed from side to side, like she was dancing.

They all laughed. Onome glanced at him from the corner of her eye. He was looking at Omoefe, and Onome was happy that he had come around to see her.

"Madam of Ludo, I can't play with you today, but when I come next time."

"Ehn, when will you come?" Omoefe asked.

"Ah, I'm not going to tell you. I want to take the Ludo master by surprise," he said with a broad smile.

Omoefe laughed. "You can't beat me. Nobody can beat me."

He laughed now, and that laughter made him even more handsome, Onome thought. She watched as Omoefe and Pastor Maxwell joked for a while before she was pulled back to reality when she heard Omoefe say, "Okay, we shall see," as she walked back inside the house.

Suddenly, Pastor Maxwell turned to Onome. "I have to go now; sorry I can't stay. Ermm... I won't be here for some time because I'm going to see my parents."

"When are you coming back?" Rukevwe asked.

"Ermm... let's say about a month from now," he said. Onome's mind screamed, *A month!* It made her sad to think she wouldn't see him for that long.

There was a moment of silence.

"One month, Pastor?" Rukevwe repeated.

"I'll be back soon anyway," he said, his gaze fixed on Onome.

"Okay, we will miss you ooh, Pastor Maxwell," Rukevwe made a funny face. He smiled and gave her a hug.

"Ah, I will miss you too," he replied.

Onome couldn't find the words. Of course, she would miss him terribly. But how could she tell him? Her thoughts raced. *Is he going home to tell his parents he's getting married? Has he spoken to Prisca yet?*

"Okay, let me go ehn, Onome," he snapped her out of her thoughts. "Promise me you'll go to the services. There'll be another Pastor covering for me, he's really good."

"Yes, I will, I promise," her voice shaky.

"Okay, I'll check on you when I get back, ehn," he gave her a hug, this time holding on longer than before. As he pulled away, he looked at her one more time, but she couldn't bring herself to look at him. She was afraid she would cry.

"Okay, you people should take care of yourselves, ehn?" he said, waving as he left. Rukevwe took a deep breath, turned to look at Onome but said nothing, then walked back inside.

Onome continued to watch him walk to the gate, until he disappeared out of the compound and out of her sight.

Chapter 28

It was a Sunday afternoon, the television was on, and it was news hour. Chief was in his quarters with the Senior Pastor. It had been a month since he returned from the hospital. At Omerie's request, he had stayed home and rested most of the time, but what he insisted on was attending church every Sunday, which they agreed to. He had also insisted on speaking to the Senior Pastor, and thankfully, the Senior Pastor was in town that first Sunday Chief went to church. After the service, he went to his office where they spoke at length about their last meeting.

The Senior Pastor had dismissed the event as soon as Chief brought it up, saying he was more than certain Chief was not himself. He suspected something was wrong, so he had asked his team and the church to intercede for him. The words "he was not himself" played on Chief's mind. Yes, indeed, he was not himself. It took some time in the hospital for him to come to this realisation. It became clearer after his investigations into Rume. What a woman he had married. To think she was seeing a so-called Prophetess, who was concocting various potions that Rume was using to facilitate her evil plans. What a fool he had been and how little he knew about the woman he married. Rume. Right then, he wondered where she could be. He heard she could not be found at the family house in the village where they lived. Even her mother didn't know where she had gone to. He did not care, as long as she was out of his life. He had already arranged to return her bride price and made sure her family was told she was not allowed to be anywhere near the children.

Chief sighed. The Senior Pastor looked at him now, with a concerned expression on his face. Just then, there was a knock on the door, which was slightly open. He immediately turned his gaze to the door. Through the half-drawn curtain, he could see the feet of two men standing outside. He knew who one of them was, of course; he had asked him to come, but he didn't know who the second person was.

"I think they are here," Chief said quickly to the Senior Pastor.

"Ehn, okay," the Senior Pastor said, adjusting himself on the chair.

"Yes, please come in," Chief said, also adjusting himself on the chair.

They stepped in one after the other. Richard stepped in first, and Chief realised he was much taller than he thought. There was a look of surprise on his face as he looked at Chief, then he suddenly turned his gaze to the Senior Pastor and then back to the much older man who had stepped in now.

"Good afternoon," Richard said to both of them.

"Good afternoon, Chief," the older man greeted immediately after. Turning to see the Senior Pastor, his mouth slightly opened with a surprised look on his face. "Ah, Pastor, is this you?" he asked as he immediately walked across the living room toward the Senior Pastor.

"Ochuko!" the Senior Pastor exclaimed, rising to his feet. They both shook hands. Chief watched as they exchanged greetings and noticed that Richard was watching them too.

"Please sit down, sit down," Chief said to both men.

They both thanked him and sat down, side by side on the two-seater chair.

"Pastor, I am happy to see you ooh. It has been a long time," Ochuko said.

"My brother, I have been busy, but God is helping us," the Senior Pastor replied, then turned to Chief. "I used to lead the church in the town where Ochuko and his family live."

"Ehnn, okay, I see," Chief turned to look at Ochuko with a slight smile.

"The church has not been the same since you left us, o, but we are trying by God's grace," Ochuko immediately said.

"We thank God," the Senior Pastor replied, pausing for a second before continuing, "Is he one of your children? Because I never met him when I was there," he asked.

"Ah, no, sir," Ochuko laughed.

"He is my Uncle," Richard finally spoke.

"Ah, okay, because I was not too sure," the Senior Pastor said, now turning to Chief.

There was an awkward silence. Chief was unsure what to say at first. He had spoken to the Senior Pastor, before arranging this meeting, and they had planned and rehearsed everything he would say. But now, seeing Richard today and noticing how much Onome resembled him, made him a little sad. His daughter, he thought. Yes, she is his daughter. He had been there when she was born, carried her in his arms, helped nurse her, and trained her through school. How could he not call her his daughter?

He saw both men looking at him, unsure themselves of what was going on.

Chief cleared his throat. "Thank you for honouring my invitation," he said, staring at Richard as he spoke.

"No problem, sir. I hope you are feeling well, sir," Richard responded.

"Yes, I am feeling well. My body is much stronger now."

"Ah, good. We thank God, sir," Richard said with a slight smile. There was a brief silence as Chief turned to the other man sitting next to Richard.

"Ermm, you are both welcome," Chief replied. "Please, what can I offer you?"

"No, sir, we are okay, sir."

"Ah, no naah, you must drink something, even if it's water, please," Chief insisted. They looked at each other, as if to decide what to do.

"Okay, we will have some water, sir," Richard replied.

Chief called out to the maid and asked her to bring some bottles of cold water. The room fell silent again as the maid entered, placed the bottles on the stool with two glasses, and left. Chief watched as Richard leaned forward, opening the bottle of water. He poured some for himself and for his Uncle. Chief observed as they both drank simultaneously. He adjusted himself on his chair again as they placed their glasses back on the stool. After a few seconds, he turned to the Senior Pastor, who nodded to encourage him to go ahead.

"I want to thank you, Richard... and your Uncle, for honouring my invitation to come here today." They both nodded in response.

"Richard, first of all, I want to thank you for how you have handled this matter. It has shown me that there are still a few good men around." His gaze was on Richard, who nodded at first but soon lowered his head.

"Thank you, Richard, for not shaming me," Chief said with an appreciative tone. Richard nodded again.

"I do not want to talk about my wife Rume's actions. I believe that God is the best person to deal with that, as He likes."

"Yes, yes, that's true," Richard's Uncle said, patting him on the back.

"Ehn... I think it has already happened, so let us not discuss the past. Let us now talk about how we move forward from here," Chief paused for a second. "Or do you not think so?" he asked, looking at Richard.

"Yes, sir, I definitely agree, sir," Richard replied, nodding again.

"Good, it's good you agree with me." Chief paused again. "Now, let us discuss our daughter Onome." He paused, watching Richard's reaction. He thought to himself, *This is going to be a difficult conversation,* but he could only pray that the Senior Pastor and Richard's Uncle could help them come to a reasonable agreement. All of a sudden, he felt thirsty. He reached over to the glass of water by the side stool and drank slowly. After placing the glass down, he continued.

"They tell me that you have two children," Chief asked.

"Yes, sir, one boy and one girl," Richard replied.

"Onome is your first child?" Chief asked in a low tone.

Richard nodded, not saying anything.

"I take her as my child too," Chief said, watching for Richard's reaction. Richard said nothing again.

"You see, Richard," Chief continued, leaning forward in his chair, "I do not want to give up my daughter Onome. After all these years, I have always looked at her as my daughter… so please, let us discuss how we can move forward with this situation."

He watched as Richard turned to look at his uncle and then back at him.

"Okay, no problem, Chief. Please go ahead."

***

It was nearing 6 o'clock in the evening now, and Chief was sitting at the dining table with his two wives, having their evening meal. Mabel had prepared some Banga Soup with fresh fish and starch as the swallow. Chief watched them listen intently between swallows, their eyes sparkling with excitement as he shared how the meeting with Richard had gone. It had gone smoother than he had imagined. Richard had agreed to all his suggestions: Onome would continue living in Chief's house until she finished university; they both agreed that Richard would pay for her university fees, accommodation, and all her study requirements, while Chief would be responsible for her upkeep. This arrangement would give them both a chance to care for her and allow Richard to get to know his daughter, since he hadn't been given the chance before. They would leave it to Onome to decide what she wanted to do during her holidays, especially Christmas and New Year celebrations. Chief promised that he would encourage her to build a relationship with her father, Richard, while also ensuring that it did not come across as rejection from him. They were both so pleased with everything that they decided to accept Chief's offer of a celebratory drink, bottles of Supermalt for everyone.

"You used to hate Supermalt, now look at you!" Omerie interrupted, laughing slightly.

"Abi ooh!" Mabel joined in, and they all laughed.

"Supermalt is good for you," Chief said, as if doing a Supermalt commercial. They laughed again.

"Ah, this is good news shaa," Mabel said, her smile wide. Omerie nodded in agreement.

"Well…" Chief continued, taking a quick swallow, "We thank God. Now I can sleep very well," he said, preparing to take another piece of starch.

"Ehn, I said it to Mabel a few days ago that I don't think you are sleeping at night," Omerie said, looking at Mabel across the table. Mabel nodded.

"My dear, how can I sleep, not knowing if Richard was going to cause trouble?" Chief paused, his hand hovering over the bowl of Banga soup. "I was worried," he continued. "Richard could have made trouble for this family and dragged my name through the mud in this town," he concluded, taking another piece of starch and dipping it in the Banga soup.

"You are right. He is a good and respectful man," Omerie agreed.

"Yes, very respectful," Chief replied.

They continued eating, changing the topic to things happening in the town. Just then, Beatrice walked in, dragging her feet slowly, her face down as she approached the dining table. Chief turned to look at her.

"Beaty, Beaty..." he called her by her favourite nickname, pausing as he noticed something was wrong. "What is it?" he asked, concerned.

Beatrice shook her head and wiped her cheeks, tears rolling down.

"Ah, Beatrice, what is it?" Chief heard Omerie ask. Mabel slowly got up from her chair and walked over to her.

"Let her sit down," Chief said. "Beaty, sit down and tell us what has happened." He watched as Mabel guided Beatrice to sit across from him, the tears continued to roll down her cheeks.

"Ah, Beatrice, will you not talk?" Chief said, his irritation growing as he washed his hands in a bowl of water. What could have happened? Did something bad happen to her? Or maybe one of his children? No, never. Nothing bad would happen to his children, he rejected that thought.

"Beatrice, talk naah, do you want to trouble your Uncle, ehn?" Omerie said.

Chief watched as Beatrice sniffled, wiped away some tears, and then looked up at him. "Uncle, it is that boy Michael."

"Michael?" he paused, trying to recollect who Michael was. "Oh..." he said, remembering now. "You mean your husband-to-be,

Michael?" he asked, but didn't wait for a response. "Ah, did something happen to him?"

"No, Uncle, nothing happened to him," she said through sobs.

"Then why are you crying?" he asked, getting irritated again. Beatrice sobbed harder.

"What is it now, Beatrice? Please talk to us," Omerie urged, almost pleading.

Chief watched as Beatrice sobbed loudly before eventually speaking.

"Mr. Odafe's daughter is pregnant for him ooh," she said, bursting into tears again.

"Ah, our neighbour pikin? Nah lie be that!" Mabel exclaimed, both hands on her head. Chief turned to look at Omerie, who shook her head slightly. Chief was silent.

"Where did you hear this?" Mabel asked.

Beatrice stopped crying for a moment, raised her head, and said, "It's all over town. They say that Mr. Odafe's daughter isn't the only girl pregnant for him. They say he has a child with one girl in Lagos city and another child with a girl at Ughelli town." She put her hands on her head and exclaimed, "Oh God, I am finished, I am finished ooh, my enemies have finished me!" She cried louder.

Chief watched again as Mabel tried to console her. *Young children with enemies after them*, he thought. He shook his head.

"Mabel, please take her to her room," Chief said. Mabel helped Beatrice up as she continued to cry.

"Beatrice, don't cry, ehn? Go and rest, your Uncle will discuss this with you later," Mabel said, guiding her slowly away.

"My enemies o, my enemies have finished me o" Beatrice cried out placing her hands on her head.

Chief heard Omerie take a deep breath. He turned to her. "Did I not tell you? I said that boy looked like a stupid and useless boy" he said.

"Yes, Chief you said it ooh" Omerie replied. Chief sighed.

"But Chief, these stories could be lies ooh."

"Which lies? I believe them," he said, rising from his chair. "I told you I've always suspected it. He looks like a good-for-nothing boy, but you all kept saying, 'No, o, he's a good, respectful, hardworking boy from a rich family.' A good and respectful boy who goes around impregnating young girls, abi?" He grabbed a napkin to wipe his hands.

"All that big man talk the other day didn't fool me at all," he added, clicking his tongue. "Anyway, I'm glad we found out now, and not after the marriage." I would have killed that stupid boy."

"Ah, I believe you," Omerie said, slowly getting up from her chair and calling for the maid. As Chief walked to sit in the living room, he began to reflect. What was he really saying? Hadn't he done the same thing to Omerie? He'd gotten other women pregnant, but the only difference was that it had happened within a marriage. At least he'd been responsible. As he continued to ponder the current situation with Beatrice, it made him realise just how hurtful it must have been for Omerie, even though he had done things 'the legal way' with the other wives he married. She loved him, and he loved her, but he had hurt her badly

He heard her footsteps as she joined him in the living room and sat down next to him.

"Are you going to watch anything?" she asked, pointing to the television, which was off.

"Omerie."

"Um?" she replied, turning her eyes to look at him.

"I'm so sorry for what I've put you through," he said, pausing. "I'm sorry," he repeated. He watched as tears welled up in her eyes. He stood up and walked over to her, wrapping his arms around her and letting her rest her head against his chest. Gently, he began to pat her on the back.

Chapter 29

I f God is for you, who can be against you? So, we must continue to trust God. He is in control of everything," the visiting Pastor said as he prepared to close the Wednesday evening service.

"Amen?" he asked.

"Amen," Onome responded along with the rest of the congregation.

"Amen. Now let us pray. Please stand on your feet," he instructed.

As Onome stood with the others, she noticed the choir rise as well. Prisca was at the front, smiling and whispering to a girl next to her. Onome couldn't help but reflect on how their friendship had become strained. She had visited Prisca a few times, but each time, Prisca was either heading to choir practice or going to the market. On one occasion, Onome had offered to accompany her to the market, but Prisca had declined, claiming she was going somewhere else afterward. Onome remembered reassuring Prisca that she wasn't after Pastor Maxwell; that she would never do that to her. But deep down, Onome knew that she had come to like Pastor Maxwell. In fact, she loved him. But she had reached a point where she had to believe that God had a plan for her, that there would be someone for her one day.

"Okay, let us bow our heads in prayer now," the Pastor's voice interrupted her thoughts.

As Onome bowed her head, she heard the Pastor begin to pray.

"Our Father, we thank you for this service..."

Her thoughts wandered as she listened. The visiting Pastor had been filling in for Pastor Maxwell for over a month now. The last they'd heard, Pastor Maxwell had been delayed in returning, but he was doing well. Onome had been sad when she'd heard that news; she had been eagerly awaiting his return. She had started counting the days since he left, and as soon as a month had passed, her heart would race every time she made her way to church, whether for Sunday or Wednesday service. It was almost as if Senior Pastor knew people were beginning to wonder if he would return, so he had informed every one of the delay. He hadn't mentioned when he would be back, which left Onome feeling even more uncertain. She missed him deeply and had made a habit of praying for him every day.

"Amen, amen," the visiting Pastor said, finishing the prayer. "Let the choir sing us a closing song. Please, let us join them."

Onome watched as Prisca, with a wide smile, belted out each verse of the song. She didn't seem to miss Pastor Maxwell at all, Onome thought. Maybe Prisca knew more than the rest of them. Onome had been practicing her expressions in the mirror, preparing for the day when they would tell her they were getting married. She knew she would cry later, but she would try to be strong in their presence.

"Ah, Chidimma is here," she heard Rukevwe's voice beside her. She had completely forgotten that Rukevwe had come to church with her and had been sitting quietly all this time. Rukevwe pointed to the right. Onome turned to look. Since the service wasn't packed, she easily spotted Chidimma, a girl who had become their friend in the past few weeks. As if sensing she was being watched, Chidimma immediately turned toward them and waved, smiling. Onome waved back, signalling for them to talk later.

She quickly turned her attention back to the Pastor, who was speaking again. The choir's song was coming to an end, and he started to speak once more.

"We thank you, Lord. Yes, we thank you." He gestured for the choir to stop.

"Let us go in peace, and please remember we are still collecting donations of clothes and shoes for the orphanage. Bring any old clothes and shoes to drop off at the front," he added, pointing to a side of the room. He paused, awaiting a response. Onome heard a few people say, "Yes, okay."

"Okay, go in peace," the Pastor said.

As soon as he finished, everyone began moving around, looking for people they knew. Rukevwe had left her now to speak with Chidimma. Onome glanced around, unsure of what or who she was looking for. Her gaze landed on the choir. Prisca was with other members of the choir now, and Boniface had joined them. She'd seen him at least twice since they last spoke, but he hadn't said anything to her. He seemed to get along well with everyone, especially Prisca, who laughed and playfully hit his arm.

Onome shook her head. She should go home. She was feeling sad again and didn't feel like talking to anyone. As she walked toward the door, she passed the book table. It had grown bigger and wider, now stacked with many books. People were gathered around the table, and Onome decided it would be a good idea to find a book to read. She began searching through the pile of books and found one that seemed interesting. She tucked it into her bag. As she turned to leave, she nearly collided with Prisca.

"Sorry," Onome said, feeling she had stepped on Prisca's foot.

At first, Prisca didn't say anything. Onome noticed that Boniface had joined them.

"Ah, Onome," Boniface said with a smile. "How are you? Long time!" he greeted.

"I'm fine," Onome replied, returning the smile.

"I've been seeing your father at church every Sunday. We thank God he is now well," Boniface added, his face serious.

Onome nodded, her gaze drifting to Prisca, who remained silent. Boniface turned to look at Prisca, and Onome watched as his hand moved to hold hers. To her surprise, Prisca welcomed it. Onome couldn't hide her shock.

"Erm... yes, we thank God," Onome said, quickly shifting her gaze to her bag as if she were adjusting the book already secured inside.

"Are you going home now?" Prisca finally spoke, her tone soft.

"Yes," Onome replied, avoiding Prisca's gaze.

"Okay, maybe we can walk together. I'm going home too," Prisca said, though her voice held an uncertain note.

Onome's head snapped up. She was surprised. She turned to look at Boniface, who seemed to be waiting for her response.

"Okay," Onome said, turning toward the door. She wondered if Boniface was coming along too. She stepped outside the church and stood, waiting for them to join her. But it was only Prisca who stepped out.

Onome glanced behind her. As if reading her thoughts, Prisca said, "He's not coming."

They began walking together in silence. Onome didn't know what to say to break the quiet, so they continued for a few minutes until Prisca spoke again.

"Have you registered for the next JAMB exam?" she asked.

"Yes, I have," Onome replied.

"Which centre are you writing it at?"

"I was told to go to the Sapele centre, at the next town," Onome answered.

"Eyaa… that's far ooh," Prisca remarked with a concerned tone. Onome nodded but said nothing.

They fell silent again for a few seconds.

"What about you?" Onome asked.

"I'm writing it here at Rose Primary School," Prisca replied.

"Ah, you're lucky ooh," Onome said with a smile.

There was another quiet pause. As people from the church walked past them, Prisca placed her hand on Onome's shoulder to get her attention. Onome stopped, and Prisca immediately moved close, wrapping her arms around her in a warm hug.

"Onome, please forgive me, I am sorry," she said, hugging her tightly.

Onome stood still for a few seconds, surprised at this. She wondered if Prisca was crying, but thankfully, she was not. Then Onome put her hands around Prisca too. They stood there for a few minutes before letting each other go. She looked at Onome.

"Do you forgive me?" she asked.

"Of course, naah, are you not my best friend?" she said, seeing that it made Prisca smile. They started walking again, remaining silent for some time.

"Hmm… I have many things to tell you ooh," she said.

"Okay," Onome replied. At that moment, she thought to herself, it was as if they had never stopped talking.

"Are you ready for gist?" Prisca asked.

"You and your gist shaa, which one is this now?" Onome said with a smile, and they both laughed. "I think I know shaa," Onome added.

"You know?" Prisca asked, turning to look at her with surprise.

"Yes naah. It's Boniface, or is it not?" Onome gave Prisca a funny look. Prisca laughed.

"Okay, wait, wait, let me tell you," Prisca said. They continued walking as Prisca proceeded to tell her all she missed during the time they were 'not so close,' according to her.

***

Onome stepped out of the examination classroom, breathing a sigh of relief. The exam was over, thank God. She had been preparing and studying for some time, not being able to sleep, and worrying about what questions were going to be asked. The JAMB examination was known to be quite difficult, as it covered multiple topics stretched across different areas. She could safely say that she answered all the questions, now she could relax. She took a deep breath again. Now, she could go home and sleep. Her father had told her that he would send the driver to pick her up, as it was a town 2 hours from them.

There were quite a few cars parked in the school parking lot. She looked around for the driver but couldn't see him. He must still be on his way, she thought. What could she do now, she wondered? Maybe she should find a place to sit down and wait. She looked around again and saw a shop with some seats, under a tree. Maybe she could buy something to eat and drink there while waiting for the driver. She went over to the shop. It wasn't busy, so she bought some snacks and a drink. She found an empty table with a few chairs; she arranged her plate and drink on the table, and began to eat.

She had only been there for a few minutes when she heard, "Supermalt! Your favourite drink." She lifted her gaze to see who it was. She didn't need anyone to tell her who it was. It was him. It was Pastor Maxwell, standing across the tiny table in front of her with his arms crossed and a smile on his face.

"I can see you're having meat pie as well. I hope the exam wasn't too hard," he chuckled as he continued speaking. He pulled a chair across from her and sat down, placing a set of keys on the table.

Her heart was beating fast. *He is back!* she thought to herself as her heart leaped a little. She could hardly believe he was right in front of her. How come he was here? Why was he here? she asked herself.

"Is everything okay?" he asked, staring at her now. She nodded her head, putting her hand over her mouth, as she had taken a big bite of the meat pie at that moment. She dropped her head down as she chewed slowly. *How is it that he is here?* she asked herself again.

As if he could read her mind, he said, "Your father asked me to come and pick you up. I was at your house."

She continued chewing, now staring at him as he spoke. Almost two months had passed since he had been away, and she had been praying for him to return. Now, here he was. She thought she was dreaming. As she looked at him, she noticed he had put on a bit of weight, and it suited him. He wasn't wearing his usual white shirt and black trousers. He was wearing jeans and a blue t-shirt with the word "Strong" written on it. He looked really handsome.

"He had to go somewhere with the driver," he continued, his eyes not leaving hers, his gaze completely fixed on her, still smiling. She placed the meat pie on the plate it came with, picked up her bottle of Supermalt, then took a sip and placed it back down on the table.

"How was the exam?" he asked.

"It was fine. It was alright," she replied.

"You answered all the questions?"

"Yes, all of them."

"Very good," he said, looking pleased.

There was a strange silence.

"How did you manage to find me?" Onome asked.

"I saw you as I was looking for a place to park. I couldn't shout your name because you were too far. I noticed where you were going and thought to come and find you around here. Then I saw you sitting here," he said, smiling broadly now.

She smiled, taking her gaze away and looking down at her meat pie.

"Don't worry, finish it. I'll wait," he said, pointing at her plate of meat pie.

She shook her head. "I've finished. I'll take the rest home," she said, starting to wrap up the meat pie. She didn't feel like eating anymore.

"What about the Supermalt?" he asked, curiously.

"Erm, I'll take it too," she said as she slowly pushed the chair back to stand up.

"You're ready to go?" he asked in a slightly disappointed tone.

She stood there and slowly nodded. He paused for a second. "So, you're not happy to see me?" he asked, still sitting down, staring at her.

She paused. Yes, of course, she was happy to see him. Did it not show? She thought. Could he not see that her legs and hands were shaking? This is why she wanted to go home, she thought. She wanted to hug him. She was hoping at that point he would stand up and give her a hug, but he didn't.

"Yes, I am happy to see you," she finally responded, her head down again.

"Onome," he called. When she didn't look up, he called again, "Onome, please look at me." Then she looked up.

"I missed you ooh," he said, his gaze now so soft. "Did you miss me?"

She paused a little. *This is the time to be brave*, she told herself.

"Yes, I missed you," she said, still with her head down.

His smile was broad now. "Really?" he asked. She slowly nodded.

"Please sit down, let's talk," he beckoned, his tone serious. She sat down slowly, wondering what he wanted to say.

"I'm sorry I didn't come back as I planned. My father was very sick."

"Eyaa, sorry," she said, lifting her gaze now.

"Thank you. You see, I had to stay home to look after him and help my mother too."

"Sorry," she said. "Is he feeling better now?" she asked immediately, starting to relax a little.

"Erm, he is much better now."

"Okay, thank God."

He nodded. His gaze remained on her.

"Onome, I am really happy to see you ooh," he said, his gaze soft as he looked at her. She said nothing.

"Onome," he said, pausing briefly, "I like you ooh, do you know?"

"You like me?" she asked, surprised.

"Yes, Onome, I like you. I like you very much," he replied immediately. "You see..." He continued, placing both hands on the table. "I want to marry you," he said, intently staring at her. She had her mouth slightly open. This must be a dream, she thought. Pastor Maxwell likes her? Pastor Maxwell wants to marry her? How? She knew Prisca had moved on and was now going out with Boniface, but she never thought he liked her.

"Onome?" he called.

"Yes" she answered.

"What is the matter? Because I can see something is wrong."

She took a deep breath, not sure how to answer the question.

"I did not know that you liked me," she said, looking down.

"Hmm...." he said, taking a deep breath. "I was hiding it," he continued. Onome looked up now. He suddenly picked the keys from the table; she wondered if he was nervous. "I noticed you a long time ago, the first time I saw you with Prisca." His voice was slightly shaky.

She vaguely remembered that day. She had been at Prisca's house that evening as Prisca prepared to go to the evening service on Wednesday. Prisca had invited her, but she had said no. They had walked to the church as it was on her way home. They had seen Pastor Maxwell at the church entrance speaking to a young boy. He had lifted his head to look at them, stared for a while, and then turned his attention to the young boy. Onome did not read any meaning into it and had carried on home.

"I noticed you and wanted to get to know you. I prayed to God that if you are His will for me, He will make everything go well," he paused again and then continued. "I did not see you again, but then a month later, Senior Pastor took me to your house to introduce me to your father. In fact, I did not know it was where you lived or that you were Chief's daughter. I found out later, and I knew God was at work. I kept visiting your house and hoped that I would see you. I prayed for an opportunity to get to know you, and God gave me that opportunity the day I helped you carry that bag of food to Madam's house. After that day, I knew I wanted to marry you. I was just waiting for the right time to tell you and tell your father." He stopped, hesitating. "I was not sure that you liked me," he stopped talking again and looked at her, waiting to see her reaction. Tears had formed in her eyes while he was talking. She was thinking to herself: So all this time, he liked her and wanted to marry her? The tears began to drop down her face.

"Onome, why are you crying?" he asked gently. He sat up, pulling his chair over and placing it next to hers. He pulled her toward him to comfort her.

He gently pulled her head to rest on his chest, her hand wiping her tears.

"Nothing," she said, wiping away a few more tears.

"I hope you are crying because you are happy?" he asked with a concerned tone. She nodded, not looking up.

"Okay, that is good," he said. She could tell he was smiling. "You like me too, abi?" he asked. She nodded her head, unable to speak.

"Okay, that is good, because I have asked your father if he will agree for me to marry you."

She raised her head to look at him, leaning away slightly. Her father? But which one? She thought. He doesn't know. He doesn't know that my father is not my biological father. Or does he? No, her father would not discuss that with anyone. But what did her father say to him, she wondered. She was looking at him strangely now.

"Is everything alright?" he asked with a concerned tone.

"Ermm..." she paused. "What did my father tell you?"

"Well, he said he has heard me, that I should come back in a few days, but I should come and tell you first, so I know if you want to marry me."

Onome took a deep breath and moved away from him to sit fully on the chair. He shifted slightly on his chair to look at her.

"What is it, Onome?" he asked. "Did I say something bad?"

"No," she said, shaking her head but not looking at him.

"Then what is it?" he asked again. "Do you not want to marry me?"

"Yes, I want to marry you, but..." she said softly.

"But what?" he asked.

She shook her head, staring down at her hands.

"What is it, Onome, ehn? Tell me."

She raised her head to look at him. Should she tell him? But no, it is up to her father. If her father did not say anything, then why should she? Her father knows best. She has to let her father tell him.

"I think we should wait until you see my father in a few days," she said.

"Okay, I will wait," he leaned back in the chair now. "But I want you to know that whatever it is, we can go through it together, you hear?"

His tone was serious. She looked at him, seeing the assurance in his eyes, and she felt a sense of peace. She believed him.

"Okay," was all she felt she needed to say. He took a deep breath and smiled. He pulled her to his side, her hair against his cheek.

"We will be fine, you hear?"

She nodded with a smile. There were no tears now. She was happy.

"And... you can call me Maxwell now," he said smiling and she could not help but laugh out loud.

***

Maxwell parked the car just outside the compound. Onome opened the door and got out. It had been a two-hour drive back from the school where she had taken her JAMB examination, and she was happy because it gave them time to talk about many things. She hadn't realised how funny and loving Maxwell was. Maxwell, she called him Maxwell now, and she loved it. She loved his name, and more than that, she loved him.

She smiled as she saw him waiting for her to join him so they could walk in together. As she approached, he stretched out his hand, and she placed hers in it. Together, they walked to the gate, which was slightly open. Onome watched as Maxwell pushed the gate open, but Musa wasn't there. They walked inside, and Maxwell guided her to her father's quarters. As they approached, the sound of voices grew louder, and Onome saw Musa rush out, almost bumping into Maxwell.

"Ah, sorry oga. Abeg I no see you, sir," Musa apologised.

Onome watched as Maxwell tried to steady Musa from falling. At that moment, she left Maxwell's side, wondering what was going on. She heard Maxwell ask Musa what was happening, but she didn't wait to hear Musa's response. As she stepped into the living room, she saw Sister Beatrice and Aunty Mabel beside Aunty Omerie, trying to lift her up. Onome rushed to help. Aunty Omerie was screaming, and Onome didn't need to be told, she was in labour. Just then, Maxwell came in, and Onome noticed he was unsure of what to do.

"Pastor, thank God. Please, did you come with your car?" she heard Aunty Mabel ask.

"Yes ma," Maxwell replied immediately. "I will go and bring the car inside," he rushed off.

They had managed to lift Aunty Omerie and were slowly helping her through the living room.

"Onome," Aunty Mabel called.

"Yes, ma," Onome responded.

"Oya, take this money, go and take a motorcycle to Chief's office quick-quick, tell him that your aunty is in labour and we've taken her to the family hospital. Hurry up, hurry up, ehn!" Mable said, putting some money in her hand.

"Yes, ma," Onome said, taking the money and rushing out of the living room. Outside, Maxwell was just driving in with the car, but she waited for him to park and get out. She quickly went over to him.

"I'm going to tell my father in the office," she said in a rush.

"Okay, how are you getting there?" he asked.

"I'll take a motorcycle; Aunty gave me money. Let me go quickly," she said, turning and walking quickly toward the gate.

"Be careful ooh," Maxwell called after her.

"Okay," she responded without turning back. As she exited the compound, she began to run, needing to reach the next road to call a motorcycle. There was a reason Aunty Mabel asked her to take a motorcycle, it was much faster. As she approached the road, she saw a motorcycle passing by and signalled for it. As soon as it came around, she quickly got on, ensuring she was securely seated. She gave the driver the address of where she was going. It was a 20-minute ride to her father's office. When the motorcycle arrived, she got off and paid the driver.

Her father's office had a high fence with a gate that was open. She walked in but was quickly stopped by the security man.

"Who be that?" he asked.

"Nah me, sir."

"Ah, nah you, Onome? I never see you since ooh. I think say you don go university sef."

"No, sir, I never go yet. Abeg, my papa dey here?" she asked quickly.

Placing his hand under his chin, thinking, he said, "Ehn, I think your papa dey warehouse ooh, but you fit check am for office first shaa."

"Okay, sir, thank you, sir," she said, rushing off.

"Okay ooh, welcome, ehn," the man said.

Onome decided to check for him in his office, which was just a few minutes away from the gate. As she walked quickly, she noticed it was a busy day, employees were loading cartons of beer and crates of soft drinks onto customers' lorries. She greeted them as she passed. She hadn't been to her father's office compound in a long time and didn't recognise any of the employees, but she knew they were workers because of their uniforms. She walked past them quickly and reached the building. It was a bungalow, and his office was at the front. The door was closed, so she knocked a few times, but there was no response. She decided to go around the corner to the back of the building, to the warehouse.

As she neared, she could hear her father's voice shouting commands. She paused for a moment to gather herself; how would she tell him? She had never had to break this kind of news to him before. "Papa, Aunty dey labour," she practised. "Papa, Aunty has gone to the hospital, the baby is coming." After taking a deep breath, she continued walking. She could see her father now, standing at the door of the warehouse with a few cartons of beer in front of him. He looked like he was counting them.

As she approached, he turned around, likely having heard her footsteps. He looked at her, trying to place her face. His expression shifted to a frown as he turned away from the cartons of beer.

"Onome, what has happened?" he asked, as if he already knew. "Ehn, what has happened?" he asked again, now standing in front of her.

"Erm... Aunty... Aunty has been taken to the hospital," she managed to say, not quite as she intended.

"The baby?" he asked, not even waiting for a response. He started calling for the driver. He called several times, even after the driver had already answered.

"Bring the car, bring the car, quick-quick!" he shouted. Turning back to Onome, he asked, "Which hospital?"

"Aunty said the family hospital," Onome quickly responded.

"I should have left this car at home," he said, putting his hand over his face. "They chartered a car?" he asked.

"Erm, no. Max... Erm, Pastor Maxwell was there, so he has taken them to the hospital," Onome explained.

"Ah, thank God for the Pastor," he said. Just then, the driver drove up and parked the car in front of her father. He was about to get in but stopped. "No, no, I have to go there quick-quick," he said. "I'll take a motorcycle." He shut the door of the car and began walking toward the gate. Onome watched as the driver rushed ahead of him.

"Oga, make I go call one for you, sir?" the driver asked as he rushed off.

Onome stood there unsure what to do now. She heard her father call her name.

"Sir," she answered.

"You can come with the driver in the car, let him take you there," she could hear as his voice faded away while he walked around the corner of the building, heading towards the gate. She stood by the car, waiting for the driver. She wasn't sure how long she had waited, but as he approached, she thought, *my father is right. It will take a long time to get to the hospital by car. I want to be there with him at the same time.*

As the driver approached, she said to him, "I will go and call a motorcycle. I want to reach the hospital quickly."

"Ah, but oga say make I carry you come the hospital naah," he said, sounding angry.

"Abeg naah, no vex, I wan reach there quick quick," she almost pleaded, walking away from the car. The driver sighed.

"Oya, make I go call bike for you. Come," he said as he led the way. They quickly walked out of the office compound, and it didn't take long for him to call a motorcycle. She securely got on, and it sped away. She was happy. She wasn't sure how long it would take to get there from her father's office, but she believed it wouldn't take long as it was a small town. She was right; they arrived in no time. She got off, paid the driver, and rushed through the hospital gate. It was the same hospital her father was admitted to. She quickly walked in and, in no time, saw Aunty Mabel and Sister Beatrice. She quickly went to join them.

Aunty Mabel pointed to a chair beside her, and Onome sat down.

"How is everything?" she asked her aunty.

"Everything is fine. She is in the theatre room now," Aunty Mabel said.

"Okay," Onome replied, looking over at Sister Beatrice, who was staring straight at the wall. It seemed her mind was elsewhere. Onome stared at her for a little while. Sister Beatrice had been quiet and withdrawn since the story about Michael; everyone knew. It had become the talk of the town. What a shameful thing to have happened to Sister Beatrice. To think Michael was like that. "What a terrible person," she thought. She had believed she was in love with him, but God saved her from falling into a terrible trap. She sighed.

Onome turned her gaze around the area where they were sitting, wondering where her father and Maxwell were. She wondered if Maxwell had gone back to the church. She was unsure if she should ask Aunty Mabel. Just then, she saw her father walking towards them. He must be coming from the theatre, she thought. She got up from her chair to let him sit.

"You're here already?" he asked with a surprised tone.

"Yes, papa, I took a bike," she answered, a little nervous.

"So, is the driver coming?" he asked.

"Yes, he's coming," she replied, still nervous.

"Okay, when he comes, you people will go back to the compound," he said and sat down. Onome did not want to go home; she wanted to stay until Aunty Omerie delivered the baby. How would she tell her father? He'd probably say no.

The driver came after a while, and Aunty Mabel and Sister Beatrice got up to leave as her father signalled to them. Onome got up and slowly walked towards the exit but then stood still. She wanted to stay, she thought. Should she ask her father if she could stay? She took a deep breath, turned around slowly, and walked toward her father, who had his arms folded around his chest, his head leaning back, his knees shaking. She could tell he was worried. *Lord, let him say yes*, she prayed silently.

"Papa," she said.

He slowly lifted his head to look at her. She took another deep breath.

"I want to stay and wait," she finally said.

He stared at her for a few seconds, then sighed before pointing to the chair beside him for her to sit. She walked slowly to the chair and sat down. The driver came back, and her father told him he could go without her. They sat quietly for some time, then her father sat up straight.

"So, the pastor came to pick you up from the school?" he asked.

"Yes, Papa, he said you told him to come," she replied, a little nervous. Maxwell had said her father asked him to pick her up from the school, did he not?

"Yes, I did," her father said.

She slowly adjusted herself on the chair.

"Has he told you?" her father asked.

"Ermm…" She wasn't sure if he was asking about Maxwell's plans to marry her.

He turned to look at her. "Did he talk to you about marriage?" he asked.

"Yes, sir," she answered.

"Good," he said, turning his face away. "Ehn, what did you answer?"

She felt strange talking to him about this. She didn't want him to turn and look at her again.

"I said… I will marry him, sir," she whispered.

He nodded his head as if in approval.

"He is a good man," he said. She nodded back, though he couldn't see her.

"I've asked him to come in a few days so he can speak to your father," he said, his tone dropping slightly as he leaned back on the chair. She turned her head slightly to look at him, his eyes were closed. She turned away to look at the nurses walking up and down around the waiting area; it wasn't busy. Her mind wandered to Maxwell now. He must have had to go back to the church. She wondered if he would come back to the hospital. She looked at the clock, it was almost 5 o'clock in the afternoon. They had a long wait, she thought. She decided to copy her father, leaning her head back on the chair. To her surprise, it was comfortable, and she decided to shut her eyes to rest.

***

She opened her eyes now, realising she had fallen asleep. She looked at the clock, it was 7 o'clock. She turned to look at her father; he was asleep. She needed to use the toilet. Thankfully, a nurse was standing a few steps away. She walked over to ask for the toilet. It wasn't too far from the waiting area. She quickly walked there and was out a few minutes later. As she approached the waiting area, she saw Maxwell sitting beside her father, with his back to her. They seemed to be having a serious conversation. She could tell her father had said something to Maxwell because he turned around to look at her.

She slowed down, walking slowly, unsure how to react to Maxwell with her father there. She noticed her father was watching her, but he was smiling, which she thought was strange.

"Ah ah, why are you walking like that? Are you not going to greet your husband?" he asked.

She saw Maxwell smile and put his head down. Her father put his hand on Maxwell's back, laughing softly.

"Abi no be your wife?" her father asked, leaning down to speak to him as he laughed softly. Onome was shy now, putting her head down. How was she supposed to greet him now?

He stood up suddenly, walking slowly toward her. She stood still, wondering what he would do. He stopped a few steps away.

"How are you? Have you eaten?" he asked, his tone soft.

She shook her head. She had completely forgotten to eat.

"Okay, I'm going to get some Egusi and Eba for your father. What should I buy for you?" he asked, touching the side of her hand.

She wasn't sure what she wanted to eat. "Anything is fine," she said.

"What about Jollof rice and chicken?" Maxwell asked.

"Okay," she shrugged her shoulders.

"Ah, with some plantain and Supermalt?" he said playfully, smiling.

She couldn't help but laugh softly, putting her head down.

"Okay, let me go and get the food."

"Should I come with you?" she asked.

"Ermm…" He began to speak, then turned to look at her father. Her gaze moved to him as well. "Maybe you should stay with your father. I'll quickly go and come back," he said.

"Okay," she replied. He touched her hand again and turned around, walking away.

She walked back to the chair and sat down beside her father. He was back to resting, his head leaning back, his eyes shut. She decided to do the same.

"You must start learning how to greet your husband when you see him. You cannot be doing shy-shy ooh, you hear?" he said, not even opening his eyes. She thought he was asleep.

"Yes, sir," she said quietly.

They sat in silence for some time until Maxwell arrived with some food. They were very hungry and grateful. They were able to eat in a separate area in the hospital. She noticed that Maxwell had bought himself some Jollof rice and chicken too. They ate without rushing. The doctor said he would let Chief know if there was any news.

She sat beside Maxwell and ate quietly, watching as her father and Maxwell talked about anything and everything. Maxwell would turn to her from time to time, asking if she was alright and if she was enjoying the food. She nodded, too hungry to speak. She wondered if this was what a boyfriend and girlfriend relationship was about.

She worried, unsure what to do or how to act. Her father was right, her shyness would not help her. She would need to learn how to be a wife. Maybe she could learn from American movies or ask Prisca. She wondered how Prisca would react when she found out. Would Prisca care?

Well, she thought, Prisca was now going out with Boniface, and they were planning to get married. She shook her head. Prisca would be fine.

She will be getting married also. The excitement had made her forget her plans to marry after she finished University. Right now, it didn't matter because she trusted Maxwell to allow her to further her education after they are married.

She continued eating while listening to Maxwell and her father as they talked.

Later, they were back in the waiting area. Maxwell decided to stay with them. She tried to get him to go home and rest, but he said he had taken an excuse from the Senior Pastor who said it was okay. It was now 10 o'clock. They were tired and soon fell asleep, her head resting on Maxwell's chest with his arms around her.

They were soon awakened by heavy footsteps and a voice calling her father.

"Chief, Chief!"

They woke up suddenly. Her father sat upright immediately.

"Ah, Chief. Sorry to wake you," the doctor said, standing in front of her father. Her father stood up quickly.

"Doctor, any news? Ehn, any news?" he asked, grabbing the doctor's hand. Onome knew from his tone that her father was very worried.

"Relax, Chief. There is good news. Congratulations, Chief. You have a bouncing baby boy!"

"Ayyyyy!" her father shouted, jumping around. "Thank you, God ooh! God, I thank you! Jesus, I thank you!" he kept saying, looking up to the ceiling with his palms together as if in prayer. Onome could see tears forming in her father's eyes. She started to tear up too. Maxwell was by her side, his hands on hers.

"Congratulations, sir. We thank God," Maxwell said to her father.

"Thank you," her father said, turning to look at him.

"Chief, you can come and see them now," the doctor said.

"Yes, Doctor, please, let's go, let's go ooh!" her father exclaimed, starting to walk away from them, almost dancing as the doctor led the way. He stopped then, and Onome looked at him as he turned around to face her.

"Onome, oya, come, come!"

She smiled and rushed to his side as the doctor continued leading the way. She turned back quickly, realising she had forgotten about Maxwell. He just smiled at her and signalled for her to keep going, saying he would wait. She watched him take a seat before continuing to follow the doctor.

When they got to the room, Aunty Omerie was lying on the bed, looking as if she was asleep. Upon their entrance, she opened her eyes and looked at them. Her father quickly went to her. Onome saw his eyes becoming teary again. He touched her hand and then her face. Onome heard him whisper something to her, though she couldn't hear what he said, but she saw Aunty smile.

Onome quickly peeked into the baby cot and saw the baby sleeping. Her father turned to the cot, calling, "Ogheneruona, my son, my son." She saw her father carefully picked him up and place him in his arms, rocking him gently from side to side. Aunty Omerie smiled, her face looking so tired. Onome noticed that her aunt's gaze moved to hers. Aunty Omerie smiled at her, and Onome smiled back.

She then saw her aunt turn back to her father and their son—her brother. Her brother, she thought. Yes, he is her brother.

She decided it was better to leave them now. She turned to the door and walked out. She headed toward the waiting area. As she walked slowly, she saw Maxwell from afar, bent forward, reading a newspaper. She stopped to look at him, his head was bent intently, he had a little frown on his face, as he read the newspaper.

It was 1 o'clock in the morning, and he was still with her at the hospital. She took a deep breath. So much had happened, and it was all good things. When she left in the morning for the JAMB exam, she had said a prayer asking God to bless her day and make it great. He did, he made it more than great.

She smiled, looking up toward the ceiling. She whispered, "Thank you, Lord."

She started walking toward him. He lifted his head as he heard footsteps, and as soon as he saw her, he quickly stood up, a concerned look on his face.

"Is everything alright?" he asked. She nodded.

"Come and sit down; you look very tired," he said, pulling her to sit beside him. As she sat down, she placed her head on his shoulder. He placed his arms around her and leaned back fully in the chair, resting his head. She knew he was tired as well. She figured he had closed his eyes now. She felt his arms tighten around her. She was happy he had decided to stay with her.

She moved her head slightly up his chest, her arms tightening around him now. Right then, she remembered—she wouldn't have been able to do this if she had the rash on her skin. Maxwell never knew. She would tell him one day. She knew what had happened—God had healed her.

She closed her eyes and took a breath. Quietly, she said a prayer:

"Lord, I thank you for healing me, for blessing my family, and for bringing Pastor Maxwell into my life. I love him. I hope it is alright with you if I marry him. Please, God, help me to be a good wife. Thank you. Amen."

~~The End~~

About the Author

Hi, I am a Nigerian-born writer based in the United Kingdom; a passionate storyteller from an early age; I began writing plays that sparked my love for drama and narrative. Whispers of the Heart is my debut novel, marking the start of my journey as a published author.

In addition to my writing, I host Your Journey, Your Testimony, a podcast that shares inspiring stories of hope and faith. When I am not writing or podcasting, I enjoy exploring new places, reading, and spending time with friends.

Connect with Me

FOLLOW ON INSTAGRAM: @yourjourney_yourtestimony
CONTACT ME VIA Email: juliedeborahauthor@gmail.com